THE

RULES

OF

HALF

THE
RULES
OF
HALF

a novel

JENNA
PATRICK

SparkPress, a BookSparks imprint
A Division of SparkPoint Studio, LLC

Published by SparkPress, a BookSparks imprint,
A division of SparkPoint Studio, LLC
Tempe, Arizona, USA, 85281
www.gosparkpress.com

Published 2017
Printed in the United States of America

ISBN: 978-1-943006-18-2 (pbk)
ISBN: 978-1-943006-19-9 (e-bk)
Library of Congress Control Number: 2017930642

Cover design © Julie Metz, Ltd./metzdesign.com
Formatting by Katherine Lloyd/thedeskonline.com

To Chad,

For pushing me to fight for my dreams,
even though it meant putting your Camaro on hold.

I couldn't ask for a better partner in crime.

Hell is yourself
and the only redemption is when a person
puts himself aside to feel deeply for another person.

—Tennessee Williams

CHAPTER ONE

Seven hours and two hundred cornfields after hitching a ride out of Chicago, Regan Whitmer could finally see the light. It was the same old-timey traffic light she'd memorized from the pictures online, blinking just over the questionable, wooden bridge that crossed a shallow creek. In the distance, she could make out the silhouette of a town—striped awnings and tall, brick buildings with the occasional banner strung from one side of the street to the other. The moment Regan saw it, she knew Half Moon Hollow was a place she could get lost in.

"You can let me out here," she shouted over the gospel music to Betty Lou.

Her plump getaway driver stopped the Buick inches before the bridge and pushed her rhinestone-lined glasses into her white curls. "Honey, are you sure? I feel just awful leaving you here by yourself."

"I'll be fine," Regan said, climbing from the car. She lugged her scramble-packed bag of clothes across her shoulder, closed the door, and leaned into the window. "Thanks for the ride."

"Oh sweetie, I only did what Jesus would do." Betty Lou smiled and held out the purple WWJD bracelet she'd given Regan around the state line, and Regan had covertly shoved into the valley of the seats a few counties later. "Remember, if you get lost—"

"He has the map. . . I know." Regan rolled her eyes and slid the bracelet over her wrist as she backed away from the car. "Have fun in Atlantic City. Hope you hit it big."

As soon as the Buick's rattle faded in the distance, Regan threw the bracelet far into the cornfield that bordered the road. It wasn't anything personal against Jesus; Regan figured he helped a lot of people who were in trouble, even if she'd never been one of them. The bracelet just felt more like a pair of handcuffs after living in her stepfather's religious jail.

She crossed the wooden bridge and headed toward town, the sour smell of dirt and old straw a harsh contrast to the exhaust fumes she was used to. No hum from the L train muffled the crunch of her feet against the gravel road, nor sirens reminded her someone was worse off than she was. The only sounds were the birds chirping in the air and the rustling of cornfields. It made Regan uncomfortable, lonely. It made her question coming here to find her father.

She still hadn't decided how to break the news to him. Perhaps: *Knock, Knock. Who's there? The daughter you never knew you had.* Or maybe: *Nice to meet you. I'm your kid.* And there were the bigger questions that tugged at her brain too. Was her father everything her mother had described? Did he have a family of his own—a beautiful wife and kids and a dog that fetched the morning newspaper? Was there any room in his perfect life for her?

Would he even want her if there was?

Reaching the edge of town, she shook the uncertainty from

her head and examined the streetscape before her. So this was Half Moon Hollow—the population just under fifteen hundred, according to the weathered, wooden sign hanging from one rusty nail. Where those fifteen hundred people were, she did not know. If not for the banner advertising an upcoming festival, she'd have thought Half Moon Hollow abandoned long ago.

She set off down the vacant street, glancing in each window she passed. A hardware store, a pharmacy, a bank—all closed—each with blue and yellow garlands draped around the windows. There was nothing to help her, no one to ask for directions, nowhere to turn. Only one rusty Jeep without any doors parked in the road up ahead. She sank to the sidewalk with her head in her hands, defeated.

Get up, Regan.

She stiffened at her mother's voice. Not this again. Regan hadn't heard her since climbing out the window last night, had hoped she'd left her behind with the rest of her ghosts.

Go. Find a map, her mother pressed.

"Uh, in case you haven't noticed, there's no visitor's center here in Half Moon Hollow."

We need to keep going.

"What do you mean *we*? There's no *we* anymore. There stopped being a *we* the day you left me with Steven. Now, get lost!" Regan threw a handful of gravel into the air toward the invisible ghost of her mother, or whatever it was. The first time she'd heard it, a few months back, she'd blamed it on a gas station burrito she'd eaten. The second time, a severe case of survivor's guilt. By the third, Regan had stopped explaining and started thinking up ways to get rid of her.

Hearing her mother stirred up all the anger again, anger that always led back to sadness. And Regan had no more tears left to waste.

11

"Pardon my meddling, but are you lost, Miss?"

Regan turned toward the strange voice. A tall man in cut-off overalls and a white T-shirt stared back with a toothy grin. Any other time, she'd have found him creepy, but, lost and sweating in the August heat, he looked like her hero.

His grin started to slide, and his bushy brow rose. "You must be one o' them Hawkins High kids from the city, huh?"

She brushed the bangs from her eyes and nodded, though she had no idea where Hawkins High was. Right now, she'd tell him she was from Mars if he'd help her.

"Well, the new high school's about a mile up the road that way," the man continued, tossing a navy-blue bag into the back of the rusted Jeep. "If you hurry, you can still make it."

"Make what?"

"The football scrimmage. Where else you think everyone is today? A tractor pull?"

"Right. Football." Regan hopped to her feet and tossed her bag across her shoulder, not entirely sure what a tractor pull was. "This might be a stretch, but is there a bus I could take?"

He blinked. "Nah, no buses 'round here. But I can take ya, if you want."

"No, but thank you." Regan spun on her heels and headed in the direction he'd pointed, hoping her father lived somewhere near the new high school.

"Mmm-kay," he said suggestively. "But I am heading that way on my route today."

Regan paused. Route? She spun back toward the Jeep, eyes landing on the faded U.S. Postal Service sticker she hadn't noticed before. "Who needs a map when you have a mailman?"

"Say again?"

She shook her head. "I said I think I'll take that ride after all."

"All right then." He waited at the passenger's side as she approached, then helped her inside. "Name's George."

"Regan. Nice to meet you."

George tilted his head. "Well that's a funny name. Regan like the president?"

"Yep. Just like the president," she said, because explaining her mother's obsession with *King Lear* was a long-winded conversation she didn't want to have twice in twenty-four hours. Explaining it to Betty Lou had been enough.

George walked around the Jeep and climbed into the driver's seat. "Shouldn't take but just a few minutes to get to the high school."

"Yeah, about that . . . you mind if we make a pit stop first, George?"

He shrugged. "Sure thing. Where to?"

Regan pulled the crumbled piece of paper from her pocket. "One twenty-four Baxter Street?"

"One twenty-four Baxter Street? Well, that's the old Fletcher place."

"That's right. Fletcher. Will Fletcher." She pulled her seatbelt across her chest and looked straight ahead, but he didn't start the car. "Something wrong?"

"Nope," George stated, turning the key. "But I can't say the same about Will Fletcher."

"Mr. Fletcher, there is something seriously wrong with you."

Will's grin faded. This wasn't the first time someone had told him that, and it for certain wouldn't be the last, but it still stung. "Wrong is a relative term, Your Honor."

"Not in my courtroom, it isn't." The judge removed her glasses and pinched the bridge of her nose. "Would you mind telling me what, exactly, would provoke you to think it would be okay to play a guitar *naked* in the new town fountain?"

"That the piano would be a pain in the ass to get in there?" The courtroom erupted with laughter, and Will turned for his customary bow. He'd managed to draw quite the crowd today. Not his biggest, but he was up against the first football scrimmage of the season. And, above all else, this town loved its Howlers' football.

He finished bowing to the crowd and turned to offer one to Judge Riddick, but of course she didn't laugh. And neither did his sister or Dr. Granger, who stood beside him.

"I was kidding," he whispered, and then looked toward the judge. "I was just kidding, Your Honor. I think it's clear I *wasn't* thinking."

Truth be told, Will didn't know why he'd climbed into that fountain or how many police officers it had taken to pull him out. One minute, he'd been getting a haircut at the barbershop, and the next, he'd woke up with his wrists tied down to a bed and a severe case of cottonmouth. Maybe he'd remember someday, maybe he wouldn't. That was how his mania worked.

"Your Honor, please excuse my patient," Dr. Granger said. "He's still adjusting to the new medications."

"I understand that, Dr. Granger, but the question still remains—why wasn't Mr. Fletcher on medication to control his illness in the first place?"

The answer was simple—because Will hated the medication. He felt groggy and irritable and lackadaisical all at the same time. Like he wanted to scratch out someone's eyes, with no idea why, no inkling how to do it, and no desire to get started any time soon. Off the medication, Will felt free. He could do anything, be anyone.

He could forget everything.

"Your Honor," Janey piped in, "My brother has a long . . ."
And complicated past.

Will turned his eyes to the floor, pushing his mind to better places as he always did when Dr. Granger and Janey summed up his life into a series of misunderstandings and tragic circumstances. It didn't hurt to hear their words, nor did Will deny any of it. He simply didn't approve of the way they explained it, like he was the victim of his sad story. He'd ruined his career. He'd destroyed his marriage. He'd shattered his family. Perhaps his illness played a role, but that illness inhabited the blood and cells and neurons inside him.

Will *was* his Bipolar Disorder.

But it was easier not to argue over a technicality, so instead Will thought of happier times. He thought of swimming in Half Moon Creek and picnics afterword at the dam. He thought of his mother's homemade, blueberry pie and his father's old transistor radio crackling in the background. He thought of a time when he was just little Will Fletcher—future wide receiver for the Half Moon Howlers. Not crazy Will Fletcher—the example parents cite to their children when explaining the meaning of *stranger danger*.

"Mr. Fletcher, do you understand?"

Damn, were they finished already? He'd just gotten to the good part: when he'd met Ellie on the playground at school. "Sorry, Your Honor, I wasn't listening," he said, slightly irritated.

"Apparently." Judge Riddick tossed a Tic Tac into her mouth and rolled her eyes. "I'm turning you over to the care of your sister and your doctor and sentencing you to six months of community service, in addition to the six *years* you've already racked up."

Will smiled. "Excellent, Your Honor."

"And . . ." the judge continued. "You have to serve it in some fashion other than volunteering at the animal shelter."

"What?" Will and Janey both exclaimed.

"You heard me. No dogs, no cats, no hamsters. I don't even want you helping a turtle cross the road into Half Moon Creek. This time you're going to use your sentence to help out *humans.* Do you understand?"

Will sighed. "Yes, Your Honor."

She beat her gavel against the wood block, the sound a sledgehammer against Will's foggy head, and exited the courtroom to an eruption of laughter. Even the audience knew how ridiculous her punishment was.

Dr. Granger patted Will on the back, as if offering his condolences, then gathered Will's stack of medical records. "Hang in there. The side effects will go away with time," he said.

Sure it will. Just like all the other things you promised would go away.

"Janey, you got a minute to chat?" Dr. Granger asked. "Outside?"

"Uh, sure. Will, I'll be right back."

Will waved her off, still staring at the leather chair Judge Riddick had vacated. No one in this town wanted his help. No one even liked being in the same room with him. They scattered like ants hiding from a thunderstorm when he came around, unless of course he did something crazy; then they brought the popcorn bucket. And back on his meds, what were the odds of that? This would land him right back in jail.

Or worse yet—Creedmoor Institute.

A shudder ran down Will's spine just thinking of that place. The crying. The howling. The screaming. Time swallowed by a perpetual dream state of days spent staring at the open canvas of a blank wall, as he ached for a storybook life much different than the one he'd created. The torture of waking up only to remember he was the villain of this story, not the hero.

He'd never go back to that place. He'd die first.

"You ready?" Janey asked.

Will turned with a start. Boy, was he ever.

Janey led and Will followed down the dark corridor toward the glass doors of the courthouse. As always, she waited to comment until they were alone outside, where no one could hear them. "Well, this should be interesting."

"Hey, I got this. I'll just volunteer at the cemetery."

Janey barreled down the stone steps, shaking her head.

"What?" Will said. "The judge didn't say the humans couldn't be *dead*."

"You're missing the point. It's supposed to be a punishment. Something to teach you a lesson and help the people you so often offend. And you just find another way to insult them."

He hurried to catch her. For a little thing, his sister walked fast. Will had trouble keeping up, even at six feet tall. "Hey, you know as well as I do that no one wants the town crazy anywhere near them."

"You're not the town crazy." Janey unlocked his car door and met his gaze. "You're sick. I don't know why everyone can see that but you."

"Because no one has to live inside my head day in and day out." He grinned. "Well, at least not *everyone*. There are a few strange characters that keep showing up."

"Damn it, Will!" Janey punched his arm and then stomped around the car, her short, blonde hair a wild mess. "Not funny. Not funny at all."

"What?" he asked, climbing inside. "Now I can't make a joke?"

"Not one that'll have you thrown in Creedmoor." She got

in the car and turned the engine over. "Dr. Granger said you're down to your last chance as it is. The court wouldn't hesitate to throw you in there if you were hearing voices like *him*."

Will frowned. He knew Janey was referring to their father just by the way she'd said *him*. It was a disconnected, bitter, empty word. Will didn't blame her, really. His sister may not have inherited their father's illness as Will had, but she'd certainly taken the brunt of it.

"I need to drop the sketches for the fall issue in the mail on the way back," she said, backing out of the parking space. "Need anything else before we go home?"

Well, if she was offering . . . "Mind if I stop by and see Emma?"

Janey hit the brakes. "Would it matter if I did?"

The question clearly rhetorical, Will didn't bother responding. It had been a week since he'd last visited Emma. He would go, with or without his sister.

"Of course not," Janey conceded, retrieving a bouquet of flowers from the backseat. The stems were joined together by a bright-purple ribbon. "Here. Picked these from the garden this morning."

Will placed the daisies in his lap, the aroma filling the air around him. "Thanks," he said, rubbing the ribbon between his thumb and finger. "She loves purple."

Janey pulled the sunglasses from her head to the bridge of her nose and watched anxiously as Will walked back down the path toward the car. Visiting Emma did something to him, spun a wheel of emotions inside him and Janey never knew where the arrow would land. Fun Will. Annoying Will. Sad Will. I-Hate-The-World Will. Janey felt like an eight-year-old on the way home from the bank, holding a mystery lollipop. Was it sour apple or root beer?

Would Will be her sweet, older brother or the bitter bastard she hated so much?

She took a deep breath as he climbed into the car, his expression sober. Like all other days, she wouldn't speak first. She'd wait for a sign from him then choose her response wisely. It could be a smile or a sigh, uncrossed legs or a nervous twitch, a humble *thank you* or a teeth-gritted *fuck you*. Today it was a simple flip of the radio to the oldies station. Oldies were good. Had he turned it to the heavy metal station, that would've been bad, and love songs disastrous.

"Emma doing okay?" she asked.

Will nodded and offered the faintest of grins. Today she had Humbled Will.

About to put the car in drive, Janey noticed the time. "Damn."

"What's wrong?" Will asked.

She shook her head. "Nothing," she said. Telling Humbled Will she'd missed mail pick-up, because he'd taken too long with Emma, would result in Angry Will. So instead, she'd have an angry agent. Janey'd promised to send Gretchen sketches for *Ziggy Rothchild: Cowboy at Large* over a month ago. Being a comic book artist had its perks, but the freedom to draw at her brother's pace wasn't one of them.

"Sorry," Will said.

Janey stiffened. Had she said all that aloud or had Will figured it out? "For what?"

"For everything." He rubbed his jaw, staring out the window. "I just don't know why. I don't know why I do all these things."

She deflated. Of course. She'd forgotten that Humbled Will sometimes came with Self-Pity Will. How foolish of her to think he'd actually remembered the mail time, to think he'd thought of her needs for a change. "It's okay," she said, hiding her disappointment from him.

"Just don't give up on me, okay?" he added. "I don't have anything else. I need you."

With those three, little words, Janey's disappointment melted into resolve. She turned toward him, tugged his chin her way, stared at him. When had the dark stubble on his face grown gray? His gunmetal blue eyes seemed grayer too, and the plump-rose color of his cheeks had hollowed and faded years ago. That was why she was there.

"Never," she finally responded. "It's you and me against the world, Bro."

He started to speak, but Janey shook her head once, let go of his chin, and put the car in drive. They'd go to bed tonight, lay it to rest, and never speak of this manic episode again, the way they didn't speak of any others. The conversation would be left to the rest of town. *Guess what crazy Fletcher did this time? Acorn doesn't fall far from the tree.* Or her personal favorite— *That family is nuttier than a squirrel turd.*

Still, Janey would take the mania over the depression, any day of the week. She'd grown used to turning a deaf ear to the comments, but she'd never get used to the emptiness of Will's eyes as he stared out the window, for the fourth straight day, from the same chair, in the same corner of the same room. Or the queasiness in her stomach every time she left the house, wondering if he'd be gone by the time she got back.

The depression, frankly, scared the hell out of Janey. And since Will just had his third manic episode in a row, she knew the odds weren't in her favor for the next.

Exhaustion had set over Will by the time they returned home that afternoon. Though he'd only been gone a week, the old farmhouse looked different—the white paint more chipped, the front porch more uneven, the single-paned windows more fragile. Or maybe it was the same as he'd left it, and he had changed.

A breeze blew past as he climbed from the car, sending the curtain from his upstairs bedroom dancing across the porch roof. "My screen must've come loose again," he said, spotting it in Janey's rose bush below.

She glanced up, taking stride beside him. "Let's hope the family of cardinals living on the porch didn't make themselves a home up there."

"You had to go there, didn't you?"

She shrugged. "I don't think it's too much to ask for my talented brother to build me a birdhouse. Do you?"

"It's on the list." He tugged on the screen door, which croaked like a giant tree frog, proving her point all the more. Oiling it had been on Will's list for two years.

Janey grinned. "Go get cleaned up. I'm fixing Salisbury steak for dinner. Sound good?"

Will's mouth watered. His menu in the county hospital had consisted of foods suitable for a plastic spoon, like boxed mashed potatoes, corn kernels, and cheap macaroni and cheese. His sister always knew just what he needed, always knew how to gloss everything over like it had never happened. "Sounds perfect."

Almost too perfect.

He watched as she disappeared behind the kitchen door, then looked around the living room with a sweeping glance. Tissues on the end table, a quilt balled up on the sofa, a wine glass on the floor—all clues Will relied on to tell the truth, because Janey never would. Yes, she'd been crying. Yes, she'd been drinking. Yes, she'd slept downstairs where her phone had better reception, on the off chance she'd receive a horrific phone call in the middle of the night.

Will would never know the depth of what he'd put Janey through or understand why she'd sacrificed so much to save him. But one day she'd realize she'd given it all up to cure a demon that couldn't be cured, didn't want to be cured. What would he do then? How would he survive? Who would take care of Emma? Shaking the pointless speculation from his head, he climbed the stairs to the second floor. That would never happen. It was just the lithium playing tricks on him, evoking old fears and paranoia that he could typically ignore. It reasoned with parts of him that couldn't be reasoned with—parts that *shouldn't* be reasoned with. One more reason he shouldn't take it.

He approached his bedroom at the end of the hall, the same bedroom he'd grown up in, with the same furniture and the same football trophies on the shelves. Avoid change, stick to the familiar, think of good memories—all Janey's rules, though Will often wondered if she'd made them more for herself than for him. Changing this house meant taking ownership of it, and, for some reason, his sister wouldn't do that. Their mother died years ago, but Janey still referred to it as Mom's house. Maybe Will wasn't the only Fletcher praying to see a ghost.

He rounded the corner into his bedroom, took two steps inside, and nearly collapsed to his knees at the sight. Will's prayers had finally been answered.

She slept backward on his bed, facing the wall, her black, Converse sneakers atop his pillow and long, red hair flowing across the footboard like the rays of a sunset. She wore a dirty pair of blue jeans with a ripped back pocket and the faded concert T-shirt of a band he did not recognize. Her age was a bit off, but who was Will to question God's accuracy, God's reasoning, God's gifts to him?

That's when it occurred to Will that this might not be a ghost at all.

He backed into the hallway and clenched his eyes shut. God didn't make mistakes. God didn't give gifts like this to people like him. Will was hallucinating. Had to be. It was the only logical explanation for a teenage girl to be asleep on his bed.

"Will, what is it? What's wrong?" Janey asked somewhere behind him.

He shook his head, eyes still locked shut.

"Answer me. What happened?"

He opened his eyes. The girl still lay there, now with her face turned toward the ceiling. Her skin was the color of ivory tusks, accented by rose-colored freckles scattered about like a constellation. She shined like a bright summer's day.

This wasn't a hallucination. This was a cruel, cruel joke.

"Will!" Janey shouted.

He put his finger against his lips to request her silence, then glanced back at the girl. She stirred at his sister's yell, but didn't wake. "There's a . . . a . . ."

"There's a what?" Janey asked.

He met her gaze and mouthed, "There's a girl in there. Asleep on my bed."

Janey reared back. "A . . . *girl*."

"Yes."

"Asleep on your bed."

He nodded, tiptoeing to where his sister stood. "Yes."

Janey leaned against the banister. "And what does this girl look like?"

"Red hair, pale skin."

"Like Ellie's?"

"Yes, like—" He pursed his lips. "I'm not hallucinating. There's a goddamn girl sleeping on my bed. With red hair and pale skin." He looked Janey over. "About your height and weight."

"Will—"

"Go look, damn it!"

"Okay, okay. Fine." Janey pushed off the staircase. "But if there's no girl—"

"Janey, if there's no girl, I'll check *myself* into Creedmoor."

She took a deep breath and tiptoed down the hallway to his doorway, Will right behind her. There, in his room, stood a teenage girl about Janey's size with red hair, pale skin, and blue-gray eyes, glassy as a pond.

"Well. Shall I check us *both* into Creedmoor?" Will whispered.

Regan woke to the sound of an argument. Not brawling, like the moral debates her mother used to have with Steven, but loud enough to rouse her from a deep sleep. Who was speaking? Where was she? How had she gotten there? She sprang to a sit, shaking the sleep from her groggy head. The dirty, chipped, wood siding. Blue shutters. The Fletcher residence, or so the reflective stickers on the dented gray mailbox had read.

Fletcher. Will Fletcher. She was in her father's house.

It all came back to her, like a film reel flashing pictures before her eyes. Her growling stomach had begged her to go inside. She'd eaten overly ripe bananas and a half jar of peanut butter. She'd lain down on the bed with the quilt made of scattered bloodred and bruise-blue patchwork, resembling her life all too closely. She'd closed her eyes and searched for a way to tell him so that today wouldn't contribute another patch.

She'd fallen asleep, apparently, still without the perfect words to say. Now it was too late.

A woman appeared first in the doorway, then a man. He was tall and thin—almost too thin—and his skin was the color of bone. He looked old and tired, like a worn-down shoe. Not the knight in shining armor her mother had described, she thought, staring at the man cowering behind the short woman.

He whispered something into the woman's ear that Regan couldn't make out.

"Go call Tom. Tell him we've got another one," the woman ordered. "Then go to the barn and listen to some music."

He hurried off, leaving Regan and the woman alone. Good. Regan had always done better with women. "Are you Mrs. Fletch—"

"What the hell are you doing in my home?" she asked, stomping over to Regan. "This isn't funny anymore. You hear me?"

Regan blinked. "I'm sorry?"

She forced Regan by the elbow into the hallway. "Why don't you kids just let my brother be? Don't you think he's suffered enough?"

"Please, just let me explain," Regan pleaded, attempting to free herself. "I came to—"

"I know why you came," the woman said, steering her down the stairs. "You came to see what you could make the crazy man do next. Well, this is the last time you and your friends will make a spectacle of Will Fletcher."

"I don't know what you're talking about. Stop!" Regan tugged free, causing the woman—her aunt—to lose her grip and fall to the floor with a loud thud. "Just listen to me. Please."

Her aunt quickly climbed to her feet. "I said, get the hell out of my house now."

Regan folded her arms. "No. Not until you hear me out."

Her aunt yanked the closet door beside her open and ducked out of view; the barrel of a gun appeared a second later, taking her place. "Get out now. I don't want to, but I'll pull the trigger."

Maybe Regan should've been scared, but this wasn't the

first time she'd had a gun pointed at her head. And the shakiness in her aunt's voice screamed bullshit. "Go ahead. Shoot your niece if you want to."

She lowered the gun, and her jaw. "What did you say?"

"I'm your niece." Regan eased toward her, tugging the faded, brown paper from her pocket and holding it up. "You see? His name is on my birth certificate. Will Fletcher is my father. That's why I'm here. To meet him."

Her aunt glanced at the paper, then back up at Regan. "How is this possible?"

Regan shrugged. "My mother said he saved her from a car crash. That's how they met."

"That's not what I meant," the woman said, though Regan never really thought it was. Her aunt glanced nervously toward the kitchen door. "You have to leave. Now."

"What? Why?"

"Leave. And don't come back," her aunt repeated, crowding her toward the door.

"Please, just ask him. Ask him about the peanut butter and pickle sandwich he made her, or the all-night superhero movie marathon they had, or the . . . the . . . the . . ." Regan paused, mind blank. "I can't remember the rest, but I know he will. Just ask if he remembers Michelle—"

"Whitmer," he said.

Regan turned. There her father stood, with a set of headphones on his neck and an MP3 player in his hands. "Yes," she said in a low voice. "Michelle Whitmer."

He began to approach, but his sister stepped between them. "I told you to call Tom."

"I did. He's in a meeting," he said, eyes still set on Regan.

"Then go out to the barn and listen to some music while I deal with this."

"I tried. Juice ran out." He placed the MP3 player in his sister's hand, while stepping around her. "I can't believe I didn't see the resemblance before." Will lifted his hand toward Regan's hair, but placed it on his stubbly chin instead. "Wow. You look just like her. Janey, doesn't she . . . well, I guess you wouldn't know." He glanced back at his sister, who was biting down on her lip as she teetered back and forth on her feet. "What the hell is wrong with you? You gotta pee?"

"Will, please go out to the barn," she pleaded.

"No, Janey. Now, will you stop being so rude? This is no way to treat a guest."

"Fine," she said, dropping down into a chair. "But don't say I didn't warn you."

"Yeah, yeah." Rolling his eyes, he turned back toward Regan and held out his hand. "I'm Will, but you already knew that. And this nervous nelly behind me is my sister, Janey."

Regan took his hand, examining the lines of his face. His eyes were kind and the same gunmetal blue as Regan's, just as her mother had always told her, and his salt-and-pepper hair was thick. She could see why her mother had fallen for him.

"And you are?" Will beckoned.

"Sorry." Regan's face flushed with heat. "I'm Regan."

"Regan, like—"

"Yes, like the president," she answered before he could finish.

"Bummer. I thought maybe she'd named you after King Lear's daughter." Will grimaced, placing his hands on his hips. "So, where's Michelle? I haven't seen her in ten years or more."

"Fifteen," Regan corrected. "And she died. Six months ago."

"Oh." He sank to the arm of the couch like a balloon losing air. "How? Cancer?"

"She had a sick heart," Regan said. It wasn't a complete lie.

Will frowned. "Well, I'm so sorry to hear that. They say

27

heart disease is the leading cause of death for women, you know. Our mom died the same way."

Somehow, Regan seriously doubted that.

"So, what brings you to Half Moon Hollow, Regan? Don't tell me Michelle left me an old mixtape in her will. Or maybe some of the money we stole from that bank." He chuckled a moment, his smile fading when his sister crossed her arms. "I'm kidding. I swear."

Regan glanced at Janey, then back at Will. She didn't know what a mixtape was, or why Will Fletcher would have to reassure his sister he hadn't robbed a bank, but one thing was obvious— he hadn't heard the first part of the argument. "Mr. Fletcher—"

"Will, please. Call me Will."

Regan grimaced. Now or never. "How 'bout, *Dad?*"

"*Dad?* But why would you . . ." His smile fell.

"It's me. I'm what Michelle left you." She closed her eyes, no courage left to view his reaction, then threw her hands in the air. "Surprise!"

A moment later, Regan heard a large thud.

CHAPTER
TWO

A dull pain resonated from the back of Will's head as he opened his eyes to find Janey sitting beside him. "What happened?"

"You blacked out. Bumped your head on the coffee table." Janey helped him to his feet. "Your blood sugar is probably low. You need to eat and then rest."

Blood sugar. Yes, that explained it. Which meant all that nonsense was a nightmare. There was no girl asleep on his bed, Janey hadn't ordered him to call the sheriff, and his MP3 player was fully charged in the barn, loaded with calm music for the next time he began to lose it. But the real, concrete evidence was the other detail.

Will wasn't that girl's father. He knew this for absolute certain because he'd promised Emma he'd never make that mistake again.

Janey helped him to the kitchen and lowered him into a chair, then placed a pill in his hand and a glass of water on the table. "You okay?"

He nodded, tossing the pill into the back of his throat and downing the water.

"Here. You might need this," Janey said.

Will glanced down at the paper towel she held, which could only mean one thing. "Damn it, Janey! Clonazepam?"

"I thought the situation called for something stronger than aspirin."

"Situation?" He yanked the paper towel from her hand, expecting the drool to come at any moment. "I blacked out! Give me some coffee!"

Janey folded her arms across her chest. "You don't remember anything, do you?" she asked, something in her tone telling Will he didn't want to remember anything. And then she stepped aside to reveal the girl on the back porch, red hair glowing in the afternoon sun like the embers of a fire coming to burn him alive.

A nightmare, yes, but one he would not wake from. "No. No. No!"

"Fight it, Will!" Janey ordered, grabbing his chin and directing his eyes toward hers. "You can fight this. Just focus on breathing. In, out. In, out."

He did as he was told, staring into his sister's jade-green eyes until his racing heart returned to a steady thump. How she calmed him, Will would never know.

"Everything is going to be okay," she said, her hand still tight around his jaw. "We just need to take this one step at a time. Right?"

Will nodded, but only to appease her. He couldn't argue anyway; his mouth grew more saturated by the second. The damn Clonazepam did that to him—the ability to corral his scattering thoughts at the bargain price of a pool of drool.

"Now, I'm going to call Tom again. I'll be right in the living room if you need anything." Janey smiled, rubbing his cheek with her thumb. "Everything is going to be all right."

Will nodded again, though Janey had already gone and he didn't believe her anyway. Nothing about this was right. Not the girl sitting on the back steps, picking at her frayed shoelaces. And not the realization that she had to be around fifteen or sixteen, placing him in Michelle's dorm room right around the time of her conception.

Looking back, Will knew he'd been in a manic state. He hadn't slept in days, and his roommate had grown tired of his rambling, so Will had taken up residence in a booth at an all-night diner near campus. A screeching sound had turned his attention out the window, just in time to see the car crash into the power pole, and Michelle's head into the windshield. He'd told the waitress to call 911, and rushed out the door.

Through the electrical sparks showering down, Will had seen her slumped over the steering wheel, a trickle of blood careening its way from her forehead to her chin. Had it not been for the red hair, he might've left her there, waited for the ambulance to arrive, but all he could see was Ellie when he looked at her. No way would he have left her. Even back then, the mere sight of Ellie was enough to pull him over the edge.

Will only remembered pieces after that. The EMT placing a bandage on her forehead. Her cluttered dorm room. An argument over who played the best Batman. Two days later, he'd woken up naked beside her with a headache and his stomach sickened with guilt. He'd dressed, careful not to wake her, and tiptoed to the door. The last thing he'd seen was her name, written on an English essay upon her desk—Michelle Whitmer. Will had sworn he'd never allow himself to forget it, or the freckles on her cheeks, or the essay she'd titled, "The Daughters of King Lear." He wouldn't forget because, if he had, it would make cheating on Ellie that much more atrocious, that much more vile.

Janey inched back into the kitchen and placed her cell phone on the counter. "Tom's still in his meeting. He's going to call me when he's done."

Good. Then this will all be over.

"She may need to stay in Mama's room until we get this sorted out," Janey added.

He met her gaze. "You're not actually considering letting her stay here?"

"Well, I'm not going to send her back onto the streets."

"Then send her home," he argued.

"She ran away for a reason, Will. If I do, she'll just end up on the streets again."

Will clenched his jaw, ignoring the saliva dripping to his chin. "I don't agree with this."

"Well, I'm sorry." Janey snatched the paper towel from his hand and wiped his chin, despite his attempt to evade her. "I make the rules in this house. That was the deal, remember? If you don't like it, you can stay out in the barn with the other stubborn ass."

Regan picked at her frayed shoelaces as she glanced out over the Fletchers' backyard. She'd never had a yard before. Somewhere to swing on a swing set or roll herself sick down a hill, and the old red barn would've made a nice home for the bicycle she'd never had. The odd scarecrow, staked out on bird patrol over the garden, protected the vegetables she'd only known from a can, and the clothesline strung from the house was probably much more effective at drying clothes than hand dryers at truck stops.

It was all so different. Not just the yard and the clothesline, but the yearning in the pit of her stomach for it all to be hers.

She'd never felt that before, nothing close. She didn't even care that her aunt had pointed a gun at her, or that her father hadn't spoken to her since he'd woken up from his little nap. Regan wanted this, and she hoped they felt the same.

Go talk to him, her mother demanded.

Regan glanced through the screen door at Will and Janey still quietly debating in the kitchen. "She told me to wait out here," Regan whispered, turning her gaze back toward the barn. "Besides, I don't think he wants to talk to me."

It's not what you think.

Regan rolled her eyes. She'd heard that more than once from her mother and made the mistake of trusting her, but in the end Regan's gut had been right. Steven wasn't the savior who would give them a good life. Holden Wright wasn't the boy who would show Regan how it felt to dance on the moon. And her mother hadn't bought that gun for protection.

I'm sorry.

A tear crested the corner of Regan's eye, which she quickly wiped away. She'd heard that more than one time from her mother too. Promises made, promises broken, apologies and forgiveness given—Regan's fifteen years of life with her mother summed to a revolving wheel of disappointment.

But Regan didn't have to forgive anymore. She wouldn't.

The screen door burst open from behind, startling her. Will staggered out with a lamp under one arm and a pillow under the other, mumbling something about a barn and an ass, but didn't look her way. Two seconds later, the door opened again and Janey stepped outside. She leaned against the porch rail, tucking her fingers into her old, ratty jeans as she squinted toward the sun. "You can stay. At least until we figure out what to do."

"Really?" Regan asked, a hint of something in her voice she hadn't heard in a while. Maybe hope, maybe surprise. Then she turned her gaze back to Will, who'd stumbled all the way across the backyard to the barn.

"Don't worry about him. Will's just a bit . . . complicated."

"But this is his house, and—"

"It's my mom's house," Janey corrected as she opened the door. "And she'd be mighty upset if I didn't invite her granddaughter to stay a while. So, please . . . just let me show you to your room, okay?"

Regan followed her through the house, listening as Janey pointed things out and commented on their significance. The fridge without any soda, the pantry without many sweets, the living room without cable TV, the stairs lacking a good coat of paint and a half-decent carpet runner. To Janey, everything seemed to be missing something. But to a girl who'd once slept on shady hotel lounge chairs and ate dinner straight from dented tin cans, it was the Ritz.

Her new room was at the end of the upstairs hallway, just before her father's. It smelled funny, like the church's basement back in Chicago, and the flowered wallpaper and dark furniture decorated with doilies reminded her of old lady Snodgrass's apartment on the first floor of her building. Regan sometimes took dinner there as part of her penance program with church; sometimes she stayed until she was sure Steven had fallen asleep. Toward the end, Mrs. Snodgrass was the only friend she'd had.

"I know it's a bit old-fashioned, but I guess I could never bring myself to change it after Mom died." Across the room, Janey pulled the lace sheers, stained yellow with time, back on their bronze hooks. "We can change it to something more your age, if you decide to stay."

"It's perfect," Regan lied, because by *decide to stay*, her aunt surely meant *if we decide to keep you*. She needed to appear as independent as possible for this to work. Not eat too much, not speak too much, and stay out of trouble. The first two would be easy; the last she wasn't so sure about. Trouble had a way of disguising itself to Regan. Holden Wright was proof of that.

"It wasn't loaded, you know."

Regan met her gaze, Holden's image fading along with the sting in her heart.

"I don't even keep bullets in the house." Janey ran her hands through her short hair, leaving a messy disorder of blonde behind in their path. "We've just had a lot of . . . trouble, with the local kids in town. Had I known—"

"It's okay. I won't tell anyone," Regan assured her.

If there was one thing Regan Whitmer was good at, it was keeping secrets.

Janey watched from the front-porch swing as Tom Blythe climbed from his patrol car and removed his sheriff's hat. Tom was one of the few people in town she trusted. After all, he and Will had been best friends since before they'd learned how to toss a football around. Perhaps their relationship had evolved into something different over the years, but Tom was the only one who gave her family the time of day.

Even if it had taken him two hours to get there.

"Hey, Tom," she said, getting to her feet.

"Janey." He paused on the bottom step, eye level with her, and smiled. He always did have a nice smile. If circumstances were different, and Janey weren't the gay sister of the man he continuously arrested, they might've had a relationship. "Well, where is she?"

"Went to bed straight after dinner. Looked like she hadn't slept in days."

"Yeah, running away will zap the energy right from ya, I suppose." Tom sat on the steps, directing Janey to do the same, and removed a tiny notebook from his shirt pocket. "Well, here's what I found out. Regan Whitmer, age fifteen, no other living next of kin to speak of except you and Will, mom committed suicide last January."

Janey flinched. "Suicide?"

"Yep. Shot herself in the head. Right in front of Regan, apparently."

Janey flinched again, this time covering her gaping mouth with her hand. She'd found Will, bleeding in the hallway, after his suicide attempt and couldn't sleep for days. Janey couldn't imagine the torment of having watched him do it.

Tom sighed. "I take it she forgot to mention that."

"No. She just said . . ." Janey paused, remembering back. Regan had told Will that her mom's heart was sick and they'd assumed she meant heart disease. "My God. That poor girl."

"That ain't the half of it," Tom said, rubbing his jaw. "Up until three years ago, the only address I could find for Regan or Michelle was some pay-by-the-month hotel in Chicago. The girl's record was clean, but her mom wasn't no saint. I found prostitution charges, panhandling charges, and shoplifting charges. Then she marries some self-professed assistant pastor at a church called His Light, and, let me tell you, that guy's a real peach. I called up to talk to him, and he hadn't even realized she'd run away. Apparently, she'd been locked in her room for two days doing, what he referred to as, *spiritual devotion*."

Janey could only stare. There were no words.

"Look," Tom said, closing his notebook. "Just because she put Will's name down—"

"She's his," Janey said. If the girl's eyes weren't proof enough, her stubbornness was.

"But—"

"Trust me," Janey said. "She's his. And even if she isn't,

how can I send her back there after hearing all that?" Just the thought turned her stomach into knotted ropes. Janey'd been in both places after her mom died—living with a father unfit to care for her and in a system that didn't protect her. She and Will might not be ideal caretakers for Regan, but they were better than the alternatives.

"Well, I don't think you'll get much of a fight from her stepdad. When I asked if he wanted her to come home, he said, and I quote, 'only God can save such a damned soul.'" Tom stood and stretched. "Listen, I haven't reported this to social services and I don't plan on it. As long as Will's listed as her birth father and no one contests it, you shouldn't have any problems. Best to not rock the boat, if you know what I mean."

Janey knew exactly what he meant. If they reported this to social services, there was a high probability Will would be deemed unfit. Janey could file for custody of course, but she'd already been down that path with Will, and it wasn't a cheap one. "Thanks, Tom."

Tom nodded, spinning his hat around by its brim a few times. "You know, if you keep on giving up your life to rescue Will, sooner or later you're going to start to resent him."

Janey forced a smile. "He's my brother. He's all I have left."

"Maybe that's the problem," he said, then placed his hat on his head.

As Janey watched Tom walk back to his patrol car, emptiness grew inside her. Emptiness and, perhaps, a little guilt. The truth was she already resented Will at times. She told herself it was stress and worry, but, deep down, she knew it was resentment.

But the guilt she felt would be no comparison to the guilt she'd feel if she sent Regan into foster care. Janey had lived that hell for a short time after her mother died and had fought the demons that came out with her ever since. There were times at night she could still feel her foster brother's filthy hands on her, hear his inappropriate whispers, smell the liquor on his breath.

She would never allow those sort of memories to haunt another woman's dreams. Especially her own flesh and blood.

Will turned off the sander and yanked the headphones from his ears. *Safety first,* Janey always said. Maybe if he let his hearing go, he wouldn't have to listen to her crap day in and day out.

He blew the sawdust from the wood slab, the mess of hairy splinters standing on end like a cool chill down his spine. He could've kept going until it was smooth, but he liked doing this part by hand. It reminded him things could still be accomplished the hard way. That rough pieces could be whittled to dust without the aid of something else. That somewhere inside him was the power to turn things into what he wanted, instead of the emptiness of accepting what he'd become.

He shoved his hands inside his gloves and glanced around at the hundred half-finished projects around him. Some were still splintered, some only lacked stain, but all were started with a purpose that had somehow gone astray along the way.

And that was the problem. That had *always* been the problem.

When he heard the rickety, old, barn door open and close, he jumped back to his—what was he making again? A nightstand. Because Janey wouldn't let him take the nightstand from his room, or anything else, for that matter. He'd be sleeping in the loft on an old cot he'd dug up with no place to put his reading glasses.

"Hey. Brought you some dinner," she said.

"Not hungry," he grunted and pushed the sanding block down with the grain. Maybe he should've just thrown his headphones back on. Then she would've left the plate and bolted.

Now he had to deal with whatever real reason had brought her out to the barn.

"I'll leave it here for later." Janey placed the plate on his workbench and slid her hands into her back pockets. "So, Tom just left."

"And?"

"And it sounds like Regan's going to be staying with us for a while."

"Great." Will blew more dust from the slab. "Looks like everything's working out for poor, little-old Regan, isn't it?"

Janey pursed her lips. "You know, I'd blame this attitude on the meds, but, deep down, I know you're just being an asshole."

"Excuse me?"

"She's just a kid, Will. *Your* kid. And you want me to just throw her out on her ass. And for what? So you don't feel uncomfortable?"

"Oh, come on," Will retorted. "I don't want that."

"Okay, fine." Janey leaned against his work table, crossing her arms. "Then tell me what you want, Will. Tell me what you what me to do."

Now that was the million-dollar question, wasn't it? *What would you like me to do, Will? How can I help you, Will? What will make it better, Will?* No one ever listened when he said *nothing,* because there had to be something, right? Why couldn't they just accept that maybe, just maybe, there was nothing anyone could do to help him?

"Will!"

"I don't know, Janey!" he shouted, launching the sanding block against the wall in the process. She got that look in her eyes, the one he hated seeing more than anything. The one where he could hear her words clear as day, though she wasn't saying them aloud. He'd never hurt Janey, at least that he could remember. Maybe he had in one of his episodes, and she didn't have the heart to tell him. Regardless, it killed him to think she was afraid of him.

"I don't know what I want you to do," he repeated, a few decibels lower this time. "But I know I can't be a father to that girl. And you know it, too."

"No one asked you to be a father. Just be her friend."

He shook his head. "I don't know how to be anyone's friend."

"That's not true! What about Mimi and Rocky up at the shelter?"

"Oh, great. What am I supposed to do, teach Regan how to roll over?"

Janey smiled. "Just make her feel welcome and safe."

Will grimaced. Up until the last word, she might've actually been getting somewhere. But safe? Will could never make Regan feel safe. That was too big a responsibility to carry. Far too much to ask from a guy who could hardly match his clothes.

"I'm sorry. I just can't. I wasn't meant to have a job like that."

"Will . . ."

He shook his head, pulling the pencil from behind his ear to mark an arbitrary point on another piece of wood. He wanted to let his sister know that no boulder she rolled his way would deter him from his path. He'd made up his mind—Regan was better off without him.

"Okay, fine," Janey said, pushing off the work table and retreating toward the door. Just before her exit, she paused and looked back. "By the way, thought you'd want to know, Tom told me how Michelle died."

Will looked up, but didn't speak.

"She committed suicide," Janey said, matter-of-factly.

Will shuddered, Janey's boulder hitting him square in the gut. "Suicide?"

"Yeah. Shot herself in the head." Janey slid the barn door open, rolling one last boulder his way before walking out. "In front of your daughter."

Will sank to his stool, the weight of truth too much to bear. Not only had Michelle died by choice and not an unfortunate circumstance, she'd added an exclamation point by doing it in front of her daughter. What kind of a person did that to someone they loved?

He hung his head, his scarred wrists coming into view. The answer to his question was clear, but painful. A coward like him. That's the kind of person who did that. Perhaps he hadn't slit his wrists in front of Janey, but he'd known good and well she'd be the one to find him dead, and he hadn't cared.

Another reason he should stay away from Regan. She'd been through enough, and he could only offer more hurt and disappointment. One day she'd realize it; the people Will loved always did. She was better off without him.

Will forced himself to his feet and paced over to his pile of half-finished projects. The china hutch he'd promised Ellie as a forgotten anniversary gift; the new picture frames he'd promised Janey after destroying hers in a fit of rage; the cedar chest to replace the one his father had made, since Will had used it as a boat in Half Moon Creek. He went through every project until he found the one he'd been looking for; the only one he'd ever finished.

He pulled the canvas tarp to the side, just enough to see the carefully carved ivy at the top. The wood was cold and damp from five years on the floor of the barn, yet it burned his fingertips as he traced a path through the lines. This was what happened when he forgot who he was. This was why he would never make that mistake again.

After the memory had branded itself deep inside him, Will replaced the canvas over the crib's headboard and sank to the floor beating his head with the palm of his hand. The tears were coming; he couldn't stop them and didn't want to. It was the voice, screaming inside, he wanted to silence—his own voice, echoing a truth he couldn't escape.

I'm not meant to be a father. Wasn't then and I'm not now.

CHAPTER
THREE

Three days after she'd arrived in Half Moon Hollow, Regan's father was still holed up in the barn. She'd seen him a few times—like early in the morning, when he flounced to the house in his bathrobe, or around lunchtime, when he disappeared down the road for a couple hours—but that was the extent of their interaction. Which is why, when Will came inside that morning during the middle of a downpour, Regan dropped a box of cereal all over the kitchen floor.

"I hope that wasn't the last box of Oatey Os," Will said, stepping over her as she cleaned it up. "She already ate all the damn granola bars."

Regan deflated. For a moment, she'd thought he'd actually spoken to her. How foolish.

"Will, it's okay. Really." Janey walked into the pantry and came out with a broom. "We can get more at the store tonight."

Regan waited for Will to leave the room, then glanced up at Janey, who was sweeping the floor beside her. "The store? Mind if I come?"

Janey knelt down with a dustpan and a grin. "Absolutely. Need something special?"

Regan bit her lip, heat flooding her cheeks.

"Ah. Guess I'll have to get used to not being the only girl in the house anymore." Janey winked, easing Regan's embarrassment only slightly. "If you need something before then, look under the sink in the bathroom."

Regan forced a smile, then nodded.

While her father had been absent the past few days, Janey had been the hostess-with-the-mostest. *Do you need more pillows? Did you have enough warm water? Do you want more pancakes?* Not what Regan expected from a wild child with vintage t-shirts, holey jeans, and a bleached-blonde pixie cut. She encouraged Regan to head into town to meet people, but never left the house herself. She even worked from home, though Regan had no idea what she did. And, in the mornings, she could swear she heard Janey crying in the shower, but she always emerged with a smile—like somehow the water had washed away whatever grime her life left behind.

Boy, what Regan wouldn't give to learn that trick.

"Where is my damn umbrella?" Will asked, marching back into the room and locking eyes with Janey. "Did you give her that too?"

"Christ, Will. It hasn't even rained since she's been here." Janey got to her feet, dumped the dustpan in the trash, and pulled a rusty coffee can from the freezer. "Just call George. He'll drive you to work today."

The same George who, as it turns out, was the town mailman, cabdriver, and designated errand boy. Yesterday Janey had paid him to pick Will's vitamins up from the pharmacy.

"I don't know why you just can't drive me," Will muttered. "I hate driving with George."

"Why don't you just drive yourself?" Regan blurted out, before she could stop herself.

Will and Janey looked down at her like she had two heads and a tail. It was the same look her mother had given her when she'd asked why Santa Claus was passed out beside the liquor store. The same look Holden had given her when she'd asked how many girls he'd loved.

Regan felt the same way she did then, too. Like the monkey in a big game of keep-away.

Janey broke her gaze first, pulling cash from the can and placing the makeshift piggy bank back in the freezer. "I have work to do. I don't have time to take you today."

"Maybe I'm just concerned about the environment. She ever think of that?" Will said to Janey, swiping the money from the counter. "Aren't kids these days supposed to be environmentally conscious? Save the earth and not rely on the man for oil and all that?"

A million responses flew through Regan's head that she was too afraid to say aloud. Like how that antique lawn mower he used probably burned a bigger hole in the ozone in one swipe than driving Janey's little Honda did in an entire year. Or how could he possibly know what was important to Regan when he hadn't bothered to ask?

"I'll be at Hadley's at six," Will said, heading for the door. "Don't be late again, or I'm taking the produce section."

"Wait a minute. Aren't you forgetting something?" Janey said.

Will stopped, midstep, and turned toward Janey with an irritated look on his face. "What? You want a goodbye kiss before I go to school, Mom?"

Janey pointed to the counter, where a glass of water and four pills, each a different color and shape, sat on a napkin.

"I already took them," Will said.

"Well, that would be pretty hard, considering they were locked in my room." Janey crossed her arms. "Take them. Now."

With a heavy sigh, he stomped over to the counter, tossed all four pills in his mouth at once, chased them with the water, and then stuck his tongue out for Janey to inspect.

"Thank you," she said.

"Can I go now, Mom, or do you want to make sure I made my bed too?" he asked, but he didn't wait for her response. He stomped back through the kitchen door like a teenager who'd just been exiled to his bedroom. If Will would just give Regan the time of day, he might realize they had more in common than he'd thought.

Regan looked back toward Janey, who stared at her with an odd look on her face.

"He doesn't like taking pills," Janey said.

Regan shrugged, resisting the urge to scratch her armpits and make *ooh-ooh-ah-ah* sounds like the monkey she was. "Okay."

Janey opened her mouth, as if to say something else, but quickly closed it and pulled the apron from around her neck. "Well, I'll be upstairs working if you need me," she said, then tossed the apron on a hook and headed out the swinging door and up to the second level.

Once Regan heard the last footstep on the stairs above, she stood up. She walked over to the freezer, tugged on the handle, and pulled the makeshift piggy bank from the cold. She could take whatever money was inside and run until she couldn't run anymore. Her father probably wouldn't even notice.

You're not a thief, her mother's voice retorted.

"Yeah, but I'm not a monkey either."

It will get better. Give it time.

Regan rolled her eyes and placed the can back in the freezer.

"Time is all I have left," she said. "You took everything else, remember?"

Lindsay Shepherd celebrated her divorce by looking for someone new. Someone who loved to cuddle and didn't mind watching *Jeopardy* beside her on a Friday night. Someone who couldn't care less that she lived with her mother, or that she wasn't a size two anymore. Someone who would spend hours listening to her and never offer unsolicited advice.

Someone who would be loyal.

She knelt beside the last cage and sighed. How could she pick between all of them? They all fit the bill. The only real stipulation was that the cat didn't shed, because she'd never hear the end of it from her mother. *Look at all this cat hair, Lindsay. My eyes are puffy and red, Lindsay. Why can't you do anything right, Lindsay?*

But they were all in need. All lonely. All looking for someone to take them home and all hanging by their last shred of hope. They were all just like her, and she had to pick between them? It didn't seem fair. Nothing seemed fair.

"Which one would you pick?" she asked, glancing back at the girl holding the clipboard.

"Oh, I'm not a cat person. My husband's allergic." She pulled the clipboard to her chest, resting it on her huge, pregnant belly. Lindsay couldn't help but stare. It was like talking to someone with a broken tooth. No matter how hard she tried to ignore the bump, her eyes always wandered there. "Is there anyone at home you could ask? A husband or a child?"

As if the salt couldn't get any deeper into her gaping wound.

"No. Just me." Telling this woman she lived with her mother would make it worse. "Can you . . . uh . . . just give me a minute to think about it?"

As Lindsay watched her waddle out the door, she wondered if the girl realized how lucky she was. Beautiful, blonde, early twenties, married, baby on the way. She'd just started her life, and the possibilities were endless.

Shaking the bitter truth from her head, Lindsay bit her lip to hold back the quivers and continued the task at hand. This would've been something David handled, not her. He would've known the exact color to pick and what breeds shed more than the others. He would've had a name preselected and a playhouse built of yarn balls and scratching posts, because that's what David did. Now she had to make a decision like this on her own.

Lindsay took a deep breath. She could do this. She could find something *she* wanted. She paced back down the aisle glancing into the cages, looking for the ugliest cat she could find.

"What's wrong, Pepper? You look so sad."

Lindsay paused at the voice—deep with masculinity, yet gentle and smooth from concern. She stepped back, searching through the cages to the tiny room on the other side, until she spotted the figure of a man.

"You miss Mr. Henry, don't ya?" The man continued, petting a thin, smoky-gray cat in a bottom cage. "I know, buddy. I know."

"Excuse me?" Lindsay said.

The man's shadow went stiff, but he didn't speak.

"Did, uh . . . did something happen to this cat's owner?"

"Had a stroke. Got sent to the old folk's home in Claremont last week."

"Oh my. That's terrible." She approached the cage and kneeled down, finding the man's blue-gray eyes, but he quickly turned away. "I recently lost someone too. I'm looking for a friend to keep me company."

There was a long silence, long enough to ask herself if she'd been referring to the cat or the man with the smooth, masculine voice. Long enough to convince herself it had to be the cat, because she didn't even know this man on the other side of the cage.

"Would you like to meet Pepper?" he finally asked, eyes coming back into view.

Lindsay nodded. "Yes, I'd love to."

A few seconds later, the door opened at the end of the aisle. Lindsay hurried toward it, something telling her this was a limited time offer, and met the voice on the other side of the cages. He was tall and lanky, but had an intimidating, strong jaw lined in dark stubble.

"I'm Lindsay," she said, holding out her hand. "I just moved to town."

He glanced at it for a moment, as if checking it for contagions, then grabbed hold and led her to the open cage. "This here is Pepper. Pepper, this is Principal Shepherd."

"Oh. I didn't realize you knew me already."

He shrugged. "You were the second order of business at the June town council meeting. Everyone should know you."

"The second?" Lindsay ran her hands across the cat's soft mane, feeling the purr vibrate against her hand. "What was the first?"

"Sod for the new football field."

"Oh." She was glad to know landscaping was more important than her. "So, tell me more about Pepper. Does she shed?"

"Pepper's a *he*." He turned on her, lips pursed and arms crossed. "And if I told you he sheds, would that make you change your mind?"

"I . . . I don't know. . . I—"

"Because that's kinda shitty, you know. Judging a cat based on something he can't help."

Lindsay stared. Were they really having this argument?

"That would be like me judging you on those silly freckles or that ridiculously noticeable widow's peak." He closed the cage and locked it. "Doesn't feel so good, now does it?"

She smoothed her hair, spending extra time on the widow's peak she'd never paid attention to before. Shedding or no shedding, there was no way she'd leave here without this cat, no way another man would make another decision for her. "I'll take him."

Will examined the bananas one more time, making absolutely certain no green could be seen, and then placed them in his basket. Next were the apples. He didn't recall this being on the long list Janey had rattled off before she stomped toward the canned good section with Regan, pissed he'd insisted on the produce section since she was late—*again*. Janey didn't much care for Will's fruit and vegetable selections, especially the apples.

They had to be just right. Not too red. Not too shiny. Not too hard. And he wouldn't even consider them without at least one bruise present. The way he figured it, those apples were destined for the trash at the end of the day, so it was his duty to save the ones he could. Janey would've called them half-rotten, but not Will. They weren't in the best shape, but he could never forget about the other half, the good half. It wasn't fair.

He picked six out and weighed them, ignoring the crowding old woman grunting beside him. The garden was full of tomatoes, so he skipped past those and went for the peppers.

"Pepper," he muttered, feeling a slight sting in his chest. It had always been hard bidding farewell to the parolees, even back when he was the head veterinarian at the shelter. Perhaps his role had been reduced to nothing more than a shit scooper, but his love and devotion to the animals had never changed.

And while he was happy Pepper had found a new home, Will still wasn't sure about Pepper's new owner and her ridiculous widow's peak. Okay, so maybe it wasn't that ridiculous. In fact, it was barely noticeable. And her freckles had reminded him of his mother, along with her pale-green eyes and mousy-brown hair. But Will had been hard pressed to find something else in such a hurry. Maybe she had bad breath, or said *irregardless* instead of *regardless*. Maybe she laughed like a hyena or had a click in her knee when she walked. And maybe, if Will had given her long enough, she would've started to look down on him like everyone else in this town did.

He leaned against the pepper stand with a sigh. Who was he kidding? He'd been a downright ass to Principal Shepherd, and all she'd wanted was advice on choosing a cat.

The old woman grunted impatiently again. Couldn't she wait? People usually steered clear of him, but she was like a damned turd that wouldn't flush.

"You finished?" Janey asked, pulling up beside him with Regan and the cart.

Will reached straight for the toilet paper and held it in the air. "I'm not afraid to use it."

"I beg your pardon, young man?" the old woman said.

"Get off my ass, hemorrhoid!"

Regan let out a loud laugh as the old woman retreated, which irritated Will. She'd already taken over the house, the meals, the bathroom. Now the groceries? What next? He hoped she didn't plan on getting into his will, because all he could leave her was a lot of veterinary school debt and a barn with an ass inside.

"Come on," Janey said. "Before you insult someone else."

But I was just getting started.

They'd almost reached the registers when it happened. It

had been weeks since he'd seen her, maybe months. Will had started to wonder if she'd left for good this time, or had just gone on another one of her hiatuses. Didn't matter, really—the hole was there whether she was on the other side of the world or right next door. Seeing her reminded him how infinitely deep it was.

"Ellie," he said, low enough so Janey couldn't hear. But the quick notice Ellie took of him from across the store made him question how loud he'd been. It was only a glance, nothing to bring him any hope or peace. It was just enough to make him wish he were invisible.

"Who's Ellie?" Regan asked, jumping into his line of sight.

"Ellie?" Janey echoed. "Did you see Ellie?"

Will glanced over Regan's head to where Ellie had stood a moment before. As he'd expected, she'd disappeared. "No."

"Will—"

"I said no, Janey!" He gave her his best don't-fuck-with-me-right-now look and then reached into the cart, grabbing random items to toss onto the conveyor belt.

"Sure sounded like you said Ellie," Regan muttered. His look had no effect on her, but, then again, she'd never seen him lose his shit before.

Ignoring her sidebar comment, Will turned back to Janey and grabbed the box of tampons from her hand. "Well, this explains a lot."

"And what's that supposed to mean?"

"Well, since I had toiletries last trip, I know I bought you a new box of these *last* week. So like I said—explains a lot."

Janey's skin burst into bright shades of pink as she yanked the box from his hand. She wouldn't dare yell in public; she'd save that for the trip home, which he'd gladly take in exchange for another long Ellie discussion. "For your information, these aren't for me!"

"Well they aren't mine!"

She waited for him to catch up and, when he finally did, Will wasn't the only one embarrassed. Now all three of them were shades of pink.

"Fuck, I'm sorry," he muttered, his first words to his daughter in three days.

She rolled her eyes as she turned to Janey. "I'll be at the car," she said, then hurried from the store with her eyes trained on the ground.

"Did you see that? She just completely ignored me," Will said, a slight sting in his chest.

"Yep." Janey placed a box of Oatey Os on the conveyor belt. "Sucks having a taste of your own medicine, doesn't it?"

Regan went straight to her bedroom when they returned from the store that evening, and she didn't come out until Janey had settled into her office the next day. She wouldn't listen to any more apologies or excuses for her father. She wouldn't fake another smile and pretend she understood something she didn't. She wouldn't spend one more day in that house feeling like the monkey in the middle, because it simply wasn't fair for them to have secrets. Not when she couldn't have the slightest bit of privacy when it came to her menstrual cycle.

Today, Regan would catch that ball of truth, even if she had to rip it from their hands.

She stood at the kitchen window, waiting as the eleven o'clock hour approached. Like always, Will darted from the barn in his usual white T-shirt, jeans, and ball cap. He carried flowers today. Purple irises. That was new. He paused midway to the house and glanced back toward the barn for a moment, then mumbled something to himself and went on his way.

Or maybe he'd been talking with Ellie, whom Regan had

determined was a dead wife or girlfriend. Why else would Janey care if he'd seen an old flame at the grocery store? It was bound to happen in a small town. But if Will hallucinated Ellie, that would be cause for concern.

Follow him, her mother said.

Without hesitation, Regan stormed out the door and up the drive, catching the red shade of Will's hat as he rounded the corner. She followed, using the oak trees as her shield.

When Will turned up the walkway toward the stone church, Regan stopped in her tracks. She'd sworn to never go inside another church. Not after Steven had made her confess her sins in front of the congregation. If this was where Will spent his lunches, he could do it without her.

But Will didn't go inside the church. He kept going on around the back, toward another path that disappeared behind a tall, iron fence overgrown with dark ivy.

She hurried up the path, then followed the fence along the outside until she heard Will's voice on the inside. She pushed aside some ivy and found a peephole, spotting the red hat no more than ten feet from her. He knelt next to a rock.

No. Not a rock. A headstone. Regan was right about Ellie.

For the next forty minutes, Regan leaned against an oak tree and listened to him chat with Ellie about useless things. The flowers he'd picked for her. Janey's new comic book deal with the newspaper. Some cat named Pepper and a woman with a widow's peak. He rambled from one subject to the next, barely taking a breath in between, then suddenly went silent.

Regan waited for him to go on. He couldn't be finished. There was still one subject left. Her. Who she was. He hadn't told Ellie about Regan yet.

She peeked through the ivy. Will was gone.

She waited until she was sure he had left, then followed the fence back around, through the iron arches leading to the cemetery. She spotted the purple irises and hurried to the grave to verify what she'd already figured out herself.

But she was wrong. This gravesite wasn't Ellie's.

Regan read the headstone three times, just to be certain.

EMMA JANE FLETCHER. FOREVER CRADLED IN GOD'S ARMS. BORN AND DIED, 2011.

CHAPTER FOUR

R egan walked back to the house in a haze of confusion and anger. She'd had a sister—important information to share with family—but Will and Janey had never mentioned Emma. There weren't even any clues in the house to give it away, not that she'd seen anyway. Were the reminders too painful to look at? Is that why they hadn't told her? Why did Will go to the grave every day if he wanted to forget? The questions swirled around Regan like bonus tickets in a blaster booth at the arcade, but she couldn't grab onto them. Until the single, most important question came around.

What happened to Emma?

She stepped into the house, unsure how she'd found her way back. There was no sign of Janey or Will, so she started her search through the living room. First through the coat closet and then through the drawers of the end tables. Nothing. No hidden photographs or bronzed baby shoes. No old baby rattles or teething rings. There had to be something he'd kept, even if it wasn't so obvious. Something he could look at when he wanted to remember. Where would he keep it?

The barn. He'd keep it in the barn.

Regan stepped into the kitchen and walked toward the screen door, just in time to see Will charge from the barn with Janey hot on his heels.

"Absolutely not," Will shouted.

"It's just for a few hours. I'll be home by midnight," Janey responded.

"It's way too soon, Janey."

"Too soon for what? To ask you to keep an eye on your own kid?"

Regan rolled her eyes. She was fifteen. She didn't need a babysitter.

"But what if she gets hungry?" Will asked.

Nor did she need a chef.

"Then she'll eat," Janey retorted.

"And what if I get hungry?"

Janey laughed. "Then make yourself dinner. You're a grown man."

At that, Regan laughed too.

Will crossed his arms. "I don't find this funny at all."

Regan covered her mouth, even though he hadn't been talking to her.

"That's because you're not in my shoes," Janey said, then turned and continued toward the porch. "I'll have my cell phone on if you need anything."

Regan hurried to the table and began to casually flip through a sales paper.

"Hey there," Janey said, stepping through the door. "Where did you run off to?"

"Just looking around town. Trying to learn my way."

"That's good. I'm glad." Janey smoothed her skirt, though Regan was unsure why since it was leather. "Listen, I have to run up to Columbus and meet with my agent today. She's passing through town. There's plenty to eat in the fridge. Just help yourself." Janey grabbed her keys from the counter. "And Will's in the barn if you need anything. Okay?"

Regan forced a smile as Janey walked out. The last time she'd come to Will for help, he'd moved out there.

Once the click of Janey's heels turned to the crunch of gravel, Regan walked back to the window. Will was gone again, the rip of his wood saw the only evidence of his presence. She glanced around the kitchen, spotting where his pills had been sitting the day before.

Regan darted up the stairs and into her aunt's bedroom in search of those pills. She looked through the nightstand, the closet, the dresser, but came up empty. Then, just as she was about to close Janey's underwear drawer, the shine of metal caught Regan's eye. She pulled aside the velvet lining of the drawer to reveal a tiny silver key attached to a chain. Snatching it, she gave the room a sweeping glance.

The air vent, her mother said.

Regan's eyes locked on the vent below the window. Could her mother be right? Could all of the answers be there? Regan had hidden all her secrets in an air vent back home. Her diary, her love letters from Holden, her secret key to the room in the church basement where they often met. Regan wondered if, someday, someone would find those secrets locked away. Believe, as she once falsely did, that she and Holden had been in love.

She paced over to the vent and dropped down beside it, using the tiny key to unscrew it from the wall. Inside sat a wooden box, a little smaller than a shoe box, with the letters J.M.F. engraved into the lid and a tiny lock securing its latch. Regan placed the box on the floor in front of her, unlocked it with the key, and opened it.

Four medication bottles lay on top. Two of the drug names she didn't recognize, but the other two she did—lithium and Depakote. They were used to treat Bipolar Disorder. Regan had researched them online after her mother died, after the shock had turned into guilt and she needed a reason to believe it wasn't her fault. A reason she still looked for.

Her mother hadn't been out of her bedroom since the day after New Year's, since the horrible day Regan had made her confession at the church. Steven had told Regan not to disturb her mother, but she hadn't listened. She had to be sure her mother was okay. She had to be certain she still had her mom, even after losing everything else.

Regan had popped the lock on her mother's bedroom door with a coat hanger and inched inside. Her mother sat on the bed, staring into nothingness with the same stoic expression she'd had in the pews the week before. Only that day, it hadn't been a bible in her hand, it had been a gun. The same gun her mother had bought for protection a few months before. By the time Regan had walked back out, her mother was gone.

The medic had told Regan that her mother probably suffered from severe depression, perhaps even a disorder like Bipolar. That even if Regan hadn't broken in that day, her mother still would've killed herself. That, despite all the guilt Regan felt, the suicide wasn't her fault.

Regan believed it all but the last part.

Keep going, her mother said, pulling her from the memory.

Regan pushed the pills aside and dug farther into the wooden box. Old sketches of a cartoon character Regan didn't recognize, a photo of Janey kissing a woman that proved what Regan had already guessed, an old, dried-up corsage in a plastic bag. And, at the bottom, buried beneath all of these good memories, was the one bad memory.

Read it, Regan's mother said.

"Emma Jane Fletcher, age two months, died in her sleep yesterday. She is survived by her parents, Dr. William Fletcher and his wife Ellie, her aunt, Ms. Janey Fletcher, her uncle, Mr. Timothy Bradford, and her grandfather, Mayor Arthur Bradford. Funeral will be held at St. Mark's Cemetery, Saturday at noon."

Regan glanced up, a sorrowing feeling blanketing her, more questions flooding her mind. If Will was a doctor, why did he shovel dog crap from cages? How had a guy like him ever won over the mayor's daughter? How does an innocent two-month-old baby die in her sleep?

SIDS? her mother offered.

Regan nodded in agreement. An unmarried couple who lived in Regan's apartment building back in Chicago had lost their infant son to that, though Steven had insisted it was a punishment from God because they were living in sin.

"Asshole," Regan muttered.

We should go, her mother urged.

Regan placed the items back inside the wooden box the way she'd found them, bad memories on the bottom and good memories on top, followed by Will's medication. She latched it shut with the lock, placed it back inside the hole in Janey's wall, and got to her feet.

Now, if Regan could only find the secret hole in her father's wall, maybe he'd let her in.

Lindsay placed the last box onto her desk with a sigh. This office was smaller than her last. The town had spared no expense on the locker rooms and coach's office, but when it had come to the principal's office? Well, she'd just have to store her things in the janitor's closet between the mop bucket and the bottles of bleach.

It had taken all day, but, by dinner, she'd managed to whittle the heap of boxes down to one labeled Awards in black magic marker. She glanced around at the office walls—one full of windows, another lined with bookshelves, another decorated by a rather large corkboard. The only wall with empty space stretched straight in front of her.

Good thing she didn't have that many awards.

She lifted the flaps of the box, pulled out the large items first—her master's degree, her teaching certificate, her Educator of the Year award—and placed them on the floor against the wall. She'd remember to bring a hammer next time. As she returned to her desk, one of the frames fell over, the sound of cracking glass stinging her ears.

Just her luck, it was the fancy Educator of the Year award with the etched detailing.

Lindsay held the award over the trash can, shaking the broken pieces loose, then pulled off the frame. Unfortunately, that wasn't all that came with it.

David must have placed it there when he'd had it framed—the photograph of them at the awards dinner. Even with her fancy dress and joyous smile, she didn't match him. It was something about his dark hair, blue eyes, and olive skin tone that pulled her in. Would she ever have that again? The handsome man or the smile?

"Well, now. Looks like you're just about settled in."

Lindsay glanced up to see Mayor Bradford standing in the doorway. "So nice to see you again, Mayor. What are you doing out this way?"

He pushed his hands into his pockets and smiled. "I had a meeting with Coach Johnson, so I thought I'd swing by to see if you need anything."

A bigger office? A new certificate frame? A better life? "No, think I'm all set."

"Good, good." He stared at her a moment, still smiling. She hadn't noticed how round he was until now. Not just his face, but everything about him. Like a big beach ball. And with that blue suit, he kind of resembled the blueberry girl from Willy Wonka. And then all Lindsay could think about was that damned pie her mother had baked last night.

"I do hope you're planning on attending the Founders' Day Festival this weekend," he said. "It'll be a wonderful time to introduce you to the community before school starts."

"Yes, of course. My mother is entering the pie-baking contest."

"Oh, how wonderful. My daughter's the one who started that, you know?"

"Really?" she asked, trying to show interest in him, instead of fixating on the blueberry pie waiting for her at home.

"Yeah, won the first three contests herself. Probably would've won the last five had she entered." He paused and did that thing with his fingers that annoyed her—like he was rubbing a piece of silk between them. "Well, I suppose I'll let you get back to it."

"Alright then. Thanks for dropping by."

Mayor Bradford stopped just shy of the door. "She'll be judging, you know."

"I'm sorry?"

"My daughter will be judging. Came all the way back from her mission trip in Rwanda a week early, just to make sure she could."

"Oh, that's . . . great." A pie-baking contest hardly seemed like a good reason to rush home, but what did Lindsay know? "I'm sure you've missed her. Must be exciting."

"Yes, it is." There was the thing with the fingers again. "I could put in a good word for your mother, if you'd like."

Lindsay stared at him. Was he really trying to give her a leg up in a pie-baking contest? "Thank you, Mayor Bradford, but I'm sure she'll do just fine."

"Well, she probably doesn't need it anyway." He nodded and moved forward. "My Ellie has a keen taste for a good pie."

Will shielded his eyes from the afternoon sun as he looked across the yard toward the kitchen window. There Regan stood, same place as five minutes before when he'd checked, concentrating on something in front of her that Will couldn't see. A big, fat steak maybe. Perhaps a bowl of ice cream. His stomach growled just thinking about it.

He'd felt this way once before, at ten or eleven, standing in his bedroom doorway counting the number of steps to the bathroom. It had seemed so far away at that age. He'd have to pass his parents' bedroom door, pass Janey's, pass the hall closet his dad kept locked, and pass the cracked, oval mirror hanging across from the bathroom. He'd hated that mirror, hated the way his face appeared when he looked inside it, like displaced halves that would never find their way back to each other.

He'd inched down the hallway, holding himself in a way Mama wouldn't have approved of; going faster would've been disastrous. He shouldn't have watched that scary movie before bed or drunk that gallon of iced tea, and he shouldn't have glanced in his parents' room as he passed by.

Will could see it just as clearly twenty-five years later as he had that night. The candles glowed orange against the ivory walls and lace curtains. There was the faint hint of a whisper somewhere beneath the hum of the ceiling fan. And then there was that smell his parents' room had—a mix of his mother's lilac perfume and the straw clinging to his father's work clothes.

He'd known what candles and whispers meant; he had cable TV. Suddenly, it hadn't mattered that he had to pee, because sheer curiosity ran through his veins. Did his parents really do that sort of thing? Will didn't want to know, but, at the same time, had to.

He got on all fours and crawled inside, careful to avoid the squeaks in the wood floor he'd learned by sneaking into their bed after nightmares. But that night their bed was empty. They were on the other side, next to the window, sitting on the floor. It seemed odd to him, being on the floor, but he supposed the floor was as good a place as any.

He crawled around the bed, listening more intently as he neared. But when he turned the corner and saw his father's eyes, Will knew this wasn't like what he'd seen on TV. He'd never seen eyes so daunting. They'd looked like the eyes of that psycho from the movie he'd watched before bed. Full of anger. Full of hate.

"William! Get out of here!" his mother suddenly cried.

But Will couldn't move. Not even when his father's crazy eyes met his. Not even when Will felt the warm liquid puddle beneath him.

"Shh! Listen!"

Will recoiled at his father's low, harsh voice and held his breath to obey.

"Henry, please wake up," his mother begged. "You're still dreaming."

His father shook his head, but Will didn't know if it was in disagreement or an attempt to wake himself, then froze mid-shake. "They're coming!"

Will dove straight for his mother's lap. Wet or not, he needed to hide from whoever was coming through that door.

"It's fine, baby. Daddy's just dreaming," she whispered, planting a reassuring kiss on his forehead, then turned back to his father. "Who, Henry? Who's coming?"

"Please don't let them take me."

"Who, goddamn it? Who?" She yelled that time, which scared Will even more. She never yelled, except at the television when the lottery numbers ran.

"The angels!" he yelled. "They're coming!"

"Mommy?" Will cried.

"Henry, please! You're scaring Will."

His father turned to him, eyes calm and still, kind, even. "Don't be afraid. They don't want you," he said, and Will believed him because his father never lied. "They want me."

"Henry!"

"Listen." A half grin crept up his father's cheek, sending a tear down from his eye to meet it. "They're singing."

Will didn't remember much after that. He didn't remember his mother cleaning him up or putting him back to bed. He didn't remember waking up the next day or everyone acting normal. He didn't remember, but he was sure it had all happened.

Because the morning after, as Will passed the cracked mirror that split his reflection in two, he worried that he'd heard those angels singing too.

His stomach growled again, pulling him from the unpleasant memory and reminding him of the current problem at hand. He checked the kitchen window. Regan still stood there, an obstacle to his needs, just like that mirror all those years ago. What hell would plague him if he made the mistake of facing her? Would she foretell his future as the crack in his reflection had?

No. It wasn't worth it. He could live a night without food. He'd gone without it for a few days at a time before he'd been diagnosed—no sleep, no food. Just a lot of coffee and cigarettes. He could do it again now, even if he wasn't a spring chicken anymore. Craziness didn't discriminate against the aged; in fact, Will would say his father had grown worse as he got older.

His stomach growled a third time.

"Damn it, Janey!" He burst out the barn door toward the back porch. She should know better than to leave him alone with this . . . this *girl*. And for what? So she could go shack up with her girlfriend for a few hours? This wasn't fair. This wasn't fair at all.

Spaghetti, that's what Regan was fixing. The smell of boiling pasta hit him as soon as he opened the door. Spaghetti was usually Will's thing because it was all he could make, and the fact Regan was making it irritated him just a bit.

"The water's boiling over," he said.

Regan jumped and spun in one swift motion, dumping a container of parmesan cheese onto the floor. Good, she was afraid of him too. She should be afraid of him.

Will turned the stove to medium, but it was already too late. "You overcooked it!"

"Maybe that's the way I like it!" she spat. "I've certainly seen weirder things. Like a man who likes bruised apples!"

"Touché." He flipped off the front burner, moved the large pot to the back, and glanced around the kitchen for something else he could criticize her for. "Do you like cold sauce with your mushy noodles, or are you planning on eating them plain?"

"I hadn't decided yet," she retorted, dropping to the floor to clean up the mess of ground cheese. That's when Will saw the unopened jar on the counter by the window, sitting beside a wet dish rag, a butter knife, and a piece of the rubber liners from the cabinets. Janey would have Regan's ass if she knew she'd messed with her cabinets.

"Need some help opening that jar?" he asked.

"I can get it myself."

Will walked to the window and examined the tactics Regan had tried to open the jar of sauce. So, this is what she'd been doing for twenty minutes while he starved and her noodles turned to mush. She was creative, he'd give her that. He imagined she'd started with the wet cloth first, then tried to dislodge it with the butter knife, and, finally, ended with the rubber liner to get traction. All things he would've tried if he were a scrawny, weaker version of himself.

Regan snatched the jar from in front of him, red-faced. "I said I could get it."

He took it from her hands and popped it open with one quick twist. "There. Now there's no point in arguing."

"I could've done it," she muttered.

"Maybe. But I wanted to eat this century." Will reached into the pantry, pulled out a new canister of parmesan cheese and a fresh box of noodles, and placed them on the counter. "Save the mush. I'll give it to Jack for dessert."

"Who's Jack?"

"Jack. The donkey."

"You have an *ass* named *Jack?*" she asked with a grin.

He blinked. "Would you prefer Bob or Rick? Maybe Fabio?"

Regan rolled her eyes. "Never mind."

Will headed to the fridge, hiding his grin. Yes, he had an ass named Jack. Hardy-har-har. He might eat dinner with Regan tonight, but he refused to make jokes or small talk.

"Oh," Regan said as he closed the fridge. "You add green peppers to your sauce?"

He glanced at the pepper in his hand. "You allergic or something?"

"No, it's just . . . my mom put green peppers in her sauce. And I hate green peppers." She opened the new box of pasta. "So did she, actually."

"Then why did she put them in?" he asked.

"It's how Steven liked it." She dumped the pasta into a clean pot. "She wasn't one to complain. Especially about the person putting a roof over our heads."

Will looked down at the green pepper a moment, then turned around and placed it back inside the fridge. From what Janey told him, Steven was a real tool. Will had never met the guy and he wanted to punch him. "I don't remember Michelle being such a pushover."

"Yeah, well, people change. You're not exactly the Will Fletcher she described either, you know." Regan filled the pot with water. "Except the animal thing, of course. Though she embellished a little, because she said you were going to veterinary school."

Will dumped the sauce into the pot and stirred, opting to leave the salt in the wound and the explanation of his fall from grace for another day.

"She told me once that's why I was such an animal lover." Regan smiled a smile obviously not meant for him. "We were staying in a shelter on the west side—I must've been around seven—and she caught me sneaking my halves to a stray German Shepherd that hung around out back. Said it was something you would've done."

Will's spine stiffened. "Your *halves*?"

"Yeah. It was kind of mine and Mom's thing." Regan placed the pot of pasta on the stove and turned it on. "Save half for later so—"

"So you always have something else," he muttered.

Regan turned toward him. "Yeah. How did you know that?"

He shrugged. "Lucky guess."

"Anyway, that's when she told me about you. It's kinda strange for kids when they realize they have something in common with their parents." She leaned against the counter a moment and crossed her arms. "You know what I mean?"

Will shrugged again then turned his gaze out the window toward the barn, toward the woodshop where his *halves* resided in piles on the floor—all waiting for a better day to be sanded or stained. He thought of his father teaching him how to use the saw for the first time, the first time he'd smelled the harsh chemicals of lacquer, the first birdhouse he'd made for his mother.

And then he thought once more of that night up in his parents' room, when Will wondered if he'd heard the angels too. And Will prayed, for Regan's sake, that animals and a silly rule about halves were all she had in common with him.

Janey glanced back at Gretchen, asleep on the hotel bed, and quietly pulled the door shut behind her. She'd catch hell for leaving without saying goodbye, but it was easier this way. If she woke her, Gretchen would try to convince her to stay. Then they would fight, because Janey would be forced to admit that Will still came first and always would. Janey would receive the obligatory three-to-four-week silent treatment, until one day when Gretchen would call as her agent and sneak in an apology during their conversation.

Janey would forgive her, because that's what Janey did.

The elevator slid open and she stepped on, ignoring the stares from an old couple inside. As the doors closed, she saw her reflection in the shiny chrome and understood why. Her hair was in disarray, her mascara was smeared, and she was missing an earring. Add in the leather skirt, black, lace bra peeking out from her blouse, and cheetah print stilettos in her hands and Janey looked like an escort. Or perhaps mistress was a better word.

When the elevator doors opened, she squared her shoulders and stepped into the lobby with her head high. The transformation back to *Crazy Will Fletcher's Sister* would begin on the two-hour car ride home, but for these next few minutes she would continue to pretend she was the woman she used to be. Hot, new comic book artist, trendy New Yorker, a shiny link in the giant circle of friends she once had.

In truth, that was the real reason Janey forgave Gretchen. She was the only reminder Janey had of who she was before she'd become *Crazy Will Fletcher's Sister*. In those few hours before the fighting began, she felt like the old Janey again, not the nagging bitch she'd become over the past four years. Janey needed that time, as short and as infrequent as it was, to make herself whole again. Without it, every single piece of her belonged to her brother's illness.

The same hotel manager who was always on duty smiled as Janey neared the exit. "See you next time, Ms. Fletcher."

"Next time." Janey slid her shoes on at the door and stepped out into the dark night, pretending he was the doorman back at her and Gretchen's apartment in New York. Pretending "next time" was just a few days away instead of the two or three months it would be. But, by the time she reached her car a few aisles down, the whistle blew and pretend time was over.

Janey knew the text message was from Gretchen because of the ringtone—literally a whistle. She looked toward the east wing of the hotel and counted up until she found the corner suite on the fourth floor—their usual room. Sure enough, Gretchen stood in the window, a bed sheet wrapped under her arms.

"Damn." Janey retrieved the phone from her purse, entered

her lock code, and read the message aloud. *"Nice move. Tell the warden I said hello. G."* Janey glanced back up, but the window was empty. And now, so was she.

"Great," Janey muttered, lowering herself into the car. "Just fucking great."

To be fair, circumstances had been different when Janey first met Gretchen. Janey had just moved to New York, and they had exchanged numbers at a comic book conference. Three months later they'd moved in together. They'd traveled the world, kissed beneath the starry skies of thirty countries, listened to waves crash against crystal-white and onyx-black sand beaches. For the first time in her life, Janey had been free to be who she was meant to be.

Until the night she'd received that horrific phone call from her brother, and her life was forever changed by three little words. Emma was dead.

"When will you come home?" Gretchen had asked, as Janey packed for the airport.

"I'm not sure. After Will gets back on his feet," Janey had answered, not knowing at the time that he never would.

Nearly five years later, here she was, leaving again.

With a heavy sigh, Janey backed out from the parking space and began her long ride back to Half Moon Hollow. But as for her transformation back to *Crazy Will Fletcher's Sister?* Gretchen had done that in one quick jab to the gut.

By the time Janey pulled into the driveway at home, it was after one. The house was dark, only the moonlight illuminating her way to the backdoor. She considered checking on Will, but decided against it. He must've gone to bed early, as she didn't hear the whine of his saw.

Inside the house, she dropped her keys on the counter and poured herself a glass of water. Apparently Will hadn't starved while she was gone. He'd made spaghetti for dinner; Janey smelled oregano in the air, and the pots and pans sat drying in the dish rack. Usually, he left the mess for her to clean up, so this pleased Janey. She placed her empty glass in the sink and headed through the swinging door. But, two steps inside the living room, Janey froze stiff.

Her brother slept on the couch, with his pillow beneath his head at one end and his long legs hanging off the other. He wore pajama pants, and one sock dangled from his foot while the other lay across his slippers on the floor. His reading glasses sat on the table beside him.

Will hadn't fallen asleep here on accident; he'd slept here on purpose.

A wide grin spread over Janey's face as she pulled the quilt from the couch and placed it over him. Leaving Will alone with Regan for twelve hours had accomplished more than five days of her constant nagging. Maybe Will wasn't as fragile as Janey'd thought all this time. Maybe he just needed to be pushed out of the nest.

Maybe then, one day, Janey could leave her brother alone for good.

CHAPTER
FIVE

Will finished off his last rationed cup of coffee and set it on the vinyl placemat, waiting for his sister's standard checklist of reminders. It's not that he needed them— he'd been doing the same damn thing for four years, save a few seasonal chores here and there. But it made Janey feel important to rattle them off, so he obliged. Wasn't like he had a choice in the matter.

Thing was, they'd sat there for nearly an hour, and she hadn't said much of anything. Other than "Good morning," and "How did you sleep?" she'd just smiled with that same silly grin and glanced back and forth between him and the Sunday comics. And Will had grown impatient waiting for his list.

Janey poured herself another cup and held the pot up with a smile. "More?"

"What's wrong with you?"

"I'm sorry?"

Will leaned back in his chair, arms crossed. "It's ten thirty."

"So?"

"So, you've yet to remind me of my medicine."

"Let me get this straight," Janey said, placing the pot back in the coffeemaker. "You're criticizing me for *not* hounding you to take your pills?"

"*And* offering me a cup of coffee when you've already poured me two."

"I have?"

"Yes. And you're the one who says I should—"

"I know, I know. You should only have two." She grinned. "I just couldn't help but notice you slept on the couch last night."

Ah, hell. That's what this was about? The smile, the forgetfulness, the near breakdown of Fletcher family law was all because the mushy pasta had given Jack gas and forced Will to sleep inside last night?

"Well, somebody had to supervise that girl while you were out gallivanting. She could've burned down the house, or . . . or . . . or had some wild party while you met with your agent," Will said, using his fingers as quotation marks.

"Because she has so many friends in town?" Janey shook her head, ignoring his Gretchen comment like always. "You're being paranoid."

Will pursed his lips. He hated that word, and Janey knew it. Not because he disagreed, but because he didn't think there was anything wrong with being paranoid. Much better to err on the side of caution than let things go too far. He'd learned that the hard way. And he wasn't about to let her turn this on him. "Don't forget, you're the one who wanted to keep her."

Janey nearly spit out her coffee. "She's not a dog, Will. And when did you become so concerned with the teenager who's been living here for the past week, hmm?"

"I'm not. We just don't need any more trouble in this house.

And she's already got the cards stacked against her, being the crazy man's daughter and the niece of . . ."

"The niece of what? The only lesbian in town?" She shook her head. "I knew that's what this was about. God forbid Regan realize I'm gay."

"Oh for Christ's sake. It's not about that, and you know it!"

"Then what's it about?"

At that point, Will had no idea. "Regan. This is about Regan."

Janey picked up his empty coffee cup. "Well, if you're so concerned about Regan fitting in, you'll have no problem escorting us to the Founder's Day Festival today."

Will met her gaze, a little taken back. "You don't actually plan on going to that."

"Why not?"

"Somehow, I don't think we're on the guest list. Unless they're looking for entertainment. Someone they can dress up in a clown suit to make funny balloon animals for the kids."

"But this is about Regan," Janey echoed in a deep voice.

Damn it. He'd walked right into that one. Regardless, this had disaster written all over it. And for what? A stack of mediocre ribs and a slice of . . .

"I'll go!" Will said, with slightly more enthusiasm than he intended.

Janey turned with a skeptical look on her face. "Just like that?"

"Yes. But under one condition."

"Why do I have the feeling I'm not going to like this?" She crossed her arms and sighed. "What's the condition?"

Will smiled at his sister. There was only one reason he would agree to go to this thing. One reason he'd agree to do anything, really. And if Ellie had come back to Half Moon Hollow, she'd be judging the pie contest at the Founder's Day Festival. After

THE RULES OF HALF

all, she'd started the tradition. "You have to promise to let me off my leash if I go."

"Go where?" Regan asked, walking through the kitchen door in her pajamas.

"The Founder's Day Fest," Janey said, her eyes still set on Will in a game of stare-down.

"Really?" Regan glanced between them. "When?"

Will got to his feet, pulling his eyes from Janey first. "Right after I get back from my walk," he said. "So, be ready."

A rumble in Regan's stomach reminded her of the one o'clock hour approaching, and of the peanut butter sandwich still sitting in the brown bag beside her. She'd learned a lot about her father during her second covert trip to the cemetery. Like his million and a half reasons for preferring dogs to cats, oak to pine, bar soap to shower gel, and books to movies. She'd learned tomatoes gave him heartburn, chicken biscuits gave him gas, and that he hated when Janey bought green bananas. She'd learned these were the types of things Will talked to his other daughter about and, more importantly, there were two things he didn't talk to Emma about.

Regan or Ellie.

With a sigh, Regan leaned back against the old oak tree and removed the sandwich from the bag. She'd brought it as an excuse in the event Will caught her—no, she hadn't followed him; it was pure coincidence she'd picnicked beside the cemetery his deceased daughter was laid to rest in. Unlikely maybe, but questioning her lie would mean admitting all of his. Regan didn't know much about her father, but she knew enough to deduce he wouldn't do that.

Save half.

Regan stiffened, midchew, at her mother's voice, then glanced at the sandwich in her hands. She'd almost forgotten about the rule of halves. It came in handy many days along the highway and many nights in overcrowded shelters, when it was just the two of them pinching pennies and rationing every ounce of food. That was long before Steven rescued them from the streets. Long before her mother realized how empty her life really was and decided to end it.

How ironic it was that before Steven, when they had nothing, her mother felt full.

Save half, her mother repeated.

"Fine," Regan muttered, hopping to her feet and tucking the remaining half back into the plastic bag. She'd save it for tomorrow when she came back, as she'd already decided she would. She'd come back the day after and the day after if that's what it took to get to know Will. She'd come back and fight off the guilt of spying on him, even if she had to pretend she was the dead girl lying in the ground he talked to. She'd come back because it was still better than being what Regan was to him.

Not a damn thing.

She left the old oak tree behind and followed the ivy-covered fence toward the road, as Will rattled off his to-do list to Emma. Just as she'd reached the end, the sound of retreating footsteps caught her attention.

Regan hurried to the sidewalk, glancing one way and then the other before spotting a tall boy sprinting up the sidewalk. He wore a navy-blue baseball cap and football jersey to match, the name Barrett printed above the large, yellow number twenty-one. At the church steps, he paused and glanced back toward Regan, a scowl on his face that resembled an old man's whose grass she'd just trampled over.

What was his problem? Who was he? A friend of Will's, maybe? Did Will even have any friends? Had he spied Regan spying on Will? Would he rat her out if he did?

Regan took a step in the boy's direction with one last look around the fence at Will still kneeling beside Emma's grave. She took another step.

Don't, her mother ordered. *Look.*

Regan glanced toward the boy, just as he disappeared behind the arched, wooden church doors.

Leave, her mother added.

Without question, Regan obeyed. Because she'd followed a boy into a church before, and came out a different person. Because the last time her mother had said those three words in that order, Regan had been too selfish and stubborn to listen.

Because when she woke at night, the haunting image of her dead mother still branded in the dark, Regan knew it was the consequence of both those bad decisions.

Janey never would've attempted this had it just been her and Will, because he was right—no one wanted them at the festival. But there was something about seeing Will on that couch last night that had given her hope. Besides, if hell was freezing over, Janey wanted a homemade corndog and a cinnamon-covered funnel cake before it did.

With a deep breath, she stepped onto Main Street and glanced over the crowd, Will and Regan standing just behind her on either side. She imagined they were a band of superheroes charging into battle, the Fierce Fletchers they would call them, and today they would take back every bit of respect that had been stripped from their family over the years. Yes, it was a long shot. Okay, it was a near impossibility. But Janey had to have hope. She had to believe that the rest of her life wouldn't be defined by the memory of her father's sickness or the reality of her brother's. The rest of her life and her niece's.

She put on a big, reassuring smile and turned around to see Will heading in one direction and Regan in the other. So much for that whole banding together thing.

"Hey! Where are you two going?" she asked.

They both paused and turned; Regan responded first. "Thought I'd go look for that . . ." She glanced at Will, then back at Janey with a pair of pleading eyes.

For the mysterious boy she'd asked Janey about, as they'd waited for Will to return from the cemetery. And what could Janey say, really? It was the first attempt Regan had made to meet people. "Okay, well, just be back at the bingo tent in an hour."

Regan nodded, then jogged off.

"The bingo tent in an hour," Will echoed. "See you then."

"I'll be in the pie tent if you need me," Janey called after him.

Will turned around, slowly. "The pie tent. Really."

"Yes. The pie tent."

"But you hate pie."

Janey crossed her arms, but didn't respond. They both knew she wasn't heading to the pie tent for the sweets. Neither was he. She'd figured it out when he'd climbed in the car, freshly shaven and smelling like a Christmas tree. The only reason Will had come was to look for Ellie.

"Fine." Will set off in the opposite direction. "Just fine."

"I'll get you a piece of blueberry!" she hollered, but all she received in response was a hand in the air. Had Will given her the finger?

Janey made her way through the crowd to the yellow-and-white striped tent, the aroma of sweet crust and fruit flooding her senses as she stepped inside. She counted eleven booths, all with a different kind of pie. Cherry, lemon meringue, pecan, apple, strawberry, peach, blueberry, and those were only the ones she could see.

Lots of pie, lots of people. But still no sign of Ellie Bradford.

Janey didn't recognize the two women sitting at the blueberry booth—one older and the other a younger version of the first. They both had kind eyes and inviting smiles, two things the rest of the townspeople no longer offered Janey and Will. It wasn't until George came through the back of the tent, carrying a stack of pies and calling the younger woman "Principal Shepherd," that Janey remembered this was more than just Regan's introduction to the town.

"Are these the last of them, George?" Principal Shepherd asked.

"Yes ma'am. Only the one labeled judging left."

"Thanks." She leaned into the older woman. "You see that, Mom? I told you everyone would love your blueberry pies."

"Yes, dear. You were right. Now can you please just take orders? One per customer."

Principal Shepherd smiled up at Janey. "Thirty-five and she's still telling me what to do."

Janey thought of Will. Janey *always* thought of Will. "I'm sure she means well."

"Not so loud! You'll only encourage her!" She handed a piece of pie to Janey and then held out her hand. "I'm Lindsay Shepherd."

"Janey Fletcher." She watched Lindsay's hand for the recoil that usually followed, but it never came. Lindsay Shepherd didn't have a clue who she was. Yet.

Janey clasped Lindsay's hand. Her skin was soft and warm, a contrast to Janey's hard calluses from years of sketching and farming. Or maybe it felt so good because it had been ages since someone offered to shake her hand in this town.

"Hey, Fletcher, you gonna get a piece of pie or what?"

Janey stiffened. *Bob Yates.* She'd know his chewing tobacco–mumbled voice anywhere.

"Oh wait, I forgot," he continued. "This isn't the kinda pie you like, is it?"

A group of men erupted in laughter behind her, men just like Bob whom referred to parts of a woman's body as food, like pies and melons and pepperonis. Just another reason Janey would stick to women. She dropped Lindsay's hand, doing her best to ignore them and the confused look on Lindsay's face.

"Where's the crazy man?" Bob said. "At home watching *Looney Toons?*"

At that, Janey spun around, jaw clenched. "You know, if you were half the man my brother was, maybe you wouldn't be standing in line behind *me* to get pie."

The men booed, and there was nothing Bob Yates could do because he wasn't smart enough to keep up. "Just get out of my way," he demanded, sliding past her to the front of the line, where he winked at Lindsay Shepherd. "Piece of that blueberry pie please, honey."

Lindsay glanced between them, then handed a second piece of pie to Janey. "Oh, so sorry. But given the choice I'd rather give my pie to her."

"Looks like the new town principal's a lesbo too." Bob Yates pushed himself off the table with a grunt and stomped off. "We don't want your damn pie anyway, do we fellas?"

But the men didn't follow; they only stared at the ground. Janey marked that as a win in her book, with an assist from Lindsay Shepherd.

"Thanks. You didn't have to do that," Janey said, turning back to her ally.

"Don't mention it. People like him just need to be put in their place from time to time."

"I've been looking for a place to put Bob Yates for years."

Lindsay giggled, the sound flooding Janey's ears with warmth. She wanted to hear it again, but, put on the spot, she couldn't come up with anything funny to say. Where was Will when she needed him? He was never short of wit.

"Would you like to come over, maybe? For dinner sometime?" Janey blurted out instead.

Lindsay smiled. "Dinner sounds lovely."

"Yeah?"

"Yeah. Why not?"

There were a million reasons why not, but Janey wouldn't give her any. "Perfect. Great. Fantastic." How many more overly enthusiastic words could she spit out? Feeling the heat creep up her neck, she turned to an empty table and jotted her address on a napkin. "When?"

"Tuesday," Lindsay's mother said, whom Janey had all but forgotten was there.

Lindsay turned toward her mother, arms crossed.

"What?" Her mother said, handing another piece of pie out. "Tuesday's my turn to host card night. Figured you'd rather not be at the house."

Lindsay turned back to Janey. "Tuesday's fine. Now, if you'll excuse me, I'm being beckoned to meet the mayor's daughter."

Janey's eyes began to search, even before the weight of this statement sank in. It had been another part of her training, along with medications, food triggers, and sleep cycles—find and eliminate all of her brother's catalysts.

And there the biggest catalyst stood, in the back of the tent, straightening her auburn hair and smoothing her pink skirt, a big, blue judge's ribbon attached to her white-knit jacket.

Ellie Bradford was here. Ellie Bradford wasn't a figment of Will's imagination. Ellie Bradford had come home to finish off her brother.

The sidewalks of Main Street were too crowded to walk on, being lined with vendors selling knickknacks and gadgets no one could possibly have a use for. Regan's mother had loved events like this. She'd dragged Regan around, getting ideas for their next big venture. Paper windmills, decorative vases turned fish tanks, tin men made of old soup cans they'd dug out of the trash—they'd done it all. Of course, none of the plans ever panned out, until their last festival, where her mother had found Steven on a corner handing out pamphlets for His Light. He was the venture that gave them a home and all the heartache that came with it.

He got us off the streets, her mother said. *Remember what's important.*

Surviving—that's what her mother referred to. Ironic, considering she was now dead. Had her mother forgotten how to survive when Steven came along? Had she been ill-equipped to survive in his world? Or, had she realized surviving wasn't the same thing as living? Regan would never know, but she did know she wouldn't end up like her mother.

It was easy to find a meal to eat, a shed to sleep in, a winter coat to wear. Her mother had taught her to scavenge well. What was hard was finding someone who cared enough about her to share all those things, without all the hoops. Regan wasn't even sure she'd know that someone if they stood right in front of her, because her mother had never taught her to scavenge for that. But Regan would find it, even if it wasn't in Half Moon Hollow. Even if it meant letting go of everything she was, and molding into who she was meant to be.

"I'm not like you," Regan finally responded, though she had no idea *who* she was.

Her mother giggled, adding another crack to Regan's heart.

"Glad I'm so amusing."

Only you can decide who you are, Silly Sue.

Another crack. Her mother hadn't called her that since she was a kid. Where the "Sue" had come from, she didn't know. Tears welled in her eyes. "Please, just leave me alone."

"Really? But I'd just worked up the nerve to come over here."

Regan stiffened at the voice that wasn't her mother's, then glanced over her shoulder to see a boy standing five or six feet away, wearing a blue-and-yellow football jersey with the number twenty-one on it.

It was the boy from the cemetery today.

"Just wanted to introduce myself," he said.

"Yeah?" She wiped the tears from her eyes as she turned to face him. "Is that why you ran away from me today?"

"You saw me, huh?"

"No, I just took a wild guess," Regan retorted.

A grin tugged at the corner of the boy's mouth as he neared, the weight of his stare cementing Regan's feet in place. His eyes were an odd shade of green that, next to his sandy hair, freckles, and olive skin, made them look like two gems shining in the desert sun. He was beautiful.

"Yeah, well, sorry about that. We don't get many new kids around here," he said, tossing an orange softball back and forth in his hands before holding one out. "Name's Lane."

She grabbed hold, trying to disguise her nervousness as a cold chill. "Regan."

"Like the president?"

What was it with these people? "No. My mom was a liberal."

He nodded, his grin falling to one side. "Was?"

"Yeah. Was."

A question played across his lips that Regan knew she would not be able to answer.

"Lane! Come on, man! You gotta see this!" another boy shouted.

"I swear, they can't do anything without me," Lane mumbled, then threw his hand up in acknowledgment. "Hey, we're running a dunking booth to raise funds for a scoreboard for the new football field. You should come over."

"Really?" she asked, with more enthusiasm than intended.

"Yeah, you get three shots for a dollar. And it's for a good cause."

Regan deflated. Of course he was trying to drum up business, not trying to get to know her better. That made more sense. "Actually, I gotta get back."

"Ah, really?"

No, not really. "Yeah. But good luck with the chalkboard."

"Scoreboard," he corrected.

She bit her lip. "Right, scoreboard."

"All right then. See you around, Regan with the red hair."

"See ya." Regan waited for him to turn before she added *Lane with the lovely eyes.* He was far more clean-cut than the boys back in Chicago who talked to her, with their baggy jeans, disheveled hair, and faded, concert T-shirts. Lane was the kind of boy her mother had told her to shoot for, the kind she now tried to avoid. He was trouble, despite the eyes.

Go back, her mother's voice interrupted.

Regan paused on the edge of the curb, gritting her teeth. "He's not interested in me."

Just turn around.

Regan let out a big sigh and spun around. Just as she'd thought, Lane was already lost in the crowd of people laughing it up at the poor sap in the dunking booth. The poor sap who looked an awful lot like . . .

"Will!" she yelled, taking off in a sprint toward the crowd. "No! Will!"

"Come on, crazy man!" a boy yelled. "Play us a song like you did in the fountain."

"Stop it! What are you doing?" Regan yelled, squeezing between the jerseys and cheerleading uniforms in her way. But no one paid her any attention, not with the crazy man climbing back onto the platform, only to be dunked again. Why didn't he climb out? Why was he letting them make a fool of him?

Regan pushed the last two football players out of the way and grabbed a cheerleader's hand just before the bitch punched the bull's-eye again. "Leave him alone!"

The girl yanked her hand free. "Says who?"

"Says me," Regan snapped, closing the gap between them. "Unless you want the crazy man's daughter to show you just how crazy *she* can be."

"Is that a threat? Are you threatening *me*?"

Regan clenched her fists ready to charge. "Abso-fuckin-lutely."

The girl took a step back, her face red as a beet against her blonde hair. "Who the hell—"

"Court, just let it go," Lane said, stepping through the crowd as it parted.

"Don't you dare tell me what to do, Lane Barrett!"

"Wouldn't dream of it." He stepped between them, his back to Regan. "But remember what Sheriff Blythe said the last time."

Courtney glanced between them, eyes landing back on Regan. "Since you're new here, I'm going to give you a break. But next time, you better remember who you're dealing with."

Regan turned back toward the booth, helping Will climb from the tank.

"You hear me, skank?" Courtney added. "I'm a Bradford. And no Fletcher ever talks to a Bradford that way."

A Bradford. Like Ellie. Great. In some weird, fucked-up way, Regan could be related to this sorry excuse for a girl. The hits just kept on coming in Half Moon Hollow.

Regan snatched a towel from a pile on a picnic table and led Will from the silenced crowd toward an empty park bench just outside the road blockades. "You okay?"

Will nodded, shivering.

Regan tossed the towel over his shoulders. "Wait here. I'm going to go find Janey."

"Please d . . . don't tell her about this."

"I think she's going to know when—"

"I'll th . . . think of something. I just . . . don't want t . . . to ruin her day."

Of all the things to be upset over, this is the one he'd picked? Not the crowd laughing at him. Not the ice-cold water that had turned his lips blue. He was worried about ruining Janey's day. And here Regan had thought he only worried about himself.

And Emma.

She sat on the bench beside him. "What were you doing, anyway?"

"I was hot."

"Bullshit."

He shrugged. "They said they needed a new scoreboard. Thought I could help. Everyone in town is dying to dunk the crazy man."

"So? Why give them the satisfaction?"

"Because, fuck them," Will spat.

Regan whipped her gaze toward his, truly seeing her father

for the first time since she'd arrived in Half Moon Hollow. This had nothing to do with the summer heat or a new scoreboard for the football stadium. Will wanted those people to make a fool of him. She knew this because it's what she would've done, what she *had* done. Playing the part everyone cast her in was far easier than proving them wrong.

It made her wonder how much of Will's behavior was a front to keep everyone away.

"That was stupid, what you did," Will said, shaking water droplets from his soaked hair. "Now they all know who you are."

That concern hadn't crossed her mind in the heat of the moment. All Regan had thought about was getting to her father, sticking up for the guy who wouldn't stick up for himself. And, whether he'd ever admit it or not, Regan knew Will would've done the same for her. Because they were built of the same stuff. Not just blood and genes, but regrets and fears and shame.

Only you can decide who you are, her mother's voice echoed.

Regan shrugged. "So what if they know who I am?"

Finally, so did she. She was her father's daughter. That's who she was, and that's who she wanted to be.

Will climbed the ladder to the loft, his security detail following behind. When Janey had suggested he go lie down, he hadn't expected she'd be coming along. In fact, Janey hadn't done anything he'd expected since she'd sprinted around the corner toward the park bench, demanding he go to the car immediately. She hadn't even noticed he was wet until halfway home.

It wasn't until they'd pulled into the driveway that it occurred to Will they weren't running *to* anything. They were running *from* something.

"Do you mind?" he asked.

His sister turned to face the corner of the loft. She'd seen him naked on more than a few occasions, but never when he was of sound mind. And if there was one thing he wanted Janey to know, it was that he was 100 percent in control of every movement he made right then.

"I wish you'd come sleep inside."

Chills rushing over his skin, he peeled the wet clothes from his cold body and tossed them into a pile on the floor. He didn't need to answer; his harsh sighs and brisk movements spoke louder than words. And, when he climbed beneath the covers of the cot, he made an extra effort to toss around three or four times for added effect.

Janey checked over her shoulder before returning to his side. Normally, he liked when she pulled the covers up to his chin and tucked the sides in tight. It was like a cocoon; he was unable to bust out into the world and hurt anyone else. But, tonight, he only felt suffocated.

"Don't. I'm too hot."

"Will, you're freezing," she said, continuing with her tucking. "You want to tell me why you were soaked to the bone?"

"You want to tell me what fire you were running to?" he retorted.

Janey placed her hands on her hips without responding. When had they started lying to each other? Why couldn't they just call bullshit and get it over with?

"Of course not," he muttered, rolling toward the woodplank wall. "Because that would mean you'd actually have to admit she's here, wouldn't it?"

"Who?"

"Oh, give it up, Janey. I know you saw Ellie. And I'll save you the suspense by telling you I didn't, okay? So there's no need for the suicide watch, Warden."

"That's not fair!"

"Fair? *Fair?*" he yelled, staring daggers at her. "I'll tell you what's not fair! A thirty-five-year-old man not deciding what he eats, or how many cups of coffee he drinks, or who he can and can't talk to!"

"Imagine what would've happened. You know how you get."

"Do I? She's been home twice in five years. *Five fucking years!* Christ, Janey, we were married. We had a child together. We *buried* that child together. You can't just erase it, and neither can the rest of the town."

Janey took a deep breath. "Will, the last time I let you near Ellie Bradford—"

"Fletcher, damn it! Ellie Fletcher!"

"—you ended up in Creedmoor with forty-seven stitches in your wrists and eating through a feeding tube," she continued. "And let's not forget what happened to Ellie."

There it was, the card that trumped all others—Ellie's dislocated elbow.

He hadn't meant to hurt her. He'd rather die first, which was part of the reason he'd ended up in Creedmoor. But he'd had to convince her that the divorce papers were a mistake. He'd just wanted to stop her from leaving again. But he'd pulled too hard, like always.

"I won't let that happen again," Janey said.

"How do you know it will happen again? I'm on my medicine. I'm better now."

"You're not better. You're just under control. And seeing Ellie will only jeopardize that, so forgive me for not wanting to go down a road I know leads to nothing but pain and heartache for this family. I just can't go back there with you anymore, Will. I won't."

"I don't recall asking you to go there with me the first time," he reminded her.

Janey met his gaze, eyes narrowed. "Well then, it's a good thing you had no say in the matter, because otherwise you'd be lying in a grave next to Emma."

Will fell against the pillow. "I'm tired. I'd like to sleep now."

"Will . . ."

"Just go, Janey."

"Fine. We have a busy day tomorrow anyway." Janey got to her feet with a sigh. "Don't forget your appointment with the probation officer at nine. And I need to get Regan registered for school." Janey paused, glancing out the loft window toward the house. "She must have a million questions. What should I tell her?"

He shrugged. "That she has more freedom than I do?"

Janey moved across the loft and stepped onto the top rung of the ladder. "I know you don't believe me, but I do what I do because I love you. There's nothing I want more than to let you make your own decisions. But I can't do that until you prove to me that you're capable."

"You're right," Will muttered, as she descended the ladder. "I don't believe you."

It was a catch twenty-two. How was Will supposed to prove he could see Ellie if Janey never gave him a chance to? How could Janey ever give him the chance if she didn't believe he was capable of doing it? There had to be a way.

Will stood and walked across the wood floor over to the window. Through the dusty filth on the glass, he could barely make out Regan looking out from his mother's room. If it weren't for the shine of red hair in the setting sun, he probably wouldn't have noticed. She waved. Before he could catch himself, Will waved too.

They stood like two species separated by universes, but still attached. He couldn't turn away. Maybe because she'd rescued him from the crowd. Or maybe it was the way she'd seen right through him after. She knew he'd climbed into that tank with a purpose. She knew he'd do it again given the opportunity. She knew *why*.

And she hadn't run. Hell, she'd tossed him a towel.

Will spun on his heels and headed for the ladder. The only way Janey would loosen the reins was if he went the direction she wanted him to go, and, right now, that direction was toward Regan. That girl just might be able to fix him enough for him to appear whole, or at least semi-glued together anyway.

Then maybe Ellie would look at him like she used to.

Janey pulled the curtains back, the morning sun spilling through the office window toward the closet like a spotlight to her darkest parts. The light bulb inside had burned out years ago; she'd just never replaced it. Maybe because she kept forgetting, maybe because she was trying to. Either way, she didn't want to go inside any more now than she had in the past, but she had to. It was time; she'd already kept the secrets locked away for too long. Regan deserved to know.

Balancing against the wall with one hand, she slid the other into the dark and searched for the seam of the loose wallpaper behind which her mother used to stash small presents. Janey must've been eight or so when she'd gone snooping one December and found the cold metal of a pistol hidden away instead of the smooth silk of a ribbon. That had been around the time she'd realized something was wrong with her father. Around the time she began to fear him.

She tucked her fingers beneath the flap of wallpaper, into the hole it was meant to cover, and retrieved the dusty gift box Ellie had given her the day she'd given the divorce papers to Will. Everything was still inside—photographs stained with

Will's blood, the church program listing her and Emma's names side by side, the tiny, gold baptism ring Janey'd given to her new goddaughter. Emma's baptism was the only untainted memory Janey had of her niece. It was the last time she'd held Emma in her arms, kissed the crown of her soft head, smelled the lavender shampoo used on her strawberry-blonde hair. Janey had never seen anything so beautiful. And hadn't since.

She'd put the box of keepsakes below her bed that day. It hurt too much to look at them, but she felt better knowing they were near. She'd hoped the next time she'd look inside she'd be able to smile, maybe even laugh. But it was Will who'd opened the box the next time, not Janey.

That was the first time her brother had tried to commit suicide.

Janey placed the lid back on top, lips quivering at the memory of her brother soaked in his own blood. How he'd survived she'd never know, just like she'd never know what he was looking for that night or why he'd opened the box. But when she'd seen the anguish on his face after, she was certain he'd never come out of it.

God, how she wished the old Will would come back.

She cradled the box in her hand and headed down the hall to Regan's room, praying it would be enough to explain. "Regan? Are you awake?" she asked, tapping on the door.

No response.

Janey pushed the door open to find an empty room. That's when she heard the faint sound of a radio coming from down the hall. She headed for Will's room to investigate, but it too was empty. Nothing but an unmade bed, a tiny pile of dirty clothes, and his alarm clock playing a tune from his dresser. How many times had Janey shown him where the clothes hamper was? How many times would she have to beg him to make his damn bed, or even sleep in . . .

Janey flipped the alarm clock off and marched down the hall to the stairs. When had Will come inside last night? *Why* had he come inside? How had she not heard him? Janey didn't know whether to be angry or happy.

There were crumbs on the peanut butter–smudged counter, but the kitchen was empty, except for a napkin pinned to the fridge with a note in Will's scribble.

"Son of a bitch!" she shouted, rushing into the living room and out the front door.

But it was too late; they were already gone.

CHAPTER SIX

"Sixty-seven," Lindsay muttered, clenching her folder. That was the number of blank stares she'd received in this morning's faculty meeting. The teachers had all summer to prepare for her new block scheduling system, but acted as if she'd informed them the earth was round for the first time. With school starting in less than a week, Lindsay feared that her implementation was doomed.

And this couldn't fail—not after she'd spent the month of May convincing Mayor Bradford it would work—because if Lindsay lost her job, what would she have left?

"Uh, Ms. Shepherd!" the secretary said as Lindsay stepped inside the main office.

"Not now, Tammy. I have something to attend to." Like closing her office door, turning down the blinds, and beating her head against the desk. That would help.

But the man she ran into as she rounded the corner had other ideas, like playing fifty-two pick up with her folder of handouts.

"Damn!" she exclaimed before seeing the student in the chair beside the man. "I mean . . . *oops!*"

The red-haired girl raised an eyebrow, staring at Lindsay with beautiful, blue-gray eyes. It was an odd color, yet familiar, and popped against the heavy eyeliner she wore. Lindsay had seen girls like this before, hiding behind a wall of black clothing and dark makeup to tell the world to go fuck itself, when all they really wanted was someone to notice them.

"Sorry. The secretary told us to wait in here," the man said, kneeling to help her retrieve the papers. And there were those same eyes.

The odd man from the shelter. What was his name? He'd never told her. He seemed different today. Still too thin and a little pale for summer, but freshly shaved, and his dark hair was combed. Without the gray stubble on his chin, he looked ten years younger.

"How's Pepper?"

"Pepper?" she asked, still staring at his chin.

"You *did* take Pepper home, right?" he asked.

Lindsay flushed. "He's good. Though he's taken a liking to my mother more than me."

"Don't take it personally. Pepper just likes old people."

"He liked *you*," she retorted before she could stop herself.

He shrugged. "Well, I'm not normal."

That was refreshing to know. Either Lindsay had to let her gray roots grow out or act like a crazy person. "So what can I do for you today, Mr. . . . ."

"Will."

"Okay, *Will*," she responded. Will was his name. "And this is?"

"Regan." He approached the girl with an odd smile, as if hooks yanked it up without consent, and patted her shoulder so gently that Lindsay wondered if he'd even touched her. "Regan is my . . ." He paused a moment, then gave his head a quick shake. "Regan is my . . ." He paused again, staring up at the ceiling, as if searching for a word. "Regan is my . . ."

Lindsay waited, mouth slightly ajar like she did when students fumbled around for a tardy excuse.

"Daughter," Regan finally answered, sinking farther into her seat. "I'm his daughter."

Lindsay reared back. Daughter? That was the word he'd had so much trouble coming up with? The role he couldn't seem to define? She'd expected something long-winded and convoluted, like *Regan is my second niece from a third marriage, twice removed*. Was he drunk? Maybe high on something? Or could he not answer such a simple question because the answer wasn't so simple to him?

It made Lindsay uncomfortable. More so than she already was around this strange man.

Will mumbled something Lindsay couldn't make out, then sat in the chair beside Regan. "She needs to register for school," he said.

Lindsay glanced between them a moment, still confused. "Well, let me get you an enrollment packet," she finally said, then backed out of the room slowly, unsure if she should leave. She'd had situations like this before, back in Pittsburgh. Beaten children, molested teens, parental neglect—Lindsay had seen many types of abuse in the fifteen years she'd been in education. And the one thing they all had in common was the empty feeling in the bottom of her stomach. The one she imagined would be called "maternal instinct," if she'd been born with the ability to be a mother.

Foolishly, she'd thought moving to a small town would make it all go away—both the troubled kids and the emptiness.

"Just help her in any way you can," she said to herself, then pulled the packet from the file cabinet, slammed it shut, and returned. "Here you go. Just fill these out and get them back to us as soon as you can." She turned toward Regan and offered a smile. "I'm Principal Shepherd, by the way. This is my first year at Half Moon High, too. So you won't be alone, I promise."

Regan half grinned, her eyes sparkling for a moment before fading back to gray. It was more of a response than Lindsay had expected, but not what she'd hoped for. As much as she wanted to fix the girl, a day of attention couldn't undo a lifetime of whatever she'd endured.

"Well, if there isn't anything else you need . . ." Lindsay said, sitting at her desk.

"Actually, there is just one more thing." His hooked smile returned as he pulled a crumpled, yellow piece of paper from his pocket. "My probation officer asked me to give you this. Said you'd be expecting me."

Regan gripped the steering wheel, checking her surroundings like the getaway driver for a bank robbery. It made her nervous being this close to the football team and cheerleaders after yesterday, but Will couldn't have cared less. Despite the pointing, he took his time measuring and sketching the location of the new scoreboard. How ironic that his punishment was to build the very thing his instability had helped raise the funds for.

Will opened the car door, mumbling random numbers, then fell into the seat beside her, staring straight ahead. "Let's get going. We're on a schedule."

Of course. They needed to be home by eleven for his daily walk. He'd made sure to remind her of its importance three times before they'd left on their random errand spree.

Regan tugged on the gear, but it wouldn't budge.

"You need to turn it on first," Will noted.

Right. She knew that. Maybe this was only the third time she'd driven a car, but she knew *that*. She'd just been distracted. She turned it over and put it in drive.

"Uh . . . aren't you forgetting something?" he asked.

What now? She checked her mirrors again, locked the doors, and turned the radio on.

Will shook his head, then reached over her shoulder and grabbed the seatbelt. For a moment, Regan had thought he was placing his arm around her. No such luck.

Still, that was the fifth time today he'd touched her; she'd kept count. First in the kitchen, when he'd picked a piece of lint off her shoulder, then twice on the way over when he'd pointed to the speed gauge and accidently bumped her arm. It wasn't a warm hug or an encouraging rub on the shoulder, but it was something. She could pretend it was more.

But then there'd been the hand on the shoulder in Principal Shepherd's office. How was Regan supposed to take that? Had it all been part of the act?

"What are you waiting for?" he finally asked. "What's wrong?"

She turned to him. "What's going on here?"

Will glanced from side to side. "We are supposed to be driving home."

"Janey's been pushing you to spend time with me since I got here. Why now?"

"I told you. I wanted to—"

"Do something nice for Janey." She shook her head. "You can't bullshit a bullshitter."

"Hey! Watch your mouth, young lady!"

"You see? Right there. Why the sudden interest in what I do or say?"

Will sighed, then mumbled something under his breath.

"What?"

"I said, I just thought we could be friends." He met her gaze. "I figure after you stuck your neck out for me yesterday, you're probably gonna need a friend, yes?"

She nodded, wary.

"And, to be honest, I could use a friend too. Someone who'll keep me out of trouble."

"And you think *I'm* the right one for that?"

He shrugged. "You seemed to do a good-enough job yesterday."

Regan gave a short laugh.

"Look, I'll level with you." Will ran his hand through his hair and sighed. "Janey's suffocating me. And the only way she's going to loosen up is if I start to play nice with everyone, including you. So, are you going to help me out, or not?"

She considered this a moment, then released the brake. "I need to think about it."

And she did—the entire way home. It wasn't exactly an intriguing offer, babysitting her thirty-five-year-old father. After all, he should be keeping her out of trouble at her age, shouldn't he? Rescuing her from bullies at the festival. Spying on her during her daily, mysterious walks. Not the other way around.

On the other hand, she'd spent more solid time with her father today than she had since she'd met him. That had to count for something, right? Even if it was all one big farce. And maybe he'd teach her something, like how to work with wood or cut the grass. Anything to save her from the isolation of her bedroom which, after a week, had grown to be pretty damn boring.

The minute they pulled into the driveway, Janey charged for the car. "Where the hell have you been? I've been worried sick."

"Relax." Will winked at Regan, then climbed out and shut the door. "We just ran a few errands. Didn't you get the note I left?"

"You mean this note?" She held up the napkin Will had left her. "Janey, Went out. Regan has her permit. Your brother, Will."

"Snappy, isn't it?"

"No, Will! No, it's not! Do you know what would've happened if Tom had pulled you over? *You* are not a licensed driver anymore! It doesn't matter if she has her permit or not! You can't drive with her." Janey stomped around to the other side of the car where Regan sat. "And you! I expected more than this out of you!"

"It's not her fault, Janey. I told her it would be all right," Will said.

"You know, it doesn't matter." Janey opened the driver's side door. "Move over. We need to go get you registered for school."

Regan climbed out, glancing toward Will. "But . . . we've just come from there."

"I told you we ran a few errands," Will said. "Went by the probation office too."

Janey took a step back and crossed her arms. "You're lying."

Regan pulled the school registration packet from the backseat. "No. He's not."

Janey flipped through the packet, growing redder by the page, then handed it back. "You two are grounded."

"Grounded?" Will and Regan asked, in sync.

"Did I stutter?" Janey said. "Yes. Grounded. For a week."

"You can't ground me. I'm a grown man," Will said. "And what exactly are you going to ground Regan from? She already sits in her room all day."

Regan tilted her head. Had Will just stuck up for her? And more importantly, how did he know what she did all day? Did he spy on her too?

"Fine, then manual labor it is," Janey responded. "Tomorrow, you two will get up bright and early and paint the barn. Is that clear?"

Will shook his head. "You know, I don't get you. You tell me to be more responsible, but when I do, you act like I did something wrong."

"Is. That. Clear?" she said again.

"Yes. It's clear," Regan responded for him, not allowing Will the chance to talk his way out of it. A girl could learn a lot about her father in a day's worth of painting, a few hours' worth of errand running, or a lunchtime of spying.

Janey nodded, then stomped off toward the house.

"Damned if I do, damned if I don't," Will muttered, kicking gravel loose on the drive.

"That thing you asked me in the car? You can count me in." Regan slammed the car door shut. "But we do this my way."

The depression had always been easy to spot; it was the mania Janey had to look for. It could be a number of things. An empty clothes basket. A stack of novels. A crossword puzzle book. Simple items at first glance, but, when examined further, meant trouble. Had Will slept in his pajamas last night or pulled an all-nighter rereading his Stephen King novels? Was the crossword magazine a month old, or had he completed every puzzle from last Sunday's edition?

She fell onto the cot, wiping her brow. Going through Will's personal things was wrong, but she had to be sure. It wasn't like him to change his mind so quickly. One minute, he'd wanted nothing to do with parenting Regan, and the next he'd enrolled her for school. Janey wanted him to show an interest and take some responsibility, but something was definitely up.

"It's not up there."

Janey jumped at the faint sound of Will's voice, echoing from below. But before she could think of a defense, she spotted Regan's eyes through the rungs of the ladder.

"I thought you said the loft," Regan responded, giving Janey a slight shake of her head.

"*Under* the loft." There was a rustling below. "I got it. Let's go."

Regan stared at Janey a moment longer before descending. How long had she been watching Janey? Long enough to see her going through Will's journal? Will's drawers? Long enough to hear the sigh of relief when Janey had come up empty? Regardless, Regan had known Will wouldn't feel quite so thrilled about Janey's spying.

Janey walked over to the tiny, open window and peered at the yard below, just in time to see Will spread the tarp he'd found. The last time the barn had been painted, Janey had been about Regan's age, maybe a little younger. Janey's father had worn those same farming overalls and fisherman's hat. He'd asked Janey to start on the same board and work her way toward the door in the same direction.

"You're doing it wrong," Will said, taking the paintbrush from Regan's hands.

Janey's father had corrected her too, though not for the same reasons. Her father's corrections had been more about changing Janey than changing whatever task she was doing wrong. It made her wonder if there ever had been a part of Janey he'd approved of.

"You're supposed to go side to side. Haven't you ever seen *The Karate Kid*?"

"With Jaden Smith?" Regan asked.

"Jaden who?" Will shook his head, then stroked back and forth along the wood plank. "See? Back and forth."

Regan retrieved her brush, dipped it in the can for a coating of fresh paint, and mimicked her father's motions as best she could. "Like this?"

"Yeah, yeah. Like that." Will moved the tarp down a few more feet and placed the can on top, shaking his head. "Jaden Smith. Do you know anything about the eighties?"

"Not particularly, seeing that I was born this millennium."

Will shook his head again. "Next you'll be telling me you don't know who Billy Joel is."

"Sure I do. Wasn't he that *Sling Blade* guy married to Angelina Jolie before Brad Pitt?"

"That's Billy Bob—"

Regan giggled, interrupting his correction.

"Oh, you think that's funny, do ya?" Will picked the water hose up and sent a warning shot in Regan's direction. "You still think it's funny making your old man feel old?"

Regan turned, spine stiff as a board, but Janey didn't know if it was from the shock of cold water or the words Will had used. They'd certainly given rise to the hairs on Janey's neck. He'd just referred to himself, perhaps for the first time, as Regan's father.

In one quick motion, Regan dipped her brush into the can and slung the excess toward Will, paint splattering from his head to his bare feet.

"Hey!" he shouted, returning fire.

And, there below the window, Janey watched as an outright battle began. A battle between water and oil. A battle between young and old. A battle between father and daughter.

The way it should be.

~

Lindsay smoothed her skirt again, checked the address on the side of the door one last time, and rang the doorbell. After another stellar day at work, she'd almost cancelled. But Janey Fletcher was the only person in town who'd attempted to get to know her since she'd arrived, and Lindsay was damn well going to take advantage of it.

Besides, she'd begun to feel like one of the Golden Girls, hanging around with her mother on cards night.

She rang the doorbell again and gave a slight knock. A mumbled yell followed, which Lindsay thought was either *Help me, I'm on the floor* or *Janey, get the damn door.* If someone didn't answer this time, she'd assume it was the first.

A moment later, the door swung open and Lindsay's heart dropped.

It was like something from a horror movie. He slid the blade of his utility knife into its sheath and wiped his red hands against his dirty t-shirt, looking her up and down like she'd interrupted a slaughter. And then a loud clap of thunder cracked against the sky and shook the windows and shutters on the old farmhouse, raising more terror in the pit of Lindsay's stomach.

What the hell had she walked in on?

"I'm sorry," she choked out. "I must have the wrong house."

Will opened the screen door and stepped to the side. "Janey'll be down in a minute."

So, this wasn't some terrible mistake? Janey lived in this house. With him. Lindsay checked the address on the side of the house and then glanced back at the open doorway, blinking as if he'd disappear. But he didn't go away.

It all came together. That redneck man in the pie tent referred to Janey Fletcher's crazy brother. And the yellow slip from his probation officer had read *Fletcher, William.* How could Lindsay not have put two and two together?

Another crack of thunder interrupted her thoughts.

"You're gonna get wet if you stay out there," he warned.

Lindsay inched past Will, warily. The red coating his hands was paint; the mix of fumes and male sweat made her dizzy as she walked by.

"I didn't realize you and Janey were—"

"Brother and sister," he finished.

The door to what Lindsay assumed was the kitchen swung open and Regan walked in, covered in red paint from head to toe. "I finished the—oh, hey."

"Good evening," Lindsay said with a wide smile. "How are you tonight, Miss Fletcher?"

"No, no. Not Fletcher," Will corrected. "Whitmer. Regan Whitmer."

Lindsay had already known this. She'd seen it on Regan's registration papers, been a little perplexed by it. She was accustomed to seeing different names between mothers and children, but not fathers. Calling her Miss Fletcher was simply Lindsay's way of prying without prying. "Sorry. I thought you said she was your—"

"She is!" Will snapped before she could finish.

"Will . . ." Regan said, with a slight shake of her head.

He grimaced, moving to place his hand on Regan's shoulder, and then restated, a few decibels lower, "I mean, she *is* . . . my . . . daughter."

Well, at least this time he hadn't forgotten, but Lindsay still didn't have a clue about the last name.

"Could you point me in the direction of the restroom?" Lindsay asked.

Regan gestured toward the stairway. "Up the stairs, first door on the right."

Lindsay darted for the steps. She had to get out of there.

Maybe to splash cold water on her face and remind herself it was only two hours out of her life. Maybe to buy enough time to come up with an excuse to leave. She'd figure out which when she reached the bathroom.

The first door on the right was half-ajar, so she pushed it the rest of the way open cautiously. Inside, Janey Fletcher stood in front of the mirror, wearing an ivory, lace top and pair of skinny jeans. Tears streamed down her cheeks as she scrubbed at the red paint on her face, leaving a mess of pink welts behind.

"Sorry. I didn't realize you were in here."

"No, no. It's fine. I'll be out of your way in a sec." Janey swiped the mess of toilet paper into the trash can, wiped her nose with the red-stained washcloth, and passed Lindsay as she stepped into the hallway.

"Uh, is everything okay? We could do dinner a different night," Lindsay asked, praying to God Janey rescheduled. Perhaps this was her ticket out of here.

"Everything's fine. It's just..." Janey broke into tears, staring down at the floor. "It's been so long since someone's come over for dinner. I just wanted it to be perfect. I even made my mother's pot roast and ran into Claremont to buy that nice wine that goes so well with it. Now you want to leave and it's all ruined."

"No, no. It's not ruined." Lindsay wouldn't lie and say she didn't want to leave.

Janey turned her magenta face up. "Look at me! And I'm the one who insisted they paint the barn today! So really, this is my fault." Janey wiped the tears from her cheeks. "Can't I just have one day when everything goes as planned and everyone is happy?"

"No. You can't," Lindsay admitted, the truth as harsh as the way it sounded. But it was a lesson she'd learned being David's wife for eight years, and being her mother's daughter since birth. Nothing ever turned out as she'd planned. She'd never possessed whatever it was that made either of them truly happy. Lindsay was done wasting her precious years trying. She was done allowing other people's issues to define her actions.

Including Will Fletcher.

"So quit trying," Lindsay continued. "And just make *your-self* happy."

"You make it sound so easy."

"It *is* that easy," Lindsay said, setting off for the stairway.

"Where are you going? I thought you had to use the bathroom?" Janey asked.

Lindsay shook her head. "I think I'll have that glass of Claremont wine instead."

Regan liked to watch him in his workshop. He was different when he was sanding, building, creating—like a man with a mission instead of one running from one. His eyes were focused, and his hands didn't shake. When Will worked, he was just a man, not a crazy man. He was the father Regan's mother had promised he'd be.

He is *a good man,* her mother's voice echoed. *Give it time.*

Regan rested her head against the barn door, cracked wide enough for her to see inside. Time was all she *had* to give. Time to dream, time to hope, time to try. But time was finite; no one knew that better than Regan. She'd given her mother time and had quickly run out of it.

It wouldn't have mattered, her mother argued. *I couldn't be helped.*

"Maybe," Regan muttered. "Or maybe you were just like Will."

It's not the same.

Regan clenched her eyes shut, signaling the end of their conversation. She refused to believe that. There had to be an explanation other than that Regan had driven her mom to put a bullet in her head. Maybe mentally ill people were drawn to each other like adrenaline junkies or drug addicts. Was the idea so farfetched, or was Regan looking for a scapegoat?

"Tough decision, isn't it?" Will asked.

Regan raised her eyes toward him. "What?"

"You've been standing in the doorway for fifteen minutes. Either come inside or don't, but the draft is stirring up the dust."

Regan glanced toward the house, then back at Will before stepping inside and pulling the door shut. "Hiding out?" she asked.

"I don't play well with others." He rubbed the sanding block down the piece of wood. "What about you? Shouldn't you be inside doing, I don't know, girly stuff?"

"I really don't like girly stuff." Regan slid her butt onto a workbench. "Besides, I wasn't sure if it was, you know, a date."

Will stiffened, dropping the sanding block into a pile of sawdust, creating a small cloud. "I didn't know you knew. I mean, about Janey."

"It's not so hard to figure out."

"Well, even so. I don't think you have to worry about Janey and Principal Shepherd being on a date." Will retrieved his sanding block. "Janey's sort of . . . involved."

With that Gretchen woman, of course. That wasn't hard to figure out either. Regan had heard Janey leaving apologetic messages on her phone the past couple of days.

Will took another swipe with the sanding block and studied the lines of the wood carefully. "There. Just about finished."

"Looks great." Regan searched up and down the slab of wood a moment, looking for clues before conceding. "What is it?"

He shrugged. "I have no idea."

She burst out laughing before she could stop herself.

"What?"

"Nothing, I just . . . never mind." She cleared her throat, glancing around the room at all the other odd pieces that didn't have a purpose. Some flat and square, just like this one. Some long and wavy. All beautiful in their own right, regardless. It was a graveyard of inspiration, or perhaps the beginning structures of something grand.

"I'm curious." Will removed the wooden object. "What you've figured out about me."

Regan stiffened, meeting his gaze. "Nothing."

"Oh, come on. A sharp girl like you?" He rested his palms on the worktable. "You must've come up with something."

"Nope." She turned her head before he could figure out she'd lied. "Where did you learn to do all this anyway?"

"Where else?" he asked.

Shop class? The nuthouse? The slammer? She wasn't judging, but these all seemed to be places one would pick up a skill such as this.

He placed a fresh piece of lumber on the bench, marking a few spots with a large pencil. "My father taught me."

Well, Regan wouldn't know what that felt like, would she? The only thing her mother had taught her was to barter, and she'd rather forget the random religious lessons from Steven that resulted with her feeling worthless. So she licked her dry lips and said, "Oh."

Will slammed the pencil onto the wood and sighed. "Come on. I'll show you."

Regan felt tingles of hope and fear bubble in her chest at the same time. Hope that her father wanted to teach her, fear that she'd screw it up and he'd never ask again. As always, the fear won. "It's okay," she said. "I wouldn't do it right."

"That's the same thing I told my father." A slight grin

tugged at the corner of his mouth. "And I'm going to tell you the same thing he told me—if you're going to stare at me, you might as well learn something while you're doing it. Now, come on."

"But I wouldn't do it right."

"Just shut up and get over here."

Regan hopped down to the dusty, concrete floor. She wanted to take after Will in more ways than just having the same eyes. She wanted to have that same power to create endless possibilities and mold them into more than just a rough piece of wood—more than what she was.

Will pulled some earplugs from a drawer and handed them to her, then retrieved a set of glasses from the table behind him. "Here, put these on."

Funny, he hadn't worn either item any of the times she'd watched him work. But she did as she was told, understanding from his stern expression it wasn't an option.

"Now, the first thing you have to remember is to always go against the grain."

She glanced up at him. This didn't sound right at all. "Against the grain? Isn't that counterproductive though?"

"Not in *my* shop it isn't." He stepped in behind her, placing her hands where she needed to hold the lumber and flipped on the saw blade. "You ready?"

She wasn't ready.

Will buried his head in his hands and stared at the cold, white, sterile hospital floor, trying to overcome the knotted mess in his stomach. But out of the corner of his eye he could see the red sawdust on his shoes, glued in place with her blood.

He'd asked Regan if she was ready and she'd nodded, hadn't she? Maybe it was the vibration of the rotary saw he'd felt. He'd pushed the board with her, paying close attention to keeping it in line with the mark he'd drawn. And when he'd seen she understood, he let go.

Oh, God. Why had he let go?

Regan had turned toward him and smiled—satisfaction gleaming in her eyes. It was only for a second, but he'd seen more of who she was than he'd allowed himself to see since she'd been there. It was peaceful, yet terrifying. By the time he'd glanced away, it had already happened. The blood sprayed. She screamed. Will rushed her to the house inside his arms.

Not once did it occur to him that this was his fault until the doctor took her from his hands. Now it was all he could see, plain as day, like all the other times. Might as well have a box to check on the hospital admission forms: "Reason for Visit? Will Fletcher fucked up again!"

"How you holding up?"

Will opened his eyes, cringing. Why was she even here? Didn't she have some papers to grade or something? And why was there a part of him that was happy to see her?

"Fine," he responded.

Principal Shepherd sat in the chair beside him and held out a cup of coffee.

"I can't. Janey would have a shit fit."

"Over coffee?"

"No, over the Styrofoam cup," Will spat. "Makes me do crazy things."

Principal Shepherd stared, not amused.

Will took the cup from her hands. "It's the caffeine. Just makes me a little . . . fidgety."

She stared a moment longer, then turned her attention toward her suitcase of a purse beside her. She dug around inside and pulled out a metal flask.

Oh, a drink. What Will would give for an actual drink.

When was the last time he'd had one? The night Ellie had left him sleeping alone on the cold floor of Emma's room with nothing but a note that read, "I'm sorry."

What did Ellie have to be sorry about? He was the one responsible. He was the one who couldn't let go. He was the one who couldn't live again when the life he wanted was no longer possible. She wanted more, *deserved* more, than the zombie-like existence he'd given her.

"Want some honey for your coffee?"

Will stared, trying to trace the thoughts that led him to Ellie. Always to Ellie.

The flask. Will gave a shake of his head. Who carried honey around in a metal flask?

"Will, are you drinking coffee this late at night?"

Shit. Will turned toward Janey to respond, but Principal Shepherd got there first. "He was holding it for you."

"Oh." Janey took the cup from Will's hands. "They're stitching her up now. The blade nicked the tendon but didn't tear it in half, so they're going to let it try to heal on its own."

"So, she's okay?" Will asked.

"She'll have a bunch of stitches and a few weeks playing patient. But yes, she's going to be okay."

Will rubbed his face and leaned back in the chair, exhaling a breath he hadn't realized he'd been holding for the past five hours. She'd be okay. This was just a warning that he was too close, forgetting his place. And now it would be easy to return things to normal because Regan surely wouldn't touch him with a ten-foot pole after this.

"She's asking for you in there," Janey said.

He looked up. "I'm sorry?"

"Regan is asking for you," Janey repeated. "Do we need to turn down your headphones?"

He pursed his lips. "No bullshit, Janey. Why does she want to see me? To tell me what a sorry excuse for a father I am? To tell me how badly I hurt her?"

Janey offered a smile, the one she gave when he'd said something completely irrational and she had to talk him down. "Because she's hurt, and you're her father."

Damn it, how did she do that? Always saying the same thing he'd said but with a different meaning? It irritated him. Janey was wrong; Regan had to hate him. She'd trusted him and he'd nearly cut her damn hand off. How could she not hate him?

He jumped to his feet and marched toward Regan's exam room, determined to prove his sister wrong. At the hospital curtain, he took a deep breath, accepted his fate, and tore it open with a force more dramatic than necessary. But once he saw that smile—that beautiful, hopeful, surprised smile—it took all the energy Will had not to drop to his knees right there.

"Hey," Regan said.

"Hey." He closed the curtain behind him and staggered inside, unable to look away from the sunlight shining from the hospital bed. Was she actually happy to see him?

Will hadn't noticed the woman in scrubs stitching up Regan's hand until Regan spoke to her. "This is him. This is my father."

The woman glanced at Will, then back at Regan's hand. "So this is the brilliant woodworker? Regan told me how good you are. Said she hurt herself trying to be like you."

Will swallowed hard, but didn't respond. Maybe that was the problem—she'd tried to be like him. He could've told her that would be disastrous.

"Okay, dear, you are all stitched up." The woman tossed a medical tool onto the steel tray and stood, removing her gloves. "I'll let the desk know and we'll get you checked out, okay?"

Will watched the nurse walk past, unsure if he wanted her to leave right then. With someone else here, he was still safe, but with her gone, anything could happen. For all he knew, this was just an act—Regan's smile, kind words. All of it.

"You're not going to leave, are you?" Regan asked.

He turned back around to face her, slow and unsure. "Do you want me to stay?"

She stared at him for a moment, then nodded.

"Then I'll stay," he whispered.

Regan glanced around the room then scooted over and patted the empty space beside her, which Will quickly sat down in. If he gave it a second thought, he might run.

"Does it hurt?"

She shook her head. "They numbed it up pretty good."

"Can you move it?"

She shook her head again. "I'm too scared to try."

You and me both, kid, Will thought as he buried his trembling hands between his knees and the hospital bed.

"You're not going to leave, are you?" she asked.

Hadn't they just been over this? "I'm here still, aren't I?"

"Yes, but I meant . . ." Regan exhaled and met his gaze, eyes wide. "you're not going to go back to hating me, are you?"

Will deflated, the rock in his gut sinking him back into his guilt. "I never hated you, okay?"

Regan nodded, then rested her head against his shoulder. It felt like he should hug her, but when Will pulled his hand from beneath him, it grew heavy and weak. He settled for a pat on the leg, followed by an awkward silence.

"I lied to you back there. About not figuring anything out about you." She turned her eyes toward his. "You have Bipolar Disorder, don't you?"

Will hesitated, then nodded. "That's what they say."

"Do you know when it's happening? I mean, the mania and the depression?"

"Sometimes. Sometimes I don't know until a week later when Janey tells me. It's different every time." Will paused. "Why do you ask?"

She shrugged. "I keep thinking that maybe that's what my mom had too. She could be the most loving, amazing person one minute and then, without any warning, curl up into a ball and cry for two days." Her voice tapered off to an uncomfortable silence. "You knew her. Do you think she was sick? Back then, I mean?"

Will looked toward the painting on the far wall of a girl in a field of flowers. What were the chances that Michelle and he had both been suffering from Bipolar simultaneously?

"Because I worry sometimes it was me," Regan said. "Maybe I just wasn't enough."

With those five words, what was left of Will's armor crumpled like a tin can. He'd never been enough. With Janey, with Ellie, with Emma. But there was always one moment before his mania, between standing in his grim reality and leaping into that idealistic world, when Will had hope. Hope that when he came back, he could bring that world with him.

He never remembered the hours that made up four or five days without sleep, the pages of one hundred books he'd read, the songs he'd sang over and over to defeat the silence. They became blurred pieces of memory, like a dream he hated to wake from. But that moment right before, he'd always remember vividly.

Sometimes, Will wondered if he'd *chosen* to step over the line.

But Regan didn't need to hear that. Right now, Regan needed to hear her mother hadn't left her behind by choice. "You know, there are lots of illnesses out there."

She nodded.

"It took my doctor a long time to diagnose me."

Regan nodded again, the movement heavier, slower. "The truth is, I really don't know if your mom was Bipolar, and you never will either. But her reasons—whatever fucked-up, crazy rationalization went through her head before she decided to end it—had nothing to do with you. It wasn't your fault, Regan."

Without warning, she buried her face into his chest and began to sob. Will wrapped his now-steady arms around her and pulled her close, as if he could absorb all her pain. Her soft hair tickled his arms and smelled like a mix of sawdust and daisies.

It smelled like home.

CHAPTER SEVEN

"Ten minutes and counting!" Janey shouted, stuffing the peanut butter and jelly sandwich into a plastic bag. It was the first day of school for Regan, the first day of Will's latest community service sentence to help humans, the first day Janey would be alone since Regan arrived. If Janey weren't so nervous about sending them off, she might be excited for the few hours of freedom. "Will!"

"Quit yelling. I'm right here."

Janey spun around, slinging grape jelly from her knife onto his shirt.

"And now I have to change again," he said.

Funny. There was a time not too long ago when he would've considered the purple stain a character statement. Now Will was freshly shaven, his hair was combed, and his jeans didn't resemble swiss cheese. She'd better not get used to it. The other foot was bound to come slamming into her blind eye any day now.

"There's a fresh load in the laundry room. But hurry. Nine minutes, thirty seconds."

"I know where the laundry is. And stop doing that. You sound like you're counting down to the end of the world." He walked off.

"Will Fletcher heading out into general society on his own today?" she muttered, spreading the peanut butter on Regan's sandwich. "I just might be."

"He'll be fine."

Janey glanced up at Regan's voice. "Easy for you to say. You won't have to go bail him out after he's run naked through the halls in blue-and-yellow paint doing the Half Moon howl."

"Hey, that was a senior prank!" Will yelled from the other room.

That was beside the point. What was once a prank to an eighteen-year-old kid would now be another campfire story about the Half Moon Crazy. Janey had seen it before, too many times. The same rules didn't apply to Will that applied to everyone else in this town.

"Will streaked down the hallways?" Regan plopped down in a chair. "That's awesome!"

"Not awesome. Suspendable," Janey said.

"Trust me. I don't need any help being the freak on the first day of school." Regan used her good hand to pull a cereal bowl from the stack on the table and reached for the Oatey Os without hesitation. When had that happened? If Janey didn't know better, she'd have sworn her niece felt at home.

"Regardless, you have no idea how quickly the tide can change with him," Janey retorted. "And with no one there to talk him down—"

"*I'll* be there," Regan interrupted.

What was this? Gang-up-on-Janey day? Make-Janey-look-like-an-overprotective-fool day? Show-Janey-she-wasn't-needed-anymore day?

At the last thought, she closed her mouth, smoothed her apron, and went back to her bagged-lunch preparation. She refused to believe that. Everyone was all helpful and optimistic until the bombs went off, then Janey'd look around and no one would be left standing. It's how it had always been. No clean shirt or bowl of cereal would convince her differently.

"Okay. I think I'm all ready," Will announced, stumbling back through the door. "The end of the earth can proceed, now."

"That's a nice T-shirt, Will," Regan mocked.

"Thank you." He sat beside Regan and poured himself a bowl of cereal. "I think."

Janey glanced at the wolf on his oversize T-shirt. When had he bought it? It looked brand-new, but had the words Senior 2000 at the bottom. "Is that your senior shirt?"

"Yeah, why?"

"I just can't believe it's in such good shape."

"I never wore it," he mumbled through a mouth full of Oatey Os. "It didn't fit then."

"It doesn't fit *now*. It's a size too big."

"Really?" Will glanced down. "Well, get a load of that. It was a size too small back then. Guess I lost some weight."

No. You just lost your mind and the weight went with it.

"Speaking of clothes . . ." Janey retrieved the purple box she'd hidden in the pots-and-pans cabinet two days ago. "Something to wish you good luck on your first day."

Regan stared at the box a moment, an odd grin on her face, then slowly lifted the lid. When she pushed back the tissue paper, her smile faded.

"Oh, you don't like it?"

Regan held the blue, cotton tank top up in the air by the spaghetti straps, examining the lime-green dragonfly stitched into the chest. "No, it's . . . beautiful. I just . . ."

"Is the size wrong? You look like the same size as me, so I tried it on, and the jeans."

Regan turned her startled gaze back toward the box at the word *jeans*. When she glanced back up, there were big tears in her eyes.

"I told you," Will said to Janey. "You should've gone with the black one."

"Honey, what is it? It's okay if you don't like it," Janey said, ignoring Will's sidebar comment. "We can take it back and you can pick out what you want."

Regan shook her head, took a calming breath, and spread the tank top on the table, rubbing her fingers over the letter *S* on the size sticker. "Mom usually got my stuff from the shelter. I've never gotten anything with tags still attached. Not sure I know what to do with this."

In one quick motion, Will reached over and tugged the sticker off, followed by the tag hanging from the label. "That's what you do with it."

With a giggle, Regan wiped her cheeks of tears, hopped to her feet, and threw her arms around Janey's neck. "Thanks, Aunt Janey."

Janey embraced her niece, a little taken back. That was the first time she'd called her Aunt since she'd arrived. The words fluttered inside Janey's heart like a bug. After Emma died, she'd feared she'd never hear those words again, but there they were.

"You're my niece. It's my job to spoil you." Janey kissed her cheek. "Now hurry and change because we have exactly five minutes and twenty-nine seconds."

Regan nodded with a wide smile and took off with the clothes in hand.

Janey turned back to Will and placed his pills on his placemat in front of him. "You know she didn't mean it literally, right? About the tags?"

Will popped the pills in his mouth without arguing and washed them down with the rest of his orange juice. "Neither did I."

Janey wasn't exactly sure what he did mean. Perhaps he'd meant that Regan should jump right in. Or maybe he'd meant that she should tear away the old, disappointed parts of her past and prepare for a life more fortunate. Either way, it didn't matter. Regan had understood exactly what he'd meant.

It made Janey wonder what other firsts would come on this day. It made her hope they would all be wrapped inside a pretty box, as Regan's first lesson from her father had been.

"How's your first day going, Miss Whitmer?"

Regan turned toward Principal Shepherd at the entrance to the cafeteria. That was the third time she'd asked her that today, and every time Regan gave her standard noncommittal response. "As well as a first day could go."

"That's wonderful. I'm so glad to hear that," she responded with that same overpowering grin she'd given the other two times. "And remember, if you—"

"—ever need to talk, your door's always open," Regan finished. "I know."

Principal Shepherd's smile faded a bit. "So, how's the hand?"

"Still stitched up." Regan waved her gauze-taped hand in the air.

"If you need additional time on your assignments—"

"Thanks, but it's not my writing hand," she interrupted. "And Will said he'd help out with anything I needed."

"Will?"

"Yes, Will. My father."

"I know, but . . ." A voice on Principal Shepherd's walkie-talkie interrupted her before she could respond. "Well, it seems I have a dispute to attend to in the gymnasium. Maybe we can finish this conversation at a later time in my office? Maybe over a cup of cocoa?"

"Sure," Regan said, and then waited until Principal Shepherd turned before she rolled her eyes and stepped into the cafeteria. The woman was nice and all, but she needed to loosen up on the Mary Poppins act. Regan didn't want to be saved, especially not from Will. And even if she did, a cup of hot cocoa wouldn't do it.

Inside the cafeteria, they all stared at Regan, just like they had all morning. As she got out of Janey's car, while she changed books at her locker, as she sat in class, and now as she inched her way through the tables, scoping out where to eat her lunch. Whose lucky day would it be? Whose table would the crazy man's daughter bless with her presence?

Go to him, her mother said.

Regan passed the last table and kept going, onto the outside patio. When she reached the edge of the patio, she went farther until she reached the end of the school. When she reached the end of the school, she headed toward the cemetery. The only place that felt right to her anymore. The one place she could eat her lunch in peace and guarantee she wouldn't be the topic of conversation. To the one person who understood she didn't want to be saved.

The cemetery wasn't as far a walk from the school as it was from the house. Will was already there, wearing his sweat-stained Howlers T-shirt, his face pink—he'd forgotten to use sunblock despite Janey's multiple reminders.

On the far side of the ivy fence, Regan settled into the familiar groove of the old oak tree. She hadn't noticed until today how the roots splitting off at the bottom fit like a glove around her narrow frame. It was as if God had made the tree just for her.

Today, Will told Emma about football. Not so much the rules or the plays, but more about the person he was when he'd played. The rush of running down field, knowing no one would catch him, the adrenaline that erupted as he stepped into the end zone, the feeling of belonging when his teammates carried him on their shoulders. It was odd to picture Will being anyone's hero in this town, and it was even stranger to think he might have enjoyed it.

A mockingbird somewhere above her began to screech. What had he just said? Something about pep rallies and cheer-leaders. Regan tried to make sense of the jumbled mess she caught between the bird's calls. It wasn't anything life changing, but she'd taken the risk to come here and wanted every ounce of her father she could soak up.

And then he said it. Her name. It was so quiet and quick Regan almost didn't catch it.

She pulled the rubber band from her hair and shot it at the bird in the tree, missing, but still managing to cause a stir. The bird flew away and Regan leaned in toward the fence, listening more closely to the words the ivy protected on the other side.

"You'd like her, I think. She's nice, you know? She's not like the other kids in town. And she's pretty protective of your old man, so I imagine she'd be the same way with you. You should've seen her stand up to all those kids at the festival."

Will paused—a long, weighty pause for Regan. This was the first time he'd told Emma about her. Wasn't there more? Didn't he think more of Regan than just *nice*? Didn't he want more from Regan than just *protection* from the mean kids in town?

Didn't he love her, even just a little?

Kneeling in the two grassless circles he'd worn into the earth beside Emma's grave, Will pointed his pink face toward the sun and shut his eyes. He was silent and still for a moment, then suddenly leaned forward, pressed his forehead to the gravestone for a moment, then sat back. Tears spilled down his cheeks.

"I'm sorry. I didn't mean to . . ." He wiped his face with his T-shirt and took a deep breath. "Anyway, back to this football thing. . . ."

Regan returned to the groove of the oak tree, unsure whether to smile or cry. Maybe Will hadn't said anything bad, but she wished he had. Wisecracks about her makeup and carrottop references to her hair would be far better than the truth she faced now.

It wasn't Will's approval Regan needed before she'd gain his love. It was the approval of a girl who'd been lying dead in the ground for five years.

Will stuffed his wrench into his tool belt as he stared at the visitors' side of the scoreboard. The home team would have to wait for tomorrow and the planter boxes the day after.

The sound of the dismissal bell caught his attention in the distance, or rather a beep—it wasn't a bell as he remembered. That had been bugging him all day, along with the million other things that weren't the same. The iron fence surrounding the stadium, the artificial turf, the concession buildings tucked nicely under the bleachers, which removed the perfect make out spot. Will smiled at that one. He and Ellie had spent many nights under the bleachers.

There had been a time when school was the only place he'd felt normal. Not just normal—extraordinary. He'd walked the halls in his jersey, always holding onto a football with one hand and Ellie with the other, and he'd felt larger than life. Coach called him *son* and his teammates called him *brother*. He'd been part of a family here, and that had made it all too easy to ignore his fucked-up home life.

Had Regan dodged the albatross of Will's illness today, as he'd once dodged his father's?

A commotion behind him chased the unwelcome thought from his head. Will turned to see a group of football players approaching with gear in hand. That he didn't miss. Drills for three hours in eighty-degree heat with a stack of homework waiting at home. He turned to pick up the rest of his tools from the ground.

"Hey look, the crazy man's on school grounds. Isn't that against town rules?"

"Yeah, no shit. And I'm not sure I wanna strip down to skins if he's watching. You know, they say gayness runs in the family. The queer might enjoy it too much."

Will clenched his jaw as the crowd of boys laughed. He'd grown immune to the lunatic comments through the years, mostly because he couldn't argue. He didn't even care that they'd called him gay. But any insinuation of pedophilia got under his skin.

"Hey, speaking of gay, crazy man, you think your sister would be up for a threesome?"

Will raised his cordless drill in the air and gave it a spin as a warning. They could say what they wanted about him, but, when it came to Janey, he drew the line.

"Whoa, you got a permit for that weapon, crazy man?" the same kid asked. Will thought his name was Nick, but he wasn't sure. "I'm going to have to ask to see it."

"You think you're man enough to come get it, tough guy?" Will asked, placing the drill into the holster on his tool belt.

"Nick, come on, man. Coach is gonna be pissed if we're late."

Will found the voice in the crowd. Lane Barrett. He'd recognize his old neighbor anywhere. Years ago, Will had thrown the football around with him every day.

"Listen to your buddy, Nick. Wouldn't want the crazy man to get angry," Will muttered.

"Hey, what's going on?"

Will turned at Regan's voice, the one thing he didn't need.

"Nothing. These kids were just saying hello on their way to practice."

She looked between him and the young men for a moment, then said, "You ready to go?"

He nodded, grabbed his toolbox, and set off behind her down the path.

"Hey, crazy man's daughter, there's something I gotta ask.... How do you sleep under the same roof as that guy?"

"Nick! Let's go!" Lane yelled.

"I mean, he doesn't exactly have a good track record with daughters, you know."

At that, Regan paused, and Will braced himself for the questions. *What's he talking about, Will? Why didn't you tell me you had another daughter, Will? Why haven't I met this other daughter, Will?* And when Will answered, she would say, *You disgust me, Will.*

Maybe he deserved it. He should've told her by now about Emma, just like he should've told Emma about Regan before today. Turned out there was never a good time to say, *You had a sister, but she's dead and it's my fault.*

But when Regan turned around, she didn't ask any questions; she didn't even look Will in the eyes. She stared straight at Nick, nostrils flared and eyes narrowed, ready to attack.

"Ooh, fellas, look. Crazy man's daughter's about to get a little crazy again."

Regan threw her book bag to the ground and charged forward, running right into Lane Barrett as he stepped between them. "Whoa, Regan. It's all cool. We were just leaving."

"Then go on and get out of here."

Lane corralled the group, but Nick refused to shut up. "Is that what happened to your hand? He try to cut it off in a blender?"

"Fuck you!" Regan launched past Lane, knocking him to the ground in the process, and slapped Nick square in the face. The crowd went silent as he clenched his cheek.

"Hey! Hey! Break it up!" Principal Shepherd yelled from across the field.

"I think it's time for us to go," Will muttered, tugging on Regan's arm.

"Don't you ever talk about my father again, do you hear me?" Regan straightened her tank, then retrieved her backpack from the ground. "Or Emma!"

Will met her gaze. "How did you know—?"

"Go ahead, but don't say I didn't warn you," Nick yelled as Lane dragged him by the arm. "Go ahead and stick up for the baby killer!"

Before Will knew it, he'd turned around and slammed Nick to the ground, trying to bury the truth with him.

CHAPTER
EIGHT

B aby killer.
The words jumbled around Regan's head like a bumblebee,
stinging every place they touched, as she sat on the floor
in an empty office at the police station. The accusation was a
mistake—a tiny detail blown way out of proportion. It had to
be. Emma had SIDS, just like the baby boy in their apartment
building, just like her mother said.

Didn't she?

"Mom?" Regan whispered. "Mom, please answer. I don't
know what to do." But just like every other time Regan really
needed her, her mother wasn't there.

"Whitmer, your ride's here," a deputy said from the doorway.

Gripping the chair beside her, Regan pulled herself up off
the tiled floor. She glanced inside the other offices as she followed the deputy down the hallway. No sign of Will.

Janey waited at the front desk, tapping her fingers against the
wood-grain counter as Regan rounded the corner. "You okay?"

Regan nodded. "Aunt Janey, I . . ."

"Not here!" Janey snapped. "Not here."

From the opposite end of the hallway, Will approached, wearing a pair of handcuffs and keeping his gaze set to the floor.

"You okay?" Janey asked him as the bailiff removed his cuffs.

Will nodded, but didn't speak.

"Come on, let's go."

The ride home was as silent and cold as the floor Regan had sat on; the disorienting sound of that bumblebee buzzing in her ear was all she could hear. *Baby killer. Baby killer.* She closed her eyes to fight the nausea and didn't open them until she felt Janey shaking her awake.

Will was already halfway to the house, eyes still trained on the earth. Regan waited until he was inside before climbing from the car, praying he'd be gone by the time she got there. She couldn't deal with this right now—not with him or with Janey. What would she say? How would she ask? She had to put her thoughts together before jumping right in.

Once inside, she darted for the stairs, and Will headed toward the kitchen.

"Wait! I'm not finished with you," Janey yelled, slamming the screen door shut.

Regan came to a halt, inches from her getaway. But when she opened her mouth to defend herself, Will's voice filled the room instead.

"Sis, I really need to—"

"Sit!" Janey ordered. Regan inched up another step before she added, "Both of you!"

Regan took a deep breath and descended the stairs, taking the farthest seat on the sofa from Will. *Baby killer. Baby killer.*

Janey crossed her arms over her chest. "Who wants to go first?"

Regan looked toward Will long enough to see he had no intention of answering and then set her gaze on the far wall, silent.

"Nothing?" Janey said. "Okay, fine. Will, since you know the drill, we'll start with you. What the hell were you thinking, jumping on a kid like that?"

Will shrugged. "He was being a prick."

"They're all pricks at that age! You were a prick at that age. That's not a good enough reason. Try again."

"Well, he wouldn't shut up!"

"And what exactly was he saying? That you were crazy? Hell, everyone thinks that."

Baby killer. Baby killer.

Regan clenched her eyes shut, trying to chase the words from her mind.

Baby killer. Baby killer.

Is that why he was so crazy? Is that why he hadn't wanted anything to do with her? Is that why he wouldn't speak Regan's name at the cemetery?

Baby killer. Baby killer.

What did this leave her with? What sort of future could a girl possibly expect when she came from parents who'd both taken a life?

"Baby killer."

The moment Regan said it, the buzzing ceased. The bickering turned to silence, and the dizziness to tranquility. She opened her eyes. "Were you ever gonna tell me about Emma?"

"That is none of your business," Will said, eyes locked on Janey.

"Well, I didn't tell her," Janey said.

"No. You didn't," Regan confirmed. "And that makes you no better than him."

"That was Will's decision to make, not mine. And if I *had* told you, it was highly possible you wouldn't have stayed."

"And that's *my* decision. Not yours." Regan turned to Will. "Is that why you don't ever talk to her about me at the cemetery? Because you feel guilty I'm alive?"

Will's eyes widened. "You . . . you spied on me?"

Oh yeah. The other half of the lies. Will wasn't the only one who'd hidden the truth. "I . . . I didn't mean to spy. I just—"

"How long?" He stood and inched toward her. "How long?"

"I don't know, I—"

"*How long?*"

Regan jumped. He sounded hurt. Betrayed. "Since you saw Ellie at the grocery store. But I didn't know the other part until today."

In a sudden move, Will whipped his hand back and smashed a lamp to the floor, letting out a loud growl that Regan imagined sounded like a dying wolf.

Janey inched toward him and placed her hand on his shoulder. "Will, let me get you a—"

He shook his head and pushed her hand away.

"But it will calm you down."

"I don't want to calm down," he snarled, meeting her gaze. "All I want is for you to keep that spy away from me. Do you understand?"

Regan jumped to her feet, fists clenched. "How did I end up taking the blame for this? I'm not the only one who was dishonest!"

"Regan, please. Don't," Janey pleaded, stepping between them.

"No, goddamn it! You might let him push you around, but I'm not going to let him do it to me!" She stepped around Janey and stared at Will. "You haven't exactly been the epitome of truth, Dad. How many opportunities did you have to tell me about Emma, hmm? How many? And you never once brought her up."

"I had my reasons," Will said.

"And so did I. But you think you get special treatment. You think what you did is less dishonest than what I did because you have an excuse. Well, I'm not buying it anymore, Dad. Because you're not crazy. You're just too damn scared to move on with your life without her."

"Shut up."

"Will, calm down," Janey said.

"She's gone. And I'm here, but you can't even see me."

Janey grabbed Regan's hand. "Please, stop."

Regan shook her off and stepped closer to her father. It was now or never. "She's dead, Dad. Emma is dead. Let her go."

The slap came squarely across Regan's cheekbone. The sound registered before the pain did—the thunderous crack only a man's large hand could give. And then the heat of shame, the shudder of breathless shock, the sting of betrayal.

Regan cradled her face in her palm, still staring at the floor and trying to believe what had just happened. He'd just hit her, something she'd sworn she'd never allow to happen again.

She sprinted for the stairs, for her bedroom, for clarity. She didn't look at the red mark still stinging her cheek; she'd seen it before. She didn't throw herself down on the bed and cry; she'd spent enough time letting other people own her tears.

Run, her mother ordered.

Now she provided advice? After the damage was done? When Regan knew exactly what to do and didn't need her help?

Regan locked her bedroom door and charged straight for the closet.

"Regan? Are you okay?" Janey asked from the other side of the door.

Don't answer. She doesn't really care.

Regan pulled the bag, containing all the things she'd come here with, from beneath the new clothes Janey'd given her.

"Sweetie, it's the illness. He didn't mean it."

How many times had Regan heard that before?

Too many to count, her mother's voice answered.

"Please talk to me," Janey pleaded.

"Just leave me alone," she shouted at both of them. She wouldn't stay for Janey and she wouldn't leave for her mother. It was time Regan made her own choices.

And she chose to never look back again.

Will's feet came to a halt at the door of the barn; his racing heart picked up speed, his limbs shook. What the hell was wrong with him? Why couldn't he move? He was inches away from his safety net and Janey would be here any minute. He was useless out here, vulnerable. He had to get inside, to a place where he was king and made all the rules. There were two places that were his—only two. And since Regan had just destroyed the other, the barn was all he had left.

Behind him, he heard the screen door creak open and slam shut. *Move, damn it, move.* Focusing all his force to his legs, he willed his feet forward and knocked the door open with his elbow. He wouldn't let Regan have this too, not after learning the kind of person she truly was: a liar and a spy. So what if her blood had tainted his saw blade and her smiles had poisoned the air. He'd find a way to remove her from this place. Remove her from his heart.

He latched the door shut, sliding the long, iron pin through the hole on the other side. Fuck Janey's rule of no locked doors. In fact, fuck Janey for not sticking up for him.

A loud thump emanated from the door. "Will! Open up, *now!*"

"I'm warning you, Janey. Just go away."

"Or what? You going to slap me too?"

Will cringed, guilt seeping in at the image of Regan cupping her cheek. There was no excuse for his behavior, other than that he'd done his job. His only responsibility was to protect his relationship with Emma. It was sacred, like guarding the gates to heaven.

"You shouldn't have done that," Janey said.

"You're right. And she shouldn't have spied on me!"

"And you should've told her about Emma before now."

But wasn't it just a given? Like breathing, having blue eyes, or using the bathroom? Will was the guy who'd killed his daughter. It was a part of him. Not just an action, but a characteristic. It defined him. He only remembered fragments of a time it didn't. Should he really have to say it aloud when it was written all over him?

"Will, you can't just pretend it never happened."

"Fuck you!" Will shouted, punching the door. "You have no right to say that to me. Not when I spend every minute of my fucking life reliving that day. *Every* minute."

"I meant with Regan. She needs to know—"

"That she shouldn't trust her own father? I tried that route, remember? I tried staying away. Because *I* recognized I can't do this. You're the one who's been running around here acting like I'm somebody I'm not. *Not* me."

There was a long silence, unusual for his sister. Where was her defense? Her know-it-all answer? Her useless pleas for him to move on in a life that had nothing to offer him? Where?

Will weaved through the piles of wood to the side of the barn he rarely spent time in, swiping a path of dust off the dirty window to peek outside. Janey sat on the old picnic table, her head in her hands. It wasn't until she wiped her face that he could see the tears.

God, he hated when he made her cry.

Will sighed, letting his gaze wander from her as she walked toward the house. That's when he saw a figure standing in Mama's old room—Regan's room—and all of his anger came flooding back. She looked down on him, just like everyone else did. So Will needed to treat her like he treated everyone else. Like nothing.

Nothing.

Tears flooded his eyes as he backed away from the window, farther from this delusion and back into his dark reality. He didn't stop until he had nowhere else to go, back pressed tight against his fate, against the reason he never went to that side of the barn.

Janey had begged him to get rid of it a million times, but he could never bring himself to do it. To him, it was more than just an old BMW; it was a crystal ball. It represented all his lives—when he'd been high on the perfection of life, the moment he'd come crashing down like an airplane to the ground, and the fiery hell he'd been living in ever since.

This car was the last part of him that still had all the pieces.

Will pulled the tarp to the floor, shooting a dust cloud of memories into the air, swirling around him. When they settled, he wiped off the back-passenger window and glanced inside. Emma's pink and gray car seat was still there, in the rear position. It was covered in bugs—the cartoon sort. Purple and yellow butterflies, green and blue dragonflies, red and purple ladybugs, all stitched into the fabric. A mirror would've hung in front of her, and, on the handle, a toy frog on a string would've made funny noises when she reached for it. The cross-stitched blanket with her birth date was still beside it, and the diaper bag he was supposed to take into daycare was still on the seat. Everything just as he'd left it that day.

Everything except Emma.

In truth, Will didn't know if this was how he'd left it. He didn't even remember driving in to work that day. Dr. Granger had said the work hours had been too much for him. Being the only vet in a town built on farming could be exhausting. He'd assisted with four births that week, two of which were cows that had required all-nighters. He must've gotten the call about the fifth delivery around six that morning.

He didn't remember Ellie asking him to take Emma to daycare. He didn't remember dressing Emma in her peach outfit with Peter Rabbit on the front. He didn't remember kissing Ellie goodbye and wishing her good luck on her first day back to work for her father.

He didn't remember the record hot day, unusual for late September, or the stubborn calf that didn't want to be born. He didn't remember driving home, never once looking in his rear-view mirror, or crashing on the couch when he got home. He didn't remember the dreams he'd had, if he'd had any at all, or if they were anything compared to the nightmare he'd woken up to.

From there on, everything was vivid. Will still woke in the middle of the night, hearing Ellie's scream calling him in the dark. He could still feel the woven texture of the couch, brushing against his hands as he rose up, and the hot, thick night air blowing past as he raced out the door. He could see Ellie slumped into a ball on the ground, clenching Emma's cross-stitched blanket in her fist, while the BMW's door hung open beside her. And then he could feel the earth moving beneath him—parting to reveal that special part of hell reserved for fathers who forget their own children.

Someone called 911, though, to this day, Will didn't know who. The ambulance and police sirens yelled in the background. Will sank to the ground beside his wife, but she never looked him in the eyes. Not once.

Will remembered thinking it was all a mistake—this wasn't his daughter. Emma was rosy faced, like the color of the tulips he'd planted when he found out Ellie was pregnant. This baby was blue and clammy, like the color of a late-afternoon thunderstorm rolling in the distance, the color of wet ash. This baby wasn't giving him those tiny, sleepy smiles his daughter gave, the ones he'd sworn were real even though the pediatrician had said they were a part of a baby's sleep pattern, the ones that made it exciting for him to have the night-feeding shift.

This baby wasn't breathing.

They said the heat took her around noon, about the time Will removed the calf from its mother. They said that even if he had looked in the rearview mirror on the way home, it would've been too late. They said it was an accidental death, but that didn't make Will feel any less a murderer. He still felt that way.

Will sank to the dirty barn floor, tears magnifying the clarity of his fate. They might not punish him here on earth, but God would find a way in the end. Will would burn in hell for what he'd done to Emma, and rightfully so. And if Regan was half as smart as Will gave her credit for, she'd run for the hills before his demons sucked her down with him.

"Mr. Barrett, could you come in here, please?"

Despite the shiner under his left eye, Lane Barrett gave Lindsay a deer-in-the-headlights look and set his backpack on the floor as he walked into the office. "I know it's after hours, but I forgot my math book in my locker."

"Glad to hear you're being so attentive on the first day of

school, but that's not what I want to discuss with you." Lindsay moved her mug full of pencils to the side, clearing a place to sit, then leaned against her desk with her hands clasped. This was her nonthreatening pose. Had she sat in her chair with her back stiff and hands folded over her desk, that meant a storm was coming. "Coach says you're the voice of reason for the players. If they're out of line, you're the one to step up and say so. That true?"

"Guess I don't have time for the bullsh . . ." He bit his tongue, sinking into his seat. "I don't have time for playing around. If they're messing around, that means more laps. More laps mean a longer practice. And I've got a job I have to get to."

Lindsay nodded. "Lane, the reason I'm asking is I need to talk to someone about what happened at the field today. Someone I could trust to be honest. Can you do that?"

He nodded slowly.

"Today you said the black eye was an accident, is that true?"

He nodded again.

"And you said it wasn't Mr. Fletcher who hit you?"

Lane cleared his throat. "It was Regan."

Lindsay raised her brow. "Regan . . . hit . . . you?"

"Not on purpose. She shoved me away and her elbow found my eye. That's all." He glanced down and fingered a tiny hole in his jeans. "She was just defending her dad, you know? The guys . . . they can get pretty mean when it comes to Will Fletcher, especially Nick. He's my stepsister's boyfriend and, well, Courtney has good reason to hate Mr. Fletcher, I suppose."

A slew of questions surfaced at the base of Lindsay's tongue, none of which she would allow to form. Gossiping with a student was not an example she should set. She'd research the link between Courtney Bradford and Will Fletcher when she got home.

"Nick deserved it, if you ask me," he said, interrupting her thought.

Lindsay met his gaze. "I don't believe there's ever an excuse for fighting."

"Maybe that's because you've never been the guy who always has to fight." He glanced at his watch. "You mind if I go? Got a job to get to."

"Yeah, sure," she responded, even though she wanted him to stay and answer the million other questions surfacing—the ones she couldn't look up on the internet. Like how did he know what it's like to have to fight, and how did he know she didn't? Was he referring to Will or Regan with that observation? How had he managed to grow so wise?

When he'd gone, Lindsay fell into her chair. Her first day and she'd broken up two fights, one of which had resulted in the police being called. But the walls still stood. The teachers hadn't walked out. No strange viruses had been uploaded to the computers enabling them to show only porn. She'd place this day in the good column.

"Knock, knock."

Or maybe not. "Mayor Bradford. To what do I owe this visit?"

"Just wanted to drop in and see how the first day went." He moseyed inside, wearing his standard bow tie and striped suit, and helped himself to a seat, placing a briefcase on the floor beside him. "And to discuss the altercation that took place today."

Well, word certainly traveled fast in this town. "Nothing to discuss. The police were called and are taking care of the situation."

"And the Fletcher girl? Has she been suspended?"

"Whitmer," Lindsay corrected. "And no. I decided it would be more detrimental to suspend her than to work with her."

Mayor Bradford leaned forward and clasped his hands

together, resembling a blackjack dealer in Vegas, with the smile that said *I have you by the ass.* "Ms. Shepherd, it's standard procedure to suspend a student who instigates a fight."

"I understand. But there are conflicting stories about who might have started it."

"Are you suggesting that Nicholas Watkins, the star punt returner for the football team, started this fight?"

Lindsay's face flushed. "I'm simply saying I didn't witness who started the fight, and therefore didn't think it fair to tarnish either of their records with a suspension. And with all due respect, sir, I'd appreciate it if you'd let *me* handle decisions at this school and I will leave the town to you."

Mayor Bradford's smile sank to a hard line. "Of course."

"Good. Now if you'll excuse me—"

"And *since* you mentioned the town, there's another item I'd like to discuss with you." He pulled a manila envelope from his briefcase and placed it on the desk. "I believe the altercation here today warrants your signature."

Lindsay unlatched the envelope, sliding out the papers inside. A lot of legal mumbo jumbo in front, a stack of signatures behind. "Is this—?"

"We've been working a long time on this. Long before today's incident. Earlier this month, it was nudity in the town fountain. Today, he attacked a group of kids."

"I hardly think he *attacked* them, Mayor. He—"

"The town no longer feels safe. And it's my job to make sure every citizen feels safe."

"But you can't possibly think he'd ever—"

"I don't think. I *know.*" Mayor Bradford waved a hand in the air and stared out the window. "It's happened before, and, if it wasn't for my daughter Ellie's kind heart, I would've found a way to do this then."

Lindsay tilted her head. There was no point asking, he'd just cut her off again.

"Did I mention there have been some complaints from the teachers, already? Apparently, this new block scheduling you've implemented isn't going over well." He met her gaze, that same blackjack-dealer grin dancing on his lips. "As principal of Half Moon High, it would greatly improve our case if you signed our petition, Ms. Shepherd. Greatly."

Lindsay glanced down at the papers. All the words mixed together in a blur of black and white, all except the words in the middle of the first page in bold letters.

PETITION FOR THE COMMITTAL OF WILLIAM FLETCHER INTO CREEDMOOR PSYCHIATRIC HOSPITAL.

As Janey lay in her bed that evening, the weight of the day settled over her like a blanket of stone. Every bit of progress she'd made with Will and Regan over the past few weeks had been erased in one afternoon, and it was Janey's fault. She should've told Regan sooner, but, as always, she'd put Will's feelings before her own. Not because her brother bullied her or she was too weak to stand up to him, but because that's what Janey did. Because Will would do the same for her.

Before Emma had died, Will had been Janey's tour guide at every misstep through life. The one to show her which way to go, to dust her off when she fell face first into the dirt, to push her along when she couldn't move. Will's name was the one she'd put down on her senior survey in the line next to Person You Admire Most. He was the first person she'd called when her comic book sold, and the only person she'd thanked in the acknowledgements.

Her older brother was her hero, and she was never embarrassed to call him that. She would've shouted it from the rooftops if she'd had to, because, the way Janey saw it, she was lucky. Most people didn't discover their heroes until that hero was no longer there to save them.

Maybe Janey let Will say things to her she shouldn't, but wasn't that the reward all fallen heroes should get for their service? Permission to be crotchety and to tell the world all the honest truths they've learned in life? That no matter how many times you save someone, the only thing they remember is the one time you didn't?

But she couldn't expect Regan to understand, couldn't even explain it in hopes she might. She was a fifteen-year-old girl who'd never had a hero to save her. Not from hunger or the cheap motel she'd grown up in. Not from a sick mother or the stepfather who'd turned his back when she needed him most. That's why she'd come looking for Will, wasn't it?

How desolate Regan must've felt when it sank in—the man supposed to give her hope didn't have any left of his own to give.

Janey pushed her quilt to the side and climbed from her bed. She'd obeyed their wishes to be left alone long enough. She wouldn't allow someone else to fail Regan. She wouldn't allow Regan to give up on Will. She would find a way to put them back together, because Will and Regan needed each other more than they would ever know.

Before she could talk herself out of it, Janey tapped on the door. When she didn't hear a response, she tapped again. "Regan, are you decent? I'm coming in." But Regan wasn't there. In fact, her bed was made, not a throw pillow out of place or a wrinkle in the comforter. Which made Janey nervous, because when she'd brought Regan's laundry to her room earlier today, the bed hadn't been made.

Janey hurried down the hallway and back, pushing open every door, then descended the steps two at a time. Normal teenagers didn't clean their rooms after a fight; normal teenagers ran away. She knew firsthand.

When she came up empty inside the house, Janey circled outside and shouted Regan's name in between the whines of Will's saw. When that failed, she headed for the barn and pounded on the door, still locked. "Will, have you seen Regan?"

Another quick rip of the saw was all she received in response.

"Will, goddamn it! Tell me if you've seen her!"

A long silence, and then the door opened. "Maybe she finally got the hint that I don't want anything to do with her."

"You bastard!" Janey shouted, beating her fists against his chest to push her way inside. "I swear if anything has happened to her—"

"And you think I did it, right? The crazy baby killer strikes again?"

Janey covered her mouth. The thought had never crossed her mind, not once. "Will, I swear, that's not what I meant."

"Go fuck yourself, Janey," he spewed, picking up a fresh piece of lumber. "I'm not gonna waste my time explaining myself to some traitor."

"Is that what you think? That I took her side over yours today?"

Will shrugged. "Call it like I see it, sister."

Janey stomped toward him, fists clenched. "You can huff and puff all you want. You can throw your fits and call me every name in the book. But I'm not going to let you push away the first person who's made you feel real since Emma died. You hear me? I'm not!"

"Real?" He chuckled. He actually chuckled. "For someone who can pick a piece of my bullshit out of a pile of manure, you sure missed a big one."

Janey took a step back. "What's that supposed to mean?"

"That it was all just an act. Every bit of it. I knew the only way you'd get off my ass was if I played nice with her, so I did. And you fell for every bit of it." He made two marks on the piece of lumber in the shape of a cross. "I couldn't care less where Regan's gone or why, or if she ever comes back. And that's the damned truth."

Janey closed the gap between them. "You may never admit it out loud or even to yourself, but what you just said, about not caring what happens to Regan?"

He glanced up at her over his work glasses.

"*That*, my dear brother, was a line of your bullshit. Not the other way around."

A bag of pretzels, two bottles of water, a candy bar, and a map. Regan placed the items on the conveyor belt at the register and dug into her backpack for the cash she'd stolen from the coffee can. How far would fifty dollars get her? She paid the cashier and stepped down to bag her items, someone else's hand grabbing the pretzels before she could.

"Road trip?" the bagger asked, his voice too familiar.

Regan clenched her jaw, meeting Lane Barrett's gaze. The shiner she'd given him today covered his left eye, but the smile on his lips didn't hint that Regan had given it to him. "No."

"Sure looks like road-trip material to me," he responded, holding the map next to his face.

Regan yanked it from his hands. "So, Sherlock? I like geography."

Lane rolled his eyes, then finished bagging her items, keeping the bags out of Regan's reach. When finished, he untied his hunter-green apron and placed it on a hook beside the cashier. "See you tomorrow, Shirley."

Shirley grinned between them. "Say hi to your mom for me."

Lane nodded, then grabbed the two bags and smiled at Regan. "Ready?"

"For what?"

"It's customary here at Hadley's to hand deliver our last customer's groceries."

Great. Just what she needed. "That's really not necessary."

"I think so." He nodded toward her bandaged hand. "Where ya heading? Slumber party?"

"Right. Slumber party." Regan spun on her heels, falling in step beside him. "Look, I'm sorry about the eye, but I really don't need an escort."

"Nonsense. Never know what crazy people lurk around the corner."

"Suit yourself," Regan answered without slowing. "But I think it's only fair to remind you that *I'm* that crazy person."

"I don't believe that."

"No? Then why am I racing off to a slumber party where someone just said my name into a mirror three times on a dare?"

He let out a loud laugh. "Strong-headed *and* witty. Ain't I the lucky one?"

Regan paused in the middle of the road, locking eyes with him. "Why don't you just come out and say whatever it is you want and then leave me be, huh?"

Lane stared a moment, lips slightly parted. It occurred to Regan this must be new to him—a girl telling him to get lost. Boys like him were used to getting whatever they wanted without much of a fight. "I wanted to apologize for this afternoon. The guys were out of line."

"Apology not accepted," she retorted. "That it?"

"Not exactly." He fidgeted with his fingers a moment before sliding them through his sandy hair. "I also wanted to see if maybe you'd like to go see a movie after the game on Friday, but, since you won't accept my apology, I doubt that's going to happen."

She hefted her bag farther onto her shoulder. "Draw the short stick, did ya?"

"I'm sorry?"

"Well, that's what you're doing, isn't it? Keeping up your end of a bet? Why else would a guy like you be interested in someone like me?"

Lane blinked. "You don't know anything about me."

"Trust me," Regan said, biting back a growl. "I know all I need to know."

"I'm not like the others."

"Prove it!"

He glanced down the road in both directions, then grabbed Regan by the hand and set off to the right, down a stone path. "Come on."

"Where?"

Though he didn't answer, Regan still followed, with no idea why.

CHAPTER NINE

Regan's mother had told her there were times in life she'd find herself at a crossroads. "Go left toward the rainbow and you'll find a pot of gold," she'd said. "Go right and you'll find a bag of precious rubies. Stay at the crossroads and you'll miss both." They'd been sitting in the ladies' room of the parish, both dressed in white, fluffy dresses and tiaras, waiting for the pastor to say it was time. Her mother was living proof of the theory; she was about to marry her pot of gold or bag of gems, though Regan wasn't sure which.

But Regan's mother never told her the other half of the story. That sometimes rainbows vanish before you find the pot of gold. That gems sometimes turn out to be hot coals. That if you travel too far toward one treasure, the path to the other fades, so choose wisely. These were lessons she'd taught herself, lessons she recalled as Lane led her by the hand back to the place of her crossroads.

Why was she still holding his hand?

It had to be the same road. Regan recognized the old wooden

sign pointing toward historic Half Moon Hollow, though, this time, she walked in the opposite direction. She'd thought about that day many times since she'd arrived. Deciding she would find her real father after her stepfather had locked her in her room. Hitching a ride out of town with an evangelist named Betty Lou, the irony almost too much to bear. Pulling up to a crossroads, the same crossroads she now walked back to.

What if she hadn't gotten out of the car? Would she be better off?

She hesitated when Lane set off through a farm field.

"What's wrong?" he asked.

Regan blinked. Alone in the dark night with a boy she hardly knew, heading into a field of cornstalks taller than her, all the while wondering why she still held his hand. The question was—what wasn't wrong?

When she didn't answer, he smiled and tugged on her hand. "Come on. Let's go."

The chirping of the crickets seemed to grow louder, the farther they weaved down the beaten path. Through the dim moonlight, Regan could make out the roofline of a building in the distance. And then the rows of cornstalks came to an end, falling off into a ravine.

"What is this place?" she asked.

"The old Half Moon Creek dam."

Regan glanced at the trickle of water spilling over. "Not much of one."

"They built a new one upriver a few years back." Lane continued on toward the old building. "This kind of became the local make out spot after that."

"And you brought me here because, why?"

"*Just* to talk," he defended, pulling the rotting door open. "Scout's honor."

She glanced back toward the beaten path, then inside the dark cabin.

Go on. Go inside.

Trying not to flinch at the sound of her mother's voice, Regan squeezed past Lane through the doorway into the tiny cabin. There was one chair in the middle of the room, a few half-gallon buckets against the far wall, and spiderwebs the size of small trees.

Why was she here?

"My dad used to take me fishing down at the creek and come here to clean up the catch before we headed home. Mom didn't like the fish smell in the house." He sank to the floor, pulling his knees to his chest. "He left when I was eight."

Regan sat beside him. "I didn't know that. Sorry."

"Don't be. He was an asshole."

"But he was still your dad," Regan said.

A bit of a smile surfaced on his lips, so small Regan wondered if the shadows of the night were playing tricks on her. When he went back to mumbling into his knees, she was certain of it.

"But you know what's funny? I don't remember any part of the day he left. All I remember is how, after he left, everyone in town treated my mom like it was her fault. Like if she would've been a better cook or kept the house tidier, maybe he wouldn't have left us."

Regan glanced away, trying to think of what to say to someone she had a hard time pitying. She settled for, "Yeah, well, people suck."

"People suck," he repeated in a whisper, a hint of that same smile showing again. "Your dad said the same thing to me once."

"Yeah?" she asked in the least interested manner she could conjure, even though his statement sprouted a thousand questions. "Sounds like something he'd say."

"He and Ellie were the only ones who didn't treat me like some reject bastard. Ellie even set Mom up with her brother. Then everyone had to like me, since he's the mayor's son and all."

Ten thousand more questions sprang to Regan's foggy head.

"I even liked all the attention at first," Lane continued. "Until they got married, and Courtney Bradford became my stepsister. Superficial brat."

Courtney Bradford was Lane's stepsister? Was there anyone in this town *not* wrapped up in her father's tragedy?

Regan exhaled sharply, reminding herself she didn't care. "Why are you telling me this?"

He met her gaze, lips in a firm line. "Because I know what it's like for everyone to judge you based on your dad, and I don't want you to believe half the shit the town says about him." He glanced down at her hand resting on the floor and slid his over it. "And because it's the only way I know how to prove I'm being genuine."

His fingertips felt like warm rainwater, spreading over hers, creating a million tingles. Her faced flushed from uneasiness; her heart sped with hope. She was a ball of contradictions, rolling downhill. This was wrong, so terribly wrong.

"You don't even know me," she finally managed past the lump lodged in her throat.

"Sure I do. You're sophomore Regan Whitmer. You were born in Chicago. Your favorite color is black and your favorite author is Poe."

"Congratulations, Einstein. You read my bio in the school paper today."

"You didn't let me finish." He smiled a half grin, then pinched the collar of her blue jacket between his fingers. "You *say* you like black, but you always wear something with blue in it. Poe might be your favorite author, but it's not because you're some dark, scary chick like you want everyone to believe. It's because when you read his stuff, you remember there's someone out there worse off than you are."

Regan deflated, the truth a sharp needle into her side.

"You cut your sandwiches in a diagonal and always save the upper half for later."

"How did you know . . ."

"You think God forgot about you along with the rest of the world, so you don't bother to look his way either. You don't really care, because there's only one person you want to have notice you anyway, and he's too blind to see you standing behind someone else. You're scared what he'll think if he *does* see you, so you hide behind an oak tree so you'll never have to find out."

The anger bubbled inside Regan like lava, until the steam shot her straight up in the air like the lid on a teapot. "You asshole! You've been spying on me? That was *my* private time! You had no right to take that away from me!"

"If you want to get technical about it, *you* took it away from *me*." He got to his feet. "That was *my* damn oak tree until you came along."

"*Your* tree?"

"Yes, my tree. I've been eating lunch in that same spot for the past two years now."

"Spying on my father!"

"Said the pot to the kettle!"

Regan reared back. "What does a pot or a kettle have to do with this?"

"Never mind," he sighed, digging his hands into his hair. "You're missing the point."

"Well, maybe it's not sharp enough!"

"Or maybe you're just blind! God, why do you have to be so

...so...so damn...stubborn!" Lane yelled, throwing his hands into the air. "The most goddamned stubborn girl in town! The other girls would do anything to have me follow them around."

"Well, I'm not all the other girls."

"Which is why I like you so much. You're not like my stepsister and her minions. Your decisions come from your heart, even if they won't launch you to the front of the popularity line. You stand tall next to your father no matter what the cost, just because he needs someone to stand there." Lane inched toward her, lips trembling, and took her face in his hands. "Why is it so hard for you to believe I like you?"

Because I've been here before. Because I think I like you too. Because I don't have anything left for you to break.

"Please, say something."

Regan opened her mouth to respond, the million questions she'd had dissolving like sugar on her tongue. And then without warning, her lips were locked tight with Lane's.

Lindsay turned onto Main Street again and looked down the same alley she'd looked down the last three times. The moon had shifted; light no longer shined a pathway for her to see. Regan could've been giving her the bird, and she never would've seen it. "Do you know what time she left? Maybe she's already made it to the highway."

"I don't know," Janey answered, voice as crackled and weak as it had been when Lindsay answered the phone. She'd only gotten pieces of the puzzle then—Regan and Will had a fight, at some point she'd run away, and since Will didn't drive, Janey needed someone to cart her around town while she looked. Lindsay was the only person she'd called. Which reminded her . . .

"Janey, maybe you should go to the police."

"No!" Janey snapped.

Lindsay stopped the car in the middle of the empty road and met Janey's gaze. They'd searched for two hours without any luck, and Lindsay had to get up for school in less than four. As much as she wanted to help, Janey didn't make it easy.

"Look," Janey said. "If they find out Regan ran away, they'll take her away from us for sure. Will's not exactly the father of the year, you know."

Lindsay released the brake pedal, but not because she understood or agreed. Sometimes, kids were better off without their natural parents—she'd seen it a million times. But that wasn't for her to judge. Right now, all that mattered was finding Regan safe.

"You didn't tell her, did you?" Lindsay turned down First Street and headed toward the main highway. "About the baby."

Janey's eyes widened, and her lips parted with a question.

"Mayor Bradford came by my office tonight. Told me to be careful associating with your family." Lindsay would save the rest for another time.

"Then why are you here?" Janey asked.

Lindsay considered this, unsure of the answer herself. It was political suicide for a principal to associate with a man who'd killed his child. But she'd also been the one shunned by her friends and family; some were afraid barrenness was contagious, others were unable to go on living their normal happy lives beside someone who'd never have one. And her ordeal was nothing compared to this. Not being able to give life to a child was far less painful than taking life away from one.

Lindsay was surprised Will had survived at all.

"My family doesn't need your pity, Lindsay."

"If pity was the only reason I was here, I wouldn't want to be here." She grabbed Janey's hand and smiled. "I think we both could use a friend, don't you?"

Janey glanced down at their locked hands. "Yes. I do."

Lindsay stepped on the gas pedal. "Then let's go find your niece."

"You did it first," Lane teased. "I make it a habit not to kiss any girls unless I ask."

Regan rolled her eyes. Why had she kissed him? Why had she liked it so much? "But you said I'm not like the other girls, so maybe your stupid rules don't apply."

He chuckled, resting his head on his arm and motioning for her to use his other as a pillow. "I think, with you, the rules *definitely* need to apply."

Regan lay beside him and gazed at the moonlight streaming through the tiny window. How much time had passed? It felt like seconds, yet they'd been through both of their life histories. She'd told him about her mother and Steven. He'd told her about his drunken father and being the mayor's step-grandson. She'd told him how lonely it was growing up an only child, and he'd told her how Courtney and little Mikey made him wish he still were.

"Won't you get in trouble, not coming home?"

"Nah, my folks are at a cheerleading competition with Court." He released his arm from beneath his head and glanced at his watch. "Ellie's staying with me, but she still has another four or five hours knocked out on her Ambien."

Ellie. It was weird hearing someone else say it so normally. Like *Mary* or *Bob.* No guilt behind it, no feelings. Just a normal name to a normal person, sleeping and eating and breathing like everyone else. Not a goddess, not a ghost. Just Ellie.

"What about you? You gonna get in trouble?" he asked.

"I'm not going back." She rolled to his side. "Tell me another story about him?"

Lane was quiet for a moment, then let out a long sigh. "There was this time Ellie made a pot roast. She wasn't very much of a cook, so this was a big deal. She asked my mom for the recipe, worked all day on that damn pot roast, and then I saw black smoke coming out of the windows. Fire trucks came, police came, and, about the time they were carrying that charcoaled pot roast out of the house, Will came home.

"He rushed toward Ellie sitting on the porch steps with Emma, but Ellie hurried back into the house and slammed the door before he could get to them. He yelled, 'Ellie, what the hell's wrong with you? Let me inside!' But she didn't answer him. 'Ellie,' he said again, 'at least tell me if you're okay!'

"'I'm fine!' She answered. 'But you're not coming back into this house!'

"'Why? What did I do?' he asked her.

"'You've always got to be so damned perfect! The perfect husband, the perfect father, the perfect vet, the perfect *cook*. I just wanted to do something for you. And I ruined it!'

"'No you didn't, sweetie. You're perfect.'

"'Just go away, Will. I can't keep it up anymore. I can't. I want a divorce!'"

Regan perked up. "She told him that?"

Lane nodded. "Ellie always said stuff like that. Especially after she had Emma."

"Well, what did he do?"

"Will ran down the steps to the firefighters standing around the burned pot roast and whispered something into the chief's ear. Next thing I know, they're carrying that damn pot roast back up the steps to the porch. Will sits down beside it, snaps a piece of burned meat off, and tosses it into his mouth."

"No, he didn't!"

Lane nodded. "And then he took two more bites. 'You see Ellie,' he yelled, 'It's perfect! Doesn't even need any ketchup.'

"I think he ate half that pot roast before the door finally opened. Ellie came out, carrying Emma in one of those wrap things around her chest, sank down beside him, and gave him the longest, hottest kiss I've ever seen someone give a person."

Regan swallowed hard, the thought of Lane kissing her again making her shiver. "So, then they lived happily ever after?"

Lane tensed, suddenly chilly. "At least for another month."

For a moment, Regan had allowed herself to get lost in Lane's story. She'd allowed herself to think of Will as a perfect father and a perfect husband, to imagine she was a part of that fairy-tale world. But, as all girls eventually realized, not every hero had a bright, happy ending. Sometimes, the hero had to settle for less darkness than he'd started with.

With a sigh, Regan raised herself up onto her elbow. "I think I'm ready."

Lane met her gaze, a question hanging on his lips.

"Tell me what happened to Emma."

Will had been standing in the driveway for fifteen minutes, staring at Janey's car and weighing all the options. What harm could it do to make sure Regan was all right? Didn't mean he was giving in. Didn't mean he wanted to sign up for the daddy-daughter dance down at the school. He'd simply be a fellow citizen looking out for his town's youth.

Just two problems—how would he get there and what would he do if he saw her?

He grunted, leaning against the hood of the car. Maybe he should wait for Janey. It was possible she'd thought to look at the water tower and the old dam. Will didn't know much about

Regan—he didn't *want* to know much, and this didn't change that—but he did know she didn't seem the type to enjoy roller-skating or air hockey down at the arcade.

"Going out to look for her?"

Will turned with a start to the unfamiliar voice. Lane Barrett squatted on the old willow stump in the front yard, with a black eye no less. Will prayed he hadn't done that to the poor kid. And why the hell was he here at five thirty in the morning anyway?

"I told her you cared, but she didn't believe me."

"You've seen her?" Will asked before he could stop himself.

He nodded. "Spent the night with her."

Will clenched his jaw and took two steps forward before he'd even realized it.

"*Not* like that," Lane added quickly. "Just stayed with her at the old dam, trying to talk her into coming home."

"I *knew* it! The old dam!" A sharp squeal escaped Will's lips as he took off for the house. God, he loved it when he was right.

"Wait, aren't you going to go get her?"

Will shook his head. "Nope."

"But what if something happens to her out there?"

"It's okay. I'm sure she's got a better chance without me."

"That's funny," Lane yelled. "You said the same thing when *my* father abandoned *me*."

Will came to a halt. It was something about that word—abandoned. It took him back to that day. Lane had been sitting on his front porch, like he had been the three nights before, looking down the street as if he'd see his father's truck any moment. Ellie had told Will to stay out of it, but Will couldn't stand to watch the hope drain from the kid's eyes, like a grape shrinking in the sun. So he'd grabbed his old football from the closet and headed over.

After an hour of tossing the ball around in silence, Will had finally said, "I know you don't believe me right now, but your dad did you a favor. You're better off without him."

Lane had smiled then and responded, "Glad someone else besides me thinks so too."

That was when Will had realized it wasn't hope draining from Lane's eyes; it was guilt building inside them. Not all kids fall asleep at night thinking their families are unbreakable; some lie awake, praying the breaking will finally end. Sometimes the best parenting a parent can do is throwing in the towel and leaving the job to someone more qualified.

It made him wonder—had Regan's eyes done the same each hour he hadn't come after her? More importantly, could he live with not knowing?

"Are you still happy he didn't come home?" Will called to Lane over his shoulder.

"No," he admitted. "I'm pissed he was too much of a coward to swallow his pride and admit he needed help."

Will turned toward him, eyes trained on the ground like a toddler who'd been scolded. "Did she ask? I mean, about what happened to Emma?"

"Not at first. But then I told her about the pot roast and then . . . well . . ."

Will nodded, a slight grin playing on his lips. He'd almost forgotten about the pot roast.

"I'm sorry. It probably should've come from you, but . . ." Lane sighed. "I guess I just thought it might help if she knew."

"Did it?"

"I don't know," Lane admitted. "But she hasn't left yet."

"Maybe she was just tired."

Lane chuckled. "I doubt that would stop Regan from doing what she wants to do."

Funny. Ellie had said the same thing about Will once. It had cost him his daughter.

"Well, I gotta get back. She's gonna be up soon." Lane climbed to his feet and dusted off his jeans. "So, are you coming or not?"

The sun beckoned Regan from sleep before her body did, pouring through the tiny cabin window onto her face. She must've fallen asleep sometime after the pot roast story. Listening to Lane's heart tapping against her ear had sent her into hibernation mode. She should've been on her way hours ago, but she was still there, lying beside . . .

She rose to her elbows, glancing around the empty room. This might have hurt a year ago, even two days ago. Now, it was the norm. People didn't want Regan; she was finished with being surprised about it.

You're lying, her mother said.

A loud sigh escaped her as she lay back against the floor. Her mother was right; it did hurt. Maybe not like when her mother had died, but it was still there. A dull ache all over, like that time she'd had too much to drink. After last night, it was that much worse. She hadn't shared those thoughts and memories with anyone before. Whether Lane truly cared or not didn't matter—she'd let it out. Now, it would feel like she'd abandoned a piece of herself when she left.

"Hey! You're up."

Regan jumped at Lane's voice, a clap of thunder in the middle of her emotional storm.

"Whoa, whoa . . . it's just me," he responded to her sudden jolt. He held two cups of coffee and a paper bag. "I brought breakfast."

She eyed him warily in the sunlight. Everyone always looked different in the sunlight. "I thought you'd—"

"Run off?" He took a few steps toward her and held out the cup. "Can't get rid of me that easy. Sorry to disappoint you."

"I'm not disappointed. It's just when people leave me, they usually don't come back." She took the cup before she said any more stupid shit. What the hell was wrong with her? This guy was like a magnet, pulling out all the heavy metal that had been holding her down for so long.

He squatted on the floor beside her. "I have to get to school."

"Thought your parents were out of town?"

"Coach ain't. If I get caught skipping, I can't play Friday. If I can't play Friday, I miss the scouts. If I miss the scouts, I blow my chance at getting the hell out of this town. If I can't—"

"Okay, okay. I get it."

Lane placed his hand over hers, intertwining their fingers. "I wish you'd come with me. This stuff with your dad and Janey will work out. Just give them more time."

She shook her head, staring at their intertwined fingers. "I've been here before. Sometimes time isn't enough."

"Fine." Lane pulled her chin up, locking eyes with her. "Then give *me* more time."

Regan bit her lip long enough to stop the quiver. "I just can't."

His lips melted into a thin line of hurt. Maybe regret. It gave Regan a queasy feeling in her stomach. "Fine," he said. "Then you leave me no choice."

A moment later, the door opened and in walked Will.

"You asshole!" she spat at Lane. "You brought him here!"

Silent, Lane leaned against the wall with his hands in his pockets, eyes downcast.

"I'm not here to bring you home." Will took a step closer. "I just want to talk."

"Yeah? Well, I guess it's your turn to be treated like nothing."

Regan jumped to her feet, gave Lane the best eat-shit-and-die look she had, then pushed past her father. She was better off without them. She knew what to expect, knew how to survive.

"What can I do? Do you want me to beg?"

Regan paused at Will's voice, just near the edge of the beaten path. "I've never wanted anything from you except the truth."

"The *truth?*"

"Yes!" she responded, spinning back toward him. "I think I deserve at least that!"

Will glanced toward Lane, then back at Regan. "But I thought he already told you."

"I don't want to know what happened to Emma. I want to know why you still refuse to drive a car. Why you never finish anything you start. Why, when Janey asks how your day was, you say 'Same as any other,' but you give Emma a minute by minute recount." She shook her head to banish the tears. "And I want to know why I don't deserve to know any of it."

Will ran his hand down his face, taking a deep breath. "Because I'm scared."

"Of *me?*"

He stepped forward, shaking his head. "Of forgetting what I did to Emma."

Regan opened her mouth to respond, but no words came out.

"Because," he continued. "Because, I don't deserve to forget."

Of all the excuses he could've given, Regan hadn't expected this one. That he went to that grave every day to relive the pain as punishment. That he feared letting Regan into his heart meant pushing Emma out. That he didn't know how to enjoy life with one daughter while mourning the loss of another. And Regan realized, in that moment, he might never change.

Could she live with that? Could she live her life based on a hope that someday, maybe, she'd come first in Will's eyes?

She let out a trapped breath and glanced at the path. The

morning sun shined over the old cabin, showing her the way out from the shadow of a memory into a place of possibilities. That's when she spotted it, peeking out beneath a yellow corn stalk.

Regan placed her bag on the ground, inched toward the edge of the path, and knelt down to retrieve the purple bracelet. It was much dirtier than it had been the day she'd thrown it into the field, but it was the same one Betty Lou had given her on the day she'd arrived. She rubbed her fingers over the embossed letters, the crevices filled with tiny stones and dirt asking her a simple question. WWJD?

He would abandon her again, just like he had so many times. Maybe that's why she shouldn't do the same to Will.

"If I come home, you have to make me a promise." Regan slid the bracelet into her pocket, not ready to wear it. Nor was she ready to look her father in the eye. "A few promises."

"What sort of promises?" Will asked.

"You have to start being nicer to Janey. I'm tired of hearing her cry at night. And no going to the barn every time you get mad."

There was a long silence. "Okay."

"And you have to promise that, once my hand heals, you'll teach me how to build things," she said, determined to stay on track.

"Okay," he agreed. "Anything else?"

"Yes." Regan glanced once more at the path, then turned and looked him dead in the eyes. "If you ever lay a hand on me again, that will be the last time you ever see me."

Lindsay placed the coffee cup on the vinyl placemat in front of Janey, who sat with her head resting on the table. They'd gone up and down the interstate searching for Regan and had come up empty. Now, Lindsay was convinced she was gone. Just gone.

"It's okay," Janey whispered, voice hoarse and distant. "I know you have to get to work."

Lindsay checked the clock again, spotting her reflection in the microwave door. Her hair was pulled back in a wiry mess, her eyes heavy with sleep behind her spare, red-framed glasses. She still wore the raggedy, old Minnie Mouse T-shirt and black, cotton shorts she'd put on for bed last night. But the thought of leaving Janey in such a state made her feel even grosser.

"I'll ask around today. See if anyone's seen her. Isn't she friends with Lane Barrett?"

"Lane Barrett? The football star?" Janey said, head snapping up. "I doubt Regan would associate with someone so shallow. She's smarter than that."

Lindsay began to defend him, but thought better of it. "Well, I'll ask around anyway. Maybe someone saw her." She tossed her purse over her arm and gave Janey's shoulder a final squeeze. "I know you don't want to call the police, but—"

"I can't. I *won't*."

"Just think about it, okay? Having Regan safe in someone else's house is better than not having her at all." Lindsay pushed the kitchen door open, choosing not to mention she'd be obligated to report this to the police anyway. She'd already waited too long.

"Thank you," Janey said just as Lindsay was about to step into the living room. "Will and I . . . we don't have anyone else we can rely on."

"I'll call you later," Lindsay responded, and then continued out to hide the clench of her jaw. She'd have more than a few four-letter words to say to Will Fletcher.

When she stepped onto the porch, she realized it would be sooner rather than later.

"That's a nice look for you, Principal Shepherd," he said, climbing the steps toward her.

"You've got a lot of nerve speaking to me that way. Do you know what I've been doing all night? Driving *your* poor sister around, looking for *your* daughter, because you are too much of a self-centered, son of a bitch to do it!"

He paused, spine stiff and eyes wide. "Excuse me?"

"I think you heard me just fine. You know . . . all those awful things everyone says about you—I didn't believe them. I thought everyone was being too hard on you. And then this happens and I realize what a goddamned fool I am to give a man like you the benefit of the doubt. So, thank you Mr. Fletcher for reminding me how naive I can be about the world."

"Dad? Is everything okay?" Regan asked, walking with Lane Barrett into Lindsay's view.

Lindsay didn't know whether to cry out in joy or throw up.

"It's fine, Regan. Ms. Shepherd just stopped by to see if we were okay. Isn't that right?"

Heat rose from Lindsay's chest, up her throat to her cheeks. When she tried to speak, her voice came out as a low-pitched crackle. This is why she didn't get involved in other families— she always came out looking like the ass.

"Regan? *Regan!*" Janey burst through the screen door and passed Lindsay like a bullet.

"I'm okay," Regan gasped through Janey's death grip. "Just needed a night to think."

"You had me worried sick." Janey released her from the embrace and grabbed hold of her shoulders. "Don't ever do that again, okay? Whatever happens, we can always work it out."

Regan stared hard at her aunt a moment before nodding, tears springing from her eyes.

Suddenly, Lindsay didn't care about her red face or bruised ego. She didn't care she'd be going to school showerless, or that she'd have to wear her hair in a ponytail. She didn't care she'd been up all night searching for a girl, only to have the one person who didn't deserve to find her stroll in like he'd had her all along. Watching Regan melt into Janey's arms was well worth all of it.

"Well, guess I'll hit the sack." Will stretched and yawned at the same time. "It's exhausting being so self-centered."

"Don't sleep too long." Lindsay set off down the sidewalk, ignoring Will's jab. "You've got a scoreboard to finish."

CHAPTER TEN

"Two fifty."

Regan blinked at the cafeteria lady, then glanced down the line at the impatient students waiting behind her. Where was Lane? This had been his damn idea in the first place. She was fine with her standard peanut butter and jelly, but he'd insisted the best way to hide was not to. Or something like that, anyway. It always sounded believable when he said it.

That theory would work better if he'd show up to pay like he'd promised. Now she was stuck at the front of the line with a tray of slimy meatloaf she didn't want and no way to pay for it. She regretted giving all the coffee-can cash back to Janey.

"Two fifty," the cafeteria lady said again, scratching at her hairnet.

"I got it," Lane hollered, snaking his way through the line with a tray.

"You're late."

He paid the lady and scooped up Regan's tray for her. "Sorry. Coach wanted to see me."

"About what?"

"Nothing important," he said, but the way his eyes turned guarded told Regan it was.

She followed him to the same table they'd sat at every day that week—which by now everyone knew not to sit at—and straddled the bench. "They're all staring at me again."

"They're not staring at you." He shoveled a spoonful of corn into his mouth. "They're staring at me."

"Because you're with me."

"And if I didn't let it bother me yesterday, I'm not going to let it bother me now."

Regan deflated, stirring her gravy around with her spork. It wasn't just now or yesterday. It was between every class, during study hall, at the library, in anatomy when he volunteered to be her lab partner. Lane had more eyes on him than that month-old potato in Janey's pantry.

"How can you just act like this doesn't bother you?"

He glanced around the room, his gaze stopping on her. "The only thing that bothers me is that *you're* uncomfortable. Now eat your meatloaf or you'll be starving at practice tonight."

Regan raised her brow. "I'm sorry. . . . What?"

"Practice. It's phase two of my plan."

"I wasn't aware we'd finished phase one."

"I told you—the best way to fade into the background is to get lost right in the middle."

That was how he'd said it. Only this time, it wasn't so believable.

"It'll be fine," he said, returning to his pile of corn. "All the football players' girlfriends come to watch practice."

"And that relates to me, how?"

Lane sighed. "If you don't want to come, just say so."

"That's not the part I have a problem with." She pushed her

tray away, suddenly too nervous to eat. Or maybe anger made her nauseous. How many times did she have to say it? Regan was not his girlfriend.

"We agreed that's not what this is," she said, *again*.

He reached for her muffin, smiling. "Just like you agreed not to kiss me anymore?"

Damn. Why had she kissed him last night? And the night before that, and the night before that? And this morning when they were alone under the stairwell. And yesterday on the front-porch swing. And . . . my God, had she really kissed him so much?

She shook the daze from her eyes and retrieved the half-eaten muffin from his hand. "You call it what you want, and I'll call it what I want. Besides, I can't come today. I'm getting my stiches out, remember?"

Lane leaned in, stopping just short of her lips. It was a good thing too, because, after that meatloaf, he'd need a breath mint, and Regan didn't have the will to turn away from his kiss. "What are you so scared of, Whitmer?"

Being alone. Being betrayed. Being cheated. Being deceived. Being exposed. Regan had a fear for every letter of the alphabet, and this wasn't the time or place to discuss them.

"Does this have anything to do with you being late?" she blurted out.

He backed away, clearing his throat. "I told you why I was late."

"No, you *smoothed over* why you were late."

"Well, if you're not my girlfriend, you shouldn't care any-way, right?"

Regan rolled her eyes, stabbing at her nasty meatloaf. This was entrapment. Good, old-fashioned entrapment. Forget physical therapy; Lane should go into law or politics.

A paper airplane flew between them, crashing into her

gravy and landing in the middle of their stalemate. Regan was only able to make out the words Express Train to Crazy Town printed in big, red, bubble letters on the wings before Lane snatched it away.

"Real nice, Nick," he yelled, crumbling the paper in his hand and tossing it to the table behind him. "But next time, don't use your homework, Slick."

"Who said I was trying to hide?" Nick retorted.

Lane scooped up his last bit of corn. "He does that again, and I'll kick his ass."

"You can't beat everyone in town up," Regan said.

"I won't have to once I kick his." Smiling, Lane climbed from his seat with his empty tray in hand. "I think I want more."

"Take mine."

"No, you need to eat."

Biting her bottom lip, Regan stared at her meatloaf as Lane headed for another tray, wondering how much more she had to give. Wondering if it would ever be enough.

"Are you sure you're ready for this?" Regan asked. "This is a pretty big step."

Will grimaced and turned toward the clerk. Janey usually did this sort of thing. Will made it a habit to limit his interaction with the general public to absolutely necessary circumstances, and this didn't qualify. "Uh, two . . . ch . . . cherry slushies, please. Large."

The kid raised his eyebrow, arranging his face to form the same I-just-saw-the-Grinch expression everyone else in town had when Will spoke to them, then hurried to the slushy machine.

"Piece of cake." Will leaned on the counter so Regan wouldn't see the shaking. "I guess cherry was okay?"

"Perfect. My favorite."

Of course it was, like the butter pecan ice cream and the German chocolate cake. They might not agree on a lot of things, but Will and Regan loved their sweets.

The clerk placed the slushies on the counter. "That's six fifty."

Will choked. "For two slushies? Is there a shot of vodka in them?"

"Keep the change," Regan said, placing seven dollars on the counter.

Will turned toward her.

"I didn't steal it. Janey gave it to me before we left. Said you'd never go if you knew how much they cost."

"She was right. Six fifty for two cups of Kool-Aid and frozen water?" He took a sip, just to be sure there *wasn't* any vodka in there. "These were only fifty cents when I was a kid."

"Yeah, yeah." Regan rolled her eyes and snatched her slushy off the counter. "And you walked a mile to school in four feet of snow, uphill both ways, right?"

"Hey, that's a fact!"

Will followed her through the general store as they picked up the items on Janey's list and slurped their slushies. He'd been following her around a lot lately, partly because he was scared she'd leave again, but mostly because he felt lost when she wasn't around. Why, he didn't really know. He hadn't been found in a very long time.

Once they reached the tool aisle where he was comfortable, he took the lead. Blades, clamps, saw bucks, protective glasses—they had it all. Except the most important piece.

"What are we looking for again?" she asked.

"A shield. It covers the blade when it's spinning." Will rubbed his jaw, backing up a few steps and colliding into someone. "Shit, I'm sor—"

"Hey, Principal Shepherd!" Regan said. "What are you doing here?"

Lindsay Shepherd smiled, waving a wrench in the air. "Leaky faucet. You?"

"Blade shield, so this doesn't happen again." Regan pointed to her scar.

"Hey, you got your stitches out!"

"Yep. Today after school. All healed up."

"Well, that's great." Lindsay smiled, glancing between them as if she were waiting for something. "Cherry slushies. My favorite."

"Mine and Will's too, huh, Will?" Regan asked elbowing him in the side.

"Cherry. Yum."

Will slurped down the rest of his slushy before Lindsay Shepherd asked for a sip, then continued with his search. He still didn't like her—even if she had baked him cookies, brought him lunch, and helped him stain the flower planters at the field.

"How are you, Will?" Lindsay asked.

"Fine."

"I received a lot of compliments this week on the new score-board and planter areas."

"Great."

"I made sure to tell everyone it was your handiwork."

"Super." How many more passive-aggressive, positive, short answers could he give before she got the freakin' hint?

"Don't mind him," Regan said. "He's a little taken aback by the rising cost of slushies."

"Oh. Well it is a wonder they're so expensive nowadays. For flavored water! I used to pay fifty cents when I was a kid!"

"Sure," Will mocked. "And you walked to school in two feet of snow, uphill both ways."

"Really, Will?" Regan asked, hand on her hip. "Really?"

Lindsay shifted her weight back and forth, her short ponytail bobbing behind her head as she did. Her cheeks were rosy pink, probably from working at the stadium last Sunday. Next time, maybe she'd take his advice and use his hundred-SPF sunscreen. "Well, I guess I should be going then. Need to talk to someone about how to fix a leaky faucet."

Regan elbowed him again. "Why don't you help her, Will?"

Will clenched his jaw. What the hell was this? Throw-Will-to-the-Wolves day? First the damn store clerk and now Principal Shepherd? *Baby steps, Regan. Baby steps.*

"Oh no. I couldn't possibly ask . . ." She glanced away a moment. "Well, I could pay you."

"Great! What time should he be there?" Regan said.

Will turned toward Regan, irritated.

"How about now?" Lindsay asked.

"Perfect," Regan answered.

They set off down the aisle together, leaving Will asking how a man who only broke things would fix a leaky faucet.

Janey checked her watch again, her leg twitching nervously. Being in Dr. Granger's office had always made her feel on display, like a child taking a test full of trick questions, a hostage held by the opinions of a man in an argyle sweater. Today was no exception, even if the walls were now a different shade, and his name plate now said Chief of Psychiatry.

"I never got a chance to congratulate you on your promotion," Janey offered, trying to kill any time she could. "It's really . . . great."

Dr. Granger tapped his pen against the desk a few times, then leaned forward. "Are you sure you told him four in the afternoon?"

If she answered yes, Will was out of her control. If she answered no, she was irresponsible. "He probably lost track of time in the hardware store."

"Thirty minutes?"

Janey frowned. Had it only been thirty minutes? It felt more like an hour, or three. She'd kill Will for this.

"Has he gone off his medication?"

"No. I watch him take every dosage."

Dr. Granger sighed as he leaned back into his leather chair. "I've known your family a long time, Janey. I've treated both your father and your brother. And if there's one thing I learned from your father—"

"Will is *nothing* like my father!"

Dr. Granger blinked, jaw tight. She hated that look. It said she'd failed miserably.

"Will is nothing like my father," she repeated in a calmer tone. "He's not trying to stay sick; he's trying to get better."

"There is no *better* with this illness. There is only *controlled.*"

"You can call it whatever you want. All I know is that, for the first time since Emma died, Will wants to live a normal life. Coming here only makes him feel *ab*normal."

"He *is* abnormal. And it's imperative that he comes in on a regular basis for evaluation. No matter how many good days he has, these sessions are a crucial part of his treatment."

Janey sighed. "There will always be the bad. I know."

"Will can't afford to have you being so naive. You have to be in control of this situation at all times—for his sake."

She nodded. Arguing would only prolong the lecture. And what would she say anyway? She knew better than anyone how quickly the tide could turn with Will.

Dr. Granger took a pad from his desk drawer and began to

scribble. "I'm going to renew his prescriptions for one month. But if he misses again . . ."

"I'll drag him here if I have to." Janey hopped from her chair, retrieved the blue piece of paper, and darted for the door before he could say anything else. She didn't need the lectures to convince her how sick Will was. Her memories served as a constant reminder. And hearing Dr. Granger compare Will to their father was like nails down a chalkboard. Will would get an earful when she got home.

Her phone buzzed in her back pocket just as she reached her car. "Hey, Gretchen."

"Are you sitting down?"

Janey opened the door and slid inside the driver's seat. "I am now."

"'Ziggy Rothchild Fights Moomy on the Moon' has been nominated for the Breckenburg award for Best Title for Young Readers!"

"Shut up!" Janey shouted.

"No, seriously!"

"*Shut up!*" Janey shouted again, this time beating the car horn on accident.

"You did it, Jane! Do you realize how fucking huge this is?" The sound of a cigarette lighter igniting crackled over the phone. When had she started smoking again? Probably the minute Janey had walked out the door. "Say something."

Did you ever quit, or was that a lie too? Janey wanted to know, but instead she said, "I'm beside myself. I don't know what to say."

"You can say you forgive me for the way I acted in Columbus."

And there it was, as always. The hidden apology. "Let's just forget about it, okay?"

"The awards are in L.A. this year." Gretchen said, moving on. "Book your flight for the Wednesday before, and we'll go out early."

Janey glanced back at the doctor's office. "I can't go."

"What? But you have to! It's a Breckenburg, Janey! It's a freaking Breckenburg!"

"Money's just tight right now," Janey explained, not wanting to argue about the rest.

"I'll buy your ticket. And we'll room together to save money," Gretchen offered in a loud voice, then whispered the rest, as usual. "I miss you."

For just a moment, Janey allowed herself to imagine what it would be like. Inhaling the lilac scent of Gretchen's hair as she drifted off to sleep and feeling Gretchen's warmth beside her in the morning as she woke up. But only for a moment.

"This is because of *him*, isn't it?" Gretchen asked.

Janey sighed, her transparent cover blown. "You know I can't leave Will by himself. Especially that weekend. You know it's his anniversary."

"He won't be alone. Rebecca can babysit him."

"It's Regan," Janey corrected, setting her jaw. "And I told you, the next time you talked about Will that way would be the last."

"I'm only saying you don't have to do this alone anymore. You have help."

"Goodbye, Gretchen," she stated with utter conviction. But the moment she hung up, regret began to set in just like it did all the other times.

Maybe Gretchen was less than tactful. Maybe she didn't understand or approve of Janey's obligations unless they involved her. But Gretchen was still Janey's only link to her old life. If she lost Gretchen, would she lose that too?

Her phone buzzed again, pulling her from her useless regret. She answered.

"I told you I don't want to talk to you. Stop calling—"

"Janey? It's Lindsay."

Shit. Janey had forgotten about dinner. "Hey, Lindsay. I think I'm going to have to cancel our dinner plans tonight. I have to go find and kill Will."

"They're here at the house helping me fix a leaky faucet. That's why I'm calling, actually. Thought maybe we could all have dinner here instead of going out?"

A leaky faucet? Will had missed his appointment with Dr. Granger to fix a leaky faucet? At Lindsay's? Oh, he'd definitely pay for this.

"Yeah," Janey responded, loosening her death grip on the steering wheel. "Dinner at your place sounds fine. With Regan and Will."

"Wonderful. See you soon."

Janey hung up her phone. She should be happy—there was someone in town unafraid to have her brother over for supper. And if Will had skipped out on therapy, at least he'd worked on his social skills. So why did this bother her so much?

Why didn't Janey want to share Lindsay with anyone?

When Lindsay had been married to David, dinner parties had been their thing. Every Friday night, he'd whipped up some spectacular meal she couldn't pronounce and invited two or three colleagues over with trophy wives she couldn't stand, and Lindsay would make laps in a pair of torturous heels, refilling glasses with wine she never had time to enjoy. That was the price for the successful attorney husband, the pricey townhome, the BMW sitting in the garage. That was the life she'd chosen, even if it wasn't what she'd always imagined it should be.

The first Friday after David left, Lindsay had fixed herself a Mediterranean dish she'd seen on Food Network, slipped into a silk dress and pair of heels, and sat alone in the dark with the bottle to herself. That was when she'd realized she had no idea what Mediterranean food really was, that silk made her look chunky when she sat, that she didn't even like red wine. That was when she realized she'd had no idea who she was.

Tonight, she knew.

"More wine?" Lindsay asked, holding up the bottle of chilled moscato.

Teeth tugging at a chicken wing, Janey nodded and held out her glass with her other hand. "Thank you," she mumbled.

Lindsay exchanged the bottle of wine for the two liter of soda and moved to where Regan battled with a drumstick like she'd never eaten before. "More soda?"

"Mm, hmm." Regan handed over her glass and chewed, as Lindsay poured.

"You've got a little something. . . ." Lindsay wiped the stray barbecue sauce from Regan's cheek and smiled. Her wings were good enough to require cleanup.

She turned to Will who looked like he'd just been crowned the winner in a cherry pie–eating contest. She'd resist the urge to wipe his face. "More soda?"

"No," Janey responded for him. "He can have water or lemonade."

Will smiled, but the veins surfacing at his neck told Lindsay it was forced. "Lemonade," he chose and, after Regan elbowed him, added, "Please."

With a grimace, Lindsay headed for the buffet to retrieve a clean glass. It wasn't that she disagreed with Janey's constant oversight; Lindsay had never seen Will lose it, and she certainly didn't want to. She still felt bad for the guy, though. Someone always responding for his likes and dislikes; him never having a voice of his own. She certainly knew how that felt.

Lindsay added an extra lemon to the rim of the glass and placed it in front of Will with a large smile. It wasn't much, but he deserved a little something extra after the pipe explosion in the kitchen. Not to mention the lecture he'd received when Janey arrived.

"Thanks," he said, after Regan elbowed him again.

"Don't mention it." Lindsay sat back down to her nearly full plate. "It's been so long since I've played hostess, I forgot how much I enjoyed it."

"Well, it's been so long since Will's been invited to dinner, we'd forgotten what *that* felt like. Didn't we, Will?" Janey asked.

He gave a quick half grin, then went back to his corn.

Lindsay knew how that felt too—being reminded she was the one at fault for all the troubles in her life. Only this was the first time she'd heard Janey be so passive-aggressive. She must've been more pissed about Will's missed appointment than Lindsay thought.

"We should make it a regular thing, you know?" Lindsay stated, buttering her cornbread. "Tuesday night dinners. We could each take turns cooking."

"Will only knows how to make spaghetti," Janey responded.

Will stared so hard at his sister it made Lindsay nervous.

"Oh, I love spaghetti," Lindsay offered.

"Will's is really good," Regan mumbled behind her corn.

"Sure." Janey downed the rest of her wine. "If you like smelling like garlic for two days."

Will slammed his ear of corn to the table. "Why are you so intent on busting my balls?"

"Because, apparently, that's the only way I can keep you in line."

The tension shot Lindsay out of her chair like a rubber band. "Who wants ice cream?"

"I'll have ice cream," Regan responded quickly.

Will glanced up at Lindsay. "You'll have to excuse my sister. She always gets on her high horse after she's seen Granger."

"Vanilla okay?" Lindsay asked Regan, not waiting for her response before she darted for the kitchen. She'd had arguments at her dinner parties before, but it was usually over a jury selection or verdict. And no one had ever used the word *balls*.

"So, how's it going?"

Lindsay jumped at her mother's voice, her wine glass dropping and shattering against the tile floor. "What are you doing here? Isn't it book club night?"

Her mother shrugged, joining her on the floor with a towel. "When Sally told me the Fletchers were here, I figured this would be more entertaining."

Lindsay retrieved the last piece of glass. "So you've just been sitting in here, watching us like we're some sort of zoo attraction?"

"I think I'd compare it more to the circus."

"Really, Mother. Sometimes you can be so crude." Lindsay shook her head, and then the broken glass from the towel into the trash can.

"That's my right as an old woman."

Perhaps it was. Her mother had been through more than any woman should: becoming a teenage mother, her husband's constant affairs, struggling as a single parent after the bastard had done her the favor of leaving. It was a wonder her mother wasn't bitter.

"By the way, you'll need to find another euchre partner for tomorrow. I'm going out."

"Well, well." Her mother inched forward, the shadows on

her face turning from disapproval to curiosity. "Did you finally accept George's offer for a date?"

"I'm going to the movies with Janey," Lindsay said. "It's not a date."

"Are you sure she knows that?"

"Mother!"

"Well, are you?"

"Yes. I'm sure."

Her mother sank onto the kitchen stool. Pepper jumped onto her lap. "They make me nervous."

"Who? The Fletchers?" Lindsay chuckled. "Janey's an absolute sweetheart once you get to know her. And Will's harmless. You just have to dismiss most of what he says."

"Is that why you signed that petition?"

Lindsay's smile dropped. She should've never told her mother about the mayor's petition. Better yet, she should've never signed the damn thing. "I told you why I signed it."

"Because the mayor blackmailed you?"

"Yes."

Her mother shook her head. "We both know that's not true, Lindsay. It was because of that girl. You thought she'd be better off without him."

Lindsay turned her eyes to the floor, ashamed. Her mother was right. But that was before Lindsay knew about Emma. Before she'd seen the sweet man beneath Will's gruff exterior. Before she'd realized that a lost soul like Regan could only be found by a lost soul like Will. How could Lindsay have been so judgmental? Her only hope was that the damn petition never saw the light of day.

"What do you want from me, Mother?" Lindsay asked, pushing the guilt from her mind. "Aren't you the one who said

I should make friends? In fact, I believe it was you who pushed me toward the Fletchers in the first place."

"That was before."

"Before what?"

"Before you made it your mission to save these people. They're not your responsibility."

Lindsay shook her head, biting back her anger.

"Look, sweetie, I just don't want you letting your desire to have a family blind your judgment, that's all. You've been through so much in the past year. Do you really want to jump into another situation you can't possibly fix?"

And there it was. The reminder of everything she'd done wrong. The blame for losing a life that was never really hers to begin with. But this time, Lindsay almost felt grateful. Almost.

"Thank you so much for the vote of confidence, Mother," she hissed, the sting of her mother's disappointment pinching at her throat.

"Lindsay—"

She held her hand in the air, cutting her mother off, before yanking the freezer door open. Then, with the gallon of ice cream, scooper, and all her imperfections in hand, Lindsay marched with pride back to her dinner party.

Back to the circus, where even a blind woman without a spine fit right in.

CHAPTER ELEVEN

This was exactly why Will wasn't nice to anybody. The minute he'd give an inch, they'd take a foot. Plain and simple. You offer to do some landscaping around the new stadium, and they ask if you can build a few benches as well. You offer to fix a leaky faucet, and they ask if you know anything about garage doors. You offer to sand a few splintered porch boards, and they ask if you'd replace the rotted rails in their fence. Will had become Lindsay Shepherd's hired hand, only he wasn't getting paid.

He rolled his eyes at his own thought as he dragged the old rail to the pile. So maybe Lindsay had offered to pay him—like he'd ever accept money from a single woman living with her mother. And, okay, Lindsay *technically* hadn't asked him to do any of it. But she could've declined his services as soon as he'd offered.

"Bringing you some lemonade," she hollered from the porch.

Will wiped a bead of sweat from his brow. Perfect. Now he had to be all normal and everything. Couldn't he have finished a half hour ago? Before she'd gotten home from work?

As Lindsay weaved her way through the midcalf high grass, he tried to remember all Regan's tips for how to act normal around other people. Making eye contact was a big one. Small talk about something other than her imperfections. The weather was a good go-to.

"It's looking great," Lindsay said, handing him the lemonade.

He tried to look her in the eye, but settled for her chin as a focal point. "The . . . uh . . . grass is getting long."

"Yeah, I haven't had a chance to cut it."

Oh, dear God. That's how it always started. He'd made that mistake before, saying: *Not much of a courtyard without benches.* To which she'd responded: *It's just not in the school's budget this year.* Or when he said: *Garage door sounds squeaky,* she'd replied: *I've been meaning to get that looked at.*

Well, he wouldn't get sucked in this time. She'd just have to find a kid in town to be her lawn boy. If he didn't stop now, he'd be remodeling her damn, hundred-year-old house, when Janey had been asking him for two years to build a damn birdhouse.

"I love Indian summers," she said randomly, leaning against a post and drawing her ankle up to scratch it.

"Got the pox?"

Lindsay blinked. "What?"

Will pointed to her ankles, covered with tiny pink bumps leading all the way up to where her cropped jeans met her calves. She'd changed clothes when she got home. She'd worn a blue dress to school today, with an apple brooch pinned to the collar. He'd seen it when he and Janey dropped Regan off for school.

She grimaced, scratching again. "Damned mosquitoes."

"Gotta love those Indian summers." Will half grinned, then

took a swig of the tart drink and glanced at her jungle of a yard. "I could come by tomorrow and cut the grass. Might help."

"That's kind of you to offer, but you've already done so much," she said, bending over to reach a bite near the bright-red polish on her pinky toe. On the next toe was a silver ring with something etched in it, maybe butterflies or dolphins or flowers. A little odd for a school principal, but who was he to say? She had lovely toes, why not decorate them with jewelry?

He froze, midsip. Why had he thought that? It was inappropriate. Maybe creepy. With all the other oddities about him, Will didn't need a toe fetish.

Discretely as he could, he forced his eyes from her toes up her body, trying to find something else to focus on. Her knees, her thighs, her hips, her waist—had she lost some weight? He closed his eyes and shook the thought from his head, trying to concentrate.

"You okay?" she asked.

He opened his eyes, staring right into the crease of her breasts, and sighed in utter defeat.

"Maybe it was the lemons," she suggested. "They felt ripe, but maybe they weren't."

"No, I think they're just right." He chuckled, a million dirty thoughts springing to his spinning mind that he was helpless to stop. "You know, I need to go."

Lindsay glanced up and down the fence line. "Oh. Okay."

"Not home. I mean to the bathroom."

"Of course." She smiled, pushing herself off the fence post and scratching a bite at the same time, this one on her shoulder—her lovely, freckled shoulders. There was just no need for such beautiful skin to be so irritated. "You remember where it is, don't you?"

"Hmm?"

"The bathroom? You remember where it is, right?"

He nodded. "I'm going to come by and cut the grass tomorrow."

"Will, you really don't—"

"Yes," he interrupted, taking a step back. "I do."

She smiled again. This one more of a half grin. "Well, okay then."

Will turned and took a step toward the house before realizing he'd have to adjust himself to walk pain free. It had been a long time since he'd gotten an erection over a real, live girl—at least one standing next to him. There was the time he'd found his father's thirty-year-old *Playboys* up in the loft, or the many nights he'd fantasized about Ellie. And there were times Will couldn't help it, like now.

But Lindsay Shepherd, of all people?

At the porch steps he paused to look back at her, still standing by the fence. So what if the blonde highlights in her hair shined like pixie dust in the sun, or if her breasts were as plump as he'd imagined beneath the lace bra peeking out of her tank top. So what if she had a tattoo somewhere he couldn't see, or if the freckles on her shoulders tasted like warm cinnamon.

It was wrong to think of her this way, to have this urge inside his hands to pull her into him and feel the curves of her body. Because no matter how badly his body thought it needed something like her, there was still his head and his heart screaming the obvious.

Lindsay Shepherd wasn't Ellie.

Sometimes alarms went off inside Regan, signaling trouble. A queasiness in the pit of her stomach. A dull ache in the back of her skull. A cold emptiness drowning the warm breath in her chest. She'd had these feelings the day she and her mother had met Steven, and in the moments before she'd opened her mother's bedroom door that cold, January night.

Regan must have missed these catalysts somewhere along the way with Lane.

It was almost time to go—she could tell by the way he kissed her. The randomness of his hungry kisses had evolved into something more deliberate, like he was memorizing the grooves in her neck and the scent behind her ear. It was the same every day, only today the sun hadn't hidden behind the wall of the old dam yet. Regan could feel the heat of it warming the cool grass around her, see the glow against her closed eye lids. Maybe today would be different.

A few more kisses, then his bottom lip dragged across her collarbone, up her neck until his mouth hovered beside her ear. This was the part she hated, when he would say—

"Do you believe in fate?" he whispered.

Regan's eyes snapped open. This was not how this usually went. "What?"

"You know . . . fate. Destiny. Everything happens for a reason."

She glanced toward her bare shoulder, the straps of her tank and bra hanging over her arm. "You really want to have a philosophical debate *now?*"

"Now is as good a time as any." Lane ran his nose across her earlobe. "Do you?"

Regan deflated, setting her gaze toward the far end of the sky as she twirled her fingers through the hair at the nape of his neck. It used to be moments like these when she knew there was something bigger. When streaks of amethyst scattered through the orange sky created a sight too beautiful to be by chance, and the breeze sang a lullaby too seamless to be accidental.

But then came the other moments.

"No," she finally answered. "I don't."

"Why not?"

Because that would mean a bullet had been created with her mother's name on it, and the purpose of Emma's life had always been death. "I just don't."

Lane shifted to his side. "So, what do you think this is?"

"What do I think *what* is?"

"You and me. If it's not fate, what is it?"

"I don't know." Regan sighed. "Two horny teenagers playing doctor?"

Lane grinned, his smile alone making her heart race. "I make you horny?"

"Shut up."

"Exactly how horny do I make you?" He trailed the back of his hand up her bare side, a wave of goose bumps springing up in its wake.

"Quit it."

"That doesn't sound very convincing." He walked his fingers up her ribs one at a time, sending a series of jolts straight through her bones.

"I'm serious," Regan said with a chuckle. "You better stop."

"Or what?" And then he was at the band of her bra, gently sliding his fingers beneath it.

"I said quit it!" Regan shouted, pushing him the rest of the way off her as she sat up.

Lane stared, his mouth hanging open. That was the third time he'd tried to make it to second base this week. His third out. He wouldn't take many more. "Is it me?" he asked.

"What? No." Regan slid her straps back up her shoulders, trying to ignore the confusion on his face. How could she explain something she didn't understand herself? The kissing she loved.

It drove her crazy. Even more crazy than she'd felt with Holden, which was the problem.

But she couldn't tell Lane that. Ever. Because then she'd have to tell him the rest.

"Look, I'm sorry," she said. "I'm just not ready. I understand if you can't wait."

Lane sat up, a tiny grin tugging the corner of his mouth. "I see what's going on here."

Regan stiffened. "You do?"

"Yeah, I'm not blind. You're only fifteen." He scooted in closer, intertwining his fingers with hers. "You think you're the first virgin I've been with?"

She blinked, unsure which part of that statement bothered her more. Not telling Lane about Holden was one thing. Blatantly lying to him about being a virgin was another. "Lane—"

"It's okay, really. You're worth the wait, Regan Whitmer."

"But—"

He pressed his lips to hers—stealing her breath, stealing her courage, stealing her confession before it surfaced—then pulled her into his arms. "Besides, how honored will I be when you *are* ready and you choose to share that moment with me?"

"You're pretty sure of yourself," she mumbled against his chest.

"No." Lane pulled away, taking her face in his hands. If his eyes searched any harder into hers, he would've seen straight to her soul. "I'm sure of fate. And you are my fate, Regan Whitmer. Whether you believe it or not."

Regan dove to his chest, clenching her eyes to hide the ache in her skull, dissolving the lies in the queasiness of her stomach, fighting the coldness filling her chest after every breath.

Janey watched from the store window as Lindsay hurried up the sidewalk toward the door. She'd learned a lot from her new friend over the past few weeks, like how to make a wreath using burlap, wire, and cut-up strips of Will's old jeans. Or that empty wine bottles could be used to keep the shape of her boots when she wasn't wearing them. Or if she put a dryer sheet in a soaking pan after Regan cooked, it would bring the burned crud right off of there.

And most importantly, if she wanted Lindsay Shepherd to be on time for anything, she had to tell her to arrive a half hour before the start time.

"I am so sorry I'm late," Lindsay said, the door falling shut behind her.

Janey smiled. "What was it today? Backup on the interstate?"

"Ha ha! You're funny." Lindsay tossed her car keys into her purse. "Actually, Will was at the house fixing my fence when I got home from work. I didn't feel right leaving."

"Oh," Janey responded, and quickly turned to glance through a rack of dresses before Lindsay could see the irritation on her face. Janey wasn't the only one spending a lot of time with Lindsay these days. It was like that time she'd gotten her first Barbie doll and knew it was a matter of time before Will would cut the doll's hair off, mark war paint over its face, and enlist it with his G.I. Joes.

Lindsay was the only treasure Janey had that her brother hadn't tarnished.

"Not because I don't trust him there alone or anything," Lindsay said, backpedaling. "Just because it's hot and . . . well, what if something happened to him?"

"Oh, I get it. No need to explain." Janey took a deep, calming breath and turned back around. "Well, let's find you a dress for the mayor's dinner, Principal Shepherd."

They set off down the aisle, side by side, in search of the perfect dress to meet Lindsay's list of qualifications. It couldn't be too formal, too casual, or too business-y. Nothing that accentuated her waist, because apparently Lindsay'd put on fifteen pounds since her divorce, though Janey thought she looked perfect. And it had to fall just right on her leg—too high and her thighs looked huge, too low and her calves did. By the time Lindsay had narrowed the options to three, Janey had reaffirmed why she hated to shop.

"Oh my God." Lindsay huffed behind the dressing room door. "I'm a giant rubber duck."

"I'm sure it's not that bad," Janey said, praying she was right. She couldn't do another day of this. "Let me see."

Lindsay pushed the door open, all yellow chiffon, lace, and bows, and squeezed herself and the god-awful dress into the mirrored area. "Isn't it lovely?"

Janey tried to contain her laughter, but how could she not laugh at a giant rubber duck? "Well, just pick one of the others."

"Did you not see the others?" Lindsay pushed the dressing room door open. "The pink one made me look like a baby pig. The black and white one, like George's prized Maurie May. This is the best one. At least a duck is a *slender* farm animal."

"You could always add a black belt and hat," Janey offered. "Go as a bumblebee?"

"A bumblebee. Right. Then Mayor Bradford would send a petition around the party to have my stinger removed."

Janey's smile fell, memories flooding her mind. The memory of Dr. Granger explaining to her and Will what the petition was for. Of her father being hauled away in a straightjacket and committed to Creedmoor for the last time. Of the guilt she'd felt later on for not having visited him before he died, despite all the torture he'd put her through.

Had Lindsay heard the stories? Did she know?

"What do you mean?" Janey asked.

"Hmm? Oh, nothing." Lindsay bent over, digging through a box of hats on the floor. "He's just always asking me to sign his damn petitions. Last week, it was to make Hank Bumgarner paint his antique store. The week before, he wanted Caleb Mitchell to trim up the rose bushes in front of his house."

That sounded like the mayor, alright. When he wanted something, he turned the town against you. The petitions allowed him to dodge the blame, like he had when Ellie had asked why he'd had her fiancé's father committed.

Coward.

Lindsay straightened, wearing a large, feathered hat and a new pinkness in her cheeks. "Well, how do I look?"

"Oh yes. That definitely makes it better."

"I can't believe people actually wear this stuff," she said, pulling the hat from her head. "What did you do when prom time came around?"

"There weren't exactly a lot of girls dying to ask me. And I doubt it would've been appropriate if there had been."

"I know what you mean. Same reason I'm not taking a date to this dinner."

Janey half grinned. "Do you have a crush on someone in town, Principal Shepherd?"

"What?" Lindsay met her gaze, her grimace turning to complete terror. "No, I just mean . . . well . . . if I did pick someone, it wouldn't be from that crowd, ya know what I mean?"

Janey nodded slowly, not sure she actually did know.

"Anyway," Lindsay retorted, clearing her throat. "There has to be someplace else we could go shopping for dresses. You must have gone to something in your life that required you buy a nice dress. A wedding maybe? Awards banquet?"

"I got my dress for Will's wedding in New York. And as for awards . . ." Her voice trailed off, the memory of her last argument with Gretchen flooding her mind and filling her with both pride and disappointment at the same time. "I'm a Breckenburg finalist."

"What?" Lindsay exclaimed.

Janey realized and regretted she'd said it aloud. "A Breckenburg is—"

"I know what a Breckenburg is. Janey, that's fantastic!" Lindsay hugged her. "You should be the one shopping for a dress. It's in a few weeks, isn't it?"

"Yes, but—"

"Then you don't have much time." Lindsay pulled away and marched toward the dressing room. "Come on. We're going to Columbus to find you a *real* dress."

"I'm not going." Janey folded her hands into her lap. "To the awards, I mean."

Lindsay spun around. "Are you insane? This is a *Breckenburg*."

"I know, but . . . well . . ."

"Well, what? Is it the money?"

"No. Well, I mean yes, that's an issue. But there are many reasons I'm not going."

Lindsay placed her hands on her hips. "You don't want to leave Will."

Janey clenched her jaw. Not Lindsay too. "I know you think it's stupid, but—"

"No I don't. I completely understand your concerns."

"You *do*?"

"Yes. You're Will's rock. It's gotta be hard to leave him." Lindsay turned to point toward the zipper on her back. "Do you mind?"

"He just needs someone here," Janey said, jumping to her feet. "And I can't leave a responsibility like that to Regan."

Lindsay pulled her hair to the side and glanced over her shoulder back at Janey, green eyes glossed over with something Janey didn't quite understand. It wasn't pity—she'd seen enough pity to know what that was. This was more than that. An understanding rooted in a connection that went far beyond a few dinners or a girls' night out. And Janey wanted nothing more than to get lost inside those eyes, surround herself with whatever it was forever.

And that was wrong. On so many levels.

"You, Janey Fletcher, are the most self-sacrificing woman I've ever met." Lindsay smiled and turned back around. "Now get me out of this before I grow webbed feet."

Janey swallowed the lump in her throat and stepped forward, staring at the thin spaghetti straps of the dress. Beneath them, Lindsay's freckled shoulders seemed so delicate, the skin smooth as corn silk and the shape a medley of perfect arcs blended together. She hadn't noticed this perfection until now, or the way it melted into the lines of Lindsay's back to create even more flawlessness. Maybe because she'd never seen her in this light. Maybe because she'd known all along and had been trying to pretend it wasn't more.

She tugged on the zipper and spun away, trying to find clean air. This was why. This was why she didn't want to share Lindsay with anyone else. Why did she feel this way? This was wrong. She'd had crushes on straight women before—it never ended well.

"Hey," Lindsay whispered, grabbing her shoulder from behind.

Janey jumped at her touch, the burn of it too much to ignore. "I'm okay. Just got a little dizzy. Must've stood up too fast."

Lindsay gave her a quick clench on the shoulder and was gone a moment later, leaving Janey aching with desire for another life she couldn't have.

CHAPTER TWELVE

"So, what are we making again?"

Will made a measurement for the side of the birdhouse, then glanced at Regan over his glasses. Had he imagined it, or was this the third time she'd asked that question? Usually, he couldn't get anything past her, which irritated Will to no end. She was worse than Janey.

"A guillotine," he answered.

Regan nodded, the same way she had the other two times he'd answered incorrectly.

"For Lane," he added.

"What? Why?"

So she was listening; he just had to say the magic word. It reminded Will of that time they'd tried to cure his father's craziness with hypnosis, but instead his father had walked around bawking like a loose chicken until Dr. Granger had said *coyote*.

Must've been a horrifying word for a chicken to hear.

"We're making this." Will tossed the craft magazine on the table, open to the photo of the pristine, red-and-white birdhouse. "It's for the family of cardinals Janey wants to evict from the porch. Thought I wouldn't feel so bad if they had a place like this to live."

Regan concentrated on the photo. "It's nice."

"Nice? It's a freaking avian spa. Any bird would be lucky to call it home," he argued.

But it was a moot point. Regan was already lost in another thought, staring at the wall with glazed eyes as if she were solving an advanced algorithm.

Was she drunk? High? Had Lane Barrett slipped Will's daughter a roofie? He'd kill that little bastard if that was the case.

Will snatched the magazine from Regan's hands, leaned in a few inches from her face, and gave one quick sniff. No herb, no alcohol; just the same old daisies. Maybe in the hair. He stepped around to the back and sniffed. Nothing again. By the time he'd circled her completely, Will had her attention.

"Did you just sniff me?" she asked.

"Just checking to make sure you were of sound mind."

"By *sniffing* me?"

Will shrugged. It always worked for the drug dogs on *Cops*, why not him? "So, you going to the football game tonight?"

Regan clenched her jaw. "Why would I?"

"Uh . . . to watch your boyfriend play? You two have a fight or something? Because you can tell me, you know, if he's been mistreating you." Will picked up a hammer, carefully inspecting the head. "There's no need to be ashamed."

"Lane is not my boyfriend." Regan slowly removed the hammer from Will's hands and placed it on a shelf. "And I can assure you, he's always been a gentleman with me. I just need to study today."

"On a Friday night?"

"Yeah. I have a big anatomy test coming up."

"Anatomy."

"Yeah." Regan flipped on the saw, carefully lined up the board by the marks Will had drawn, and pushed it through. "The skeletal system has a lot of bones to remember."

"So, this doesn't have to do with the six messages you left on Lane's phone?"

"I didn't leave six messages."

Will grabbed another board. "Shall I recite the content of those messages?"

"Damn it, Will! Is nothing sacred? Am I not allowed to keep anything to myself?"

He blinked. Privacy? In this house? Was she kidding? And since when did it become okay to curse at your old man? Will never cursed at *his* old man.

She sighed, heavy and loud, like water rushing through dam gates. "He just said he'd call me before he left for the game so I could wish him good luck. And he never did."

"Maybe Coach called them in early?"

"Maybe." Regan retrieved the next board from Will and carried it to the table. "You don't think he's seeing someone, do you? I mean . . . not that I would care if he was or anything. But if he was, you'd think he would tell me."

Lane *was* seeing someone—Regan. But for some reason, she didn't want to admit it. He'd forgotten how contradictory the mind of a young woman could be; Ellie had always been that way. It was why she'd broken up with him those countless nights, but always found her way back to his arms the next day. Why she'd married the town crazy's son, but could never break free from her father's rules. Will's mother once told him those were just the ways of a young woman's heart, and a man shouldn't question them. And so he wouldn't.

"I'm sure he's not seeing anyone," Will said, fighting the

urge to add the word *else* to the end. "He probably just got held up before the game. Being a member of the mayor's family means being on call all the time. Ellie was the same way."

"Yeah?"

"Yeah. I'm sure it's fine." Will gave her a quick pat on the back and grabbed another board. Problem solved. Maybe this parenting thing wasn't so hard after all. Hell, Regan even had a half grin on her face. "Not that you care anyway."

"Right. Because we're not a couple."

Oh dear God, when would she give this up? It had been too long for even Will, the king of the Land of Denial. "Is it because Lane never asked?"

"No! He asks every day. It's just . . ." She sighed, sitting on his work stool. ". . .that means something, ya know? Something I don't know I'm ready to give."

Will smiled. "That's my girl."

"No, that's not what I mean. Not just sex."

Will frowned.

"It means I'm giving him part of my heart. And every person I give a piece of it to ends up leaving." Regan met his gaze. "Guess I'm scared before long, there won't be anything left."

Will stared at his daughter, searching for words a normal father would say. Like how love was a gamble—sometimes you lost, but the payout was worth the risk. Or love didn't work that way—it was infinite, like a vine of ivy, growing to fill in the holes left from last season's cut.

But Will wasn't a normal father, and these were things he didn't believe himself. How could he ask his daughter to have faith in something he no longer had faith in?

"Hello? Anybody home?"

Will perked up at Lindsay's voice coming through the barn door, then glanced at his T-shirt to make sure there wasn't any ketchup or jelly or . . . what had he eaten for dinner today? When he looked back up, Regan wore a crooked smile. "What?"

"You've got a crush on Principal Shepherd."

"I do not!" Did he?

"Hello?" Lindsay called again.

"Come here," Regan insisted. "You've got mustard on your shirt."

Hot dogs. Yes, that's what he'd had.

Regan licked her fingers, then pinched the spot on his T-shirt and rubbed a few seconds. "Just so you know, only dudes with crushes worry about this sort of stuff."

Will pursed his lips, then yelled, "Yeah. We're in here."

The barn door opened and in walked Lindsay. "Well, hey Regan. I thought you'd be at the football game watching Lane."

Will gave a shake of his head toward Lindsay and quickly changed the subject. "Janey's not here. She went to buy toilet paper."

Oh my God, had he just actually said that?

Lindsay smiled. "That's okay. I actually came to talk to you."

"You *did?*" he asked, swiftly realizing it was with too much enthusiasm. "Why?"

Lindsay glanced at Regan a moment, awkwardly.

"Guess that's my cue." Regan grinned.

"What? Where? Where are you going?" Will asked, when what he really wanted to say was *Don't leave me now.*

"To the school," she muttered. "Maybe I can catch the last half."

Now? She picked now? "But what about the bird house? And anatomy?"

Regan smiled. "Bye, Will."

Will stared as the barn door slid shut, then turned to Lindsay. "So, what's up?"

Lindsay sat on his work stool. "Did you know Janey was nominated for a Breckenburg?"

Leaning against the block wall, Regan glanced down the hall, past the locker room doors painted in blue and yellow. The usual girls who hung out at Lane's practices were there, all wearing their boyfriends' letter jackets. Regan was nothing like them. She didn't have long, fluffy hair or big, brown eyes. Her ratty Converse couldn't compare with their furry boots. And even if Lane *had* given her his letter jacket, there was no way she'd wear it in this heat. Regan was the one green apple among all the red; the white goose with all the brown feathers.

"Somebody needs to introduce her to a tanning bed."

Regan didn't need to look up to know it was Courtney Bradford's not-so-discreet, fake whisper, or that the comment was directed at her.

"Where'd she get those shoes? Look Like a Boy on a Dime?" another girl said, followed by a round of Valley girl chuckles.

Regan shifted her eyes to her feet. This was nothing new; she'd always been an oddball. And their disgusted eyes and degrading words were cotton balls compared to the stones and daggers cast on her that day at His Light. She was their bearded woman without the beard, the butt of their jokes. Something she'd sworn to herself, and her mother, she'd never be again.

Someone whispered something she couldn't make out, and then Courtney said, "Don't feel bad, sweetie. My man whore of a stepbrother only dates sophomores for two reasons. A, if they're related to a college recruiter, and B, if they're easy."

Regan met her gaze, jaw clenched.

"Apparently, it's B, ladies."

Regan could feel the blood boiling under her skin like lava, the tears rushing to put out the fire lighting her face. Then she ran, from the laughter, from herself. Down the hallway, out the door, and into the night where the air wasn't toxic. She grabbed hold of the railing and sank to the bottom step, her feet no longer having the strength to continue. It was a miracle she'd made it this far; she hadn't felt her legs since that one word. That awful word.

Easy.

He can't find out.

Regan stiffened at her mother's voice.

He won't understand.

"You don't know that."

Neither do you. That's why you haven't told him.

Regan hung her head, defeated. Her mother was right. She'd had so many opportunities to tell Lane about Holden Wright, but she'd chosen not to. Maybe she was afraid of losing Lane; maybe she was just ashamed. Either way, she didn't want him to find out.

"Regan?"

Regan glanced up to see Lindsay standing on the sidewalk. So much for leaving Will and her alone to *bond*.

"Is everything okay?" Lindsay asked.

"I'm fine. I just . . ." Unable to come up with an excuse for why she was clenching the metal rail like the last dry piece of the *Titanic*, Regan broke down in tears.

Lindsay hurried to her side. "Is someone bullying you again about your dad?"

Regan shook her head. She wished that was all it was—just a few comments about Will that weren't even half true. Lies didn't hurt as much as the truth.

"Did you and Lane break up?"

"We're not a couple!"

"Sorry, sorry." Lindsay took a seat beside her. "Is he dating someone else?"

"No," she responded.

"Okay, so if this isn't about Lane or your dad, then tell me what it's about."

Regan glanced at her own leg nervously skipping on the concrete. "Have you ever done something you're ashamed of? So ashamed you don't know if you'll survive if it gets out?"

Lindsay considered this a long moment—so long Regan considered climbing under a rock—and then she came out with it. "I pissed on my ex-husband's toothbrush."

Regan reared back. "What?"

"And his new wife's," Lindsay added. "I dropped off a box of his things before I moved here—odds and ends I'd found when packing up the house. I hadn't seen him in six months or so, but I really thought I was over what happened between us and I'd be fine. I *was* . . . up until I got ready to leave and had to use the bathroom.

"They had this ceramic toothbrush holder with two Adirondack chairs molded into it—one labeled *His* and the other labeled *Hers*. David would never let me have anything like that; it was much too ordinary. Then it hit me I wasn't the *Hers*. I never really was. Everything we had was his—everything. Even if it was mine, it was what he allowed me to have. And something inside me just snapped. So, I grabbed the toothbrushes and peed on them."

Regan held in the laughter at the base of her throat. "Do you regret it?"

"Not peeing on the toothbrushes," she admitted with a half grin. "I'm ashamed I let someone else define who I was for ten years. I'm ashamed I never demanded to eat where *I* wanted, or watch what *I* wanted on TV. I'm ashamed I didn't have that stupid toothbrush holder in *my* bathroom." Sighing, she stared at the ground. "I'm ashamed I was too ashamed to be *me*."

Ashamed of being herself. Regan certainly knew what that felt like. She couldn't remember a time she hadn't felt ashamed—begging for food and money on the streets, mistaking the need for someone to notice her for being in love, dating a boy who was too good for her.

Regan placed her arm across Lindsay's shoulder. "For what it's worth, it counts now."

"Oh, thank you, sweetie. But I'm supposed to be the one consoling you, aren't I?"

"You did. I know exactly what I need to do." She just didn't know how to do it. But maybe she'd find a way to confess her past once she finally admitted who she was in the present.

"Well, guess I should be on my way." Lindsay climbed to her feet. "Unless you want me to wait with you?"

"Thanks, but I should probably wait inside." Regan glanced toward the doors, then stood tall. "That's where all the football players' girlfriends wait."

Butterflies. Tingling. Breathlessness. These were all sensations Janey had grown averse to, because these were all sensations she'd had to sacrifice in order to manage Will's illness and life. She'd forgotten what it was like for blood to rush to her head at the sight of a woman, for her lips to go numb at only the thought of one. She'd forgotten what it was like to have to force herself to concentrate on normal tasks, such as walking and breathing.

And sketching.

It was a simple series of lines—a tree house she'd drawn a million times. Yet every time Janey pulled away, the branches all resembled Lindsay's curves. Her jawline, her shoulders, her hips. Even the damn squirrel hole looked like the arch of her eyes. Janey couldn't send this to Gretchen, she'd see right through it. And that wasn't a discussion Janey was ready to have.

She crumpled the sheet of paper, tossed it into the trash can with the twenty others, and rested her forehead on the desk. How would she deal with this? She couldn't keep saying she was "busy." It had already been a week since their trip to the dress shop, and soon it would be apparent Janey was avoiding Lindsay—another topic of discussion Janey wanted to avoid.

"Janey, there's a delivery at the door for you!" Will shouted.

Janey raised her head from the desk and glanced at the calendar. Today was payday, and, since her nomination for the Breckenburg, Ziggy had been selling like crazy. Maybe a nice, fat royalty check from the FedEx man would be enough to inspire her to draw.

She headed downstairs, trying to make a list of how she'd spend it. A new set of markers, snow tires for the car, a nice dinner with Lindsay, a winter coat for Regan, a massage for her and Lindsay, a new saw blade for Will, a nice negligée for Lindsay.

Lindsay! Lindsay! Lindsay! Why couldn't she stop thinking of her? When Janey washed dishes, folded laundry, cleaned the shower. Lindsay was always there, in her thoughts.

And now she stood at Janey's front door.

"Please don't be mad!" Lindsay said.

Janey pushed open the screen door, glancing around for the FedEx man she'd already gathered wasn't there. "And, why would I be mad?"

"Because I got you a little something." Lindsay nodded toward the porch swing swinging in the breeze, a gift perched on top of it. "Happy birthday."

"My birthday isn't until March," Janey responded, but all she could think of was that the gift she wanted didn't come inside a box.

"Okay, then an early birthday present. Or just because. It doesn't matter."

Janey let the screen door close behind her, eyes locked on the shiny paper and hunter-green bow as if they were a block of gold wrapped with a snake. "What is it?"

"It's customary to open the present to find out," Lindsay said, dragging her over. "Doesn't Will ever buy you Christmas gifts?"

"Yes, but he never wraps them."

"Never?"

"Not since before Emma died." Janey sat on the swing, working hard to stay focused on the gift. "He made me a picture frame out of popsicle sticks the year after, but they wouldn't let him have scissors in the psychiatric unit. I don't know; it just kind of stuck."

Lindsay sank down in the swing beside her, the heat of her body radiating to Janey's core. "I think that's the most depressing thing I've ever heard."

Janey had never seen it that way. She didn't need fancy bows to be surprised by Will.

"Well, go ahead," Lindsay said. "Open it."

Janey bit her lip, trying to ignore the hair standing on end at the nape of her neck, and wedged her fingernail under the bow until it snapped. A moment later, she tore into it like a five-year-old on Christmas morning, a smile arced across her face.

Until she saw the fancy dress folded inside.

"It's for the Breckenburgs," Lindsay said.

"I know what it's for." Janey slammed the lid back on the box. "And I thought you understood why I'm not going."

Lindsay opened the lid and pulled an envelope from inside. "You didn't open the card."

Janey sighed, snatching the envelope from her hands. "I don't see how Hallmark is going to change the fact that—" She paused, pulling the airline ticket out and holding it in front of her.

"Issue number one solved," Lindsay noted. "Keep looking."

Janey pulled the next item from the envelope, a hotel reservation.

"Issue number two solved."

"This is too much," Janey said. "You shouldn't have done all this."

"I didn't." Lindsay snatched the card away and opened it, pointing to the signature.

Janey met her gaze, slack-jawed. "Will did all this?"

"I exchanged an old set of tickets David and I never used. Will took care of the hotel."

Which explained why he'd been asking so many odd questions lately, like if she was afraid of heights and if she preferred cotton or down. "This is . . . it's . . . well, it's amazing. But you and I both know it doesn't change the fact that I can't leave Will."

"Which is why I am going to volunteer to stay here while you're gone."

"Ha!" Janey spat. "I know *that* wasn't Will's idea."

"Well, Cinderella, every dream has its midnight clause. Yours is to tell your thirty-five-year-old brother he's going to have a babysitter while you're gone."

Janey sighed, looking at the airline ticket. She'd be back the night of the sixteenth, in time for his anniversary—D-Day, Will called it. She opened the box again, looped her fingers beneath the straps of the ivory dress, and held it up in front of her. "It really is beautiful."

"I knew the moment I saw it how beautiful you would look in it." Lindsay ran her fingertips along the lace trim. "Not that you need any help looking beautiful."

Janey dropped the dress, clenching her eyes shut. "Why are you doing this for me?"

"What?"

"The dress. The trip. The compliments." She opened her eyes. "I don't understand why."

Lindsay blinked. "Because we love you."

That was all it took. Janey's defenses went down—her body out of her control, her mind set on one course. She couldn't have stopped if she wanted to, and she moved in so fast, Lindsay didn't have time to react. It was too late. By the time Janey had regained what little control she had, her lips were already pressed tight against Lindsay's.

Janey pulled away, trying to interpret from Lindsay's expression how much time had passed. A second? A minute? Forever?

"Janey—"

Janey jumped to her feet, realizing it didn't matter. Any amount of time was too long. She had to save the situation, fast. "Sorry. It's been so long since I've had a friend; don't know if thank-you kisses are acceptable."

Lindsay stared at her a moment. "Thank-you kisses are totally acceptable, but . . ."

"But what? Oh, you thought?" Janey laughed. "No, no, no. I have a girlfriend, Lindsay. Back in New York."

Lindsay's cheeks reddened. "I just didn't expect it. You usually tense when I hug you."

"Well, don't get used to it," Janey replied. "I was just . . . excited."

"Excited is good!" Lindsay stood with the box in hand. "Go! Try it on!"

Janey retrieved the box and headed for the door, the lump of butterflies so thick in her throat she thought she would choke.

CHAPTER THIRTEEN

S he had to be forgetting something. Her dress, her shoes, her old-man cap and overalls she reserved for signings— everything was crossed off Janey's packing list and inside the two stuffed suitcases at the bottom of the steps. But still, there was that ache tugging at the back of her skull, that uneasiness in the pit of her stomach, telling her to take a look around again.

Telling her not to go.

With a long, deep breath, Janey tossed her toothbrush in her toiletry bag, zipped it up, and headed for the stairs. She was anxious, that's all. It had been so long since she'd planned for something other than Will's crazy life; she couldn't remember how to plan for her own.

"Hey, you forgot something."

Janey turned at the bottom of the steps and glanced back up the stairs. "My sanity?"

Will descended the stairs two at a time, then pulled a wrapped box from behind his back. "It's from Regan and . . . me."

She stared, unsure which was more unusual—Will getting her a gift for something other than Christmas, or that it was wrapped. And she still didn't know where he'd gotten the cash for the hotel room. "You shouldn't have spent any more money, Will."

"I didn't. Just open it."

She tore away the paper and opened the cardboard box. "Your camcorder."

"With a fresh battery and new, fancy case. Regan said the ratty, old, canvas one I had wouldn't go with your dress."

Janey smiled, not having the nerve to tell her brother that nobody used a camcorder anymore. "Thank you."

"It's the least I can do, seeing that you're trusting me not to burn down the house."

"Uh, yeah. . . ." Janey placed the camcorder on her suitcase. She should've told him before now, but half of her never believed she'd go through with it. The other half was scared to death that if she said it aloud, it would jinx it. "About that—"

But as fate would have it, the doorbell rang before she could get it out.

Will backed away toward the door. "Thought you were driving to the airport?"

"I am."

He tugged the door open and leaned against it. "Well, well. All this makes sense now."

"What?" she heard Lindsay say.

"The suitcases? I knew you weren't doing all this out of the kindness of your heart." Will glanced back at Janey. "Why didn't you tell me she was going with you?"

"I didn't tell you because . . . she's not."

"Then why—" Will's odd smile slowly faded into a jagged line of disapproval. Once the pieces all came together, he slammed the door shut. "No way."

"Will—"

"I don't need a damn babysitter, Janey!"

"Then don't look at her that way. Look at her as my peace of mind."

"That's the same damn thing!"

Janey took a deep breath. "Open the door, Will."

"No."

"I said, *open the door!*"

"And I said *no!*" He crossed his arms tight over his chest and widened his stance. "Nothing you can say will make me agree to this."

She plopped her ass on top of her suitcase. "Fine. Then I'm not going."

"What?" Will muttered, arms dropping to his side. "You can't do that. You've been working toward this your whole life."

She shrugged. "There will be another one."

"No, Janey. I won't let you give up another dream because of me."

At that, Janey's entire reverse-psychology lesson began to crumble. "Is that what you think I've been doing?"

"There's no thinking about it. That's a damn fact."

She rose to her feet and inched her way to where her brother stood tall, yet deflated. He wouldn't look at her, but Janey knew what he was thinking, perhaps for the first time in weeks. There had been so many changes, so many distractions. She hadn't stopped to notice the trace of color or the fullness that had returned to his cheeks.

"I didn't give up my dream for you. I just had to find another way to get there," she said. "And I would never, ever blame you for any of it. Not my leaving New York, or Gretchen, and certainly not for missing a stupid awards banquet."

Silent, Will glanced toward the door.

"I didn't ask her to come here because I don't trust you. I asked her because I'm a paranoid freak. Tell me you wouldn't do the same exact thing if positions were reversed." Janey tugged his chin back her way, looking him in the eye. "She's just my peace of mind. Okay? Come on. You have to give me at least that. Especially *this* weekend."

"But I told you I'd be fine," Will argued, and Janey knew he believed that 100 percent. Unfortunately, Janey didn't.

"Just my peace of mind," she repeated.

Will closed his eyes and let out a long, defeated breath before stomping over to open the door. "Welcome to our humble abode. Hope you enjoy your stay in the nuthouse."

Flustered, Lindsay pushed her way past him, suitcase dragging behind her. "Sorry I'm late. I was worried you'd already be on your way by now."

"In a few," Janey responded. Was she disappointed Janey wasn't on her way, or relieved? Janey examined Lindsay's face but couldn't tell. Either Lindsay was a good actress, or she truly believed that the kiss had been just a thank-you gesture. It was one of Janey's monumental moments of weakness.

"So . . ." Lindsay said. "Will I be staying in your room?"

Janey nodded with the best fake smile she could conjure and grabbed hold of Lindsay's suitcase. "Come on. I'll take you up."

"Oh, for Christ's sake. Give me that," Will grunted, yanking the handle out of her hands and stomping off toward the stairs.

"I think he took it well," Lindsay offered, once he was out of earshot.

Better than could be expected, actually. Janey had been prepared for a full-on, rolling-on-the-floor tantrum. "Let's go over everything again real quick."

Lindsay placed her hands on Janey's shoulders. "We'll be fine, Janey. What could possibly happen in three days' time, huh?"

"Three days?" She raised her brow. "I'm just worried about the next three hours."

"We've been over this a dozen times. I understand exactly what I need to do." Lindsay brushed the stray hairs from Janey's eyes. "Trust me to do this for you, if for no other reason than the simple fact that I would die before I ever caused you any heartache. Okay?"

"Okay," Janey responded, wondering if Lindsay could hear the doubt in her voice. Wondering if she knew Janey's heart ached just standing beside her.

Lindsay hung her work clothes in Janey's closet and glanced out the back window. In all the what-if speeches Janey had given her, Will was always in the barn. If he became angry, he'd go to the barn. If he was sad, he'd go to the barn. If he was constipated, he'd go to the freaking barn. Not once had a scenario come up where he sat in his room listening to music or watched TV in the living room. There was never a scenario with Will just being Will, not *crazy* Will.

So what was Lindsay supposed to do now?

"Damn it, Janey," she mumbled, forcing herself back to her suitcase. Lindsay had been fine with this two weeks ago, when they'd made arrangements. She'd had no worries whatsoever. Now, Janey had her more nervous than a virgin on prom night. A prom she didn't even have a date to. She'd go stag before she'd go with someone like Will Fletcher. He wasn't her type, not at all. Her type was . . . her type was . . .

"Oh my God." Lindsay sank to the bed, clenching a pair of unpacked panties. Where the hell did that line of thought come from? And, more importantly, what *was* her type?

Since her divorce, she'd discovered so many things about herself, like she preferred Caesar salads to chef and alternative music to classic rock. She'd even realized her favorite color was lime green, instead of the navy blue David insisted on every time he gave her a sweater or a scarf. But this . . . this was earth-shattering.

Had David ever been the man she'd wanted? Or had he made her believe that too?

"Settled?"

Lindsay turned with a start to find Will, standing in the doorway. "Almost," she responded, although she wondered if it would ever be.

"Good, then we can chat a bit." He leaned against the door-frame. "Look, I don't know what Janey told you about me, but I don't need a babysitter."

"I don't—"

"Ah, let me finish." He let out a long sigh. "The only reason I'm going along with this whole charade is because she wouldn't have gone if I hadn't, and I don't need anything else on my conscience. That being said, we're going to be in the same house for the next few days, and I don't want it to be awkward. Do you?"

Awkward? Really? Every minute she spent with Will Fletcher was awkward. He was one giant puzzle, and Lindsay couldn't help but want to figure him out. She bit down on her lip, trying to hide her smile. "No. Of course not."

"Good. Then, here's what I propose we do." He pushed himself off the doorframe, stepped inside Janey's bedroom, and began to pace back and forth with his hands behind his back—pure presidential style. "I do my thing, you do yours. There's no need to offer false pleasantries or pretend we have anything in common. When Janey calls . . ." He paused and met her gaze. ". . . which will be at seven forty-five every night."

"How do you know?"

"Trust me." He resumed his pacing. "When Janey calls,

we'll plan to both be here. I'll come up with a list of things we did that day together—nothing too involved because she wouldn't believe that. Maybe just a board game, or watched *Jeopardy* together."

"You like *Jeopardy?*"

"Love it. Watch it every . . ." He paused again. "That's beside the point. It doesn't matter if I enjoy it or not, it just matters if Janey will believe it."

Lindsay bit her lip again.

"And we'll have to eat dinner together every night. Janey knows I don't like to eat alone. When she asks, I had at least one green vegetable—doesn't matter which—and I always, always drink water or juice with my dinner. You got that?"

She nodded.

"What am I forgetting? Oh yes. . . . When would you like us to bathe?"

She stiffened. Janey had never said anything about bathing him. "I'm sorry?"

"Morning or night? I take mine at night before bed, and they tend to be a little long so it may be better to take yours in the morning. That's what Regan does."

"Oh." She relaxed. "Morning is fine with me."

"Good." Will clasped his hands together and glanced around the room as if there was an audience. "Any questions or concerns?"

Lindsay raised her hand, because it seemed like the right thing to do.

He nodded toward her. "Yes?"

"What happens if we *do* enjoy doing the same thing?"

"Oh, that's easy. We . . . We . . ."

Eyes cast on the floor, Will ran his hand along his jaw, while Lindsay looked on at his wonderment. She imagined a complex network of gears, buckets, dominoes, and pinballs, all working in sync inside his head. One big, giant mousetrap waiting to capture the perfect thought at the perfect time, prepared to self-implode had an imposter gotten through the maze undetected.

Will met her gaze with a wide smile. "We don't have to worry about that."

"Why not?"

"Well, you and I don't enjoy the same things."

"And how do you know that?"

"Simple logic and probability. If you place all the things I enjoy doing on a Venn diagram and then all the things Janey enjoys doing, there's no overlap. Trust me, I've done it."

Lindsay smiled. "And what does that have to do with me?"

"That's the probability part. You and my sister get along so well, which means you must enjoy doing the same things she does. Therefore, we—*we* as in you and I—*wouldn't*."

"Ah, I think I understand now." Lindsay climbed to her feet and headed for the doorway.

"Where are you going?" Will asked.

"Doing my own thing. Like we agreed." She glanced back with a smile. "It's almost seven. I'm going to watch *Jeopardy*."

"So I was thinking . . ."

Regan glanced over her geometry book toward Lane lying on her bed, one arm bent under his head and the other sprawled over his pre-calculus book. "That's never good."

"Now, wait a second. Just hear me out," he said, scooting to a sitting position. "I think you're going to like this one."

Using her pencil as a bookmark, she closed her book and placed it on the nightstand beside her. "Okay, shoot."

"Well, since I don't have a game this Friday, Mom is making

her famous chicken and dumplings. So, what would you say if I asked you over to my house for dinner?"

Regan rolled her eyes and grabbed her book, trying to resume reading. "I'd say you're crazy."

"Why? Why is it crazy for me to want my girlfriend to meet my family?"

Girlfriend. No matter how many times she heard the word, it still didn't feel right.

"Have you even thought about what it would be like?" She sat up tall, putting on her best boy-next-door smile. "Mom, Dad—I'd like you to meet my girlfriend, Regan. Her mom was a panhandler before she married a religious freak and shot herself in the head. And her father used to be married to Aunt Ellie before he killed Cousin Emma and went completely insane!"

"You think they don't already know? I skip breakfast each morning so I don't have to swallow so much passive-aggressive shit from them. 'Lane, I heard Holly Frank doesn't have a date to homecoming yet.' 'Lane, Mr. Hadley said you could have more hours at the store since you have so much free time.' 'Lane, isn't the weather in Oregon lovely this time of year?'"

Regan blinked. "What does Oregon have to do with this?"

"Nothing, I just . . . you know, never mind." He threw his legs over the side of the bed and reached for his shoes. "And since when do you care what anyone thinks about you anyway?"

"Since it started to directly impact the people I love."

Lane froze, his fingers intertwined in his laces. "What did you say?"

Regan sank into her chair, melting in the heat of her embarrassment. "Nothing."

"No, not nothing." He looked up with a half grin. "I think you just said you loved me."

"No I didn't!"

"Uh, yeah. . . . You did."

"Well I . . . you . . ." she huffed, defeated. "I didn't mean it."

"No?" Lane said, limping over with one shoe on. Once in front of her, he sank to his knees and placed his hands on her thighs, locking eyes with her. "That's a damn shame, Regan Whitmer, because I was just about to tell you I loved you too."

She tried to look away, but it was his eyes; they wouldn't let her go. How could she love him already? Her mother had said it was love at first sight with Will, but Regan had assumed it was an embellishment. How absolutely terrifying to think she'd have no control over who her heart chose to give itself to. But here she was, staring into the eyes of a boy who couldn't be more wrong for her, and there was no denying it. Regan was 100 percent in love.

"Say something?" he whispered.

She threw herself at him, the force knocking him to the floor.

"Hey, hey. No need to beat me up," he groaned, pulling her close. "I think an, 'I'm in love with you too, Lane,' would've sufficed. Or even an 'Oh my Lord, I'm the luckiest girl on earth to have a god like Lane Barrett pining for me.'"

Regan ran her nose over his, never losing sight of his eyes. "I am."

"The luckiest girl on earth?"

"No." She jabbed his side with her index finger, sending him squealing. "I'm . . . in . . . love with you. And I'm not exactly happy about it, so give me some time to adjust."

Lane shrugged. "Take all the time you want. But just remember—you said it first."

"Fine. I said it first. Are you happy now?"

"Not exactly." He flipped her over, settling between her legs. "There's one more thing I need, since you love me and all." From the kisses and the throbbing against her thigh, Regan knew what it was.

She pulled her lips from him, gasping for air. "Lane, I told you I couldn't."

"Pretty please?" he whispered, pressing his mouth into her neck when she wouldn't give him back her mouth. "It won't take long, I promise."

Just what a girl wanted to hear as she considered giving herself to a guy. "Look, there's just . . . there's something you don't know about me."

Lane brushed his nose behind her ear in the spot that drove her crazy. "What? Are you allergic to nuts or something?"

"You're a pig," she spat, pushing him to the side.

"It's nothing to be ashamed of. I'll just tell mom not to use them."

Regan stiffened a moment, then burst into laughter.

"What's so funny?"

Chagrined, she attempted a smile. "I . . . thought you were asking about something else."

He blinked.

"'I want something from you, Regan.' 'It won't take long.' 'Are you allergic to nuts?'"

He blinked again, then burst into laughter. "You've got a perverse mind, Regan Whitmer. You need to get it out of the gutter."

"Me? Your little soldier was the one trying to raid the fortress walls. *Again.*"

"Well, quit looking so hot." Lane glanced down, adjusting the bulge beneath his jeans. "Just to verify, that was a no on the sex, right?"

"Yes! I mean no!" She sighed. "I mean, it's a no on the sex."

"Okay, then what about dinner?" he asked, closing the gap between them. "I really think it would help if they got to know you. See you like I see you, ya know? Instead of the lie."

But wasn't that the problem? Both versions of her were lies.

"Look . . . Lane . . . I—"

"Would love to. Because I'm in love with you, and people who are in love make sacrifices for each other," he answered for her, pulling her in until their foreheads were touching. "Please? I really need you to do this for me."

"Checking in, Miss?"

"Yes." Janey placed her purse on the granite countertop. "It's under Fletcher."

The tall man hummed the theme to *Jeopardy* as he typed on his keyboard. Which reminded her—she needed to call home soon.

"Ah, there you are, Ms. Fletcher. You're already checked in."

"I *am?*"

He nodded toward the bellhop, "Room 1207, Karl."

"Oh, I can get those. No need . . ."

But the bellhop already piled her suitcases on a cart.

"Here is your room key and a 250-dollar spa credit," the clerk stated, placing an envelope on the counter.

"Oh, I won't be needing—"

"You're booked for our A Better You Massage with Esteban tomorrow at nine. The spa is right down at the end of this corridor, across from the Promenade where you have dinner reservations for eight."

Janey glanced behind her. "But there's just one of me."

The man smiled. "Eight o'clock, Miss."

She retrieved the envelope, chagrined. "Right."

"Might I suggest the Manchurian swordfish with creamed asparagus? It's delectable."

Apparently Will hadn't remembered her allergy to seafood.

"Is there anything else I can assist you with at this time, Ms. Fletcher?"

Janey gave a slight shake of her head and slid her purse strap over her shoulder. No, it appeared her brother had taken care of everything. What parallel universe had she orbited into?

Her cowboy boots echoed against the marble floor as she wandered in the direction the bellhop had gone. The tall, stone columns and statues reminded her of the frilly hotels she and Gretchen stayed in when they'd traveled the world.

Janey pressed the button for the twelfth floor, staring at her reflection in the mirrored elevator, as she had at the hotel in Columbus the last time Gretchen visited. She looked different now, looked more like herself, looked more comfortable in her boots and jeans than she had in her stilettos and leather skirt. Janey wasn't the same person now as she was then. She didn't need to go back to being the old Janey to be happy any longer. She knew who she was and exactly what she needed now.

She was just too chickenshit to take it.

The bellhop stood outside the elevator when the doors opened, the luggage cart already empty. "Enjoy your stay, Miss Fletcher."

"Oh wait!" Janey said, squeezing past him as she fumbled in her purse for a tip.

He held up his hand to stop her. "It's already taken care of, Miss."

Janey deflated. "Of course it is."

"It's at the end of the hallway on your right."

She followed his directions down the curved corridor. Janey half expected to find a bathtub filled with bubbles and rose petals inside, or, at the very least, a furry robe to lounge around in. Who knew her brother had it in him? This had to be Lindsay's idea.

The door was cracked open when she reached it, most likely

from the bellhop's exit. Janey pushed the door open and stepped inside, dropping her key and purse on the table.

"Hello, Janey."

Janey spun with a start, immediately recognizing the smooth-toned voice. "Gretchen."

Smiling, Gretchen crossed the room in her slow, graceful manner, her long, blonde hair glowing in the lone beam of sunlight peeking through the windows. Some things never changed—Gretchen had always managed to find the spotlight in a room. And there Janey stood, in the shadows of her towering, narrow frame.

"I don't . . . how did you . . . what are you doing in my room?"

"You mean *our* room?" She grinned. "Will called me."

So, that's how he'd afforded all this—he *hadn't*. Apparently Janey had forgotten to mention that she and Gretchen were on the outs again.

The grin on Gretchen's face slowly faded. "This is okay, isn't it?"

"I . . . uh . . . yeah. I just . . . this is . . . wow. What a surprise."

Gretchen stared at her a moment longer, then pulled her in for a long kiss.

Apparently, Janey had forgotten to mention their breakup to Gretchen as well.

What had the world come to when logic and probability couldn't get him through anymore?

First she'd kicked his ass at *Jeopardy*, then *enjoyed* the grilled tilapia he'd fixed because Janey was allergic. She washed the dishes the same way he did—all pots and pans first, because why save the worst for last? At dessert, she picked the ripest banana in the bunch for her pudding—something Will wasn't very happy about. Then she'd said she was getting her *bedroom shoes,* not her *slippers.* When it came time for her nightly glass of strawberry milk and crossword puzzle, Will couldn't take it anymore and slid on his *bedroom shoes* before he snuck to the front porch.

Maybe the game show was a fluke, but nothing else was. This chick just might be the only other person on the planet with the same, screwed-up habits as Will. It scared the living shit out of him. Who did Lindsay think she was, coming here and stealing his thunder?

Will froze midswing when the screen door opened. Lane stepped down the stairs, dragging Regan behind him. When they reached the grass he pulled her close, and then Will turned his head, because the thought of seeing Regan kiss Lane turned his stomach over.

"Promise me you'll think about it," Lane said.

Regan sighed. "I promise."

A long silence followed, which Will assumed was more kissing he didn't want to see. Then, he swore he heard Regan tell Lane she loved him. Wasn't it a bit soon for that? They'd only been officially dating for two weeks, though Regan still flinched whenever it was mentioned. It reminded Will of how Ellie used to respond when someone called her a wife.

It made him think now—when had Ellie first told Will she loved him? Was it after they'd lost the state championship his freshmen year? Or was it the night she'd snuck through his bedroom window after his mother had died? It had to be one of those disappointments. Ellie didn't offer up those words unless they truly needed to be heard.

Maybe he couldn't remember the first time she'd said it, but he *did* remember the last. And it wasn't when he'd needed to hear it most.

"What are you doing out here in the dark?" Regan asked.

Will opened his eyes to see Lane had gone. "What did you promise you'd think about?"

"I asked you first."

"So? I asked you second, and two's a bigger number."

"Oh, geez. Really?" Regan placed her hands on her hips. "He asked me to go to the homecoming dance with him."

"And you told him you'd *think* about it?"

"Well, there's a lot to consider," Regan pointed out as she sat on the swing beside him. "I'd need to find a dress, which I can't afford. Then the square dancing lessons."

"*Square* dancing? There will be no . . ." Will met her gaze, lips pursed. Though she tried to hide her smile, she was clearly proud of her wit. As was Will. "Very funny, big-city girl."

Regan grinned. "I have my moments. And *you* shouldn't be eavesdropping."

"No, no. I was out here before you two, I swear." He nodded toward the window. "I'm hiding from Janey's watchdog in there."

"Why? She's not so bad."

"Exactly! She's not so bad. And that's the problem!" He grimaced as soon as the words were out, wondering why it *was* such a problem.

Regan half grinned. "Told you. You're hot for the teacher."

"She's a principal, and that's just ridiculous. I am not." *Am I?*

"Okay, fine." Regan sniffed, then turned her gaze toward the yard and mumbled, "I've never seen you let *me* have the ripest banana."

"Because you don't like them that ripe!"

"How do you know? You never asked."

"Well, I didn't ask . . ." Will paused, remembering back two hours before.

Would you like sliced banana on your pudding? he'd asked, sure she'd say no.

I'd love some, Lindsay had responded.

Flustered, he'd reached for the bunch. *How ripe would you like it?*

The riper the better.

"Damn it," he muttered.

Regan giggled. "It's okay. Lindsay's really nice. And she's pretty, too."

Will opened his mouth to argue, but it was no use. She *was* really nice. And he'd figured out a month ago she was pretty— he'd just made a sound decision to ignore it, even if his Johnson had disagreed. But finding someone nice and pretty was a far cry from having a crush.

"I'm going to bed. Got a big day tomorrow." Regan got to her feet and stretched. "For what it's worth, I think she likes you too."

"You do?" he asked, more enthusiastically than he'd intended. "I mean how . . . how do you know? Why do you think that?"

She pointed inside. "She only wears her hair down on assembly days."

Will shook his head. "You're basing this on her hair?"

Regan shrugged. "I didn't think the goo-goo eyes she made at dinner would be enough to convince you if you didn't pick up on them then."

"She didn't make . . ." Will paused again.

Is there something wrong with your eyes? he'd asked, after Lindsay had blinked for the fourteen hundredth time.

Her face had flushed pink. *No. Just tired, I suppose. Guess I should go to bed early.*

Will checked his watch; it was after eleven, and Lindsay was in there working on crossword puzzles. "Damn it," he mumbled, burying his head in his hands.

"Just catching up, Sherlock?"

"That doesn't prove anything."

"Sure, sure. Whatever you say." Regan inched over to the doorway. "Good night, Dad."

"Good night, Regan," he responded, choosing to ignore she'd called him Dad. There were too many other surprises for him to process right now. He couldn't worry about that one.

Through the window, he watched her say good night to Lindsay, then climb the stairs. When he glanced back toward Lindsay sitting in the chair, this time she stared back at him. And when they found each others' eyes, she smiled and looked away.

"Damn it," Will repeated.

So maybe Lindsay was a little attracted to him too. It wasn't the real him, the natural him, the broken him. She'd never met the man who could explode the brightest sun into the blackest of holes, sucking her and everything else into nothingness. She'd only met the mirage who'd been built on the rules of his younger sister, the encouragements of his teenage daughter, and the fog of his numbing medications. That man was a lie.

Remove all that haze, and all that was left were the sharp, jagged edges of truth.

CHAPTER FOURTEEN

Regan distinctly remembered the day she and her mother met Steven's father. Not because it was the first time her mother had ever been good enough to meet a boyfriend's parent, but because of the little things. The lattice-crusted apple pie they'd baked. The yellow Sunday dresses they'd worn. The three-hour drive to Fort Wayne, which they spent singing all of Regan's favorite church hymns.

And then, there was the tiny, white-and-brown, single-wide trailer surrounded by a barbed wire fence, the secret code Steven knocked on the rusty door to earn entrance, and the interior walls covered in newspaper clippings and maps linked with pushpins and red yarn.

Steven's father was a total whack job.

Regan looked at Steven differently after that day. For making them wear those stupid dresses and asking them to bake a pie. For taking the only seat in the house that wasn't covered in nicotine-stained plastic, and allowing his old man to call them

Red One and Red Two. For letting Regan's mother believe she might actually be worth something, and then showing her how little that something was.

Regan swore she'd never let anyone make her feel that unworthy again.

"You okay?"

She snapped her eyes toward Lane beside her, then around the table at the three other faces staring her down. How long had she been stuck in that memory? Why had she been stuck there at all? This was nothing like that day. The Bradford's mansion was immaculate, not a pushpin or scrap of old newspaper in sight, and they were eating off fine china at a table that would seat twelve people, not off paper plates on dirty TV trays.

"I'm fine," she finally responded with a forced smile. "Why?"

Lane placed his hand on hers and nodded toward her plate. "Haven't touched your food."

"Sorry." She grabbed her fork and scooted closer to the table, without an appetite. "Just got a lot on my mind." Like why she'd even agreed to this in the first place. Had she completely lost her marbles? This was Ellie's family. *Ellie's family!*

"So, Regan, Lane tells us you're from Chicago?" his mother asked. She was a tall, thin woman with a stack of blonde hair pinned on top her head that could house the cardinal family Will was building the birdhouse for.

"Yes, Mrs. Bradford. Lived there all my life."

She smiled a smile that Regan wasn't sure was real or fake. "Please, call me Kitty. And same goes for Tim and little Mikey."

"What else would she call Mikey, Ma? Brother Mike?"

His mother grimaced. "Well, I just want her to feel welcome, Lane."

"It's fine," Regan piped up. "Really." She dug into her mashed potatoes, not ready to tackle the dumplings yet. Maybe in a minute, after they asked what happened to her mother.

"Courtney said you're the crazy man's daughter."

Lane sprayed his mouthful of water across the table, and then pounded his fist into it. "Mikey! What the fuck, man?"

"Lane! Language!" Kitty shouted.

"Well, Christ, Ma! We had this discussion."

So, Regan was the topic of conversation? How sweet. She'd never been a discussion item before, at least not that she knew of.

"Lane, he's four years old. Cut him a break," Tim pointed out.

"Don't tell me what to do, Tim. We've had this discussion too."

"I'm not telling you what to do. I'm simply pointing out that you can't rely on the promise of a four-year-old child in a situation like this."

A situation? Now she was a situation.

Tim cleared his throat, meeting Regan's gaze with a smile she knew for certain was fake. He might not have been a complete whacko, but he didn't approve of her stepping into his mansion any more than Steven's father had approved of her stepping into his rusty tin can. "Tell us a little more about yourself, Regan. Do you play any sports?"

"I'm not really the athletic type."

"Musical instruments?"

She shook her head. Pushpins or not, Regan began to feel grimier than the bottom of Steven's father's beer-can ashtray.

"What about clubs? Student council maybe? Drama club?"

"Nope," she responded, this time wearing her own fake smile. Was he kidding? Regan had enough drama in her life. She didn't need to join a damn club.

"Well, what do you plan to do with your spare time next year when—"

"What the hell is this, twenty questions?" Lane interrupted, balling his hands into fists. "Why don't you just let my amazing and beautiful girlfriend eat her meal, huh?"

Tim's smile fell to a frown, Kitty's fork to her plate. Apparently Regan wasn't the only one who still had trouble accepting that word. *Girlfriend*. Or maybe it was *beautiful* and *amazing* that had them stumped. It certainly had her stumped. Lane told her these things all the time, but it was always just the two of them, and she'd assumed it was a tactic to try to get her into bed. But here? Now? In front of his family? What was his angle?

After a long silence, Kitty retrieved her fork, put on a genuine smile, and met Regan's gaze. "So glad you could make it."

Regan raised an eyebrow. Hadn't they already been over this?

"Of course, Kitty. So sorry I'm late."

Regan stiffened at the new voice in the room, a woman's voice, coming from just behind her. Kitty's statement hadn't been meant for Regan, nor the smile.

A moment later, the woman sat in the empty chair across from her, face flushed and eyes wide. There was something familiar about her. It wasn't the woman's auburn hair or sea-green eyes. It wasn't her petite frame or perfect, ivory complexion. It was her mouth when she smiled, a synthetic shape made from years of false smiles.

It was bound to happen sooner or later. Regan was surprised it hadn't until now.

"Regan," Lane stated, voice low and weary. "This is Ellie Bradford. Ellie, this is—"

"You're Will's daughter." Ellie held out her hand. "And I'm Will's ex-wife."

The room went silent, not a fork scraping a plate or a glass clinking on china. The only sound Regan could hear was the loud thump of her heart, and little Mikey blowing bubbles in his glass of milk. The only thing she could see was Ellie's hard eyes leveling her like a bulldozer, reminding her of who she was. Red Two.

But the longer Ellie stared, the softer her eyes became, the pinker her cheeks grew. She dropped her hand to the table and frowned. "I'm sorry. That came out terribly rude. I just thought we should get it out of the way. Maybe I should . . . just . . . go."

"It's okay, Ellie," Lane responded, pulling Regan up as he stood. "We were just leaving."

"But you haven't finished your dinner," Kitty exclaimed.

"Lost my appetite back around 'Crazy Man's daughter,' Mom."

Regan followed Lane around the table, everyone's eyes locked tightly on her, her eyes locked tightly on Ellie. She was beautiful, but not in the way most would define beauty. Her beauty was more subtle, hidden behind years of being defined as something she didn't want to be, someone other than who she truly was. Like Will.

When she and Lane reached the door, right beside Ellie's chair, Regan let go of Lane's hand and held it out toward Ellie. "I'm Emma's big sister. You're my little sister's mother. And it's so nice to finally meet you."

Ellie glanced up, eyes glazing over, and placed her hand in Regan's. Her grip was weak and telling—once again, just like Will's. It was a wonder they hadn't been able to work it out. Regan wondered for a brief moment how her life would be different now if they had. Ellie would be her stepmother and Lane would be her step-cousin-in-law. Her father would be someone completely different. She didn't know if that was a good or a bad thing.

"Come on," Lane whispered in her ear. "Let's go."

Regan dropped Ellie's hand. "Thank you for dinner. It was ... enlightening," was all she had time to say before Lane pulled her out the door and onto the front porch, probably before she did anything else to make these people hate her.

"I'm so sorry," he said. "I swear I didn't know she'd be here."

"It's okay. It was bound to happen sooner or later."

He wrapped his arm around her as if protecting her from the icy smiles she knew were coming through the large, arched window. "Maybe. But not that way."

That way? Why didn't he just call it like it was? A set-up. A slap in the face. Just like Steven's father that day.

Regan wouldn't let them do this to her. Not again.

In a sudden move, she shrugged free from the shelter of Lane's arm, grabbed the collar of his button-up shirt, and pulled his lips to hers. This kiss was different than the kisses she normally reserved for public display, more hungry, more urgent, with a little bit of tongue even. She had to make a statement, to both Lane and his family. She had to show Kitty and Tim they hadn't beaten her, had to show Lane they hadn't scared her off, and she was here to stay. After all, that's what this whole evening had been about, hadn't it? That's why he'd brought her here, why he'd said those wonderful things at the dinner table. She wouldn't disappoint him, ever. Wouldn't stop until he said it was time.

Or until the door opened behind them, pulling them from their perfect, little world.

"Sorry to interrupt," Ellie said. "Lane, can I have a word with Regan? Alone?"

Lane pressed his forehead against Regan's. "You don't have to do this."

She kissed him one more time. "Yes. I do." Why, she didn't

know. The million or so times she'd run through this scenario in her head, it always ended badly.

"I'll wait up by the mailbox," he said, and then left them alone in their awkwardness.

Ellie stepped onto the porch, squinting in the late-afternoon sun. "I just wanted you to know that I wouldn't have come if my father told me you were going to be here."

Regan crossed her arms and clenched her jaw. This is why she'd stayed? To hear more insults? Really? And what did the mayor have to do with this at all?

"I don't mean it in that way. I just meant that, I would never do anything to make you feel . . . uncomfortable. Or anyone for that matter. If you don't believe me, ask him. I mean . . . if you want to ask him. He'd tell you I'm not that way. He'd tell you that . . ." Ellie sighed, chagrined. "I'm terribly bad at this."

"Ellie, just say what you want to say to me."

"Okay." She took a few steps, staring at the ground or her fidgeting hands, Regan didn't know which. "How . . . how *is* he?"

It was then that Regan realized the *he* Ellie had been referring to was Will, not Lane. That Ellie didn't like to say his name any more than Janey liked to say Ellie's.

"Is he adjusting well?" Ellie said. "I mean, to being a father again?"

"He never stopped being a father," Regan said.

"Of course not. I just meant . . ." Her voice trailed off as she glanced out toward the street at nothing in particular. "You know everyone in this town treats me like the poor woman who fell prey to the crazy man. 'Oh, poor Ellie. The crazy man's ex-wife. She should've known better than to trust him.'"

Ellie took another step forward, running her hand along a lock of Regan's hair and pausing at the end, getting lost in a moment. Perhaps wondering if this was what Emma would have looked like, perhaps if Will had loved Regan's mother more than he'd loved her. And Regan let her get lost, because she was lost too, in the soft creases of Ellie's face. They were different from her father's. His were hard, as if carved from wood or chiseled into stone. Ellie's resembled lines drawn in the fine sand of a beach, no guilt to cement them in place forever, disappearing at any moment with the next wave of water.

This was the difference between losing a child and having one snatched away. This was the difference between trying to remember and trying to forget.

This was the difference between Will and Ellie.

And then, suddenly, the wave came in. Ellie dropped Regan's hair, along with whatever thought she'd had, and turned. "I should let you go. Thank you for what you said in there, Regan. No one ever mentions Emma to me. It's like they've all forgotten her."

"*Will* hasn't," Regan said.

Ellie paused with her hand on the door, but Regan didn't stay long enough to see if she'd turned back around. She set off down the stone path toward Lane, choosing not to speak the rest of what she thought aloud. That it wasn't so long ago Ellie had divorced Will for not being able to forget Emma. That if she'd stuck by him longer, maybe they could've found a way to remember Emma together. That too much time had passed to do anything about it now.

Perhaps Regan hadn't said these words aloud to Will's ex-wife, but Emma's mother had heard them loud and clear. Regan had made certain of it.

Lindsay realized, somewhere down the oral hygiene aisle, that she was stalling. She had just picked up her third toothbrush package to read the instructions for properly removing plaque when it occurred to her. Scheduling the late-afternoon conference, offering to watch the last hour of detention, stopping by the drugstore to purchase a toothbrush that wasn't the same color as Will's—they were all tactics her subconscious was using to keep her from the Fletchers'.

To keep her from making an even bigger ass out of herself in front of Will.

What was she thinking last night? Batting her eyes and twirling her hair like an eight-year-old begging for candy. Eating an exceptionally ripe banana like a teenage girl drinking a beer to prove she was one of the guys. And then, this morning at breakfast, she'd asked him if her blouse was too sheer for a principal to wear to school, hoping she'd catch his eyes focusing on her breasts just a moment longer than necessary to make a judgment. But he hadn't. He hadn't responded to any of her advances. He was the first man Lindsay had flirted with since the divorce, and all she got in response was a shrug and an awkward fist bump.

This had been so much easier when she was ten years younger and thirty pounds lighter. When she wasn't desperate.

Her phone beeped from inside her purse, just as she picked up another toothbrush. She didn't need to look to know it was another missed call from Janey, checking on her brother's well-being. Discomfort or not, Lindsay had a job to do. She'd already spent too much time down this aisle of shame.

She paid for her new, orange toothbrush—National Dental Association tested to remove the most plaque—and headed back to the Fletchers' with a new sense of purpose. Janey would be heading home on the red-eye tomorrow night, so Lindsay would just avoid Will until then. Skip breakfast, and definitely skip *Jeopardy*. Come home late for dinner—that should annoy him enough to eat without her. He'd certainly sounded annoyed when she called to tell him she'd be late tonight. She'd take the path of least resistance and it would all be fine.

Ten minutes later, when she stood outside the back door of the Fletcher house, Lindsay realized that would not be the case.

"Hi, there!"

Paper bag still clenched in her teeth, she glanced up at Will and dropped the house key she'd been digging for in the black abyss of her purse. It was nearly eight o'clock. He should be out in the barn avoiding her by now, not greeting her by the doorway in a sky-blue polo that showed off his eyes and wood-working, toned arms.

Damn.

Will removed the paper bag from her mouth, her lip stinging a bit as it pulled loose.

Smooth, Lindsay. Real smooth.

"What's all this?" she asked, stepping inside the steam-filled kitchen.

"What's it look like?" He stirred a pot of boiling something, then moved on to the saucepan. "Dinner."

Of course it was dinner—spaghetti to be exact. She could smell the garlic and tomatoes in the air. But that's not really what she'd been asking. She wanted to know why he hadn't eaten already, why there were only two places set instead of three, if this was really just dinner or Will wanted it to be more.

Because Lindsay wanted it to be more. So much more.

"You like spaghetti, right? Everybody likes spaghetti."

She nodded, sliding onto the yellow stool beside the telephone as she glanced around the disaster of a kitchen. Maybe he was just waiting to have someone clean up his mess. "I figured you would've already eaten." *Hoped* was more the word.

"I don't like to eat alone, remember?"

That's right; he'd mentioned that, hadn't he? Upstairs,

yesterday afternoon. When he'd made up the rules for her stay. When she'd thought up ways to break them, just so he'd look at her with those eyes—the ones that gave her goose bumps. Like now.

Perhaps she should go back to the drugstore and look for dental floss.

The phone rang beside her, making her jump. "Fletcher residence?"

"Lindsay!" Janey shouted. "Is everything okay?"

"Everything's . . ." *not fine. Come home. Now.* ". . . perfect."

"I've been trying to reach you for over an hour."

"I know. I'm sorry. I was just . . ." *avoiding you. Avoiding Will.* "My phone is acting up." It wasn't a total lie; the phone had stopped ringing weeks ago.

"How is Will doing? Did he take his medicine tonight?"

Lindsay turned toward Will who held up the white oval pill she'd left on the counter this morning. "Right on time," he groaned, followed by something that sounded like "Just like the perfect bowel movement," but Lindsay wouldn't verify that. He tossed the pill in his mouth, swallowed, and opened back up—just like Janey had instructed him to do before she left.

"Yes, he did. And he's doing fine."

"And Regan?"

Regan? Yes, Regan. Lindsay covered the phone. "Where's Regan?"

"Studying with Lane," Will whispered. "Revolutionary War generals. Fascinating stuff, really, if you think about it. The way they accomplished so much with so little. Did you know—"

"She's fine," she responded to Janey, then turned away. Watching Will get lost in one of his idiosyncrasies was not the path of least resistance. "So, how's the conference going?"

"It's amazing. The food is great; the hotel is perfect. I'm

getting ready to do a signing downstairs. The awards ceremony isn't until tomorrow, but I think I have a good chance."

"Shit!" Will cried.

Lindsay turned to see smoke pouring from the oven and Will carrying something from it. "Janey, can I call you back later?" She hung up without waiting for a response and hurried to the stove, where Will hovered over a pan of blackened bread.

"Stupid," he muttered. "So stupid."

"Oh, it's just a little brown. I like mine that way." But from the sharp look in Will's eyes, her lie wasn't believable. "Well, we've got some time. We'll just make another batch."

"That was the last of the bread," he growled through gritted teeth.

"Okay. Well, we could always scrape—"

"Don't patronize me!" he shouted.

Lindsay blinked. Were they arguing over burned bread?

"How did I let this happen? I ruined everything!" He pressed his arms into the counter to support his weight and shook his heavy head, eyes closed tightly. "I know better than that. You always save half. Because you don't know how the first half is going to turn out."

Lindsay glanced down at the pan, trying to comprehend his grief. To her this would be another chalk line on Lindsay's wall of kitchen disasters, but, to Will, this was another way to scar perfection, keep him from having one thing not tainted in black.

Pot holder in hand, she tugged on the pan until she could get a solid grip. The only thing she could think to do was get rid of it, erase it like it never happened, before he opened his eyes again and had to see yet another failure. She almost had it before he latched onto her wrist.

"Don't."

"But . . ."

"I said don't bother!" he repeated, meeting her gaze with eyes so fiery Lindsay had to turn away. She stared at her wrist, waiting for him to let go. That's when she noticed the welts rising up between his thumb and index finger.

"Did you burn yourself?"

He released her wrist, walking to the refrigerator. "It's fine."

"No it's not. Look at your hand."

"Are you deaf? I said it's fine!"

"You stubborn son of a bitch!" she spat, charging toward him. "Why do you have to be so damn cruel, huh? Why? When all I'm trying to do is help you."

"I didn't ask for your help!"

"Well . . . tough!" Lindsay shouted, snatching up his hand. And, though it was apparent Will didn't approve, he didn't pull away. Maybe because the wound wasn't that bad, and he wanted a front-row seat for when she realized she was an overbearing mother hen. Maybe because he was in shock someone other than Janey or Regan had stood up to him. Either way, he was still and quiet, and Lindsay planned to cash in.

She examined the back of his hand, his fingers, his knuckles. Every crack lead to the heart of another story she wanted to read, every scar to another unhappy ending she was afraid to unveil. She traced the paths of his palm like a psychic looking for answers, but they only led to more paths, more questions, twisting their way through his calloused hands like a maze of thorns.

And then, Lindsay found the one scar that couldn't be hidden, the one tale that couldn't go untold. The brown, pearl-like skin was raised from the base of his wrist up his arm, an apex seamed by two halves not meant to equal one, but forced together regardless. It beckoned for someone's touch, craved understanding, and—before Lindsay could reason that someone might not be her—she approached the thin line of Will's hopelessness. Crossed it.

"No!" he growled, yanking free and pinning her to the refrigerator.

"I'm sorry. I just want to understand."

He beat his fist, sending magnet-pinned to-do lists drifting to the floor. "No!"

She stared into his eyes. She should be afraid, yet there was no urge for her to run, no adrenaline coursing through her veins. Just sorrow for a man who'd borne more pain than one human should have to. She wanted to be closer, take him into her, bury that sorrow inside her.

"No," he repeated, one last time, this one rolling off his tongue differently than the others. It was softer, quieter. A plea instead of a demand. It was a request not meant for her.

Lindsay inched forward, like a child toward a dove, knowing when she was detected, he'd set out in flight. And just when he began to spread his wings, she pressed her lips to his, simple and sweet, hoping the shock would be enough to keep him there, just a moment longer.

Slack-jawed, Will drew a trembling hand to his mouth and brushed his fingertips over the still-moist path of her lips. And, for just a moment, Lindsay could swear she saw a spark lighting inside his eyes. But only for a moment.

Then he ran, out the back door and down the porch steps into the dark night, dragging Lindsay's courage behind him.

Will hurried along the dirt path from the house, clenching his fists tighter with each step. No one had ever touched his scars. Not Janey. Not Regan. Not even Sherriff Blythe when he slapped cuffs on Will. That was a part of Will saved only for Emma. And his lips were a part of him saved only for Ellie.

Who the hell did Lindsay Shepherd think she was?

How had he let this happen?

And dear God, why had it felt so good?

The tenderness in her fingertips, the minty smell of her breath, the moistness of her lips against his. He shouldn't feel this way. He should be crawling out of his skin, enraged, but he only wanted more. He wanted Lindsay. And for some reason he'd never understand, Lindsay wanted him too. This was like a dream. A nightmare. This couldn't be real.

Will stiffened, his feet slowing to a crawl. That was it. None of this *was* real. It was all one big hallucination. Lindsay had never come home, Will had never burned the bread, and she'd certainly never kissed him. It was the only explanation that made sense. He'd imagined every bit of it, and now he had to find a way out of this craziness.

The barn. Yes, the barn.

Once inside, he fell to his knees and smoothed his hands across the cool wood grain of the door. The barn was his safe haven, his totem of reality, his pearly white gates. Crossing through those doors meant all was forgiven and he didn't have to hide from who he was. Inside here, no one could get him. *She* couldn't get him.

"Will! Will! Open this door!" imaginary Lindsay shouted.

"This isn't real," he mumbled, trying to keep from crying. She would go away. *It* would go away if he could just wait a moment longer.

She yelled and beat on the door, the vibrations sending his heart into a race.

"Will, if you don't open this door, I'm going to call Janey!"

Imagine that. A hallucination that knew all his weaknesses too.

Only, something wasn't right about this. This wasn't your standard hallucination; at least Will thought it wasn't. He'd always imagined seeing the headless horseman on a bloodred horse, galloping down the middle of Main Street with a blade flying through the air that had his name on it. He'd imagined being too terrified to look. So, why was there this urge in the pit of his stomach pleading with him to open the door? Why did he *want* all this to be real?

But it wasn't real. It wasn't! And he would prove it once and for all.

Determined, he stood and tugged on the handle with one quick pull. There she was, hair wild and eyes a crazed mess. Not the headless horseman, but not far from it.

Will leaned against the frame of the door and smiled. "Hey, what's up?"

Lindsay glanced him over from head to toe. "I . . . I think we should talk."

"About what?"

"This isn't funny!"

"I don't recall laughing."

She shifted her feet and fidgeted with her hands. The real Lindsay did that a lot, too. It always made Will think she had to pee. "Can I come in, please?"

He frowned. "In . . . inside here? Inside the barn?"

"Yes. Inside there."

He hesitated for a moment, but then it occurred to him. This was his safe haven. She'd disappear once inside, like vapor. And this would all be over. "Sure. Come on in."

"Look, I'm sorry," she said, walking past him. "I shouldn't have done that just now. I was way out of line."

"Mmm, hmm. Mmm, hmm." Will reached out his index finger and poked her shoulder, not once, but three times.

"Ow. What was that for?"

This was bad. This was *very* bad.

"Nothing." He put his hand up to his mouth. "You were saying?"

"I was saying that . . . actually, I was waiting for *you* to say something."

"Like what?"

"Oh, I don't know. How about 'I know you meant well, Lindsay,' or 'Don't beat yourself up about it, Lindsay.'"

The loft! Yes. She couldn't get him in the loft!

In a sharp, sudden movement, he met her gaze and lowered his hand. "I don't know what you're talking about," he said, then spun on his heels and headed for the ladder, leaving this madness behind him once and for all. He'd be safe in the loft.

But there she was, right behind him, climbing just as fast as his terrified legs could go. So much for the barn and loft theory. Dr. Granger was full of shit.

"Is that all?" she shouted, crossing her arms and stomping over to him.

He sighed, defeated. "Apparently not."

"What is *wrong* with you?"

"Do you want me to start a list?"

"I just completely *gave* myself to you. How could you just act like it never happened?"

"Well, I—"

"Am I ugly?"

"No. I just—"

"Does my breath smell?"

He stared a moment. "No, you're just—"

"What? Too chubby? Too many freckles? Is my 'ridiculous widow's peak' too ridiculous for you? What is it? Tell me please, so I can understand."

Ugly? Bad breath? Chubby? Was she freaking kidding? And her freckles were her best feature: badges telling a story, just like his scars. He stole glances at them when she wasn't looking, imagined the adventures she'd been on when she'd earned them. Snorkeling a reef, examining a Mayan ruin, hiking in the Outback. Will had no idea if she'd been to any of those places, but it was safer to think of her there, in the distance, on an apex far above his reach.

"Why?" she repeated, eyes narrowed. God, she was damn sexy when she was angry. That's why Will enjoyed riling her up so much.

He covered his mouth as if he'd said it aloud. *Oh my God. That's why you rile her up. It turns you on, you sick bastard!*

"Will!" she urged. "Why?"

"Because you're not fucking real!" he shouted, then grabbed her face and covered her mouth with his, knowing no other way to stop the yelling, the insanity. Hoping if he kissed hard enough this apparition would shatter in his hands.

But she didn't. She kissed back even harder, tangling her fingers in his hair and pressing her hips to his. And he didn't want her to stop—ever. If this wasn't real, he no longer cared, just as long as it never ended.

He felt the texture of her lips with his tongue, beckoning her to do the same. And then their tongues intertwined, circling and fleeing, until his lungs were full of her breath and his head dizzy with her heat. When his feet began to tingle, Will knew he'd reached the point of no return. Either he had to stop now or he'd go the whole way. There was no in between.

Gasping for air, Lindsay pulled away and met his gaze. Maybe she could read his mind; maybe she was having the same thoughts he was. They stood there in a staring match for what seemed to be hours, though Will knew it was probably only seconds. Then Lindsay began to open her blouse, one button at a time, slow and precise.

Will focused on her fingertips, the red of her nail polish against the ivory silk of her blouse. Each button revealed more of her skin, more of her beauty, more of his need to touch it and taste it, just like he'd imagined this morning when she'd asked if he could see through it. It had been all he could do to keep from taking her there in the kitchen.

When he turned his eyes back toward hers, they had changed again. They were fiery and calm at the same time. They were full of drunken lust, yet empty with hunger. Without breaking his gaze, Will reached his hands beneath the flaps of her shirt, finding her hips, and pulled her body to his. It had been so long since he'd touched a woman's flesh, but he remembered how the curves of a woman's body were like grooves, guiding the way to where his hands wanted to be. He followed them from her hips to her waist, making his way around to the small of her back and up to the latch of her bra. *This*, he remembered, *took a bit of practice.* And just when he'd decided to save it for later, Lindsay's fingers were on top of his, showing him where to pinch and pull and push until he felt the tension in the elastic go completely limp.

She let her hands fall to the side and shrugged the blouse from her shoulders, leaving only the white lace of her unlatched bra against skin. He traced the path where it was once pinched tight, until he felt the plumpness of her breasts glide across his knuckles. He found her nipples and brushed his fingertips across them until they went taut and hard.

Lindsay exhaled deeply and sank her mouth into his chest. He'd forgotten what that felt like, to give a woman pleasure. He'd forgotten what it was like to give them something other than pain. It was like a drug, making him want to touch her more, want to feel the hot breath of her sighs against his chest. He needed to feel her bare skin against his, nothing between them. He needed to make love to this woman.

From there, his hands were like independent beings, undressing her, cupping her, caressing her. She followed right on cue, peeling his shirt from his body and covering him in kisses as her hands traveled along the grooves of his chest. As carefully as she had her blouse, she unbuttoned his jeans and pushed them to the floor with his boxers, her hand circling his shaft.

How long had it been since he'd throbbed in a woman's hand? Ached to be inside her?

A moment later she wrapped herself around him, arms at his neck and legs around his waist, and they were heading toward the cot at a higher speed than he could handle, crushing the thin, metal rails of the cot and sending the mattress to the floor.

Lindsay laughed. *God,* her laugh.

"Guess this wasn't exactly made for two people," he whispered, chagrined.

She traced the line of his jaw with her fingers and then reached up to meet his lips. "Rules have never stopped you before."

He grinned against her lips then looked down to take in the wholeness of her. Her freckled shoulders, the beauty marks beside each of her nipples. Lindsay was beautiful. Lindsay was real. And Will was absolutely terrified.

"It's okay," she whispered, trailing her hand down his chest, his stomach, his pelvis, and finally cradling the throbbing wholeness of him again. "I'm scared too."

Will took a deep breath, pressing his forehead into hers, as she guided him to where he wanted to be, where he needed to be. And then he entered her, discovered her, found a new hiding place inside her.

Lindsay was definitely real.

"This will change everything. I promise," he whispered.

Lindsay kissed his forehead. "It already has."

Will closed his eyes and dove into her again, without the heart to admit to Lindsay the promise hadn't been meant for her. Without the courage to admit to himself he didn't know who it had been meant for.

CHAPTER FIFTEEN

"What a freaking mess, Will," Regan said, dropping her book bag to the kitchen floor. Spaghetti sauce–coated pots still sitting on the stove. A pan with some charcoal-black bread on it. Magnets strewn about the floor beside Janey's to-do lists. What had he done last night? Eaten and gone to bed directly after? Had Lindsay gotten in late and not seen it?

Choosing to ignore it, Regan walked across the kitchen to the pantry and pulled out the Oatey Os. She didn't have time to clean up his mess. She had to get to school early today to finish up the homework she'd put off to have that disaster—or dinner, rather—with Lane's family. And then she'd spent the rest of her evening making out with Lane by the old dam, hoping his kisses would make her forget what a damn traitor she was.

But they hadn't, because nothing would ever make her forget she'd met Ellie. Nothing. Hadn't she learned that lesson from her father?

The guilt had kept Regan up most the night tossing and turning; images of Will's betrayed eyes mixed with flashes of Ellie's red hair blowing in the breeze as she stood on the front porch of the Bradford mansion. She'd asked how Will was. Should Regan tell him? Maybe that would erase some of his pain, knowing Ellie didn't hate him, that she still cared.

It would kill him, her mother said.

The screen door opened behind her, putting an end to the short debate. Even if she did decide to tell him, now was not the time. "Aunt Janey would have your ass if she saw this kitchen," she muttered, pouring milk over her cereal.

"I know. I'll clean it up before I head to school."

Regan spun with a start to see Lindsay standing there, carrying a pair of navy-blue flats in her hand and wearing the same clothes she'd worn to school the day before. "Sorry. I meant that for Will," Regan corrected. Was that a piece of straw in Lindsay's hair?

"Meant what for me?" he asked, then walked through the screen door barefoot, sporting a spaghetti-stained polo and dirty pair of jeans.

And it all made sense.

Lindsay's face turned beet red. "Regan, I can explain."

"Just give me a minute." Regan shook her head, trying to remove the thought of Will and her principal doing the nasty in the barn. She was happy for Will, of course. She'd bet her hands that was the first time he'd been laid since Ellie left. But this was just weird.

Lindsay glanced back at Will, not so discreetly nodding toward Regan. When he didn't move, she approached. "Look, I know this must be very . . ."

"Freaking gross?"

Will let out a laugh and covered his mouth.

"I was going to say this must be very confusing for a girl your age."

Oh no. She was not going to explain the purpose of one-night stands, was she?

"You see, sometimes when two adults—"

She was.

Regan waved her hands in the air, cutting Lindsay off.

"Don't you want to talk about this?" Lindsay asked.

"Talk about it? I don't even want to think about it." Regan placed her bowl on a placemat and slid into her chair. "What you two do in your spare time is none of my business."

"So, you're not upset with us?"

Now, that was an odd question. Regan turned, folding her arms across the back of her chair. "Why would you think I'd be upset?"

"I don't know. Maybe you're worried you'll have to share your father from now on."

At this, Regan laughed. She'd made peace with having to share Will long ago. If she could share him with her dead sister, she could certainly share him with Lindsay Shepherd. "Nah. We're good."

Lindsay let out a deep breath that made Regan wonder how long she'd been holding it. "Good. We're good." Whether Lindsay spoke to Regan, to Will, or to herself, Regan didn't know. Then, as if this couldn't get any weirder, her principal kissed her dad on the cheek and headed toward the living room, the creaking of stairs following a moment later.

Silent, Will poured himself a bowl of cereal and sat beside Regan.

"So . . ." she said with a grin.

"So . . ." He responded, clenching his spoon in his fist. "How's Benedict Arnold?"

Regan froze, her grin sliding. "What?"

"Benedict Arnold," he repeated. "You won't pass an exam on Revolutionary War generals without knowing who *he* is."

Right. Benedict Arnold. The turncoat general. Not the turncoat daughter who'd committed family treason by dining with her father's ex-wife last night. Regan could almost feel the rope squeezing her neck. "He's . . ."

A knock at the door saved her from another lie.

Regan jumped to her feet. "That's Lane. I gotta get to school."

"Wait!"

Seconds from a clean getaway, she clenched the counter like a caught rogue. "Yeah?"

"I was wondering if you'd be at the cemetery today for lunch," he asked.

She turned toward him, confused. Didn't he know she'd quit going? Hadn't he looked every day to make sure she wasn't there?

"Because, I thought, if you were, I'd introduce you to Emma. Cause, tomorrow . . ." His voice trailed off a moment before he looked up at her. "So? Will you come?"

"I'll be there," Regan said, then threw her book bag across her shoulder and headed for the door before he saw the tears welling up in her eyes. She didn't want to make a big deal of it, didn't want him to realize what he'd just asked and take it away.

Because visiting Emma with her father was the best birthday present she'd ever receive.

Lindsay tapped on her desk, staring at the two freshmen who'd been dragged into her office after making out under the stairs. She should be informing their parents of the activities their kids were partaking in before school, but how could she? When all she could think of was how that first taste of lust made everything else not matter. How she'd been there just hours ago with Will in the barn and again in the shower before she'd left. How when they'd finished, he'd made her promise to be home early today, so he could take her there again.

It had been the single most amazing eight hours of her life. At first, he'd been so skittish. Lindsay had considered stopping him, afraid of being a morning-after mistake. But then something had changed. His trembling hands had become confident. His quivering lips had begun to press into hers with more certainty. He moved inside her with purpose, a determination shining in his eyes she'd never seen before, as if, with every thrust, he was letting go of who he was and becoming who he was meant to be.

This morning she'd expected him to pretend the love they'd made hadn't meant to him what it had meant to her. But instead, he'd climbed into the shower a different man, not a trace of the scared Will she'd come to know in sight. Without a word, he'd lifted her up against the white, tiled wall and made love to her again, with a rhythm like they'd been doing it all along.

And suddenly, Lindsay was the terrified one. Terrified because—

"Principal Shepherd?" the girl said.

Lindsay's eyes snapped open. "Yes?"

"I asked if you were going to call my dad. I don't think he'd like what I was doing."

Chagrined, Lindsay straightened. "Two weeks of detention, and if I see either one of you on school grounds before the first bell rings in the morning, I will make sure both your parents know. Now, get back to class."

No sooner had the kids exited the room when Lindsay's mother barged in, two curlers still hanging from her hair. "What are you doing here?"

"Everyone in town knows you're staying at the Fletchers. It's all the talk at the salon."

Lindsay nodded toward the curler. "Must've been . . . *shocking* . . . to hear something you already knew."

"Don't make fun of me," her mother muttered, untangling the two curlers as she took a seat. "Do you know what this sort of rumor could do to a principal?"

"Mother, I have work to do. I don't have time for your silly, social paranoia." Lindsay put her reading glasses on and pushed her mouse to the side to wake up her monitor. "So what if they don't approve of me helping out a friend."

"Helping out a friend?" Her mother laughed, shaking her head. "Honey, everyone thinks you're shacking up with one of them."

At this, her mother had her full attention. Had someone seen her and Will? Janey had warned her about the trespassers every now and then pulling practical jokes. Was it possible someone had stumbled upon the story of a lifetime last night back at the Fletcher barn?

And then the rest of her mother's words caught up with her. "*One* of them?"

"Yes. And, I have to say, if I had to pick one, I'd pick the sister. Much rather have you be into a girl than a murderer."

"Get out!" Lindsay yelled, flying to her feet and knocking her coffee over onto her desk. "Get out right now!"

"I did not raise my child to treat me this way."

"I'm not a child anymore, and I'm not about to listen to the advice of a superficial, sixty-two-year-old woman who would condemn a man like Will Fletcher."

"Why are you so hell-bent on defending this man? After what he did to that poor little baby? Your father lies dead in the ground, and you still haven't forgiven him for forgetting you at school that day when you were eight. How can you just dismiss this?"

"Father forgot me because he was in bed with another woman, Mother."

Ghost-white and slack-jawed, her mother straightened in her seat. "What?"

"Oh, don't act like you didn't know. He fucked half the stewardesses that flew on his planes. Everyone knew. *I* knew. And you just turned the other cheek. For *years*."

Her mother clenched her purse, standing to her feet. "What I did, I did for you."

"A lot of good it did me. And you wonder why I've settled." Lindsay bit her lip, glancing out the window a moment, then turned back to face her mother. "Well, I'm not settling anymore. I finally found someone good. Someone who cares about what I want. What I think. Someone who would never hurt me. And I'm not letting go."

Her mother placed her purse over her heart, a question hanging on her lips. A question Lindsay did not know the answer to until just now. It was the reason Lindsay had been terrified since she left Will standing on the front porch this morning, bare chested in ripped jeans.

"I'm in love with Will Fletcher, Mother."

The last time Will had been at the cemetery with someone other than Janey was the day they'd buried Emma. The entire town waited in a half-mile long line to drop a white rose on the mayor's granddaughter's casket. Maybe Will should've felt comforted by everyone's concern, but he couldn't feel much more than guilt. Still couldn't.

Ellie, on the other hand, had begun to look alive for the first time since she'd found Emma, glowing like a candle, even in the shackles of her black dress. Will remembered wondering how she could be so strong. He remembered praying for God to give him just an ounce of that strength. He remembered hating his wife when God didn't.

"You made it."

"Of course," Regan said, dropping her bag to the side. "I said I would."

He nodded. Since she'd come clean about spying on him, Will hadn't checked to see if she still watched him or not. He didn't want to know either way, just like he didn't want to know the real reason why he'd finally had the urge to invite her here, today of all days. In the hours since breakfast, he'd managed to convince himself his evening with Lindsay had given him a newfound force field around his heart; the shower had certainly been proof of that. Best to just listen to that little voice in the back of his head and throw himself completely into the fire before the force field disappeared.

And it would. He knew that for certain.

"Hey, Emma. It's Dad," he said, assuming his usual position on his knees. "I have something special for you today. I brought Regan with me to meet you."

Regan sank to the ground and brushed her hand along the freshly cut grass. "Hey."

"I know this is supposed to be our time, but I thought you might be sick of hearing about fleas and wood. Regan . . . she can talk to you about . . . about . . . well, she can talk to you about stuff you'd care about." He glanced toward Regan and gave her a reassuring nod. "Go ahead."

"What?"

"Talk to her."

Regan's spine stiffened, her eyes moving back and forth. "I don't know what to say."

Will had that problem once too. He'd show up and think, *She's a baby. What can she possibly understand?* That's when he started measuring the days, the weeks, the years. Adjusting his conversations to be age appropriate.

"Just remember," he whispered to Regan. "She's five."

"Okay." Regan relaxed, rubbing her hands across her thighs as if the friction would bring her insight. "Guess you'd be starting school this year. I remember my first day of school. Billy Howard thought it was funny to lift my skirt up in front of the whole class that day. And, let me tell you, kids can be cruel at that age."

Will closed his eyes. Suddenly, they weren't sitting on the hard earth of a grave, but on the soft blanket of a white, four-post bed with a yellow canopy above. With their auburn hair, Emma was the spitting image of Regan, despite having a different mother. They chatted about school and homework and recess, and Emma turned her nose up when Regan mentioned Lane. This is the way it was supposed to be. This is the way Will would picture them from now on.

Later on, as they walked from the cemetery toward the road in silence, Will wondered if this trip had been any different for Regan. Did it give her the same satisfaction it had when she hid behind a tree? Was it enough for her to let go and never come back again?

Then, just as they were about to part ways, Regan paused in the middle of the stone path with tears in her eyes. "Does it ever get any easier?"

"Does what get easier?"

"Leaving her behind?"

Will swallowed hard and shook his head.

"Then why? Why do you do this to yourself? Every day?"

He glanced back toward Emma's grave, seeing it as clearly as he had the day they'd buried her. He'd stayed behind that day, not because he wanted to see her coffin being lowered into the ground and covered with the finality of earth, but because it was his job as a parent to make sure his child reached the other side of the street before he let go of her hand. His job to stay up until midnight to make sure she came home from her first date and carry every last box into her dorm room to make sure she had everything she needed. Will might not ever have the chance to do these things, but he was damn well going to make sure Emma made it into the ground.

He'd made a promise then to be back every day at the same time to check on her.

"Because she's my daughter and I love her," he finally answered, turning his gaze back toward Regan. "I would do the same thing for you."

The tears spilled out of her eyes as she smiled, and Will knew she'd decoded exacted what he'd meant. He wanted to pull her into his arms and say it again. He wanted to hear Regan tell him she loved him too. He wanted things he didn't deserve.

"I haven't been to my mother's grave since the funeral." Regan wiped the tears from her cheeks and turned her gaze back toward the ground. "Does that make me an awful person?"

"No," he answered. "It makes you human."

"Then what does that make you?"

Insane? A freak of nature? A glutton for punishment? All logical answers. None of which seemed to be what she looked for. "I don't know. What do you think it makes me?"

Regan sniffled, wiping her nose with her sleeve. "My hero."

The irritating tone of the busy signal cut off as Janey hung up the phone and fell into her pillow. There were only two people who ever called the house, and one was downstairs at the bar schmoozing possible clients to add to her list. The other should be picking up the other end of the phone right about now.

Why the hell was the phone busy?

A knock at the door pulled her from her internal debate. She climbed to her feet and straightened her clothes before heading to the door. "Hey."

"Forgot my key." Gretchen walked past, the liquor on her breath intoxicating the air, and stopped at Janey's packed suitcase. "What's this?"

"I told you. I have to leave right after the banquet to catch my flight home."

Gretchen fell to the bed. "Oh, that's right. You have to get back before the warden catches you outside the prison."

Janey sighed. "Look, Gretchen, I don't want to fight. I need to get ready."

"Well, too bad. I think I deserve a fucking explanation."

"I just gave you one. Maybe if you'd listen to me for once, you would've heard it."

"I listen to you, damn it!"

"No, Gretchen, you hear me. You don't *listen* to me." Janey met her gaze. "I'm tired of fighting with you. I'm tired of defending my decisions to you. I can't do it anymore, and I don't *want* to do it anymore. Love shouldn't be this damn hard."

"That's bullshit. If love wasn't hard, it wouldn't be worth holding onto. You're just lazy because you spend all of your energy on Will."

"You see? Right there. You always make this about him. Always. And I can honestly say that this time it's not about him at all."

"But don't you deserve your own life, too? Don't you deserve a schedule that doesn't revolve around someone else's wants and needs, and . . . and . . . medication times?"

"Yes. I do deserve all that," Janey said. "But I also deserve to be with someone who understands I have to do all those things, and someone who will do whatever possible to lessen the burden on me. Not criticize me."

"I can do all those things, Janey. Just give me another chance," Gretchen pleaded.

Janey shook her head. "It's too late."

"No. Not if you want me. Not if you want us. It's never too late."

"Gretchen—"

She moved in too quickly for Janey to stop her, pressing her tequila-soaked mouth over Janey's. And then she pushed, just like she always did. Pushed Janey to the bed with her hands and pushed Janey to her breaking point with her will. Only this time, Janey pushed back.

"There's someone else," she gasped, as soon as she was free of Gretchen's mouth. "I'm . . . in love . . . with someone else."

Gretchen hovered over her a moment, forehead scrunched tight, then bolted for the bathroom. A moment later, she heaved.

"Pretty much the response I thought you'd have," Janey mumbled, straightening her shirt as she stood. She waited a moment, giving Gretchen time to expel all the bad thoughts and alcohol from her system, then walked to the bathroom and leaned against the frame of the door. "Are you okay?"

"Just leave me alone, you . . . you . . . oh dear God." She hurled again.

Ignoring her drunken request, Janey pushed off the door, reached for a fresh towel from the rack, and sank down beside her. "Here."

Gretchen snatched the towel, wiping her mouth, as she took a seat beside Janey. "I knew. I knew when you walked into the hotel room. You were so different. And then you kept giving me excuse after excuse."

Janey wasn't sure how to respond, so she didn't.

"What am I supposed to do now?" Gretchen asked, voice high, yet muffled with tears.

Janey pulled her head down into her lap and stroked her hair as she sobbed. "You've been doing it for five years. It's just time to make it official."

"The headless horseman?" Lindsay said with a grimace.

Will smiled, running his fingers along her naked shoulder. "Figuratively speaking."

The tension eased from her eyes. Maybe he should've lied when she'd asked what he'd been thinking last night, told her he'd been on the other side of the barn door pumping himself up for the task. But why? She'd seen every bare bit of his outside— three times now. Might as well show her the inside too.

"And what are you thinking now?" she asked.

That he shouldn't be here, but he didn't want to be anyplace else. That he felt horrible about it, but he wanted her to make him feel good again. That his heart was split perfectly in half, but this was an improvement from the million pieces it had been in.

That he shouldn't be thinking at all, because nothing good ever came from it.

Headfirst. The force field will soon be gone. Seize the moment, hero.

Which reminded him—he needed to hide the bottle of wine he'd used to chase off all those bad thoughts this afternoon, the ones creeping in now.

Just make love to her. She makes it all go away.

"William?" Lindsay beckoned.

He met her gaze. When was the last time someone had called him William? "Yeah?"

She giggled. "I asked what you were thinking now."

Oh, right. And he was avoiding thinking.

"I was thinking I could go for another round. Kinda turns me on when you call me William, Principal Shepherd." He turned on his side, pinning her against the couch and burying his face into the safety of her neck. "What are you thinking?"

"That it's strange Janey hasn't called yet."

Will deflated. Buzz. Kill.

"Maybe I should call her?" she asked.

No. That would be an even *bigger* buzzkill.

Lie. Seize the moment. Take her.

"Wait, I forgot," Will said, scrambling. "She called this afternoon before you came home and said she might not be able to get away before the awards to call."

"Really?" Lindsay asked.

No, not really. He'd taken the phone off the hook so Janey wouldn't interrupt them. But if Lindsay believed it . . . "Forgot to tell you. We were kind of busy." He grinned, pressing his pelvis against hers. "And she said she trusted you were more than capable of taking care of me."

Lindsay smiled, eyes glazing over. "She did? She really said that?"

No, not really. Like Janey would ever trust anyone to take care of him. But if Lindsay needed to hear it . . . "She *did*. And you *are*, Principal Shepherd." He kissed her, his mouth tugging on her lower lip as he retreated. "*So* capable."

With a sexy grin, she wrapped her arms around his neck and dug her hands into his hair. "Then we should probably move upstairs, William, because Regan will be home soon."

Right. Regan.

Regan will be harder to fool.

"Yes, she will," he answered, both to Lindsay and to himself.

And then, in one quick motion, Will jumped to his feet and pulled Lindsay up into his arms. "We better go hide then."

Janey woke up on the cold, sterile tile floor, Gretchen in her lap snoring like a goose. She must've dozed off listening to Gretchen's sobs. Funny, Janey usually fell asleep to the sound of her *own* sobs. Not anymore. Things were going to be different now.

She carefully moved Gretchen's head to a clean towel, then stood and stretched. The air felt calmer around her, her feet felt fancier against the floor, her heart felt lighter beating in her chest. It was like an albatross had taken wing. She knew exactly what she needed to do, and she needed to do it soon, before her senses came back to her. As soon as she got home, Janey would tell Lindsay everything and take a chance her friend thought of her as more than that too.

She was just about to turn off the bathroom light when she saw the morning paper sitting by the main door. How long had they been sleeping? She turned toward the clock.

"Fuck," she shouted, sprinting for the phone. "Fuck, fuck, fuck, fuck!"

"What? What is it? What happened?" Gretchen asked, coming out of the bathroom. "Did we miss the awards banquet?"

"Who gives a fuck about the awards banquet?" Janey cried, heart racing as she dialed the concierge. "I missed my god-damned flight."

CHAPTER SIXTEEN

The morning sun tugged at her eyes, but Lindsay couldn't pull herself away. Not from sleep. Not from Will's arms. Not from this perfect moment she'd been stuck inside for two days. She had to stay as long as she could to soak up as much as time would allow. Janey would be home in a couple of hours, and who knew what would happen after that?

She felt a slight shudder and glanced up to see if Will fought the same battle she fought. Eyes wide open and bloodshot, he seemed in a daze as he stared toward the wall on the far side of the room. Had he not slept well? Janey had mentioned he sometimes had difficulty sleeping. Or maybe it was his tiny twin bed they were both crammed in.

Not wanting to interrupt whatever internal conversation he was having, she waited patiently for him to notice her. Even with the bloodshot eyes, he was beautiful. Not in the ordinary sense one thinks of beauty, though Will was certainly handsome. There was something about the way he carried his emotions for everyone to see. He was like a work of art—the most breathtaking paintings bled emotion from the oil and canvas. This was Will. Her masterpiece.

"I love you," she whispered.

Will jumped at her voice, turning his eyes toward hers. "What?"

"I said . . . I *love* you."

Will blinked, the confusion clouding his painting like a thunderhead.

"It's okay. You don't have to say it back." She laid her head back on his chest so she could hear his heart. "I just wanted you to know."

He lay still a moment, chest pounding loud and fast against Lindsay's ear. There had been a time Lindsay had said those words simply because she needed to hear them back. With Will, it was more about letting *him* know *he* was loved. After a moment, Will mumbled something and began to slide out from beneath her.

"What's wrong? Are you mad?"

"Haven't you figured that out yet?"

"I . . . I didn't mean it that way. I meant angry."

He pulled on his boxers and shook his head. Unconvincingly.

Lindsay sat up, tucking the bedsheet beneath her arms. "Please don't do that. I swear I didn't say that to pressure you, or . . . or make you feel trapped."

"I don't feel trapped!" he yelled, reaching for his T-shirt. "This is just so . . . so . . ."

"So what? Tell me what you feel."

"*Wrong.*"

Lindsay stared. Had he just said *wrong*? He had; she was sure of it. Will believed her loving him was wrong. And how could she chastise him for that? It wasn't that long ago Lindsay had thought she was incapable of being loved too. Who would ever love a woman who didn't have a mind of her own? Who would want to waste their time building something with a woman who couldn't manage to make even the simplest of men happy?

Now she knew the answer lay within the question. She was never meant to be loved by a simple man. She was meant to be loved by Will Fletcher.

She climbed to her feet, letting the bedsheet fall to the floor and expose her naked body, then walked across the room to where he stood, fully dressed. "Look at me."

He shook his head.

She pressed herself to him as she reached her arms up around his stiff neck. "I know you think you're incapable of being loved. But you can't control the way people feel about you, and you can't just *will* me not to love you."

"I don't—"

"When everyone else looks at you and sees crazy, I see complex. When they see someone who's not worth a second of their time, I finally see someone who is actually worth every bit of mine. When they see a man who's damned, I see one who's yet to be redeemed." She pulled his wrist to her lips and kissed his scar. "Please. Just let me love you."

He snatched his hand from hers, just like he had two nights before. But this time, Will didn't push her away. This time he pulled her closer, so tightly she thought she might become a part of him. He kissed her forehead, her hair, her ear, her jaw, before finally finding her lips. And when he pulled away, he had tears in his eyes. "I need to tell—"

A scream rang out from downstairs, interrupting him.

"What was that?" Lindsay asked.

"Regan." Will took off in a sprint out the door and down the hallway.

Lindsay scurried around, looking for her clothes, finally

settling on Will's plaid robe hanging in the closet, and then ran to catch up. At the bottom of the stairs, she found Regan standing at the front door laughing, and Will staring out the window doing anything but.

"What happened?" Lindsay asked.

Regan pointed outside. "Look!"

She tucked her hands into the robe and went to stand beside Will. On the front porch were shades of yellow, red, pink, orange, and green, spraying from sun-reflecting, glistening, crystal vases with balloons attached that read Happy Birthday. Judging from the excitement all over Regan's face, Lindsay assumed it was meant for her.

"I can't believe he did this," Regan said, opening the front door and stepping onto the porch. "No one's ever given me flowers before."

Lindsay glanced over at Will who looked like he'd swallowed a rather large butcher knife. "Did you know it was her birthday?"

He shook his head, but didn't look her way.

"It's okay. We can run out and get her something. I'm sure she'll understand."

He crossed his arms over his chest, clenching at the thin material of his T-shirt as if it were two sizes too small, then nodded.

"We can make her a cake. Have some ice cream. She'll love it. Okay?"

Another nod.

"Come here and look!" Regan shouted from the doorway. "He left me a clue."

"A clue?" Lindsay asked. She waited for Will to move first, but when he didn't budge, Lindsay deduced it would be on her and hurried toward the porch. Maybe he just needed time to adjust. "You mean a note?"

"No, it's a clue, to like a scavenger hunt or something. See?" She held up a folded piece of paper labeled Clue One.

"Well, open it! What's it say?"

Regan tore open the paper and began to read aloud. "You thought I didn't know, didn't you? For your next clue, look beside the place I gave you your second I love you." She glanced into the yard. "It must be over there, beside the bird bath."

"Well, let's go find out."

Without delay, Regan raced down the steps toward the birdbath. Lindsay followed suit and turned back once toward the window to invite Will to come along. But it was empty.

"Ha, *ha*! I found you!" Regan shouted.

And foolishly, Lindsay turned around to see if it was Will. That's when she saw his red ball cap heading up the street in the distance.

It was some sort of high school prank, that's what Will thought when he saw the flowers. Someone had spent a lot of time and money playing another sick joke on the crazy man, and this was the cruelest he'd seen. Then he saw the birthday balloons knocking around like giant bubbles in the breeze, and Will knew.

The one with the sick sense of humor was God. And Will wasn't laughing.

"Did you know it was her birthday?" Lindsay had asked.

No, he didn't. But how could he have missed it? How could Janey have missed it? She'd stared at that damn birth certificate for twenty minutes to make sure it was real.

"It's okay, Will. We can run out and get her something. I'm sure she'll understand."

Yes. Regan would understand. She was the most under-standing person Will knew. But Regan wasn't the *she* he was worried about.

And that's when the guilt had crept in like thick, black smoke, filling the air with poison and tightening his lungs like a steel clamp. His heart had expanded by the second, his clothes had grown smaller with every beat. He couldn't do this. He couldn't choose. Not anymore.

"We can make her a cake. Have some ice cream. She'll love it. Okay?"

And there it was, laid out before him—the impossible choice he would always have to make from this moment until the day he died. It was too much for him to bear. As soon as Lindsay stepped onto the porch, he ran. He had to get out of there, had to explain. He had to let her know this didn't change anything; he would never forget the promise he'd made.

Will sprinted down the busy streets in town, ignoring the usual wisecracks, then hurried up the stone path past the church toward the iron fence. The closer he came to Emma, the lighter the air became, and the easier it was to breathe. He was almost there. He was almost free.

But, as soon as he crossed into his sanctuary, every square inch of breath he'd gained was sucked out of him in an instant.

He thought he was seeing things. No one ever visited Emma's grave. He wiped his eyes and blinked, but the person didn't disappear. He didn't need this right now. Today of all days. He just needed to be alone with his daughter, without this stranger crouched down beside her grave. But, as Will approached, he realized it wasn't a stranger at all.

"*Ellie?*"

She spun with a start, losing her footing and falling onto the fresh, white lilies she must've placed on the grave.

"Is it really you?" he asked, falling to his knees and reaching toward her. She hadn't changed a bit since the last time he'd seen her. The blonde highlights in her auburn hair still glowed like a halo in the sun; her ivory skin was still smooth. Her eyes were still full of disgust. He dropped his hand, just inches away from touching her. "It *is* you. Do you hear that, Emma? Momma's here."

"Please, don't do that," Ellie pleaded, clenching her eyes tight.

"Do what?"

"Act like she's still here! She's gone, Will!"

"I know. Five years today." He swallowed, reaching for her hand. "That doesn't mean she can't hear you, though. She knows you're here. She knows *we're* here. Together."

Ellie stared down at their joined hands for a moment, but didn't attempt to pull away. "You shouldn't be here. You're four hours early."

"No," he said, giving her a painful smile. "You're five years late."

"Will—"

He waved off her excuses. "It's okay. You're here now, and that's what matters."

"I can't stay." She snatched her hand away and climbed to her feet, leaving his hand aching.

"Please don't go," he begged as she walked away. "I . . . I can leave if you want me to. But Emma . . . she needs you here."

"She's never needed me. Not when she was alive and certainly not after she died. You've always been the perfect parent here, not me." She teetered back and forth a moment before turning to face him again. "She's beautiful, you know? She has your eyes."

Will frowned, confused. "How do you know?"

"I saw her. Yesterday."

"You *saw* her?" Will asked, rising to his feet. All these years of praying she'd appear to him, just once. All these years of wishing he could see her one more time, see the little girl she would've grown into. It wasn't fair. "How? How did you see her? In a dream?"

Ellie tilted her head to the side, then grimaced. "I meant Regan, Will."

"Regan?" he repeated, then quickly deflated.

"Lane told me how you took her in. That must've been hard."

Regan. The other daughter he'd forgotten about. "There are no words."

"She's lucky to have you. You're a good father."

"Stop saying that! Emma's in the *ground* because of me."

"No, she's not! She's in the ground because . . ." Ellie's voice trailed off, her mouth hung open like it used to do when she slept. Will wondered if it still did. If, back then, she'd been fighting words as she was now. "We shouldn't do this here."

Will glanced back toward Emma's headstone. He imagined she sat there, cross-legged, with her hands folded delicately in her lap, while she tried to make sense of what her parents were saying, just like he used to do when his parents argued.

"You're right. We shouldn't do this in front of Emma," he said. But, when he turned back around, Ellie was halfway up the path.

Don't let her go.

He chased her down. Just like he had four years ago. Just like he had every day since. There was no contemplation, no hesitation. She was here, and he had to find a way to keep her, because the thought of losing her again was like a knife in his heart.

"Please don't go."

She shook her head. "I can't do this. I shouldn't have come here."

"You belong here," he shouted, reaching for her arm and yanking her to a stop. "Don't you ever wonder why, Ellie? Why you can't find what you're looking for out there? It's because you belong *here*. With Emma. With me."

"Will, stop," she cried. "You're hurting me."

"Shh . . .shh." He turned her back toward him and framed her face as delicately as he could. "I would never hurt you again. Never. Don't you know that? Don't you believe me?"

"Let go of her, William."

Will glanced over Ellie's shoulder to see Mayor Bradford standing behind them in his standard suit and condescending stance. "This is between me and my wife, Art."

"She's not your wife, William. But she *is* my daughter. And, unless you want me to call the sheriff, you will let go of her now, you crazy sack of—"

"Dad, *no*," Ellie interrupted, pulling herself away from Will's grip. "I'm fine. Will and I were just talking." She turned back to Will, with something in her eyes that resembled a plea, and stepped forward. "You have to let go, Will."

"I did," he muttered. "Go."

"No. You have to *let go*. For good."

"Go get in the car, Ellie," Art ordered.

"You deserve more than this. You deserve more than me."

"Now, Ellie!"

"I'm not a child, Dad. You can't just tell me what to do."

"Then stop playing these childish games and get in the damn car."

She wiped the hair from her face, leaned in, and kissed Will on the cheek, hovering near his ear. "Please, if you ever loved me. Let go."

And then she walked away from him, toward her father, toward the car, back toward a life that didn't include Will and never should have. And, once again, Will was on his knees, powerless to stop any of it.

Powerless to stop the demons coming to drag him into the shadows.

Regan rounded the corner of Main Street heading toward Hadley's Grocery. Her fifth clue read, "Before it gets too late, meet me at the place of our first date." So far she'd received the flowers, a charm bracelet, a book, a gift card, and a new, knitted hat, scarf, and gloves. She hadn't received this many birthday presents since . . . Well, she'd never received *any* presents for her birthday, at least not new. When she was little, her mother would save the crappy toys that came from her kid's meals and wrap them up. Regan was seven before she'd figured it out.

When she reached Hadley's, Lane sat on the old, iron bench out front, holding another flower. "I already have flowers," she said.

He grinned and stood to his feet. "That's not the next present."

Regan glanced around, but didn't see anything else. Just the flower and Lane, both approaching her. "If *you're* the present then I want another."

"That's not very nice," he said bending down to kiss her.

"Neither is giving me something I already have."

"You could take the fun out of anything, you know that?" He reached into his back pocket and pulled out two tickets.

"Holy shit! Thirty Seconds to Mars?" she screamed, taking the concert tickets from him.

"Who's the best boyfriend in the world?"

"But this show is in Columbus! Tonight! How are we going to get there?"

He grinned and then stepped to the side, revealing the ugliest green truck she'd ever seen. "Bought it off Mr. Keets this morning."

"You bought this ugly-ass truck *just* so you could drive us to Columbus today?"

Lane shrugged. "I needed something for when I go on college interviews anyway."

Regan glanced inside at the dirty, tweed fabric covering the bench seat and the old, rope-style rugs on the floor. The gearshift was a little rusty, but, for the most part, it was clean. And it was Lane's. "This is perfect."

Lane pushed the rusty, chrome-buttoned handle and opened the squeaky door. "Your chariot awaits, m'lady."

Regan squealed—she actually *squealed*—as she held onto his hand for support and climbed into the truck. She began to buckle her seat belt, then quickly changed her mind and slid to the center when Lane climbed in the driver's side.

"There's no lap belt," he warned.

She shrugged. "We're just driving around here, right? Besides, this thing is a tank." *And I've always wanted to do this,* she added silently. "I'll shift." Lane turned the engine over, pulled onto the road, and wrapped his arm around her. She fit so easily in the crook of his arm, like she was meant to be there. "Thank you. This is the best birthday I've ever had."

"It's not over yet," he responded with a chuckle.

"Doesn't have to be. It's still the best." She nudged her nose against his chest. "No one's ever spent so much time on me. I mean . . . on making me happy."

"I'd do anything for you. Anything." Lane glanced down a moment, then back toward the road. "What the hell is this?"

"What?" she asked, springing back up. They were at the red light in front of the animal shelter. "What is it?"

"Stay here." Lane pushed the parking brake in, climbed from the truck, and headed toward a crowd near the back of the shelter. He'd nearly made it before Regan heard the singing.

"Will?" she whispered, scooting to get a better look out the window. Then she heard the singing again, and saw Lane weaving in a panic through the crowd. "Will!"

Regan sprinted from the truck, leaving the engine running, and took the same path Lane had through the maze of people. Will's voice grew louder as she neared, the giggling and mumbling of the crowd more distinct as she passed. When she caught up with Lane, he stood beside a large, metal shed.

"Will, come on, man. Not today. It's Regan's birthday!" Lane shouted through the door. "Come out of there."

"What is it? What's he doing?" Regan asked.

"Been in there for almost two hours," a young woman answered beside Lane. She wore an apron with a paw print stitched onto the side. "I knew something was off the minute he came into the shelter. He was shaking, and, when I asked what he was doing there, he screamed something about choices to me."

"Will! Open up!" Lane shouted again.

"Choices?" Regan verified.

"Yeah, he said 'more impossible f-ing choices.'"

"Was he not on the schedule today?"

The woman shook her head. "He always takes this day off. Every year. It's the only day he refuses to work. It's written on his damn file."

Regan stepped closer. "Why? Why today?"

"Today's the day," she whispered, followed by something else Regan couldn't make out over Lane's shouting, Will's singing, and the crowd's laughing.

"What day? I can't hear you."

"The day he killed his baby girl!" she shouted.

A hush fell over the crowd, and, suddenly, everyone's eyes were on Regan, even Lane's. It all made sense. Will wanting to take her to the cemetery yesterday. The morbid look on his face when he saw the flowers on the porch. He had no idea today was Regan's birthday. No idea he'd have to choose between celebrating one daughter's birth and mourning another's passing.

Impossible. Fucking. Choices.

Afraid she might throw up, Regan clenched her stomach and covered her mouth. Emma died on her sister's eleventh birthday. On *Regan's* eleventh birthday. And all Regan could think about at that moment was how she wished Will would choose her.

How fucking sick was that?

She looked toward Lane, pleading with her eyes for something that would make her wake from this horrible dream, maybe an excuse that would allow her to forgive herself for these guilty thoughts playing in her head. But she looked for something they both knew Lane couldn't give. There was only one man who could.

"Will!" Lane yelled, tearing his eyes away from hers. "Open up. Regan's here."

They stood silently and waited for a reply that never came. Just more singing.

And sirens.

"The crazy man is back today.

Guard your kids and stay away.

He might not have a tail or horns,

But the devil comes in different forms."

"What is that song?" Regan asked.

Lane shrugged. "I don't know. He sings it every time he flips out."

"What do you mean *flips out*? He's just upset! He's having a hard time processing all this because it's my birthday. He'll be fine."

Three men pushed past them. Regan was about to push

back before she realized it was Sheriff Blythe, followed by two deputies. "I'm sorry. I need to ask you two to stand back."

That was when Regan noticed the very large sledgehammer in his hand. "Be careful! He could be behind—" But he pounded on the door, and the other two had their hands on their guns ready to pull. "Will! Stand back!"

The door flew off its hinges. "Fletcher, come on out before we come and get you."

"The crazy man is back today. The crazy man is back today."

Regan tried to run between the large men, but they caught her before she made it to the door. "Let me go. I can talk to him."

"Not a chance," Sheriff Blythe said.

"The crazy man is back today," echoed from inside again.

"All right, Will. You leave us no choice. We're coming in." Sheriff Blythe nodded to the deputies to go inside. A few moments later, there was a loud bang like a metal bowl crashing into the floor. And yelling. Horrible yelling. Like the sharp squeals of one hundred pigs being slaughtered.

Sheriff Blythe looked toward Lane, his eyes giving a silent demand to grab hold of Regan. His mouth a hard line, Lane pulled Regan to his chest.

"Let go of me!" Regan shouted at him, squirming to get free. From the corner of her eye, she could see the sheriff pulling a syringe from a tiny box and heading into the dark shed. And then she heard more yelling. "Let go of me now!"

"You can't do anything to help him, baby."

"I just want . . . to . . . see him!"

"But you don't know . . ." Lane stiffened. "Oh dear God."

Regan froze. "What?"

He loosened his grip enough for her to turn, though she wasn't sure if it was purposeful or in response to whatever caused his shock. She squirmed around, suddenly wishing she hadn't.

The deputies were carrying Will, who was stretched out in the air as if he were on an invisible stretcher. He was shirtless and his midsection was covered only by a thin pair of boxers, but his skin was far from bare. It was covered in writing and drawings in thick, black Magic Marker, head to toe, anywhere he could've reached. Even his face. The only word Regan could make out was the one written on his forehead.

Demon.

"Oh my God. Will!" she cried, pulling herself free of Lane's grip and running to her father's side. "Will, what did you do to yourself?"

The deputies paused, but Will didn't even look her way.

"*Daddy!*" she shouted.

At that, Will met her gaze. His eyes were empty, drained of the man she'd grown to love. His mouth was sunken and emotionless, outlined in black. "Your mother was right. You *are* beautiful." He blinked, eyelids heavier on the way back up. "Get away. Get away before I kill you again, Emma. Get away!"

Regan fell to her knees as the men hauled Will into the back of the patrol car and drove off, the image of her father fading with the dust of the road.

CHAPTER SEVENTEEN

Janey was too late.

Speeding to the airport, the first flight home the next day, 102 phone calls to busy signals, 50 more to a cell phone that was turned off—none of it mattered. The bottom line was that Janey had fucked up. She should've never left Will.

"Do you understand what I'm telling you?" Dr. Granger asked.

Nodding, Janey turned her gaze toward the window, out at the gray sky. "You're saying this is more than just a typical episode."

"I'm saying that it's time we admit Will's illness may be more like your father's."

Janey tightened her jaw. "I've told you, Will is *not* like my father."

Dr. Granger placed his gold wire–frame glasses on the desk and pinched the bridge of his nose. "There's nothing to be ashamed of, here. Schizophrenia is hereditary. There's nothing you could've done to change any of it."

"Will is Bipolar. He's just had a bad day. Hell, he's had a bad five years." Janey stood and paced back and forth. "Maybe we need to adjust his medication."

"It won't help if he's not taking it."

"What do you mean? He *is* taking it."

"That's not what the tox screen indicated. And the half-life of lithium is only—"

"I know what the half-life is, Dr. Granger!"

He sat back in his chair, tapping on his desk. "Then you know that if Will skips even one dose, he can slip into a manic state. When's the last time you saw him take it?"

She couldn't remember now. Two or three days? But she'd asked Lindsay, every morning and every night. And Lindsay had said yes. None of this made any sense.

"It's been a long day," Janey said. "I just want to see my brother."

Dr. Granger nodded with a sigh. "We've sedated him. He'll be out for a while. But you're welcome to go sit—"

She headed toward the office door before he finished.

"Janey, wait!" he shouted, causing her to turn. Dr. Granger climbed from his desk chair, his old knees clicking as he stepped toward her. "I've been treating your family since I first became a doctor, and I have to tell you. . . . I've never seen anything like this."

"Don't patronize me. I'm the one who found him with his wrists cut open, remember?"

"I'm simply telling you this is different." He framed her shoulders with his hands. "It's much easier to dismiss a man's thoughts when they aren't spelled across him."

Janey tugged on the door, undeterred by his warning. "Room 526?"

Dr. Granger gave one quick nod, dropping his hands back to his sides.

The air felt thinner in the hallway. Cooler. A place more suitable to break into a million pieces. Janey charged down the long corridor toward the elevator. She refused to believe it. Yes, her brother was a mentally ill man, but not to the degree her father had been. Will didn't see angels or claim to talk to God, he just found comfort in talking to his deceased daughter. He hadn't cut himself because the voices in his head told him to, he'd cut himself because he didn't believe he deserved to live. And he'd never, *never* lock Janey inside the crawl space as an offering to a demon that didn't exist.

Biting her trembling lip, she stepped inside the elevator and pushed floor five. Janey hadn't thought about that day in years. She'd been trapped for six hours before her mother and Will came home. She didn't remember where they'd been or what game she'd been playing when her father had grabbed her by her overalls. At six, details like that don't matter.

But she did remember clinging to the crawl space door and praying the darkness didn't overcome her. She remembered screaming so loud her voice went hoarse and listening to her father's footsteps above. She remembered the brightness of the afternoon sun when her mother pulled her out, and squinting enough to see Will charging after their father with his baseball bat.

She didn't care what Dr. Granger said. This was her brother—the protector, the hero. This was why she'd fight for him any day he needed it.

When the elevator dinged and the doors opened, Janey exhaled a tense breath she hadn't realized she'd been holding. Maybe it was the minor case of claustrophobia, maybe it was because Lindsay was the first thing she saw on the other side.

"Oh, thank God you're here," Lindsay cried and pulled her into an embrace. "I am so sorry. Had I known . . ."

"It wouldn't have mattered," Janey responded, trying to convince herself of this, as well as Lindsay. Even if Janey had told her about the anniversary of Emma's death, no one had known about Regan's birthday. And that was the real trigger. "There was nothing you could've done."

Lindsay pulled away and wiped her damp cheeks. "It's just that—"

"Aunt Janey!" Regan threw herself into Janey's arms. "It was awful. It was so awful."

"Shh . . . shh." Janey closed her eyes and took in the scent of Regan's hair, the shaking of her body, the pitch of her sobs. What Regan must've gone through finding Will like that. The first time Janey had found him, she'd cried for three days. Now there was very little that shocked her when it came to her brother.

"They won't let us in to see Dad!"

"He's asleep anyway, sweetie. He wouldn't know if you were there or not."

"But I would." Regan pulled away, eyes full of anger. "I would, damn it! I want to see him! I need to know that he's okay!"

Janey tucked her niece's hair behind her ear and offered a calming smile. Something else Janey no longer had—an emphatic desire to see Will in such a state. Not because she didn't care for his well-being, but because she knew that, even if he still had all his fingers and toes, Will would never be okay. "You'll get to see him. I promise. I just need to see him first, all right?"

Lane stepped from the corner, reaching for Regan's hand. Janey hadn't realized he was there. "Baby, why don't we get out of here for a couple hours? We can get everyone some food and be back before he wakes up."

"Yeah, food sounds great. And some decent coffee too," Janey encouraged.

Regan considered this a moment, but then nodded hesitantly. "It was all just too much."

"What, sweetie? What was too much?"

"Me dropping into his life. You leaving him for the first time. Lindsay and him and . . . whatever is going on between them." She stepped into the elevator with Lane. "He wanted to be better for all of us, but it was just too much."

"Too much," Janey echoed, an uneasiness filling her stomach as she swallowed the weight of Regan's words. "Too much."

Lindsay? Will?

Lindsay *and* Will?

As soon as the elevator doors closed, she turned to Lindsay. "What's she talking about?"

Lindsay took a deep breath, but didn't speak. She didn't need to. The confession was written in her wide, glazed eyes.

Lindsay and Will.

"Are you out of your fucking mind?" Janey growled.

"Just let me explain."

Janey stepped toward her, but Lindsay backed away. "Explain what? That, when I was gone, you took advantage of my sick brother? Will's heart is only so big! It was hard enough for him to make room for Regan without completely destroying it. And you just come along and shove yourself in there. You've compromised every single bit of progress he's made."

"You make it sound like I did this on purpose."

"Didn't you?"

"No! No, I didn't. It just happened; I couldn't help it."

"You couldn't help it? Is that why you lied to me about making him take his pills?"

Lindsay blinked. "I didn't lie! He did take his pills! I saw him, every time!"

"Was that before or after you fucked him?" Janey spun on her heels. "Get the hell out of here and don't come back."

"I can't believe you think so little of me," Lindsay said, following behind her.

Me neither.

"I did *not* set out to seduce Will! And the last thing I wanted to do was hurt you!"

Then why did you?

"Damn it, Janey! Haven't you ever fallen for someone you knew you *shouldn't?*"

Janey came to a halt. She hadn't realized she was crying until Lindsay's distorted image came back into view, or that such a simple question could be so hard to answer with a giant lump in her throat. So instead of speaking, Janey took two small steps toward Lindsay, framed Lindsay's face in her hands, and gave her the kiss she should have that day on the swing.

Lindsay didn't move. And though Janey wanted to imagine it was because Lindsay was considering what Janey offered her, she knew it was only from shock.

Janey pulled away. "Does that answer your question?" she asked, then turned and marched down the hallway, never looking back at the rejection she knew was written all over Lindsay's face.

Sometime between when she'd arrived in Half Moon Hollow and now, the corn had weathered to a crunchy brown. This was once the type of thing Regan never disregarded. It symbolized the passing of time, the dying of fruitfulness, the end of the summer's sun. It reminded her everyone's days were numbered, even hers. It reminded her happiness was an illusion, lasting for a finite period of time.

How had she overlooked this?

She turned her gaze from the cornfield to her wristwatch, then out the passenger side window toward the diner. Lane had been in there for fifteen minutes; how long could it take to fix a few burgers? She should be at the hospital by her father's side. Her stomach churned at the thought of Will waking up alone.

He's not alone, her mother reminded her.

But without Emma, he truly was. Regan knew that now—she knew it the minute he'd called her Emma. She would never fill that void, never be worth the sacrifice.

Then why stay?

She'd asked herself that question more than once in the past twelve hours, and all she could come up with was "I won't fail as a daughter again."

You didn't—

Regan clenched her eyes shut, cutting her mother's argument short. It didn't matter. She couldn't go back now, couldn't do things differently. She couldn't swallow her pride and settle for the scraps of her mother Steven left behind, just to have something. She would if she could. Oh God, how she would. But she couldn't.

And she would *not* make that mistake again.

The truck door opened, offering reprieve from her regret. "Damn, I never thought they'd finish," Lane said, scooting into the driver's seat. The odor of meat and grease made Regan's stomach churn more. "Thought I'd have to throw an apron on and hop behind the grill myself."

"It's okay."

"No, it's *not!* You should never have to wait. You should always come first."

Slack-jawed, Regan turned toward him. The fire in his eyes was built from more than a long wait in line. It was built from disappointment, from anger. It was built from love.

"I could kill Will for doing this to you. Fucking kill him!"

"He couldn't help it," Regan said, defending him in a strained voice.

Lane shook his head, then, in a sudden movement, framed her face in his hands. "You deserve more than this, Regan. So much more."

But did she? After everything? Maybe this was her atonement for not saving her mother—to forever be a second choice.

Regan pressed her lips to his. Maybe she could live with that as long as she had this. "Come on. We need to get back."

Dropping his hands, Lane nodded, then put the keys in the ignition. "Need anything else before we head back?"

"A cough drop, maybe?" she responded, rubbing her scratchy throat.

"In my bag under the seat."

She searched around beneath her until she felt the handles of the bag, then tugged until it came free. The smell of his soap and cologne filled the air as she unzipped it, a much-welcome change to the greasy food she wasn't hungry for. She sifted through the items, digging farther as she came up empty. Soap, shampoo, a razor, a clean pair of boxers that made Regan blush, a large envelope with a bright-orange *O* in the corner beside the words Oregon State Scholarship Department.

"Did you find it?" Lane asked.

Yes, she certainly had. She'd found more than she could handle.

"Might be in the side pouch," he said.

"What is this?" she asked, hand trembling as she held the envelope in the air.

Lane glanced over, the color draining from his face.

"Is this what all those secret meetings were about? What your stepfather was talking about at dinner?"

He pulled to the side of the road and put the truck in park. "I was going to tell you."

"Tell me what? That you're leaving me?"

"Regan—"

She threw the envelope at his chest, cutting him short, then tugged on the door handle. She didn't want to hear him say it, couldn't take another disappointment. She had to get out of there fast, before the reality knocked her to the ground like a ton of bricks.

"Regan!" he yelled. "Regan wait!"

But she didn't slow down. She kept charging forward into the field, until the snaps of the breaking cornstalks drowned out the cracking of her heart, and the scratching of the dead leaves was far more noticeable than how she shook. Until her feet gave out from under her.

"Regan! What are you doing?" Lane huffed.

"Leave me *alone!*" she cried, beating her fists into the dirt.

"Did you fall? Are you hurt?"

"Just go, Lane!"

He scooped her up.

"I said leave me alone, you lying bastard!" Regan pushed on his chest, somehow finding the strength to break free. And she felt cold. So cold.

Lane stared at her a moment. "I didn't lie."

"No. You just conveniently forgot to tell me the truth." Regan dusted herself off, then turned to continue her retreat. She should've known better. She should've seen this coming from a mile away. She would *always* be second choice.

"Fine. Go," he hollered from the distance. "Cause I'm a little fucking tired of running after you, Regan. You hear me? I'm not doing this anymore!"

And then she was alone again, nothing but the echoes of her cries to keep her going.

Will came to himself crossing the street, carrying Emma in one arm and holding Ellie with the other. How was this possible? He didn't care. It was a beautiful day full of sun. They passed by Wilson's bakery, the bank, the post office, and then the town hall came into view. "I'll run over to the hardware store to get the part I need for Emma's bike," he said, bending to kiss Ellie. "Go visit with your father, and I'll catch up."

With an odd look, Ellie took Emma from his arms. "Don't be long, okay?"

"What's wrong?"

She nodded down the street. "That girl is staring at you."

Will glanced over his shoulder to see Regan waiting by the hardware store, a shiny, pink present in her hands. "It's only Regan. She probably just wants to give Emma her birthday gift."

This explanation didn't seem to ease Ellie's doubts. "Just hurry back."

"Five minutes." He leaned into Emma and gave her an Eskimo kiss before planting his lips on her forehead. She must've been eating a cookie in the truck—she smelled like vanilla and sugar. "Don't let Poppa spoil you rotten while I'm gone, Emma J."

"Poppa says it's his job to spoil me."

"Yes, but I like it when you smell like a cookie instead of a garbage can." Will smiled and then turned his gaze back to Ellie. "Five minutes, okay?"

She hesitated a moment, then nodded and turned in the direction of her destination as Will turned toward his. Regan still stood there beside the hardware store, but now she smiled, waved. It made Will feel content knowing she was so excited to see him.

Then Will heard a scream from behind—Ellie's scream.

He'd recognize it anywhere; it was burned into his ears, though, at the moment, he couldn't remember why. He spun around, nearly tripping over his own feet, and searched out his wife and daughter in the crowd. They were being dragged away by a tall man in black.

Will set off in a sprint only to hear another scream, this one in the other direction. He glanced back over his shoulder at Regan being dragged away by another tall man. Or was it the same man? He turned toward Ellie and Emma's direction, but they were no longer in danger. They were at the town fountain waving, as Regan had done moments before. They were safe.

But when Will spun back around to rescue Regan, the cries came again from the direction of the fountain, and the man in black was no longer pulling Regan away. Will paused and glanced down at his feet. It was some sort of test, some sort of sick game. Who would do this? Who would make him choose? He knew the answer; he was just too afraid to look.

His eyes still focused on Regan, he took one giant step back-ward until the screaming from the fountain stopped, and the tall man in black appeared behind Regan. Will focused on his face—which wasn't hard because the man stared at him like he could see through him, see every thought in his head. Maybe he could. After all, the man was *him*.

Will inched forward until the man stopped approaching, but not enough for him to disappear. If he could just find the place in the middle, divide himself in half, he could save them both. It meant he couldn't have either of them, of course, but at least they would be safe. Far away from him. Far away from the demon that always showed up when he wasn't looking.

A set of car tires squealed against the asphalt, reminding Will he stood in the middle of the street, but he didn't move. He clenched his eyes shut, fell to his knees on the double-yellow line, and prayed the car would hit him to eliminate the impossible choice.

"Will? Will?" someone whispered, shaking him from behind.

When he opened his eyes, he was no longer in the street. He was in a sterile room with white walls and a bright window that hurt his eyes to look at. He attempted to massage the ache at the bridge of his nose, but his hands were restrained at his sides against something cold and metal. "Janey!" He tried to shout, but his weak voice came out as a whisper.

"I'm right here, Will. Shh . . . shh . . ."

Will squinted until his eyes adjusted in the sun, then found his sister sitting in a blue chair beside his bed. "Are they okay? Did he get them?"

Janey leaned forward. "Who, Will?"

"Me. I mean, the tall man. Did he get them, or are they safe?"

As she nodded, Janey's lip trembled. "Everyone is safe."

Will relaxed, glancing around the room. If they were okay, why weren't they here?

"Will, what do you remember? I mean, before this."

"I was walking through town with Ellie and Emma, and we saw . . ." Will stiffened again. There was something about that statement that didn't sound right. Something was off. *Someone.* He glanced around the room again, at the bars on the windows, not a painting hung on the wall, not a get-well-soon balloon anywhere to be found. Then he glanced at his hands bound to the bed, traces of black Magic Marker trailing up his arms. "Fuck," he cried. "*Fuck!*"

"Shh . . . shh . . . It's okay. It's going to be okay."

He shook his head, trying to break his hands free of the restraints to his hospital bed.

"Will, don't! You'll knock your IV loose!"

"I don't fucking care, Janey! Get me out of here!"

"You know I can't. Not until they're sure you're not a threat anymore."

Will froze. "What do you mean, *anymore?* Who did I hurt? Regan?"

Janey frowned. "The mayor said you charged after his daughter at the cemetery."

"You mean, *Ellie?*" he growled.

"That's not how Tom said it."

Will leaned in as far as his restraints would allow. "And how would you say it, sister?"

"Will—"

"Just say it! Say her name, damn it! Why do you insist on ignoring the fact that she was once my wife, *your* sister-in-law!"

"Because you insist on ignoring the fact that every time she comes around, your entire world crumbles!" Janey retorted. "She's your kryptonite, Will. No matter how strong you think you are, you see her and you're right back on your knees in that driveway like time hasn't passed."

"That's not true!"

"No?" Janey rose to her feet with her arms crossed. "Where's your daughter, Will? Your *living* daughter? And exactly what were you planning to do about Lindsay when and *if* you managed to convince Ellie to come back to you? Hmm?"

Will clenched his jaw.

"You don't know, because all that matters when you see Ellie is finding a way to go back to this perfect life you think you had. Even back then you were . . ." She paused, clarity softening the wrinkles on her face, and then whispered, "You were delusional."

He turned away and pushed the call button on his bed rail, his chained hands barely able to reach it. "Get out."

"This isn't just about what you destroyed. This is about what you never had."

"Can I help you?" the nurse said from the intercom.

Will cleared his throat. "I want her out of here. Now!"

"Don't you understand? You're throwing away a chance at a real life because you can't let go of a life that never existed in the first place."

"*Get out!*"

"But Will . . ."

"I want you gone," he demanded, not able to look her in the face, not able to see the truth. "And don't come back."

"Mr. Fletcher, just calm down!" a nurse ordered, flying into the room. And then came the familiar sting of the needle, the pressure of hot lava rushing into his thigh, into his veins. It would all be over soon.

"And what about Regan, Will? What am I going to tell her?"

"Tell her . . . I don't want her either." The words brought another sting, this one in his heart. But it was better this way. This was the way it had to be, the way it would *always* be.

"You don't want me?"

Will forced his heavy eyes open at the cry of the falling angel, searching it out in the fog. It wasn't real. He'd imagined it. Just like his father had so many years ago.

And then his sister stepped aside, and he saw the angel with his own eyes.

"You don't want me?" it repeated.

"Don't listen to him, sweetie. It's the drugs talking." Janey walked to where the angel stood and placed her arm over its wings. "Tell her, Will. Tell her you didn't mean it."

"Tell Regan . . . Superman's dead," he slurred, no longer able to hold open his heavy eyes. "Tell her . . . he never existed at all."

Janey pulled the quilt from the back of the couch and spread it across her niece. It had taken five hours, but Regan had finally cried herself to sleep. Five hours of holding on to make sure she didn't run. Five hours of absorbing the trembling of her sobs. Five hours of keeping herself together so that Regan could completely unravel in her arms.

Now it was Janey's turn.

She crept through the kitchen and out the back screen door, her feet moving almost independently toward the place she always went to fall. The loft was where she and Will had hidden as kids when their father had a bad day, and where they'd fallen asleep sitting up talking the night after burying their mom. It was the one place she felt safe, because it was the one place her brother had always been. But this time, Will wasn't there, and Janey began to wonder if he ever really had been.

It wasn't fair. It just wasn't fair.

Ignoring the smell of ash and burned wood that met her as she opened the barn door, Janey headed straight for the ladder up to the loft. She wasn't sure what she expected to gain by going there. She just needed to be near her brother, surrounded by all the things he loved. Then she saw the leopard-print belt peeking out beneath the covers of the broken cot, and was reminded that one of those things was Lindsay.

She tore the belt free and held it in her hands, feeling the velvet texture between her fingers. So this was where her brother and her best friend had made love, who knew how many times. This was where he'd touched Lindsay in all the places Janey had dreamed of touching, and said things Janey had never had the courage to say. And worse yet, this was where Lindsay had so easily found a shortcut into Will's heart, something Janey'd been searching for, for years.

A low grumble rising in her throat, she launched the belt across the loft, over the rail to the barn floor below. She had given every part of her soul to these two people, only to have them find what they were looking for within each other.

It wasn't fair, damn it. It just wasn't fair.

She closed her eyes and took a deep breath, the campfire smell returning her to her senses. Leaning against the loft rail, she glanced around the barn and spotted the metal trash can in which Will burned his scraps. Why was it inside the barn? It was a wonder he hadn't blown the place up, or died from carbon monoxide poisoning.

Maybe that had been his aim.

Janey descended the ladder, her brain flooded with memories of childhood camping trips. She once loved that smell. It was one of the few times they had been a normal family, doing normal things. Now it would forever be associated with this, corralled inside her heart with all the other pieces of her life held hostage by Will's illness. How much more could that corral hold before its fences broke?

It just wasn't fair.

Fighting back the tears, she grabbed a broom from the wall and poked around in the trash can with the handle. Mostly scraps, a few pieces of cardboard, and then she saw it—the scrap of what he'd been trying to destroy.

It was supposed to be a surprise, but Janey had seen it the day before she'd left for L.A., only the roof was lacking then. The charred ribbon still hanging from the shingles meant he had finished it. He had finished his birdhouse, created the perfect home for the red cardinal rejects on the porch.

And then he'd destroyed it.

"It's not fucking fair!" she screamed, kicking the trash can to its side. She swung the broom like a bat, swinging at scraps of wood, half-finished projects, paint brushes, anything. She swung until she had no more rage to give, and then sank to the floor in tears.

She was exhausted, not from swinging or from lack of sleep, but from five years of trying. She was tired of sacrificing, tired of putting her life to the side so that her brother could continue to ignore his. She was tired of saving someone who didn't want to be saved.

And poor Regan. How much more heartbreak could that kid take? How much more abandonment? How long until she too laid among the splintered wood of Will's regrets?

Janey couldn't let that happen. She wouldn't.

Wiping her cheeks with her sleeve, she pulled the cell phone from her back pocket and dialed the phone number.

"Hello? Janey, is that you?"

Janey nodded, even though Gretchen couldn't see it. "We're coming home."

Lindsay held her vodka tonic like a warning sign to those passing. She shouldn't be here—not with Will in the hospital. She shouldn't be at the mayor's house on principle alone, seeing that he was partly the reason Will was tied down to a bed in the first place. But she couldn't lose her job too. It was the only thing keeping her sane.

God, she'd made a mess of things, but it all made sense when she looked back on it. The past few weeks just hadn't been the same. There had been times when Lindsay had caught Janey staring at her for no reason at all, eyes so deep Lindsay thought she'd never find her way out. Or the way Janey always seemed so tense when they hugged and appeared to be holding back a million words behind her lips when they spoke. And then the "friendly" kiss on the porch.

Lindsay had been too busy pining over Will to realize Janey had been pining over her.

"They say you're close to him?" a voice said from behind.

Lindsay spun around, spilling a few drops of her drink onto the satin fabric of Ellie Bradford's peacock-blue dress. "I'm so sorry."

Ignoring the spilled drink all together, Ellie took a step closer. She moved like a dancer, light on her feet, with a grace and elegance that matched her porcelain skin and petite frame. It was no wonder Will was still in love with her. Ellie Bradford was absolutely stunning.

Ellie gazed at the crowd like a lookout on a robbery and tucked a stray auburn curl behind her ear. "You're close to the Fletchers?"

"I am," Lindsay answered. "I mean, I *was*."

"Is he . . . okay?"

Lindsay raised her brow. "I don't really know. They wouldn't—"

"Laugh."

"I'm sorry?"

"Laugh!" Ellie demanded and then giggled like a child. A moment later, she abruptly stopped. "They're watching me. I don't have much time."

"Much time for what?"

"You've heard about the petition in town?"

"Petition?"

"To have Will committed."

Oh. That petition. "Yes. I've heard about it."

"They have everything they need now. The hearing will be next week."

The weight of Ellie's words hit Lindsay in the chest like a million concrete blocks. "But *they* can't decide that. No judge is going to commit a man just based on a few signatures."

"I assure you, they absolutely can."

"How do you know this?"

"Trust me." Ellie's eyes met Lindsay's. "I just know."

Lindsay closed her mouth and nodded.

"You need to find him a lawyer. Somebody who's not within the county limits—my father has all of them on his side. Do you understand?"

"Yes."

"Do it quickly. He won't have long to prepare for his case."

"I will," Lindsay promised.

Ellie offered another laugh. "They're coming. Any quick questions?"

"Why are you doing this?" Lindsay blurted out, trying to find *they* in the crowded room.

Ellie's fake grin disappeared into a thin line. "Because Will isn't the man they make him out to be. Never has been."

Lindsay swallowed hard. "You're still in love with him."

"I will always love Will."

"There's my Ellie!" Mayor Bradford neared them, holding out his hands as if he had an offering of some sort. "You must've snuck down the stairs past me."

Ellie smiled, planting a kiss on his cheek. "I was just telling Principal Shepherd how impressed I am with her block scheduling program this year."

"We're still working out a few bumps, but this time next year everything will be running like clockwork." Lindsay downed the last of her vodka. "I think I'm going to get another drink. Would you like to join me, Ellie?"

"Ellie doesn't drink," Mayor Bradford answered for her. "And I hate to be the doting father, but I really must steal her away to show her off around the party."

Lindsay waited for Ellie to speak for herself, but she only

grimaced. "Well, I can't argue with the man of the hour, now can I? Maybe I'll see you around the party later, Ellie?"

But Mayor Bradford had already whisked her away to the next group of people where she shook hands, twirled in her dress, and smiled as if the man she loved wasn't tied down to a bed waiting for his fate to be decided by the very people she schmoozed.

The sight nauseated Lindsay.

Lindsay waited until they'd rounded the corner into the next room, then grabbed her coat and purse from the closet. As she exited the Bradford estate, determined to save Will from the mob heading his way, two thoughts jumbled in the back of her mind. One: Ellie Bradford had divorced Will under someone else's command. And two: Lindsay never once saw anyone else with Mayor Bradford that would constitute Ellie's excessive use of the word *they*.

CHAPTER EIGHTEEN

"**B**ut they can't do that!"

"Janey, now just calm down," Dr. Granger advised.

"I will *not* calm down." Janey rose to her feet. "I want to see this list! I want to see who voted to lock my brother away in some . . . *institute.*"

"It doesn't matter who signed it."

"It does to me!" She marched toward the window. How could they say those things? How could they believe a man who caught butterflies in jars for his dead daughter could hurt a hair on anyone's head? And how, this day in age, could something like this happen? When her father had been committed, people didn't know much about mental illness. But now? In 2016? "I don't understand. I don't understand how you could let this happen again."

"Now, Janey, this isn't exactly like your father's situation. They've only brought a petition to the state asking that he be evaluated. The final decision on Will's sanity will be at the discretion of Judge Wheaton."

Judge Wheaton, a man Janey and Will had never met, would determine her brother's sanity. And this was supposed to offer her comfort? "If he decides Will is crazy, then what?"

"They admit him into a psychiatric hospital for treatment."

"Against his will."

It was more of a statement than a question, which was why Janey was surprised when Dr. Granger answered, "Not exactly."

She spun around. "What do you mean, not exactly? They'd be forcing him into treatment for an illness I don't even think he has. I'd say that's against his will."

With a deep breath, Dr. Granger leaned back in his chair. "It means that Will has decided not to contest this."

Janey stiffened. "Say again?"

"He believes that if everyone else feels he's a danger, then maybe he's better off somewhere where he can't hurt anyone."

"And who put an idea like that into his head?" Janey asked, inching forward.

Dr. Granger pursed his lips, clenching the silver pen in his hands. "It is my job as Will's doctor to fully explain all the possibilities of the situation at hand."

"It is your job to make him well. And it's my job to make sure he never has to make decisions like this. Apparently, we both suck at our jobs." Janey tore her purse from the chair and tossed it over her shoulder. "Now, if you'll excuse me, I'd like to discuss this with my brother."

"He doesn't want to see you, Janey."

She rolled her eyes. "What else is new? Will never wants to see me. And I'm his custodian, so he doesn't really have a choice, now does he?"

"This is different. He's requested that you and Regan not be permitted on his floor." Dr. Granger stood, fingertips pressed hard against his desk. "And I've approved the request."

Janey clenched her jaw. "Are you telling me that I can't see my brother?"

The weight of Dr. Granger's stare buried any argument Janey had, blurred her intentions even further. Ten minutes ago, she'd walked into this office ready to give up on her brother. Five minutes ago, she'd changed her mind. Now, Janey knew she didn't have a choice.

She never did.

"Will's also asked me to inform you that any efforts to put him inside that courtroom will only be detrimental to your case. Do you understand?"

Janey stared. She could only stare.

"It's time, Janey. It's time to let go."

A tear slid from her eye. "I don't know how to let go."

Dr. Granger frowned. "Neither does your brother, and look where that's gotten him."

Lindsay pushed the doorbell, then shifted her weight back and forth on the front-door steps. This was a bad idea. No, this was a *terrible* idea. She wasn't even sure if it was an entirely possible idea. But if there was one thing she'd learned from the Fletchers, it was this—sometimes you have to take the dead-end path if you want to find a place to break through the brush.

To her surprise, the door flung open fairly quickly. "Lindsay," he said.

She did her best to smile. "Hi, David."

He opened the storm door to offer her entrance. "Is everything okay?"

"Everything's fine," she responded, because that was what she'd always said when David asked if everything was okay. She stepped past him inside to the foyer and glanced around. They'd painted since she'd last been here.

"Renée is out right now."

Unlike you, I hadn't been looking for her, is what she wanted to say, but she bit her tongue before it came out. It would be much easier to get David's help if she could keep her emotions under wrap.

"Do you want something to drink? I could make some tea."

She followed him toward the kitchen. "Just water, please. Not a fan of tea."

"Since when?"

"Since forever," she said, placing her purse on the table.

Motioning for her to sit, David spun on his toes back toward the refrigerator. He seemed shorter than the last time she'd seen him. Maybe it was relative, like the way Half Moon High's halls felt like narrow passages in comparison to the corridors of her high school in Pittsburgh. In comparison to Will's towering stance, David was just tiny.

"So . . ." David took a seat, folding his hands on the mahogany table. "What brings you all the way back to Pittsburgh on this chilly day?"

Trying not to roll her eyes, Lindsay took a swig from the fancy, blue-glass bottle he'd placed in front of her. Why couldn't he just ask her what the hell she wanted? Why did he have to be so proper and poetic with his words? And why did his once-receding hairline seem to be moving forward? "Did you get hair plugs?"

"I'm sorry?" he asked.

"Your hair. It looks . . . fuller."

Chagrined, David raked his hand through his hair. "I . . . well . . . yes."

Lindsay crossed her arms and tilted her head. "I thought you didn't believe in all that reversing-the-aging-process mumbo jumbo."

"And I thought you liked tea."

A smile tugged at her lips, followed by a low chuckle and then a series of louder ones. All this time, she'd thought he'd found someone to suit his needs better than she had. But now she had to wonder, had David found his perfect match? Or had he found his . . . *David*?

"I'm not sure I see the humor in this," he admitted.

Of course he didn't. When they'd been married, Lindsay had dismissed him as a man of certain sophistication, but now she just saw him as a guy with a giant stick up his ass. This only made her laugh harder and miss Will's candor that much more.

"Lindsay, forgive me for asking such a blunt question, but are you stoned?"

"I'm sorry," she sighed, fighting off the laughter. "It's just, the more things change, the more they stay the same. Ya know?"

He blinked. Apparently he didn't know.

"Anyway, back to why I'm here." Lindsay straightened in her chair, dropped her smile, and took a deep breath. "I've come to collect a debt."

"But my last payment from the divorce settlement isn't due until December."

"Not that debt. The one you owe my heart."

He fidgeted for a moment, then glanced over his shoulder before leaning in. "Lindsay, I'm a married man. I'm going to be a father soon."

"I don't want *you*, David. Trust me. I just need your help getting what I do want. And, I figure, it's the least you can do after everything."

Almost offended, he deflated. "What do you need?"

Lindsay relaxed in her chair without losing his gaze. "Are you still licensed in Ohio?"

New York City. That's all Regan could think of as she stared at the shiny, big apples piled in the wicker basket and swirled her spoon around the bowl of chicken soup Janey had made.

New York. The Big Apple. A place where there were bigger freaks than her walking the streets and crowds she could get lost in. All her favorite bands played a subway ride away, and the libraries were bigger than Half Moon Hollow. There were coffee shops in New York, decent pizza parlors in New York, and freaking Time Square was in New York.

Lane isn't in New York, her mother said. *Or Will.*

Regan sighed, unsure if those were pros or cons.

Every time she thought of them, her chest swelled up like a balloon, like it had in the days after her mother died. It had been easier to discount back then, when she didn't know how it felt to be completely full. Now, it would forever feel like something was missing. Her heart, maybe. Her breath. All the things she'd once known how to ignore. She'd give anything to learn that trick again.

When would she accept it? Her head had come to terms with it, so why wouldn't her heart catch up? They didn't want her. Just like her mother hadn't wanted her.

"Why didn't you want me?" Regan asked.

But before her mother could answer, the back door opened and Janey stepped inside.

"Hey! Good evening," Janey said in her fake, cheery voice. It sorta made Regan want to dump the soup on her. "Didn't think you'd still be awake."

Still awake. As if sleeping was an option.

"How was the soup?"

Regan stood, carried her uneaten soup to the sink, and dumped the bowl of slimy noodles down the drain. "Good. Thanks."

"It was your grandmother's recipe," Janey added. "She nursed many of my broken hearts with it when I was younger."

Grandmother. It was strange, hearing Janey refer to her as that. Even stranger, seeing that Regan didn't have a father to speak of at the moment. "I didn't realize they knew you . . . well, that you had broken hearts."

Janey smiled. "There's more than one kind of broken heart."

Boy, didn't Regan know it. "Did it work for you? The soup?"

Janey's grin faded. "No. Not really."

Point made, Regan gave one quick nod, then returned to the table for the jug of milk.

"So . . . I was wondering if you'd decided anything about New York," Janey asked. "I know you don't want to leave your father, but I think it would be good."

Regan continued to the refrigerator, milk jug in hand. "Good for me? Or good for you?"

"Good for both of us."

Regan rolled her eyes as she closed the refrigerator, the magnet-pinned papers shuffling in the breeze as she did. One held her A+ anatomy test, another a photo of her in her woodworking glasses, the last a casserole recipe she and Will wanted to bake for Janey's big congratulations dinner. They were more than just paper and ink, more than letters and lines. They were proof.

This was home. *She* was home. She couldn't start all over again. Could she?

"We could start fresh. Leave all this behind us," Janey continued. "You deserve so much better than this."

At that, Regan's fragile armor began to crumble. Just a few

days ago Lane had said the same thing. How could anyone possibly know what she deserved, if they didn't know the sins she'd committed? The only one who could even come close to understanding was her father.

He'd killed someone too.

"Maybe we could go for a long weekend, just to look around," Janey offered.

"I don't want to go to New York," Regan snapped. "I want my father! Back here with me! The way things were!"

Janey stared, mouth hanging open. Regan couldn't blame her, really; she'd surprised herself with the answer as well. But this was home. She wouldn't leave. She wanted her life back, not a new one in a new city.

"Regan, I think there's something you need to hear."

"No. No more excuses. You promised me. You promised me that no matter what, we could work things out."

Janey sighed. "Not this."

"Why not? We'll wait until he comes home and just try again."

"Because, he's not coming home."

"Sure, he is. As soon as he's better—"

"No, Regan," Janey interrupted, eyes stern as a bull's. "The town has filed a petition to have your father committed to the state mental hospital, and he's decided not to contest it."

Regan deflated into her seat, eyes glazing over as she tried to make sense of what her aunt said. A petition. The state mental hospital. Her father wouldn't contest it.

Her father wouldn't come home.

"But . . . we can't just let him do this," Regan cried.

"I've been to a dozen lawyers today, and everyone said if Will doesn't want to fight, there's nothing that we can do. And frankly, I'm tired of fighting for him."

"But . . ." She met Janey's gaze. "Who will take care of Emma if he's gone?"

Janey stiffened. "Oh, not you, too. Am I the only sane—"

The doorbell sounded, making them both jump. Regan glanced at the clock, verifying it was too late for a social visit, then back at Janey. "Are you gonna get that?"

Janey shook her head.

"Why not?"

"Because, only bad news comes to the door at this hour."

"And ignoring it will make it go away?" Regan pushed away from the table.

"Regan, wait!"

Regan waved her off and headed for the front door, just as it rang again. Bad news? Her boyfriend was on his way to Oregon, her father to a state mental institution, and her mother and sister were lying in cold graves. At this point, how could things possibly get any worse?

And then she opened the door and realized they could.

"Hi, Regan," Lindsay said. "Is Janey home? Or is she at the hospital?"

Fidgeting, Regan glanced back toward the kitchen. Janey had said it would be a cold day in hell before she ever let Lindsay Shepherd back into that house. In fact, she'd said it twice. Regan didn't have any idea what all that was about, but she did know one thing—if Janey and Will weren't keeping their promises these days, why should she?

She stepped to the side. "Come on in. She's in the kitchen."

Lindsay walked past. Two seconds later, a man came through the door behind her. Was this the reason Janey was pissed? Was Lindsay screwing around behind Will's back?

"Who the hell is this?" Regan seethed.

"David Shepherd," the man responded, holding out his hand.

Regan stared at it a moment and then turned her hard gaze toward Lindsay.

"He's the toothbrush," Lindsay clarified with a wink. "And your father's new lawyer."

He was much too short for Lindsay. And balding.

This was the crazy shit Janey thought as she pulled the mugs from the cupboard. She should've escorted this floozy and her ex-husband to the door, but, instead, she poured two cups of midnight coffee—one with sugar and a dash of cinnamon for Mr. Bigshot Lawyer. Lindsay, of course, took hers black to match the color of her heart.

Gritting her teeth, Janey placed the hot mugs on the kitchen table and then slid into the seat across from David Shepherd, Lindsay and Regan on either side. "You have ten minutes."

Lindsay cleared her throat. "Well, first off, I just want to explain—"

"Your brother is in a serious pickle, Ms. Fletcher," David Shepherd interrupted. "And this is only the beginning."

Lindsay tightened and then untightened her jaw. "Still interrupting me, David."

"I'm sorry, but ten minutes isn't much time." He scooted his chair closer, placing his hands on the table. Perhaps he was balding, but this man had the hairiest knuckles Janey had ever seen. "Your brother's track record is two miles long. Frankly, I can't believe he's managed to evade commitment as long as he has. And now this petition?"

"Wait, wait, wait. How did you know about the petition?" Janey asked.

Lindsay glanced at David, silently requesting permission to share his ten minutes. "Ellie Bradford warned me. At the mayor's dinner."

The mayor's dinner. The one Lindsay had offered to give up so Janey could attend the awards she'd slept through. Or was it so she could move in and seduce Janey's sick brother? "Glad to see you took time to grieve over the loss of my friendship."

Regan grunted. "How is that any different from you making moving arrangements back to New York the minute Will woke up?"

"Stay out of this!" Janey yelled.

"Don't yell at her for speaking the truth," Lindsay retorted. "And what else was I going to do anyway? I was driving myself crazy at home."

"Better than driving my brother back to the looney bin."

"Ladies!" David shouted. Or at least, what Janey assumed was a shout. His voice was a little weak for a man. "You can fight about what did and didn't happen after we discuss the strategies for how I'm going to save Will."

"Will doesn't want to be saved." And Janey would be damned if she'd let Lindsay Shepherd come to the rescue. "You can show yourself to the door."

"So that's it?" Lindsay asked.

Janey pushed away from the table, grabbing her coffee cup.

"Five years of fighting, and that's it? You're just going to let him give up?"

Janey dropped the mug into the sink, the clash against the cast iron echoing like a bell at the start of a boxing round. "Will gave up a long time ago. I'm just finally ready to accept it."

Lindsay pursed her lips, eyes wide. "Well I don't. I don't accept it."

"Then you're in for a hell of a lot of disappointment."

"I don't believe that. And I don't believe for a minute you believe that either." Lindsay pushed herself from the table and approached Janey. "I saw it. I saw the hope in his eyes when he looked at Regan. And when he touched me, I felt his desire to hold onto something more than the pain. Somewhere beneath that iron cage is a man who wants to live again. To *love* again."

"How convenient for you." Janey crossed her arms. "You saw what you wanted to see."

"She's right. I saw it too," Regan mumbled. "He took me to the cemetery Friday."

"And then on Saturday he locked himself in a shed and covered his body in Magic Marker tattoos. Or don't you remember that?"

The hope drained from Regan's eyes like the receding tide. Janey had been caught in that current many times, fought against the crushing waves. Which only reconfirmed the decision she'd made two days ago on the barn floor and again today on the drive home from the last attorney's office.

Dr. Granger was right. She had to let go. She had to let her brother swim for himself, if she wanted to save her niece from drowning in a lifetime of disappointment.

"Trust me, Regan. I know how this story ends. But it doesn't have to be this way. We can go to New York and start fresh." Janey walked over to where Regan sat and rested her hands on the girl's slumped shoulders. "Don't let Will's illness destroy your life."

"I can't believe my ears!" Lindsay spat.

Regan glanced between the two women before settling on Janey.

Janey didn't know if that was a yes, but she'd take it. "Well then, Mr. Shepherd, it appears we won't be needing your services after all."

"Actually, Ms. Fletcher," David Shepherd said, offering a wry smile. "Unless you're the legal guardian of Regan Whitmer, it appears you *do*."

Will missed forks the most. And underwear.

The forks he could understand. There was a chance he could poke himself to death, but the underwear? If Will was going to commit suicide, he would've doused himself in gasoline and lit a match, not strangled himself with used underwear. He did have standards, after all.

Had he tried to light himself on fire? He couldn't remember. Bits of that day came back at the least expected moments— Regan's birthday shrine when the flower delivery man passed his door, or picking up that black Magic Marker when the plump RN wrote his daily stats on the dry-erase board. But that's all they were—just bits—and Will was happy to leave it at that.

He shoveled another spoonful of flaked mashed potatoes and mushy peas into his mouth before deciding he wasn't hungry. Was this lunch or dinner? Will stared out the window, looking for clues. The nurses usually didn't care as much about lunch as they did dinner—he didn't need to end up with another feeding tube down his throat.

"Mr. Fletcher?"

Great. Another doctor to diagnose him as a certified cuckoo. "What time is it?" Will muttered without looking at the man.

"Uh . . ." There was a rustling behind him. "Quarter to one."

Will's lips turned up in something that felt like a grin, but only for a moment. He closed his eyes and imagined that for dinner he'd have a hamburger.

"Mr. Fletcher, I only have an hour before I have to meet with the judge."

Will's eyes snapped open as he turned toward the voice. This wasn't a doctor at all. This was a lawyer. Even if the man hadn't mentioned a judge, Will would've known from the fancy, leather briefcase and pink-and-gray, argyle sweater-vest.

The man set his briefcase beside the visitor's chair and approached with an odd smile, holding his hand out. "My name is David Shepherd. I'm a civil rights attorney."

Will stared at the man's hand, but chose not to shake it.

"Your sister has retained my services for your hearing, as well as Dr. Sinclaire's," the man added, giving up on the handshake. "She'll meet with you tomorrow. I'll tell her to come before lunch so you're more awake."

"I'm sorry, what did you say your name was again?"

"Shepherd. David Shepherd. Your council." The man pulled a legal pad from his briefcase and scribbled a note. "You do understand what that means, yes?"

"Shepherd," Will repeated, the name soft as cotton on his tongue. "You're Lindsay's ex."

David Shepherd grinned. "I didn't realize she'd told you about me."

"Don't look so satisfied. None of it was good."

David Shepherd's smile faded to a grimace. He cleared his throat. "Well, as I was saying, Dr. Sinclaire will evaluate you tomorrow and make her recommendations."

"I already have a doctor."

"Well, Will . . ." He paused, meeting Will's gaze. "May I call you Will?"

"Knock yourself out."

"Well, Will, Dr. Granger has decided to testify for the state, recommending your committal. Under my advice, your sister felt it best to get a second opinion."

"That wasn't her decision to make." Will turned his gaze back toward the window. "Neither was hiring you. So, if you don't mind, I'd—"

"Actually, it was Janey's decision to make, seeing that she is your guardian."

"*Legal* guardian. Not guardian."

"Be that as it may, that does give her the right to make decisions on your behalf if she feels you aren't mentally capable."

"Which I *am*, so—"

"So . . . you won't mind her hiring someone to tell the court exactly that."

Will clenched his jaw, then unclenched it. This man was sharper than the argyle sweater-vest lead Will to believe. Fortunately, Will was sharper than the ass-less, blue, polka-dot hospital gown stamped Psych Ward suggested of him. "You can't make me fight this."

"No, no. I suppose you're right. I can't make you fight this." David Shepherd placed the legal pad back in his briefcase. "In fact, those are the exact words I used when Regan begged me to represent you. But she insisted. Said something about a promise you'd made."

Will swallowed the lump of guilt in his throat. "Promise?"

"At the cemetery. Something about sticking around, no matter how hard it is."

Will thought back to that day, standing on the stone path. "Because she's my daughter and I love her. I'd do the same for you." It was his job to make sure Regan safely arrived where she needed to be, just like with Emma. No matter how much it hurt.

And where Regan needed to be was as far away from him as she could get.

"She's better off without me," he muttered, the words burning his throat. Someday, maybe she would understand. "She's better off with Janey."

"Sure, sure. If the court decides that's what's best for young Regan."

The court? "Janey doesn't need the court's approval. She

needs *my* approval. This is my decision to make, and I say Janey would make a fine mother."

"Well, that's one way to look at it. Another is that a starving artist, who just happens to be a lesbian, isn't the best fit for an impressionable, sixteen-year-old girl. Not to mention Regan is still recovering from her mother's suicide, and Janey doesn't have a stellar track record of nursing folks back from incredible loss. I mean, she couldn't even get you to take your medication twice a day—how is she going to parent a teenage girl?"

Will punched his fist into the mattress. "You smug prick! How dare you?"

"Whoa, whoa. Those aren't my words. Those were Mayor Bradford's words."

Bradford. Of course.

"But, you never know. Maybe the court won't agree. He's just the mayor, right? What does the man really know about family?"

Everything. Bradford knew everything there was to know about family. At least, that's how the town saw it. But did he have that kind of pull?

Did Will want to take the chance to find out?

"Well, good luck with that, then." Shepherd threw the strap of his briefcase over his shoulder and pulled an envelope from his back pocket. "Oh, Regan asked me to give you this."

"What is it?"

Shepherd shrugged, placing the envelope in Will's lap face-down. It wasn't sealed. Will could see the bright-purple paper peeking out from under the flap.

"See you around." Shepherd spun on his heels. "Maybe."

Will tore the paper from the envelope, though he didn't know why. He didn't need this conflict right now. He didn't need anything else fucking with his head. Then why, oh why, couldn't he refrain from reading it?

"Daddy—You're still our hero. Love, Regan & Emma."

Will's heart burst like an atom bomb, blowing every bit of his reason to pieces. He felt angry and empty, both at the same time. Fierce, yet helpless. Will felt lonely, something he hadn't allowed himself to feel since Ellie had walked out on him.

Will felt human.

"Wait!" he shouted after David, swinging his legs over the bed. "Just wait."

CHAPTER NINETEEN

There were times when even Will couldn't stand the sound of loneliness. The hum of the fluorescent lights, the whistle of his breath, the added depth to every creak of a chair and slide of a foot. He could feel the sounds vibrating in the core of his bones, at the base of his skull. It didn't happen often, but, when it did, there was no way to deny he was on his own. No way to hide from the hard truth it was his fault.

Now was one of those times.

He tucked the tips of his collar into his sweater, eyes focused on the wood grain of the oak table. As many times as he'd frequented this establishment, he'd never been inside this room. That was the first clue today wouldn't be another typical court day. There was no room for a jury, no seating for the crowd he loved to play to. Just the two oak desks and a handful of empty witness chairs scattered behind them.

And that silence. That awful silence.

"How are you holding up?" Dr. Sinclaire asked, taking the seat beside him. She was the second clue today wouldn't be ordinary.

"It's too quiet," Will responded, the truest answer he could give. "Where is everyone?"

"Committal hearings are typically closed to the public to protect the privacy of the patient. Only witnesses and those with a legitimate interest can attend." She adjusted the butterfly barrette in her purple hair, the blue, rhinestone wings sparkling to match the stud in her nose. "How's the new medicine going? Don't feel groggy, do you?"

Will shook his head. Being groggy was the least of his worries.

"Good. Don't need you spacing out in the middle of your testimony."

"Fuel to the fire, huh?"

"Walter Granger would certainly think so. Me? I'd just say you're normal."

"Normal?" Will choked.

She shrugged. "Normal is subjective."

Will smiled. He liked Dr. Sinclaire. She was a little unorthodox, but sharp as a whip. And she didn't talk about his brain like it was a broken-down engine in a scrap yard.

"Zoe Sinclaire. Can't say I was surprised to see your name on the witness list."

Dr. Sinclaire rolled her eyes as she turned. "Well, you know I never miss an opportunity to prove you wrong, Dr. Granger."

"You can't really believe you know more about the function of this patient's illness than the doctor who's treated his family for thirty years."

"I would never suggest such a thing."

"Good, because—"

"But I will guarantee that I understand Will Fletcher better than you ever have."

"Same old Zoe." Dr. Granger grinned, straightening his red bow tie. "Will we see you at dinner this weekend?"

"Of course. Tell Mom I'll bring the wine."

He nodded, then took his seat at the other table.

Will leaned close to her ear. "Walter Granger is your father?"

"*Step*father," she corrected. "I don't have any of that man's genes."

Will scratched his head, turning to David Shepherd who now sat beside him. "Did you know about this?"

"Of course. Why do you think I picked her?"

"Her keen sense of style? Because no one else would defend me with a ten-foot pole?"

"Walter Granger shoved Zoe Sinclaire in and out of every psychiatric hospital in a three-county area for the entire eight years she lived with him. You will not find a licensed doctor in this state that disagrees more with that man than she does." David removed the cap from his pen and placed it on the table, then met Will's gaze with a grin. "Understand?"

"All rise! The Honorable Judge Wheaton presiding!"

Will stood, still a little unsure. Even if he disagreed, it was a bit late now with the judge, opposing lawyer, and witnesses filing into the room.

The witnesses!

"You may be seated."

Will lowered himself into his chair, heart racing. As bad as he'd wanted to see Janey, Regan, and Lindsay, he was relieved when Dr. Sinclaire suggested he wait until after the hearing. He hadn't figured out how to apologize yet, or where he should start. Even if he had, he couldn't take seeing that distrustful look in their eyes or hearing the hesitant tone of their forgiveness.

"Given the delicate nature of today's hearing, I feel it necessary to remind counsel of some ground rules." Judge Wheaton folded his hands neatly in front of him and stared across his long, pointy beak of a nose toward Will. "First, this may not be a standard trial, but I expect everyone in my courtroom to conduct themselves as if it were. There will be no showboating and no drama, and anyone who decides to challenge this may consider themselves in contempt." He shifted his gaze to the county attorney. "Second, we are here to examine Mr. Fletcher's current mental stability and determine if it warrants involuntary hospitalization. Any evidence submitted on events prior to Mr. Fletcher's previous committal is inadmissible, and I do not have the patience, nor the authority, to bend this rule. Do I make myself clear?"

"Yes, Your Honor."

"Then, Mr. Tuttle, you may begin your opening statement."

The young court attorney rose to his feet, straightening his red tie. Will was surprised the kid's voice didn't crack when he spoke. "For the past five years, William Fletcher has been more than a distraction to the small town of Half Moon Hollow; he's been an outright threat to the safety of its people. Much like a—"

"Ticking time bomb," Will muttered, simultaneously with Tyler Tuttle. Where was his creativity? Probably lost a few years back when his kindergarten teacher had told him to color the heart red while he stayed within the lines.

Will smiled at his own joke, wishing Regan could've heard it. She'd grown to appreciate his sarcasm. She might've been the only one who ever had, or ever would.

He sat back in his chair, glancing over his shoulder. If it weren't for her sitting between Janey and Lindsay, Will wouldn't have recognized her. The burgundy turtleneck and plaid, wool skirt made her look like an Ivy League college student beyond her sixteen years. Her shiny, red hair was tucked neatly away from her face with a gray band, soft curls spiraling down. Her eyes weren't hidden behind heavy black liner, but were clear and wide for the world to admire.

God, she was beautiful, and she was half him. How was that possible?

As soon as Regan found his gaze, Will turned, just in time to see Tiny Tyler Tuttle sitting down after his stellar statement of originality.

"Mr. Shepherd?" The judge beckoned.

"Thank you, Your Honor." David stood, all five and a half feet of him, and buttoned his jacket. "As demonstrated in his opening statement, Mr. Tuttle is going to try to prove Will Fletcher is a deranged lunatic. He'll dredge up a lot of examples of oddities Mr. Fletcher has performed, point out the number of times he's been arrested; he'll probably even try to convince you Mr. Fletcher's illness has already been the cause of one person's death. But the question in this case isn't whether or not Mr. Fletcher is mentally ill; I think even Mr. Fletcher would concede that point. Per the state of Ohio's statutes, the questions in this case are one: is Mr. Fletcher currently a threat to himself or to anyone else? And two: is Mr. Fletcher better off in the care of a mental health facility or in the care of family members who love him? I challenge the court to remember this today during these proceedings. Thank you."

"That's it?" Will whispered as David sat down.

"Sometimes less is more."

Will glanced at David's balding head. "Really?"

"Yes. Now, you just do your job and let me do mine."

Will nodded, then leaned in. "What *is* my job?"

David smiled. "To make sure I don't end up looking like an ass."

The first time Janey had met Walter Granger, she was nine years old. It was the fourth time her father had been admitted to Creedmoor, but the first she'd understood what Creedmoor was. She'd been sitting in the waiting room wearing her blue,

Sunday dress when a bald man in a white coat sat beside her. "I'm Dr. Granger," he'd said. "I'm the man who's going to fix your father." And even though Janey didn't know her father was broken, she'd believed him.

He'd made a similar promise after Will's suicide attempt, and Janey had believed this time would be different because they were dealing with a different illness. This time Dr. Granger swore on his life he wouldn't let her down. This time Janey had enough hope for both her and Will. But, sitting in that courtroom, as Dr. Granger testified in favor of her brother's committal, Janey realized she'd been fooled twice.

Shame on her.

"Dr. Granger, mental illness runs in the Fletcher family, correct?"

"Yes. Though Henry Fletcher, Will's father, was diagnosed with Schizophrenia."

"Can you explain the difference between Schizophrenia and Bipolar Disorder to the court?"

"Schizophrenia is a brain disorder, often associated with various types of psychosis. In Henry's case, it distorted the way he perceived reality. He heard voices, had hallucinations, and suffered from states of paranoia.

"Bipolar Disorder is a mood disorder characterized by shifts between two states—mania and depression. Depression episodes can be severe. The patient may not eat, or go to work, or even get out of bed for days. On the other hand, during a manic episode, the patient may believe himself capable of things he can't possibly do and stay up for days trying to achieve them. He may experience irrational happiness, an increase in energy, even a heightened sex drive."

Janey bit her lip. Up until recently, she'd never had to worry about that last symptom.

"And this is the disorder you diagnosed Will with, correct?"

"Initially, yes."

Tuttle reared his head back as if he didn't know the answer already. "Initially? Does that mean you've changed your diagnosis?"

"Yes, it does." Dr. Granger turned his gaze toward Janey. "I now believe Will suffers from Schizoaffective Disorder, a severe mental illness where patients have symptoms of both Bipolar Disorder *and* Schizophrenia."

"But isn't it uncommon for a man in his midthirties to be diagnosed with this illness?"

"Yes. I've suspected for many years Will suffered from it."

"So why are you just now diagnosing it?"

Walter Granger took a breath so deep Janey could feel it in her bones. "Because his sister Janey wouldn't speak of it."

"Thank you, Dr. Granger. No further questions."

David was out of his seat before Tuttle had returned to his. "Doctor, do you make it standard practice to diagnose your patients based on the feelings of their family members?"

Dr. Granger pursed his lips. "No."

"Then why, in this case, did you wait to re-diagnose Will?"

"I've known the Fletchers for years, seen their family destroyed twice by mental illness. Call me human, but part of me didn't want to cause them any more pain."

David shook his head. "Well, I think *that* ship has sailed."

"Objection, Your Honor!" Tyler Tuttle yelled. "Badgering!"

"Withdrawn." David paced a few moments, then placed his notecards on the podium. "You recently received a promotion, did you not?"

"Yes. I was appointed to chief of psychiatry at Mercy General," Dr. Granger said.

"Are you aware that Arthur Bradford—Will Fletcher's

former father-in-law and the mayor of Half Moon Hollow—
serves on the board that selected you for that position?"

"Objection." Tuttle hollered. "Relevance?"

"Counselor?"

"Well," David stated. "I just thought it would be of interest to the court that the man who started the petition for Will
Fletcher's committal was also responsible for the promotion of
the physician testifying in favor of putting him away."

"Overruled."

"Dr. Granger?" David pressed

And Janey watched in disbelief as, for the first time since
she'd met Dr. Granger, he had nothing to say.

Passing out mathematical proof that Santa Claus is a fraud outside
a preschool; showing up at a town meeting with Jack the donkey
to "show his ass"; giving a concert in the town fountain naked.

Had Regan heard these stories before she'd met Will
Fletcher, she would've agreed that they were the actions of a
dangerous man. But sitting in the courtroom that day, listening
to the sheriff recount the many ways Will had been a nuisance
in Half Moon Hollow, Regan couldn't have disagreed more.
Those weren't the malicious actions of a dangerous man; they
were only the silly idiosyncrasies of her father.

"Can you explain to the court how this last incident
unfolded?" Tyler Tuttle asked.

Sheriff Blythe took a deep breath. "I received a phone call
from Janey Fletcher at approximately 11:00 a.m. that morning.
She said she'd been trying to reach the Fletcher household by
phone but couldn't get through. Asked if I could drive by and
check in."

"And what did you find when you arrived at the Fletcher
residence?"

"Well, I never made it. I was just about to head there when a report came across the scanner that a man had locked himself inside the storage shed at the animal shelter. I knew right then it was Will Fletcher, so I headed there instead."

Tuttle nodded. "And can you tell the court what you found when you got there?"

Regan listened as Sherriff Blythe explained how everything unfolded that day. The shed, the singing, the Magic Marker covering her father's body, carrying him out and placing him in the back of the police car. It was odd, hearing the way he described it, seeing it through his eyes. Like Will was just a random perpetrator taken down on another day at the office.

But he wasn't just another person. Will was her father.

"So, it is your official opinion, Sheriff, that the town of Half Moon Hollow would be safer if Will Fletcher was committed to a psychiatric facility, correct?" Tuttle asked.

Sheriff Blythe's eyes wandered to the witnesses behind the county prosecutor's desk. Regan followed his gaze to Mayor Bradford. "Yes. That's correct."

"No further questions, Your Honor."

David stood, staring at his notepad. "Sheriff, it's on county record that Mr. Fletcher has been arrested forty-three times in the past five years. And of those forty-three arrests, fewer than half of the charges actually made it to court. Can you explain why?"

Sherriff Blythe adjusted in his seat, folding his hands across his lap. "I'm afraid I don't recall all the details of those arrests."

David looked up from his paper. "You can't explain why a man whom you feel is a danger to the town was permitted to go free so many times?"

"Objection, Your Honor. The Half Moon Hollow police department is not on trial here."

"Sustained. Watch yourself, counselor."

"Sheriff Blythe, do you recall responding to a graffiti incident at the Fletcher residence last year?" David asked.

"I'd hardly call it graffiti. It was just kids having a little fun."

"You'd call spray painting a giant cuckoo bird onto the Fletcher's front lawn . . . *fun*?"

Regan clenched her jaw, wishing she'd hit Nick Watkins just a little harder that day by the field. Wishing she would've let Lane finish him off in the lunchroom.

Sheriff Blythe grimaced. "Well, maybe fun isn't the right word."

David approached the witness stand. "Sheriff, if it really was just kids being kids, and you truly do believe Will Fletcher is a danger, why did you encourage Janey Fletcher to purchase a gun after that incident?"

"Well, I . . ." He cleared his throat. "I suppose I . . ."

David placed his hands on the wooden rail enclosing the witness box. "You don't believe Will Fletcher is a threat to society, do you Sheriff Blythe? In fact, you believe society is a threat to Will Fletcher, isn't that right?"

Sheriff Blythe glanced at Mayor Bradford then at Tyler Tuttle before returning his gaze to David and sighing.

"I'll take that as a yes," David stated. "No further questions."

"How do you think it's going?" Lindsay asked David, even though she knew he wouldn't give her a straight answer. She'd been married to him long enough to know he didn't gamble on anything, particularly his cases.

He grimaced, glancing back inside toward Will and Dr. Sinclaire, still sitting at the defense table, then closed the courtroom door behind him. "There's still a long way to go. We've only made it through the county's case."

"Yes, but they only called two witnesses," Lindsay pointed out, following him down the hallway. "That's gotta be good, right?"

"Or it could mean Tuttle thinks it's a slam dunk, so he didn't load down his case with unqualified witnesses. He stuck to the facts—all forty-three of them. It's what I would do."

"What you would do? What the hell is that supposed to mean?" Lindsay increased her speed to keep up with his pace. "You think Will should be locked up, don't you?"

"It doesn't matter what I think. What matters is that I can anticipate what Tuttle thinks and what the judge thinks."

"Well, it matters to me," she said.

David paused beside the men's room, his eyes betraying nothing as they met hers. This was why it hadn't worked out between them—because what she'd wanted never mattered, the entire ten years they were married. This was why she loved Will so much, because he thought of her needs and wants even before she did.

Lindsay turned and began her retreat, too angry to talk to David any longer.

"No, I don't think he should be locked up," he called after her, bringing her to a halt. "But cases like these can turn in a minute. All it takes is one spark to set off a bomb in there."

Without facing him, she nodded. If she'd learned any lesson from this mess it was not to assume the meaning of anything— not a look, not a touch, not a kiss. If only she'd pressed Janey about that kiss or pushed Will to tell her why he was so distraught over those damn flowers. If she'd only questioned why his once-skittish hands were suddenly confident against her body. Maybe she could've prevented all this.

Janey was right. This was all Lindsay's fault.

"I was certainly surprised to see you here today, Principal Shepherd."

Lindsay sighed, then turned toward Mayor Bradford. "Well, I am on the witness list."

"Yes, I know." He stepped toward her, rubbing his fingers together. "I must say I was a little disappointed to learn you'd be testifying on behalf of the defense—particularly after you signed off on his committal."

Lindsay pursed her lips. "Mayor Bradford, is there something you'd like to say to me?"

He smiled. God, how Lindsay hated that smile. "Why don't we go for a walk?"

She stepped in beside him, wearily. "You can take my job. I really don't care."

"I gathered that," he said. "You know, Ms. Shepherd, I've worked hard the past five years to make sure everyone knows that Will Fletcher is a danger, and it doesn't bode well for me when he develops a romantic relationship. It makes people start to see him differently. Remember who he was before all this happened. Question if he really is a danger."

"You mean, people like Ellie," she bluntly stated.

Mayor Bradford paused. "Trust me, Ms. Shepherd. You don't want my daughter coming back into Will Fletcher's life any more than I do."

Lindsay frowned, the truth striking a nerve. She would never win up against Ellie. "So what do you want?"

"What if I could give you something more valuable than your job?" he asked, setting off again down the corridor. "Something a little closer to the heart?"

"I'm listening."

He removed a folded piece of paper from his coat pocket and handed it to Lindsay. "You know, the Fletchers haven't been allowed to see this. They won't be allowed until after the hearing when it's made a public record."

Lindsay stared at the bottom of the petition, at her signature inked in blue.

"I can make sure this page never makes it into that record. Make sure Janey Fletcher never sees this page," he offered. "And from what my sources tell me, you can use all the help you can get repairing your friendship."

She swallowed. "But if I lie, she'll hate me anyway."

He shrugged. "Perhaps. But it's a lot easier to explain to someone that you lied to save your job than it is to explain why you betrayed them."

Lindsay turned away, her hand covering the scream trying to escape from her mouth. Mayor Bradford wanted her to tell the court she wasn't in love with Will and tell Janey she'd done it to protect her image and her job. Lindsay either had to be shallow and selfish, or a back-stabbing bitch. Either way, would Janey ever forgive her? Would Will ever look at Lindsay the same way again? And, in the end, would it even matter to Will's case?

"The choice is yours, Lindsay." Mayor Bradford turned. "Lose little or lose big."

The problem was Lindsay didn't know which choice was which.

CHAPTER TWENTY

For the last few days, Lindsay had managed to overlook a lot of things she didn't want to admit. That the life of the man she loved was in the hands of an ex-husband she'd tried so hard not to hate. That the random conversations she'd had with Janey were really out of necessity and didn't mean Lindsay had been forgiven. That a ruling to set Will free wouldn't get her closer to unlocking the chains around his heart.

That her signature was in permanent, blue ink on that damned petition.

"Ms. Shepherd, how do you know Will Fletcher?" David asked.

"His daughter Regan is a student of mine. I'm also a close friend of his sister, Janey."

David waited for the rest of the answer Lindsay had rehearsed. "And what, exactly, has your relationship been like with Will?" he pressed.

Lindsay thought back to that day in the shelter with Pepper, to the morning in her office with Regan, to the night she'd had dinner for the first time with Janey. The man who walked around in Will's skin then wasn't the same man she'd fallen in love with. Maybe it was the absence of his pills, maybe he'd changed, or maybe Lindsay had.

Maybe it was all of the above.

"At first, I saw Will like the rest of the town did," Lindsay admitted. "But, after I got to know him, I saw what a caring person he was. He's always offering to help me with odd jobs, and he's really good to Regan too. He just wants to live his life the best way he knows how, like the rest of us."

David nodded. "Ms. Shepherd, you were staying at the Fletchers' during Will's most recent breakdown, is that correct?"

"Yes. I stayed as a favor to Janey to help out while she was out of town."

"And before his breakdown, how would you characterize Will's behavior that weekend?"

She shifted her eyes to Mayor Bradford then back to David. This is where she was supposed to announce that she and Will had become a couple and consummated their relationship. Where she was supposed to show his tenderness, his ability to love, his humanity.

"I'm not sure I understand the question," Lindsay said, even though she really did.

David stared at her a moment, the way he used to when she'd said something stupid in front of his colleagues. "Did he take his medicine? Stick to his routine?"

"I believe so, yes."

David stepped forward, eyes stern. "Did Will do anything out of the ordinary?"

"Uh, I'm not sure." Lindsay glanced again at Mayor Bradford, this time not so discreetly, as David quickly followed her line of sight.

"You've got to be kidding me," David muttered.

"Is that a question, Counselor?" the judge asked.

David shook his head and turned back toward Lindsay. "Ms. Shepherd, did you and Mr. Fletcher become romantically involved during your stay at the Fletchers'? And before you answer, I'd like to remind you that you are under oath."

Lindsay dropped her eyes to her lap. This was impossible. This was fucking impossible.

"Ms. Shepherd?"

How could she ever face Janey or Will or Regan if they found out she'd signed that damned petition? How could she lie about what Will meant to her, what those perfect two days had meant to her? The mayor was right—it was lose little or lose big. Lose a lot or lose everything. She couldn't do this.

"Lindsay!"

She snapped her eyes to David's, the frustrated way he said her name striking a nerve somewhere deep inside her. It wasn't so long ago that her everything had included him, had been defined by him, destroyed by him. Never again. This time, *she* would decide who she was.

"The witness will please answer the question," the judge ordered.

"Yes," she sat up taller. "We did."

A low murmur spread among the few people in the courtroom, making Lindsay's spine lengthen a little, much to her surprise. It made her wonder if this was how Will had grown to be so strong. Had the disdain of these people given him purpose in a life that had no other?

"Is this relationship serious?" David asked.

She turned her eyes to Will. She didn't care. She didn't care if they found out about the petition. She wouldn't lie to him anymore. "Yes. I'm in love with him."

David grinned an approving smile—something Lindsay had never seen. It didn't bring her as much satisfaction as she'd thought it would. "Thank you. No further questions."

As David returned to his seat, Tyler Tuttle began to clap.

The judge hit his gavel on the podium. "Mr. Tuttle, I assume you have questions for this witness?"

"Yes, Your Honor." Tyler Tuttle stood, arrogance permeating through his skin. "Ms. Shepherd, you said Will took his medicine every day. Have you given any thought to why the tox screen on Will's blood showed no traces of lithium if you did indeed see him take his lithium twice a day?"

She had. Many times. And she couldn't explain it any more now than she could when Janey asked, or when David asked, or when Regan asked. "I don't know why, Mr. Tuttle. Perhaps the pharmacist made a mistake."

"Perhaps. Or perhaps all the physical activity *burned* it off."

"Objection! Badgering!" David said.

"Withdrawn from the record."

Lindsay sank down in her chair, her eyes focused on her hands. Maybe it was withdrawn from the court's record, but Lindsay certainly wouldn't forget it any time soon.

"Ms. Shepherd, I have one last question before I dismiss you. Perhaps this one won't stump you so badly." Tuttle held up a piece of paper. "Is this your signature right here?"

"Yes," Lindsay responded without verifying. She didn't need to check it.

"Can you tell the court what this document is?"

Lindsay glanced from Janey, to Regan, to Will—her everything. No matter what they decided, she knew that for certain now. "It's the petition for Will's committal."

꙳

Janey stared straight ahead, mouth hanging open, as Lindsay gathered her purse and jacket from the bench beside her. Janey couldn't look at her, couldn't stand to hear another excuse or another apology. Lindsay had betrayed her, betrayed Will. Plain and simple.

"Janey," Lindsay whispered. "Please let me explain."

"The defense calls Janey Fletcher to the stand," David announced.

Janey stood, eyes set forward, and inched passed Lindsay without uttering a single word. There wasn't an explanation Lindsay could offer that would make Janey understand why she'd signed that petition. Or how she'd looked Janey in the face and sworn to never hurt her. Or how she'd made love to Will, knowing the dishonesty that lay between them.

How could Janey have fallen in love with someone capable of that?

"Janey?" David said as she reached the witness stand. She turned her eyes toward David, fighting back the tears. "Will needs you. Let it go."

Janey closed her eyes and took a deep, cleansing breath. A moment later when she opened them back up, the only traces of Lindsay Shepherd were the courtroom doors closing behind her and the ache inside Janey's chest.

As the bailiff swore her in, Janey focused on Will. He wouldn't look her way, probably for the same reason Janey hadn't looked at Lindsay. Janey had brought Lindsay into their lives. Had she not, Lindsay's signature would be just another signature and not reason number 549 for why Will should never trust anyone.

For that reason alone, Janey would never forgive Lindsay.

"Ms. Fletcher, you've been your brother's legal guardian for a little over four years now," David said, jumping right in. "Can you describe what it's like, living with his Bipolar Disorder?"

Janey started at the beginning, recounted Will's suicide attempt, his committal, her decision not to return to New York so her brother could have his freedom. She described all the bad days she'd had with Will since and the good days that made all the bad days worth it. She explained why she'd made the decision to leave Will with Lindsay and Regan, and that she'd regretted it every moment since. And when she was done, David asked her the one question she'd been fighting over since seeing Will in that hospital bed, covered head to toe in marker.

"And Ms. Fletcher, for the record, are you willing to continue as your brother's guardian should the court decide to allow you to do so?"

"Yes," Janey said, never more certain of anything.

David nodded. "No further questions."

Tyler Tuttle stood, looking at his notepad. "Ms. Fletcher, you stated you've been your brother's guardian since he killed his infant daughter, correct?"

"Objection," David said. "Emma Fletcher's death was ruled an accident, and Ms. Fletcher stated clearly that she became her brother's guardian after his previous committal. Mr. Tuttle is simply trying to enter evidence that's already been deemed inadmissible."

"I agree," the judge said. "Mr. Tuttle, do I need to remind you of the ground rules?"

"No, Your Honor. I just misspoke. My apologies." Tuttle glanced down at his notepad. "Ah yes, here it is. You've been his guardian since his previous suicide attempt. After his ex-wife filed for divorce, and he dislocated her elbow because of it."

"Your Honor!" David pleaded.

The judge looked at Tyler Tuttle over his glasses. "Counselor, one more time and I will hold you in contempt."

Tuttle rubbed his jaw, appearing unscathed by the judge's threat, then looked at Janey for the first time since he'd stood. "You said you left Will with Lindsay Shepherd because you had a business convention to attend in Los Angeles. Can you explain what sort of convention?"

Janey straightened in her seat. "I make my living as a comic book artist. One of my comics was up for an award that they give away at this convention."

"Really? That's wonderful," Tuttle said. "Did you win?"

Janey deflated. "No. I came in second place."

"Still cause to celebrate, no?"

"Actually, I had to rush home due to Will's break. So, no."

"Huh, that's odd. But let's come back to that." Tuttle approached, holding a piece of paper. "Ms. Fletcher, this is the hotel bill from your, quote, *business convention*. Can you read the name at the bottom, highlighted in pink, beside the words *Billed To?*"

"Gretchen Parks. She's my agent," Janey said, anticipating exactly where this was going. "She often pays for my business expenses, and we sometimes room together."

"Agent and roommate, maybe. But she's also your former gay lover, correct?"

"Objection," David said. "Ms. Fletcher's sexual preference and history has nothing to do with her ability to care for her brother."

"It does when Ms. Fletcher is a flight risk because of it," Tuttle retorted.

The judge tossed a white, oval Tic Tac into his mouth. "I'll allow it. But you better get somewhere with this quick, Mr. Tuttle."

Janey cleared her throat, pulling her eyes away from the judge still chewing on the Tic Tac. The Tic Tac that looked an awful lot like Will's medication.

That's how he'd done it. That's how he'd fooled Lindsay.

"Ms. Fletcher? Were you and Gretchen Parks lovers?"

"Yes," Janey said. "But we haven't been in a long time."

"No? Then can you read the items on that bill that I've high-lighted in yellow please?"

Janey sighed. "Three bottles of champagne. Private, in-room dinner for two. A dozen red roses. Two massages." She handed the paper back to Tuttle.

"Pretty hefty list for a business convention, don't you think? Especially since you've already stated you left before any cele-brations could occur."

Damn Gretchen all to hell.

Tuttle approached, a confused look on his face. "This is what you were doing on this business trip? The business trip that was so important you decided to leave your brother in the care of an inexperienced friend and his sixteen-year-old daugh-ter? You were rekindling a romance with your former lover?"

"Objection," David stated. "He's putting words in the wit-ness's mouth."

"Sustained."

"Aren't you tired, Ms. Fletcher? Tired of putting your life on hold for your brother? Don't you want a chance at a relation-ship, maybe a family of your own someday?"

Janey bit her lip, trapping the truth inside, before she made herself look any more selfish than she already did.

"Well," Tuttle stated. "I can't say that I really blame you. No further questions.'"

"Amen," Regan said, lowering her hand. It wasn't until the bailiff smiled that she realized those weren't the right words. "I mean, I do."

"You may be seated, Miss Whitmer," the judge stated, grinning.

Regan concentrated on her fidgeting fingers as she lowered her hand again, feeling the embarrassment heat up her face. She hated being the center of everyone's attention, hated being on display, like some abstract piece of wall art for everyone to analyze and pick apart. Especially after what Tyler Tuttle had just done to Janey. Then, as if things couldn't get any worse, Lane Barrett walked into the courtroom wearing a suit and tie.

He smiled and gave Regan a discreet thumbs-up before taking a seat beside Janey, who appeared just as surprised as Regan by his arrival.

Why is he here? Her mother asked.

The answer was clear. *Because he loves me.*

But he's going to leave you, her mother retorted.

No he's not. Regan smiled. *He's just going away for a little while.*

What's the difference? Her mother asked.

Leaving is what you did. And it's time for you to go for good. But . . .

Regan's smile fell. It was time. It was time to say goodbye. It was time to move on. *Please, Mom. If you love me, you'll go. I can't live my life with you here. Just please go.*

"Regan?" David Shepherd stepped before her, commanding her attention.

Regan met his gaze. "Yes?"

"Are you sure you're ready?"

She wiped the budding tears from her eyes and nodded. After all this time, she finally was ready. Ready to let go. Ready to move on. Ready to forgive her mother.

David smiled. "Regan, how did Will react when he learned you were his daughter?"

"He was a little scared at first, but so was I." She glanced at Will, smiling. "But after some time, I think I grew on him."

"I can certainly see how that would happen," David said, then glanced down at his tablet. "What about Will and Janey's relationship? Do they get along?"

"Do any brother and sister living in the same house *really* get along?"

Mumbled laughter rolled across the room, which the judge was quick to silence.

"But, besides the standard brother-sister bickering, does Janey take care of Will? Keep him on schedule? Make sure he's taking his medicine?"

"Yes. Every day."

David stepped closer. "Regan, you're no stranger to mental illnesses, are you?"

She straightened in her seat. "My mom suffered from depression."

"So, after hearing the testimonies of Dr. Granger and Sherriff Blythe today, you can understand what their concerns are about your father?"

"Understand, yes. Agree, no."

"And why do you disagree?"

"Objection, Your Honor. Is the court really going to listen to the opinion of a sixteen-year-old girl on something this serious?"

"Yes, the court is." The judge glanced up, irritation showing in his eyes. "Is counsel really going to tell the court what it should and shouldn't deem worthy of hearing?"

Tyler Tuttle pursed his lips and took his seat.

Resisting the urge to stick her tongue out Tuttle's way,

Regan turned toward the judge. "It's like that story *How the Grinch Stole Christmas*. Do you know it?"

The judge smiled, then nodded.

"Well, it's like that. No one in this town has ever given my dad a chance. They just accept him for the crazy guy who doesn't fit in. After a while, you learn to play the part." She turned back toward David. "But he's so much more than that. He's . . . well . . . my dad."

David winked, making her feel all warm and fuzzy inside. "Regan, I have just one more question, and I want you to answer as honestly as you can." He leaned on the wooden ledge of the witness stand. "Would you say Will is a good father?"

She raised her brows. They hadn't practiced this. What was she supposed to say?

"It's okay," David said. "Just answer truthfully. Do you think Will is a good father?"

Regan looked toward Will, thinking of the way he'd ignored her the first few weeks after she'd arrived. She thought of running from Hadley's, embarrassed, and driving him around without a license. She thought of the sting on her check when he'd slapped her, and the ache in her heart when she realized she would always come in second to Emma.

But then she thought of him sitting beside her in the hospital after she'd cut her hand, building the birdhouse with him, swinging on the front porch with him the night Lane asked her to eat dinner with his family, and the way she felt the first time they went to Emma's grave together. She'd live through a thousand more bad moments to have one more of the good moments. Because somewhere along the way, her dad started to try. He started to love her.

"I'd say he's learning, and he gets closer every day," Regan finally answered. "But if they take him away from me, he'll never make it."

David pushed off the witness stand and grinned. "No further questions."

Tyler Tuttle jumped to his feet, passing David on his way to the witness stand. "Miss Whitmer, how did it feel, seeing your father in such an unstable state after his recent break?"

"It was scary."

"Scarier than watching your mother commit suicide?"

Regan's eyes widened. David had warned this would come, but it didn't lesson the blow. "No. Nothing will ever be scarier than that."

"I bet not." Tuttle placed his hands on his hips. "In your opinion, would you say your behavior in the days leading up to your mother's suicide may have contributed to it?"

"Objection," David said. "Relevance."

"Part of this hearing, as Mr. Shepherd stated himself, is to determine whether or not Mr. Fletcher could be properly taken care of outside of a mental institution." Tuttle turned to David. "I think it's relevant to question the capabilities of his would-be caretakers."

The judge nodded. "I agree. Overruled. The witness should answer."

"No. I don't believe that," Regan responded. Short and sweet, the way David had told her she should answer any question they hadn't rehearsed.

"You don't?" Tuttle verified, tapping his pen on his leg. "Well do you remember a Pastor Wright, Miss Whitmer? Head of your church back in Chicago?"

Regan deflated; every ounce of her courage ran for the hills. How did he know? How had he found out? Steven wouldn't have dare told; he'd be too embarrassed. And something like this would be a huge disgrace for Pastor Wright's family. "Yes."

"And do you remember an incident, about a week before

your mother committed suicide, where Pastor Wright caught you after you'd broken into the basement of the church?"

"I didn't break in."

"No? Then can you please tell the court what you were doing in the church's basement at two o'clock in the morning when Pastor Wright found you?"

All at once, the eyes in the room were locked on her. The judge, Janey, Will, David, the few people Regan didn't know, and, most importantly, Lane. They all waited for the truth, all waited for her to rehash the night she'd been trying so hard to forget.

"Miss Whitmer? Do you remember? Or should I get the signed affidavit from Pastor Wright to refresh your memory?" Tuttle asked, turning toward his table.

"He said he loved me," Regan muttered.

Tuttle turned to face her again. "Who?"

"Holden Wright. He asked me to come to the church that night, and when his father caught us, he lied, and said I had tricked him into coming there."

From the confused expression on Tuttle's face, Regan could tell this was not the story he'd heard from Pastor Wright or from Steven, or whomever he'd spoken with. They'd probably told him the same story they'd made her confess to the congregation. That she'd snuck into that basement with a boy she'd known from her days on the street. That she'd done it to get back at Holden for breaking up with her after he'd realized she wasn't a virgin. That Pastor Wright had caught them in time, and this was the first time it had ever happened.

"What were you and Holden Wright doing when his father caught you?" Tuttle asked.

Regan clenched her jaw. Steven and her mother had convinced her to confess a lie before, that saving Holden from disgrace and taking the weight of a hundred shameful stares on her own was the Christian thing to do. But now that she'd begun, Regan could feel the weight of those hundred shameful stares lifting from her soul. Now she would just have three to account for.

She set her gaze on her lap so she couldn't see Will, or Janey, or Lane when she answered. "We were having sex."

"Let her be," Janey said to Lane, letting the courtroom door fall closed behind her. She'd followed him out as he'd gone after Regan. Janey'd been in her niece's shoes before and knew Lane was the last person Regan would want to see. She wasn't even entirely sure Regan would want to see her after what just happened on the stand.

Lane turned, confused. "But I want to help her."

Janey had been in his shoes too—the shoes of the one trying to make everything better. If there was one thing she'd learned from her failed attempts with Will, it was that some things never got better, no matter how hard you tried. Some things were what they were, and you just had to find a way to live with them.

"If you want to help, go on home," Janey advised. "She has to sort this out on her own."

Lane glanced in the direction Regan had gone. "Will you just . . . tell her that I don't care? About any of it? And tell her that I love her?"

Janey shook her head. "That's something you need to tell her. Just not right now, okay?"

He took one final look Regan's way, then nodded and turned for the exit with his head hanging low. Janey felt bad for having judged him the way she had before all this. He was a good kid, despite the family his mother married into.

With a deep breath, Janey turned in search of her niece.

Behind a large column at the end of the corridor, she could barely make out the black flats she'd let Regan borrow this morning. Janey walked down the corridor toward her, Regan's sobs growing louder as she neared. When she'd reached her, Regan's face was buried in her knees.

"I lost my virginity to my foster brother when I was fourteen," Janey said, gingerly, sitting beside her. "He told me to meet him in the barn and he'd let me ride his horse. I didn't realize until he had me pinned to the ground that he didn't even have a horse." Janey shook her head, the shame falling over her even fifteen years later. "I've never told anyone that until now."

Regan raised her head from her knees and stared down at the charm bracelet Lane had given her. "How can I ever face him again?" she asked.

Janey thought back to all the boys she'd dated in the years after her foster brother's betrayal. She thought of the way she shuddered when other boys touched her, the way her stomach turned over when they kissed her. Perhaps it was because, deep down, Janey had known she was gay, or perhaps she'd turned to women because her foster brother had destroyed her view of men forever. She'd never know which and it didn't matter anyway, because she was proud of the woman she'd grown into.

It was all the hiding she was ashamed of. Pretending it had never happened. Convincing herself that if she told anyone, they would never look at her the same way again.

"Because, if you don't, Holden Wright wins all over again," Janey finally answered, getting to her feet and holding a hand out toward Regan. "Don't give him that kind of power."

Will glanced over his shoulder at the three empty chairs Janey, Lindsay, and Regan had sat in earlier that day. He couldn't pay attention to Dr. Sinclaire up on the witness stand, not without them here. They'd been shamed away by Ellie's father, the same way he'd been all these years.

Will wasn't stupid; he knew Bradford had constructed every piece of this trial. He'd never stood a chance against that man, had known it from the day he'd asked for Ellie's hand in marriage. And now the bastard had dragged everyone Will loved into this decade-old battle.

And for what? Why couldn't Bradford let go? What did he really have to gain from all this? Why was he so hell-bent on keeping Will and his family as the town villains?

The sound of the court doors opening caught his attention, and Will nearly burst when Janey and Regan stepped through. They hadn't left him, hadn't given up on him. Not yet. He winked at Regan, who smiled, even though she was fighting back tears, then turned to his sister.

"Thank you," he mouthed.

Janey nodded once, then took her seat.

Will waited for the door to open again and for Lindsay to walk through, but she never did. Disappointed, he turned his attention back to Dr. Sinclaire, who'd just finished explaining how screwed up his brain was.

"So, you agree with Dr. Granger's diagnosis of Schizoaffective Disorder?" David asked.

"Mental illnesses and brain disorders aren't always an exact science, but I would agree Will's symptoms lend themselves to Schizoaffective Disorder, yes."

"Do you agree with Dr. Granger's assessment that Will is a danger to society and his recommendation for institutionalization?"

"Absolutely not, and I believe it's absurd for anyone to think so," she said. "Since the death of his infant daughter, Will has put every ounce of his energy into pushing people away—his ex-wife, his sister, the entire town for that matter. I don't believe there is anyone who's more concerned about the people of Half Moon Hollow than Will himself. It's why he shovels animal feces out of pens and sings melodies in the town fountain naked."

"I'm not sure I follow," David said.

"These episodes aren't just symptoms of his disorder, but his natural armor—a defense mechanism, if you will. He believes the only way to keep everyone safe is to keep everyone away; so, whether subconsciously or consciously, it's his way of repelling everyone. Locking him up in some hospital will only reinforce this notion in his head." Dr. Sinclaire crossed her legs and scooted toward the microphone. "What Will needs is assimilation."

"Thank you. No further questions."

Tuttle stood, buttoning his jacket. "Doctor, how long have you practiced medicine?"

She pursed her lips. "Three years."

"And, just to clarify, how long has Mr. Fletcher been a patient of yours?"

"Three days."

"So, you based your opinion on three years of experience and three days with Will?"

"Yes, I did. Much the same way that you made yours based on passing your bar exam last week and *never* talking to Will."

The judge chuckled, then cleared his throat.

Will liked this woman.

"You said that Mr. Fletcher needs assimilation. Shouldn't the past five years have been enough time for him to assimilate?"

"A car has an engine, but it won't run without gas, Mr. Tuttle."

Tuttle reared back. "I'm sorry?"

"Will has always been capable of getting well, but, up until recently, he hasn't had the motivation to do it. That all changed when Lindsay and Regan entered his life."

Tuttle chuckled. "Yes, I suppose I would call them fuel to the fire since Mr. Fletcher's most recent breakdown occurred *after* their arrivals. No further—"

"You also can't expect to start an engine that hasn't run in five years on the first try," Dr. Sinclaire blurted out. "It's going to take time for Will to adjust."

"Thank you for that insight, Dr. Sinclaire, but I don't recall asking any questions." Tuttle turned around. "No further questions."

David was on his feet before Tuttle sat down. "Dr. Sinclaire, in your *professional*, medical opinion, why now? What it is about these two women that you believe has finally snapped Mr. Fletcher out of it, so to speak?"

"It's a matter of self-perception. Regan has reminded Will he's human—that he has a purpose again. And Lindsay has reminded him that he's a man." Dr. Sinclaire turned toward Will, expressionless. "Without those two things, he's just the lunatic that killed his infant daughter and the brother ruining his sister's life."

"You can't be serious."

David turned off the faucet and met Janey's gaze in the mirror. "You know this is the men's room, right?"

"You think there's something in here I want to see?" She crossed her arms over her chest. "Why didn't you tell me you were putting Will on the stand?"

"Why didn't you tell me you were getting massages and drinking champagne while your brother went nuts? Why didn't Lindsay tell me she signed that damn petition? And for God's sake, why didn't Regan tell me she was caught having sex in a church basement?" David pulled a paper towel off the dispenser and shook his head. "At this point, Will may be his only hope."

Will had no hope. How could he be his only hope? "There has to be another way."

"There's not."

"You listen to me!" Janey shouted, stepping forward. "You've never seen it. You've never seen him go from zero to nutso in sixty seconds flat. If you put my brother on the stand you'll be signing his insanity papers!"

The sound of flushing water disrupted her chain of thought. A moment later, the door to the last stall opened and out stumbled Will. Hair in disarray and beads of sweat glistening on his forehead, he glanced Janey's way only briefly before heading to the sink.

"Will?" she muttered. "Will, I didn't mean that."

He splashed a handful of water onto his face and turned off the faucet. "When are we going to stop lying to each other?"

"Uh, I'll give you two a minute," David said.

Janey watched as David walked out the door, leaving her alone with her brother and a question she didn't know how to answer.

"Do you remember when Dad took us swimming at Half Moon dam?" Will asked.

The memory flooded through Janey's mind. She couldn't have been more than five or six, but she remembered that day vividly.

"We climbed the rocks up to where the teenagers used to hang out, and there was that old rope swing up there." Will tugged a paper towel from the dispenser. "You begged me not to swing from it, remember? You even cried."

"I thought you were going to drown."

"But I didn't."

"Because you didn't jump."

He grinned. "I was drying off while you and Dad headed to the car with the picnic basket. I stared up at that swing for a few seconds and I knew I couldn't leave without doing it just once. So I climbed to the top, grabbed the rope, closed my eyes, and let go." He tossed the paper towel toward the trash can, missing. "First lie I ever told you. Definitely not the last."

For some reason, this made Janey angry. "Why didn't you tell me?"

"Because it's easier to let you think you know what's best for me," he said. "But I'm tired, Jane. I'm so tired of lying."

"Will—"

"You've got to trust me."

"And what if you lose it on the stand? What if that bastard Tuttle finds just the right button and pushes it until you snap?"

"I'm not a twig."

Janey looked her brother up and down.

"You know what I mean."

She sighed. "Why do you think this time is going to be any different than the thirty other times you've done this?"

"Because this time I'm not trying to increase my sentence." Will retrieved the crumpled-up paper towel from the floor and tossed it into the trash can. "Like I said, I'm tired of lying."

Janey stared at her brother, or, rather, this man who looked like her brother. His stern brow, his clenched jaw, his steady stance. His wool sweater, for God's sake! Who was this man before her? Who was this superhero minus the cape and boots?

Suddenly she had the urge to hug him, like she used to when he was so frail she swore she could see through him. She'd thought she'd never see this Will again. Or maybe he'd been there all along, but she'd been too busy protecting him to see his own courage.

"You need to let go," he finally said.

"I know," she said, knowing they were both referring to more than a hug. "I know."

They walked out of the men's room hand in hand. Janey closed her eyes and let Will lead for the first time in what seemed like an eternity. She could see that rope swing just up ahead, she could feel the breeze blowing off the river, she could smell the musty aroma of the boulders beneath her feet. This time she would trust her brother's courage. It was time to let Will jump, to see if this superhero could fly.

But then Will stopped. His hand shook and, even without looking, Janey could feel his confidence begin to crumble.

Terrified, she opened her eyes one at a time. There was something blocking the edge of the precipice. No, *someone*.

Will's kryptonite.

CHAPTER
TWENTY-ONE

She wore yellow.

She always looked beautiful in yellow. Her rosy cheeks glowed against the color, her eyes glistened. She shined like sunlight in a room without windows, bloomed like a daffodil in a field full of four-leaf clovers. A yellow dress is what she'd worn to their prom, a yellow suit to their engagement party. The specks of paint Will had washed from her hair were a soft, nursery yellow, just like the blanket she'd carried Emma home from the hospital in.

The goodbye note she'd written had been on her signature, yellow stationary.

"You don't have to do this," David whispered, stepping into his line of sight.

Will glanced toward Janey and Regan. In six hours, he'd seen their eyes go from skeptical to hopeful to remorseful to fearful, all because of him. He couldn't let it end this way.

He wouldn't. Not this time.

"Do your job," Will stated flatly. "Let me worry about mine."

Grinning, David pushed off the witness stand and retrieved his legal pad from the defense table. "Will, do you understand why you're here today?"

"Because the town's afraid of me," Will responded, just as they'd practiced. "Everyone's afraid of what they don't understand."

"Do you believe that's what this is? A case of misunderstanding?"

It was more a case of instigated misperception, but David hadn't liked that response much. "Yes. A misunderstanding."

"So, why don't you explain now? What would you like the town to know?"

"That if I could change who I am, I would. No one understands the burden of this disease more than I do." Will gave a sweeping glance across the room, ending on Ellie. "You have no idea how frustrating that is. I can't change what I've done or who I am. I can't get back what I've lost or give back what I've taken. The only thing I can do is take things a day at a time and learn to live with it."

"Do you think you have learned to live with it?"

"If I had, I suppose we wouldn't be here. I'm trying, but it's an ongoing process. Just when I think I can predict the next pitch, I get thrown a curveball."

David gave an approving smile, which would make it even harder for Will to do what he had to do next. "How do you feel, finally getting all that off your chest?"

Will was supposed to say *liberating*. They'd gone through a dozen or so adjectives looking for just the right word that would leave the judge with a sense of hope, a desire to believe. They'd practiced it over and over again because Will couldn't seem to get it right. It wasn't until today, after seeing Lindsay, Regan, and Janey be torn apart by all this, Will understood why. "Ashamed," he finally stated.

David stiffened, a reprieve Will had been counting on. He turned his gaze toward Janey before David could unravel what was about to happen. "You gave up everything for me, Janey. Everything. And I've done nothing but shit on you every step of the way. I honestly don't know why you stayed, or why you still want to. Why?"

"Will," David said. "You need to shut up."

"Why? It's the truth. That's what I'm supposed to do, isn't it? Tell the truth?" Will said. He was tired of lying, so tired of lying. If he was going to go free, it would be because of the truth and not some lie.

David's face turned red. "Your Honor, I have no further—"

"You deserve so much better than me," Will continued, turning his eyes toward Regan. She was all that mattered. Why couldn't he have realized it before now? "I know it. You know it. Your mother knew it. I'm so sorry I'm not the father you were looking for. I'm so sorry I couldn't be more for you."

"Your Honor!" David shouted.

"Uh, Mr. Fletcher, I believe your attorney is finished," the judge stated.

"So am I, Your Honor." Will sat back in his seat. "So am I."

"Mr. Tuttle, I believe the witness is yours?"

Tuttle stood up, grinning. What could he possibly have to ask? Hadn't Will just sealed the kid's case for him? "Mr. Fletcher, do you think you deserve another chance?"

"No," Will stated, as honest as he could. "But someone else thinks I do."

"Who?"

Will turned his gaze toward Ellie. "Emma."

Tuttle nearly choked. "Your dead daughter, Emma?"

"That's the one."

"So let me get this straight—you're stating on record, in your committal hearing, that your deceased, infant daughter thinks the court should give you another chance?"

"I know how it sounds, but . . ."

"Just answer the question, Mr. Fletcher."

Will stiffened his jaw. "That's exactly what I'm saying."

Tuttle grinned. "No further questions."

The judge turned to David, whose face was still red as a strawberry. "Mr. Shepherd?"

"Defense rests, Your Honor."

"Well then, court will recess for the day and reconvene tomorrow at nine. I'll give my ruling then." The judge beat his gavel, and the countdown to Will's loss of freedom began.

Lindsay rose from the leather chair and glanced around at the now-naked walls of her office. It wasn't that long ago she'd unpacked these boxes. The books hadn't been on the shelves long enough to collect dust. The pictures hadn't yet left a bright-white patch of paint in their absence. Her life was just as empty as the day she set foot in this town, looking for a fresh start.

Looking for Will.

Bottle of wine in hand, she climbed through the window—the one she'd just discovered opened—and took a seat on the brick ledge. Maybe if she looked hard enough into the moonlight, she could see his silhouette in the field—building, fixing, creating. How foolish to think he could mold her life into what she wanted it to be.

Was this what her life had amounted to? An endless cycle of failing and starting over, failing and starting over, failing and starting over?

"You gonna jump?"

Lindsay glanced back at Janey, standing in her office. "Sorry to disappoint you, but no. And even if I did, I'm afraid the six-foot drop would, at best, result in a sprained ankle."

Janey climbed through the window and took a seat beside her. "Heard you quit."

"Yep. I'm tired of being just another one of Bradford's pawns. Besides, no real reason for me to stay in Half Moon Hollow anymore." Lindsay took another swig from the bottle before handing it over. "So, is that why you're really here? To ask me about my job?"

Janey turned her gaze out toward the field. Lindsay wondered if she was looking for Will too, if he held her answers as well. And then Janey dug into the pouch of her sweatshirt, pulling out an orange medicine bottle and handing it to Lindsay. "I figured it out today on the stand."

"Figured what out?"

"Tic Tacs," Janey said. "That's what Will was taking. He tried fooling me once before like that, just after he came home from Creedmoor the first time."

Lindsay opened up the bottle, shaking the breath mints into her hand. It wasn't her fault.

So why didn't she feel any better about it?

"You hurt me, Lindsay," Janey said, unknowingly answering Lindsay's question.

"Janey, I can explain the petition," she defended.

"I don't care about the damn petition, Lindsay! You fell in love with my brother. And I know you're straight, and I should have never fallen for you in the first place, but I did and I don't know how to get over this. Because you have no idea what it's like when the person you love chooses your own flesh and blood over you. When you know there is no way you can even compete because God made you different."

Lindsay placed her palm on her abdomen, thinking of the baby she could not give David. "Yes. I do. Just not in the same way."

Janey drew in a deep breath, then shook her head and released it with a loud grumble. "Why is this so unfair?"

Lindsay didn't know how to respond, so she didn't.

"Do you really love him?" Janey asked, turning toward her. "Will?"

"I do. More than anything."

"Then don't leave him. Not like this." Janey climbed back through the window into Lindsay's office. "Don't leave *us*."

"But I thought—"

"I changed my mind. And fuck Bradford. Will needs you; the kids need you." She held her hand out toward Lindsay's. "*I* need you."

Lindsay stared at her friend's hand. "I can't be what you want me to be, Janey."

"I just want you to be there for me. That's all I'm asking. And to love my brother and my niece the best way you know how."

Lindsay stared at her hand a moment longer before taking it in hers. "That I can promise for certain."

Janey learned long ago that people can make themselves believe all sorts of things. That they're in love with someone they're not. That a lack of money is responsible for their unhappiness. That time has healed all wounds, even those that time itself has created. Janey had believed that the town's judgment didn't make her heart race, their pity didn't make her stomach queasy, their whispers didn't stir her tears. She'd believed if she could fix Will, she could fix herself.

As she walked through the courtroom doors the following morning, the weight of the air thin as silk around her, Janey realized all this time she'd been lying.

So this was what it felt like to be free. To know where she was going, to be at peace with where she'd been. To know who she was meant to be. A woman. An artist. A lesbian. A friend. An aunt. A sister. A hero's sidekick and, at times, a villain's keeper. She was all these things and much more.

She was proud. For the first time, she was truly, utterly proud.

"You may be seated."

Squeezing Lindsay's hand with her right and Regan's with her left, Janey took a deep breath and did as instructed.

Judge Wheaton sat back in his chair, arms gathered neatly across his stomach. "I read last night that 25 percent of adults experience some sort of mental disorder in a given year. That's one out of every four people in this country living with this, not to mention the families and friends who are affected. If you ask me, that's just too many. I wonder, has this become our go-to excuse for unhappiness? Or is it possible that so many are truly incapable of controlling the way they feel, or think, or act? I'm not sure which answer would be scarier.

"Mr. Fletcher, you've left me in a terrible predicament here. I stayed up most the night, trying to figure out what to do with you. I'd kissed my wife goodnight, turned off the light, pulled the covers up to my chin, and did something some might consider crazy—I closed my eyes and asked God to show me the way. When I woke up, I realized the answer I looked for lay within the question.

"The town claims Mr. Fletcher's insane because he goes to a cemetery every day and chats with his deceased daughter over lunch. Mr. Tuttle worked to further demonstrate this theory by saying any sane person would not believe his deceased daughter to be leading his life. So I asked myself, does that mean *I'm* insane for asking God—a being I've never seen or heard and cannot prove the existence of— to show *me* guidance?

"The town also claims that Mr. Fletcher is an outsider, that he doesn't possess the social skills to navigate society. Yet it was shown numerous times during this hearing that no one in town wants anything to do with him. So what came first? Did Mr. Fletcher shut everyone out, or did everyone shut out Mr. Fletcher?

"Regardless, it doesn't really matter why Mr. Fletcher is the way he is, or what we call his disorder. As Mr. Shepherd pointed out in the beginning, this trial isn't meant to decide that. What it is meant to decide is if the defendant would be better treated in a hospital or at home, and better taken care of by nurses and doctors, or by his loved ones. I believe in both cases, the answer is the latter. Therefore, I'm ruling against the involuntary committal."

The silence of the courtroom broke into a low rumble.

"I haven't dismissed this courtroom yet," the judge said, beating his gavel. "Would the defendant please stand?"

Even from the back of the courtroom, Janey could see Will wobbling like a bowl of Jell-O as he stood.

"Mr. Fletcher, you have endured more grief than any one man should have to endure in a lifetime. And while I do not believe that excuses you from following the rules of society, I do believe it warrants you and your family one last chance. After listening to your testimony yesterday, I also believe you will not waste this one. Is that assessment accurate?"

"Yes, Your Honor," Will responded, slightly louder than was necessary. "You have no idea how much I would like one last chance."

"Don't make me regret it." Judge Wheaton beat his gavel. "The defendant is free to go."

Janey launched from her seat like a torpedo, pulling Lindsay and Regan in her wake. And she didn't let go, not when she climbed over the wooden rail, not when she weaved around David and Dr. Sinclaire, not when she threw her arms around her brother and began to cry.

"Hey, hey! Save some for us!" Regan said.

Janey let go, but not because she wanted to. It was someone else's turn to hold onto Will, someone else's turn to believe in him. They weren't alone anymore, never would be again.

Regan dove in first, her head fitting perfectly in the crook of Will's arm. "I missed you so much," she cried.

"Not nearly as much as I missed you," he responded, a tear streaking down his cheek as he kissed the crown of her head. "I swear I'll never leave you again."

"What are you waiting for?" Janey asked Lindsay. "Go on."

Lindsay smiled, then took two giant steps forward and landed in Will's arms. A moment later, their lips met. It didn't hurt Janey as much as she'd prepared for, but it still hurt nonetheless. She'd get used to it in time, but, for now, she'd walk away.

"Ms. Fletcher! Ms. Fletcher!"

Still holding the courtroom door, Janey turned to see Dr. Sinclaire hurrying over.

"I wanted to ask . . . I mean I was hoping that we . . ." Dr. Sinclaire sighed. "We need to schedule Will's next appointment."

Janey raised her brow. "You told me to call the office, remember?"

"I did, didn't I?" Dr. Sinclaire grimaced, her cheeks turning a soft shade of pink Janey had seen many times—mostly on men she wasn't remotely interested in. This time, the shade made Janey a little dizzy.

"What I meant to say was . . . would you like to . . ." Dr. Sinclaire sighed again. "Why am I so bad at this?"

"I'd love to," Janey said.

"But you haven't heard my suggestion."

"I don't need to." Janey took a step closer. "Dinner, dancing, a rodeo. Doesn't matter. I'd still love to."

Dr. Sinclaire smiled. "I have an artist friend who's debuting at this art gallery in Columbus tomorrow night. Pick you up at seven?"

Janey glanced back inside the courtroom, Will safely between Lindsay and Regan. "Let's make it five. There's this new sushi restaurant I've been dying to try."

Regan smoothed the wrinkles from her new, blue comforter and placed the pillows on top for the final touch. It could've waited until tomorrow, she supposed, especially seeing that she'd be in bed in just a little while. But she couldn't wait. She wanted to see it then, all put together and complete. After all, it was the first birthday gift she'd ever received from her father.

Sliding her shoes off, she headed toward her dresser for her pajamas, caught off-guard by the image in the mirror looking back at her. It was her mother, or rather, someone who looked like her mother, with auburn hair gathered into a gold barrette. Or perhaps it was her father; the wide, silver eyes and pointed nose certainly attested to that.

Regan was both of them, yet neither at the same time. She hoped.

"Mother?" she whispered.

But there was no answer.

"Mother, are you there?" she asked again, though she wasn't sure what was more frightening—hearing an answer or not.

When she didn't receive a response this time, Regan leaned against the dresser and let her heavy head fall. She hadn't heard her mother since yesterday on the stand, when she'd asked her to leave. Was she gone for good? Would she hear her again? Could Regan survive if she didn't?

Was she unstable, like her grandfather, like her father, if she did?

"Emma never answers me either."

Regan glanced back up, spotting Will's reflection behind her in the mirror.

"There was a time I would've given anything just to hear her say *Daddy*. Hell, I would've settled for a *da*." He approached, carrying a box in his arms. "But, I guess I'll have to wait until I see her again to hear her voice. Just like you will with your mother."

Regan nodded, because telling her father any different would make them both crazy.

"And when she finally does talk to you, she'll tell you that her death wasn't your fault."

"I know," Regan said with another nod.

"No, you don't." Will placed the box on the dresser, then his hands on her shoulders. "It wasn't your fault. And none of that church stuff was reason enough for her to abandon you. If anything, it should've made her want to be there for you even more. Do you understand?"

Regan nodded, for the first time actually meaning it. Will wasn't a bullshitter. If her father told her it wasn't her fault, she'd have to learn to trust it.

"Good. And, just so we're clear, if you ever do anything like that under my roof, I'll ground you until you're thirty, understand?"

"Yes," she giggled, only mildly embarrassed. "So, what's in the box?"

"A birthday gift."

"Another one?"

"Another six, to be exact." Will placed the box in her hands. "Sorry, it's not wrapped."

"I wouldn't have expected anything else."

Regan pulled the flaps of the box back and dug through the crumpled newspaper until she'd reached the gifts. Five wooden blocks painted lime green, each in the shape of a letter of her name. "This is . . . wow. Did you do this today?"

"I cut, Lindsay sanded, Janey painted. Thought we could hang them on the wall after we paint tomorrow."

"Paint?"

"Yeah. Paint."

Regan grinned, leaning in to give her father a kiss on the cheek. "You know, there are only five letters in my name, Will."

"Yeah, I know. The sixth gift is waiting downstairs." He whistled loud. "Come on up."

A few moments later, Lane stood in the doorway.

"I'll be downstairs with Lindsay if you need me," Will said, exiting. "And, uh, leave the door open, okay?"

"Yes, Dad," Regan said, then crossed her arms and turned toward Lane. "What are you doing here?"

"I was never going to Oregon," Lane admitted as he approached. "That was just a ploy by my parents to keep me away from you."

Regan shrugged. "You still shouldn't have kept it from me. How many opportunities did you have? And you just let them go by."

"Just like all the opportunities you had to tell me you weren't a virgin?"

"That's different."

"How? How is it any different?"

"Because I was afraid you'd leave me if you found out!" she shouted.

Lane placed his hands on his hips. "Like I said . . . how is it any different?"

Regan opened her mouth to respond, but then the words caught up with her. Lane Barrett was afraid of her leaving *him*? On what planet would that ever happen?

"Well, that's all I came to say." Lane headed for the door.

"So why don't we both just admit we were wrong, agree to never do it again, and then kiss and make up?" she said.

In one quick motion, Lane lunged toward her and pressed his mouth to hers. And like all the other times he'd kissed her, Regan couldn't stop herself from kissing back. She didn't want to. Because it was meant to be—all of it. Lane was her fate, just like Will was her home.

"I thought you said you were tired of coming after me," she said after he'd let go.

"Guess that makes two times I lied to you." He grinned, pulling her by the hand toward the door. "Besides, *you* came after *me*."

"Yeah, yeah." Regan paused with her hand on the light switch, and glanced back at the mirror, one last time. "I love you," she whispered.

"I love you, too," Lane responded.

She flipped the switch. And, even though her statement had been meant for her mother, Regan smiled and let Lane lead her by the hand toward the light of the hallway, away from the quiet darkness of her empty bedroom.

EPILOGUE— ONE YEAR LATER

Will climbed from the car, thankful to be alive. Maybe they should've gotten her the four-cylinder instead of the six, or a minivan, or a station wagon. Leave it to Janey and Lindsay to talk him into something crazy like a sport coupe for Regan's seventeenth birthday.

"Man, I love that car!" Regan sang as she joined him on the sidewalk with the freshly picked sunflowers in hand. "Have I told you what an awesome dad you are?"

Eight times now. Will had been counting. Twice when she opened the door this morning and saw it sitting in the driveway, four times on her inaugural drive around the block, once now, and . . . when was the other one? Oh yeah, when he told her he'd sold the old BMW to get the funds to pay for it. Only that "Awesome," was more docile than the others.

They set off down the path toward the ivy-laced gate, hand in hand. The last time they'd been here, the tulips had been blooming, the trees budding; the grass had been just starting to turn green again from the cold winter. The tulips were long gone now, and the leaves were glowing in shades of auburn and yellow.

Had he really gone an entire summer without coming to see Emma? And, more importantly, was this a good thing or a bad thing? He'd have to ask Zoe about this at his next therapy session.

Will nearly ran into Regan, who had paused at the gate. "What's wrong?"

She nodded toward the direction of Emma's grave. Ellie knelt beside it, her head resting on Emma's tombstone.

Will checked his watch. Twelve-thirty. In that ridiculous restraining order, they'd agreed she'd come sometime before noon and he'd come after.

"Maybe we should come back?" Regan asked.

As if in disagreement, Will's stomach growled. "Let's go eat lunch by the oak tree until she leaves."

"The oak tree I used to spy on you from?" Regan asked.

"Sure. Why not?"

"Well, that's kind of an invasion of Ellie's privacy, don't you think?"

Will pointed to Father Bailey on the lawnmower. "Can't hear anything anyway."

Regan bit her lip, trying to hide the worry in her eyes.

"I'm fine." He set off down the fence. "Besides, I'm starving, and I don't want to have to make another trip with you in that car today."

It was half true. Janey, Lindsay, Zoe, and Lane were at the house, decorating for her surprise party. He'd nearly slipped and told already. If Will brought Regan home early, he wouldn't be so *awesome*.

They settled in under the tree and opened the picnic basket Janey had fixed for them. Regan split her sandwich and gave half to Will; Will peeled his orange and handed half to Regan. Like always. Like they'd been doing it for years. It felt so natural. Will didn't notice the hum from the lawnmower had faded until he heard the mumble of Ellie's voice.

Regan tugged on his elbow. "Let's go," she whispered.

But Will couldn't leave. There was something in Ellie's voice holding him there, something in the urgency of her words. She argued with someone.

"I've tried, Emma. I swear I've tried, but your Poppa wouldn't let me. He said he'd send me back to Creedmoor, and I can't go back to that place. . . . I barely survived it the last time."

Creedmoor? When was Ellie at Creedmoor?

Why was Ellie at Creedmoor?

Will met Regan's gaze, as if she knew the answers to his silent questions. But she seemed just as confused as he was.

"It doesn't matter anymore, anyway," Ellie continued. "Daddy is all better now. He has Regan, and he has . . . Lindsay. Telling him now would only set him back."

Telling him what, goddamn it! What?

"Fine. If you want me to leave, I'll leave. I should be going anyway. Your father will be here before long." Ellie was so close now Will could hear the rattle in her voice—the one she only had when she cried. "He's always been here for you, hasn't he? More than I have. If he'd taken you to daycare that day instead of me, you'd still be alive."

Will went still, the words freezing his veins like ice. What did Ellie mean? Why was she saying this? He was the one who was supposed to take Emma to daycare that day, not Ellie. That's what they'd told him.

That's what Bradford had told him. That's what Granger had told him.

The scattered memories flooded his mind, like a million

puzzle pieces falling in place. Seeing Ellie on her knees by the car, with the keys in her hand. Bradford showing up just a few minutes later, despite not being called. Her strange demeanor at the funeral. The pills Bradford placed in Ellie's hand every chance he got. Ellie's long mission trips to some desolate country in Africa, despite the fact she couldn't even stand an overnight camping trip in the backyard. And Ellie's note—a simple "I'm sorry"—hadn't been a simple note at all.

It was a confession.

Will met Regan's gaze. Her wide eyes and open mouth made it clear she was just as shocked as he was. They stood there like that, silent and still, until Ellie's cries had subsided and the birds made the only sound.

Will glanced through the hole to find Emma's grave abandoned, then turned back toward Regan. "Ready?"

She nodded. "We should hurry. Everyone's expecting us."

They'd made it to the front gate before Will had realized what she'd said. "When did you figure it out?"

"When you asked if I had an aversion to clowns."

Will chuckled. "It's a valid question. Not everyone likes clowns."

They continued toward Emma's tombstone, never mentioning the truth they'd just learned and never swearing to keep it to themselves. But it was understood.

This truth they would carry to more than just Emma's grave.

THE END

ACKNOWLEDGEMENTS

There are so many people who've helped me throughout this long journey. The only way I know to show my appreciation is to put your name here in print and give you your five minutes of fame. Okay, maybe that's an overstatement, but you get what I mean.

First and foremost, thank you to Chad, Avery, and Audrey Starnes for your undying love and support the past eight years. Chad—thank you for not once telling me I was crazy when I said I wanted to write a book, for sacrificing so I could work part-time, and for picking up the slack at home so I could write. You will always be the hero in my happily ever after. Avery and Audrey—thank you for the constant fist-bumps, hugs, and for understanding why I couldn't go on every field trip. You are the reasons I fight every day to be a strong woman.

Thank you to Jody Horak for being my very first reader, and making it through the painstaking first draft of my first manuscript. To Pat and Lynn Scott for not killing me when I was a teenager—I know I didn't make it easy. To Lynn and Tommy Starnes for your endless help with the girls, while I was cooped up in an office. And to the entire Tornai clan, for never leaving me with a lack of ideas to transform into words.

I'd also like to thank my friends and critique partners—Sydney Carroll, Lori Waters, Elizabeth Michels, Heather McGovern, and Jeanette Grey—for embracing my differences and letting me sit at the "cool table" anyway. Thank you to Christine Stewart for making my manuscript the best it could be, and to the people at SparkPress who helped put it all together.

And last but certainly not least, thank you to *you*, my readers, for taking a chance with the new kid on the block.

—Jenna P.

ABOUT THE AUTHOR

Raised in northern Ohio, Jenna Patrick moved to North Carolina in 1998 to attend the University of North Carolina at Charlotte where she received a Bachelor of Science degree in civil engineering. After ten years of devoting her brain to science and math, Jenna returned to her true passion—writing fiction. She and her husband reside on Lake Norman with their two daughters and two rescue dogs. *The Rules of Half* is her debut novel. Please visit her blog and website at www.jennapatricknovels.com.

SELECTED TITLES FROM SPARKPRESS

SparkPress is an independent boutique publisher
delivering high-quality, entertaining, and engaging
content that enhances readers' lives, with a special focus
on female-driven work. Visit us at www.gosparkpress.com

The Half-Life of Remorse, by Grant Jarrett, $16.95, 978-1-943006-14-4. Two tattered mendicants, Sam and Chic, meet on the streets, both unaware that their paths crossed years before. Meanwhile, Sam's daughter Claire, who Sam doesn't even know is alive, is still unable to give up hope that her vanished father might someday reappear. When these three lives converge thirty years after the brutal crime that shattered their lives, the puzzle of the past gradually falls together, but the truth commands a high price.

The Absence of Evelyn, by Jackie Townsend, $16.95, 978-1-943006-21-2. Newly divorced Rhonda, haunted by her sister Evelyn's ghost, travels to Rome to confront Marco, the man who stole her sister's heart—only to find out he's vanished in the wake of Evelyn's death. Meanwhile, Rhonda's nineteen-year-old daughter Olivia, adopted by Rhonda at birth, travels to the mysterious and lush waters of Vietnam, where she's been summoned by the missing Marco—a man she only knows from her parents' whispers. Four lives in all, spanning three continents, are now bound together in an unfathomable way—and they tell a powerful story about love in all its incarnations, filial and amorous, healing and destructive.

Hindsight, by Mindy Tarquini, $16.95, 978-1943006014. Eugenia Panisporchi, a thirty-three-year-old Chaucer professor who remembers all her past lives, is desperate to change her future. Her hope is that the Blessed Virgin Mary (who oversees her soul's progress) will grant her heart's desire, the option to choose the circumstances of her next life. But when a student reveals he shares her ability, Eugenia suddenly finds herself setting up a Facebook page and sponsoring a support group for others like her, and she discovers she must confront her current shortcomings before she can break the cycle and finally live the life of her dreams.

ABOUT SPARKPRESS

SparkPress is an independent, hybrid imprint focused on merging the best of the traditional publishing model with new and innovative strategies. We deliver high-quality, entertaining, and engaging content that enhances readers' lives. We are proud to bring to market a list of *New York Times* best-selling, award-winning, and debut authors who represent a wide array of genres, as well as our established, industry-wide reputation for creative, results-driven success in working with authors. SparkPress, a BookSparks imprint, is a division of SparkPoint Studio LLC.

Learn more at GoSparkPress.com